Medusa's Curse
By
Christopher Cartwright

Copyright 2021 by Christopher Cartwright
This book is protected under the copyright laws of the United States of America. Any reproduction or other unauthorized use of the material or artwork herein is prohibited. This book is a work of fiction. Names, characters, places, brands, media and incidents either are the product of the author's imagination or are used fictitiously. All rights reserved.

Prologue

"Security is mostly a superstition. It does not exist in nature, nor do the children of men as a whole experience it. Avoiding danger is no safer in the long run than outright exposure. Life is either a daring adventure, or nothing."

Helen Keller.

Brest, France – August 7, 1944

The mortar shell landed right next to him.

It sent a plume of dirt and rubble some thirty feet into the air. The hit was close enough to render him instantly unconscious, but not close enough to kill him. Colonel Joe MacCracken was born under a lucky star. Some people just were. He hadn't done anything particularly spectacular to deserve it. He had no intention of squandering his good fortune in the aid of others. That's not to say he wasn't a good person, honorable and duty bound. Just to say, that he was born lucky. And with that luck, as the ringing still echoed in his skull as he came around, he knew with an absolute certainty that he wasn't going to die that day, out there in that bloody battlefield.

Colonel Joe MacCracken looked like anything but regular US Army.

That wasn't surprising, given that he was everything but a real soldier. No one could have predicted where he'd end up. Certainly, no casual observer watching his life unfold. He could have landed anywhere, but the one place he'd never even considered was the coast of France during the Allied Forces' great push. It would have been equally impossible to predict that he felt happier than in any other time in his life, just to be there.

Despite the throbbing pain in his head, Joe wore an absurd smile of genuine contentment. It formed a jarring contrast with his environment, which was a mixture of permanent physical discomfort and danger. Such a straightforward display of joy didn't belong to a soldier in the midst of battle.

He didn't bother to duck down or take cover. What did it matter? If another one of those rounds landed anywhere near him, he'd be dead. Nothing that taking cover was going to do to stop it. He may as well stand tall, and face the world. His piercing blue eyes took in his surroundings with the casual interest of a tourist on vacation, rather than a soldier at war who was likely to die at any moment.

The sky was a mixture of various shades of charcoal, progressively darkening throughout the day. Sleet had been falling since dawn, turning the ground to an icy mud. Even he couldn't explain the source of his feelings. At best guess, he'd say that he'd simply accepted he didn't have a lick of control as to whether or not he'd survive the rest of the war, so he might as well enjoy it and take it as it comes.

At six foot three, he was tall with a slim, lanky figure, from which his pressed military uniform hung like an oversized coat over a hanger. Joe was a good-looking man, with thick dark hair, the slight salt and pepper coloring around the ears somehow enhancing his good looks. He had an angular, honest, and determined face. He wore a set of headphones, with a microphone hanging down across his mouth into which he barked instructions, giving him the appearance of a film director more than a Colonel in the Army.

All told, such a description of his purpose was closer to the truth.

His route to the Army couldn't have been any farther from regular, either. If there was ever a more obscure, circumlocutory induction to this miserable war, he sure as hell hadn't heard of it. Instead of West Point he'd received an education at Julliard, receiving an Arts Degree, majoring in performing arts, before going on to complete a Master's degree in Fine Arts at Yale, specializing in ancient antiquities and historical restorations. He didn't volunteer. Nor did he come into the Army the way many civilians did – through the draft. Instead, he was handpicked for his unique talents, to lead a small group of men from the Army's 23rd Headquarters Special Troops – to deceive the enemy in every way possible.

In the summer of 1944, a handpicked group of G.I.s landed in France to conduct a special mission. Equipped with truckloads of inflatable tanks, a massive collection of sound effects records, and more than a few tricks up their sleeves, their job was to create a traveling road show of deception on the battlefields of Europe, with the German Army as their audience. From Normandy to the Rhine, the 1100 men of the 23rd Headquarters Special Troops, known as the Ghost Army, conjured up phony convoys, phantom divisions, and make-believe headquarters to fool the enemy about the strength and location of American units.

Each ruse required that they impersonate a different – and vastly larger – U.S. unit. Like actors in a repertory theater, they would mount an ever-changing multimedia show tailored to each operation. The men immersed themselves in their roles, even hanging out at local cafes and spinning their counterfeit stories for spies who might lurk in the shadows. Painstakingly recorded sounds of armored and infantry units were blasted from sound trucks; radio operators created phony traffic nets; and inflatable tanks, trucks, artillery and even airplanes were imperfectly camouflaged so they would be visible to enemy reconnaissance.

Another shell landed less than a hundred yards away, sending rubble in all directions. It was a Fixed QF 88×571mmR. The shell had come from a Flak 88 cannon – one of the most ubiquitous artillery guns of World War II – an 8.8 cm high-velocity weapon equally applicable for antiaircraft and antitank use. The design, adapted in 1938, weighed about 9,600 pounds and was towed by a prime mover.

Everyone ducked to the ground, taking cover.

Only Colonel MacCracken stood upright, his back ramrod straight in defiance of the incoming onslaught and now constant, deadly barrage. He drew a deep breath. The outward edges of his lips curled upward in a tremendous grin. It was a mixture of sardonic insanity and a boyish movie-star type smile – if such a thing existed. As fire and hell rained down upon his men, he couldn't help but feel happy.

And why shouldn't he be?

After all, in drawing the angry fire of the Flugabwehrkanone 88s, he had just succeeded to convince the enemy commander of the German held French city of Brest, that his unit of just 1,100 men, armed with dummy inflatable Sherman tanks, were a 60,000 man strong double tank division. General Hermann-Bernhard Ramcke, the German commander would be forced to surrender.

Joe smiled.

With any luck, they would be inside the walls of the medieval city by nightfall.

*

Despite Colonel MacCracken and the Ghost Army's successful deception, it took another 28 days to take the city of Brest. The fighting was intense, with the troops moving from house to house. The fortifications – both French and German built – proved very difficult to overcome, and heavy artillery barrages were fired by both sides.

The Germans used artillery, rocket mortars fired by 6.22-inch Nebelwerfer 41 and flame throwers. The civilians inside the fortress tended the wounded, reloaded the machine-gun drums and belts and took up rifles to help defend the fortress. Children brought ammunition and food supplies from half-destroyed supply depots, scavenged weapons and watched enemy movements. Eventually the old city of Brest was razed to the ground during the battle, with only some medieval stone-built fortifications left standing.

The German paratroopers lived up to their reputation, as the Allies had experienced previously in battles such as Monte Cassino. While some less capable units surrendered quite easily, the Fallschirmjäger defended their ground under considerable odds, heavy shelling, air strikes and American assaults.

General Ramcke finally surrendered the city on 19 September 1944 to the Americans after rendering the port facilities useless. These would not be repaired in time to help the war effort as it was hoped. By this time, Paris had already been liberated by the Allied Armies, and Operation Market-Garden was already under way in the Netherlands.

Colonel MacCracken formed part of an official vanguard to accept General Ramcke's surrender. He was the only person from the Ghost Army at the meeting. The rest of the group were made of more traditional soldiers. Standing at the center was U.S. Brigadier General Charles Canham, a tall man with an angular jaw, thin-rimmed glasses, and a defiant stride. The Brigadier moved with the subtlety of a Sherman tank, his back, ramrod straight as he approached General Ramcke. His air about the entire charade was dismissive, as though all he wanted to do was get past the formalities, and get back to doing his job of reclaiming Europe.

General Hermann-Bernhard Ramcke, saluted to Canham. There was a look of horror in the German paratrooper's face, as he realized he was surrendering to a lower-ranking U.S. officer. Ramcke spoke good English. His eyes lowered on Canham and he asked, quietly, "Before I surrender the city of Brest, may I please see your credentials?"

Brigadier-General Canham laughed. He pointed to his nearby troops and said, "These are my credentials."

MacCracken grinned, as he suppressed the urge to laugh out loud, and watched the two opposing Generals with great pleasure. Both life-long soldiers. One, still adhering to the strictest of military protocol, as though it had been spoon-fed and forced down his throat by the Third Reich – the other, a diehard soldier, who was there to do a job and couldn't care less about protocol or formalities. Those formalities were brief and within a few minutes, MacCracken left the ceremony, and rejoined some of his men, who had set up camp beside the sandstone wall and what little remained of a once proud series of 11th Century ramparts.

One of his men had already heated up some battle rations and offered him a bowl. MacCracken took it with gratitude, and sat down to eat with his back propped up against the remnants of a sandstone wall. He'd been living on battle rations since they'd landed at Omaha, and by now he knew that every single type of meat could be compressed, preserved with copious amounts of salt, and stored in a can. He also knew, that no matter what type of animal it had once come from, it all tasted the damned same once it had entered the ubiquitous tin cans in which rations were stored. Not that it mattered one iota to him. He was just glad it was over and that Brest had finally been taken.

He finished his warm meal and settled in a position of rest. For the first time since he'd arrived on the European continent, he'd relaxed long enough to realize just how tired he was. Dusk was only just setting, but, if allowed, he would be sound asleep within minutes.

But sleep was not to be.

Instead, he was interrupted by an infantry soldier, who had come looking for him. The man was short and stocky, with a youthful face, and the shadow of beard not yet quite able to be fully grown. The boy was tentative as he spoke. He was clearly new to the army, and the importance of such things as rank were obviously heavily pressed into his mindset.

"Colonel Joe MacCracken?" the soldier asked. His tone, polite, and just shy of obsequious.

MacCracken stirred from the makeshift bed he'd formed using a mixture of his backpack and ration packs. He toyed with pulling rank, and telling the kid to get lost, but dismissed the idea as soon as he met the youth's beseeching eyes. He sat up. "Yes, son?"

"I'm sorry to interrupt you, sir." The kid's face turned serious. "My name is Jason Richardson."

MacCracken waved his hand in a curt dismissal of convention. "What is it Richardson?"

"They say you're a historian back state side?"

"That's right. Why?"

"I need you to come with me."

"Okay, why?"

"We need you to look at something for us."

MacCracken was already getting up. "What did you find?"

"There's an armored DRB 52 waiting on the tracks." The boy paused, looking at MacCracken to see if there was recognition in his eyes. Failing to see any, he explained. "That's a German steam train, built for the war effort."

"Okay," MacCracken said, noncommittally.

"The train had a single armored carriage." The kid said, "I bet you're wondering what's in that carriage?"

MacCracken nodded. His face unreadable. "I can only imagine."

His heart raced.

It was easy to imagine what had happened. Hitler's German war machine worked its way throughout Europe stripping countless priceless treasures, from artworks, historical artifacts, through to gold and silver bullion. Some of those, no doubt, had ended up in the French city of Brest. With the Allied forces working their way onto the European continent, the German commander Hermann-Bernhard Ramcke, had ordered the treasures onto a train, to be sent farther inland, where they could be protected.

"You're not going to believe what we found inside."

A wry grin formed on MacCracken's lips. "What did you find inside?"

Richardson smiled. "That, sir… is what we're hoping you can tell us."

*

The water tower rose forty feet into the air beside the railway line.

It had been built hastily by the Germans to accommodate the growing need for steam trains, which were faster to build and easier to maintain during the war than diesel locomotives. The water stop was fabricated out of oak, felled locally, instead of steel, which was in high demand in the production of military machines. Shaped like a cube, with perfect German precision, two iron pipes penetrated its shell – an incoming one, fed by a nearby pond, and an outgoing one, that rested on a single iron pivot which extended out of the shell and allowed it to swivel, in order to refill the thirsty watercart tenders that fed the steam engines that worked their way from the harbor inland, daily.

At a glance, it was easy to see the purpose of the tower. What was less visible, was the fact that the top of the tower was enclosed, covered with a small roof of corrugated iron, to protect the water supply from any impurities. A small lip, a little over two feet in height, protruded above the roof, forming a small safety barrier for the stationmaster whose job it was to routinely climb onto the roof to assess the water levels. It was at this spot, where two French lovers took refuge, their bodies invisible to those on the ground.

Nadège Rousseau glanced at her boyfriend, Raphaël Labouchère.

Both virgins, neither spoke.

Instead, in total silence, like a religious doctrine, they stared at each other. Savoring the pleasure of the sight. She was a short, brunette with big brown eyes and an impish smile. She had a slim figure, further accentuated by the last four years of undernourishment and perpetual lack of food during the German occupation. He was equally short, matching her eye to eye when they stood to face one another, with blond hair, blue eyes and a carefree smile. He had a skinny, but well-muscled, physique from two years shoveling coal at the station. Once a man's job, now attended to by someone no longer a child, but not quite an adult.

He took her hands in hiss and squeezed them gently. He smiled, reassuringly, but she noticed the slightest quiver across his upper lip. He licked them, trying to conceal his evident nervousness. She couldn't help but love him all the more for it. They were both young. They had been dating for only a couple of months. But even at her young age, she knew there was something about it that was really special. The sort of love most people don't ever get to experience.

They were barely old enough to do the things she wanted to do with him. But there was a war on and time seemed to travel differently during such times. People matured faster. They took risks. After all, who knew how much time any of them had left? But with their freedom, the risk of death, and everything else, they felt much older, and either way they didn't feel waiting made any sense anymore. After all, they might both be dead before the war ended. They still hadn't slept together, but that was all going to change tonight.

Nadège decided that she was going to have to take charge. She knew without a hint of doubt that Raphaël wanted this as much as she did, but he was too nervous and much too much of a gentleman to make the next move.

It was going to be up to her.

With that thought, she looked into his beautiful blue eyes, smiled lasciviously – and then, before she could change her mind, she quickly pulled off her summer frock. She had sewn the dress herself, out of a cotton material with green floral patterns that she'd been saving for this day. It was cut somewhere between a classic A-shape and the common Utility dress worn by working French women. And she'd managed to find a light green piece of silk to tie around her waist to complete the package.

All that work, and it was gone in under a minute.

Her heart beat faster as she stripped in front of him. He gazed lovingly at her body. She stood near naked in front of him with a what-the-hell expression on her face. With the exception of a pair of plain white, cotton, step-in panties that started above her waist and ended a full five inches down each leg. She wasn't wearing a brasserie. Nadège didn't need to. She had small, firm, breasts with equally small, red, nipples. Her skin was a cream color, with small freckles all over her body. Despite her embarrassment, she turned her hands outward, to show that she was proud to reveal her body to him.

She held Raphaël's gaze with a mixture of defiance and pleasure. Nadège was happy to see she was met by a combination of desire and impatience on his handsome face. All nervousness and embarrassment dissipated in an instant, and he quickly pulled off his coal-stained trousers and long-sleeved, buttoned, shirt, until he too was standing across from her in nothing more than his underdrawers.

Raphaël squeezed her hands again. "You look incredibly beautiful."

"Thank you," she said, glad to see the unrestrained lust painted across her boyfriend's otherwise solemn looking face.

He seemed to force himself to meet her gaze, staring into her lovely eyes. There was plenty of raw passion on both sides, but equally, she saw that he was overflowing in love for her. With a timid smile, he asked, "Now what?"

She sat down. "Lie down next to me."

He happily followed her lead.

Nadège didn't wait. As soon as he was next to her, she cuddled into the safety of his arms. Raphaël smelled good, and looked even better. Her chest was pounding with anticipation and she could hear the sound of blood surging in the back of her ears. She was breathing hard, like she'd just finished running.

It was a time for celebration.

In the distance, far below and a world away for all she cared, crowds of people were celebrating.

After Brest was occupied by German forces for more than four years, it had finally been liberated. Below them, an alcohol fueled party was raging. Allies or not, some American soldiers could behave like animals after surviving battle. If you removed the battle part of battle-lust from a thousand drunken soldiers, all you had left over was lust. Raphaël pulled her into his arms protectively. This wasn't the only type of liberation Nadège Rousseau had on her mind.

Raphaël looked at her for a long time.

She sensed what he was feeling – something that happened often – and she waited, smiling. He leaned slowly toward her and brushed her lips with his own. He put both arms around her and gently pulled her to himself, feeling her breasts against his chest.

Still with his eyes open, he pressed his mouth to hers. They both parted their lips and touched tongues hesitantly, exploring as if kissing for the first time, like the adolescents they were. She felt his hips push toward her own. She reached around him with both arms and pulled him harder. She felt swamped with more passion than he could bear. She wanted to touch and feel him with every inch of her body, and she could tell that he felt the same.

She was breathing hard.

She kissed him again. They opened their mouths, their tongues meeting hungrily with desire. Raphaël shifted his weight from his hips, pressing into her and began to start to move again. She whimpered with pleasure at the sensation. Eager to remove their underdrawers and make love fully. It was too much.

Desire turned to desperation.

Nadège went to remove her underwear, but Raphaël stopped her.

She felt frustration rise in her throat, ready to protest, and then realized why. In an instant, her desire turned sharply to fear.

There was a group of soldiers directly below.

Raphaël cupped her mouth with his hand, and whispered in his ears, "Stay silent or we'll be spotted."

Nadège rolled off him, over onto her tummy and slid across to the edge of the water tower. A small plank of oak had come free, revealing a narrow slit through which they could gaze into the unrestrained debauchery unfolding outside.

Raphaël shuffled his position to lay beside her, wrapping his warm arms protectively around her narrow waist. He kissed the nape of her neck affectionately, and they both tried to slow their breathing, as though the noise could somehow be heard and give them away.

They stared out.

It appeared that the American soldiers, ransacking a nearby train, had discovered a treasure trove. The soldiers were slowly removing various precious items and artifacts. There were paintings, and porcelain artworks, ancient antiquities, and priceless relics. All of which the Germans had most likely stolen throughout the war. The soldiers were passing things around. You could see them trying to take anything of obvious value – stealing what had already been stolen, as though it was no longer a crime.

Somewhere within the pandemonium, an officer arrived and berated the soldiers for stealing. MPs began to secure the treasure trove. The rewards of war were laid out along the ground, so that they could be identified, secured, and tagged before a decision could be made as to where and to whom, they belonged.

After a few minutes, one of the soldiers found a hideous looking mask. Light flickered across the radiant metal, as though it were made of gold – which it most likely had been. From the top of the mask flowed a cascade of serpents. Two emerald eyes with an ethereal glow, stared out of the mask, giving the serpents a green, and unnatural, tinge.

Nadège found herself unintentionally holding her breath.

In the past four years, she'd seen many horrors of war. She had known evil in a way that she'd never imagined, and yet, when she stared down at that mask, she saw evil like she had never seen before. Not just saw it.

Felt it, too.

Put the damned thing down! she wanted to yell at the soldier playing with it, placing the mask up against his face, and pretending to be some sort of devil.

Another man approached.

He was older and walked with the stride of authority. At least six feet tall, he was a lanky figure, and his military uniform hung loosely. Despite being more than twice her age, with a wearied face, he was good-looking, especially with his air of confidence.

She watched as the officer glanced at the treasure trove with genuine interest, only to have it change to rage after seeing the mysterious mask. Interest turned to anger, and he yelled at the American soldiers to seal it back in its crate before it could release its evil onto the world.

So it is evil! Nadège thought.

The senior officer traded hushed words with the MPs. "That mask needs to be sealed so that it can be locked away and protected. It's dangerous."

Even from this distance, Nadège could tell the MPs didn't quite believe the Officer's superstitious fears of the artifact. After all, it was just a mask? Wasn't it?

There was a quick, heated, argument...

And the tall officer seemed to whisper something to the MPs that made them turn silent.

After a few seconds one of the MP's regathered his wits and said, "But what is it?"

"That!" The tall man said, "Is an abomination on the world, a harbinger of death, and bringer of plagues, the likes the world has not seen for nearly three thousand years!"

"A three-thousand-year-old plague?" The MP was incredulous. "But what is it called?"

The officer stared at him, his eyes sardonic. "You're looking at pure Evil…"

"Its name!" the MP persisted. "What's its name?"

The officer threw his hands upward in disgust. "It's called the Medusa – and it was supposed to have been buried a long, long, time ago."

Medusa…

Nadège let the name settle into her mind.

She thought about the ancient Greek myth of the Medusa and wondered what it could possibly have to do with this strange artifact.

The senior officer left a few minutes later.

Nadège and Raphaël cuddled together in silence, still watching the soldiers packing up and sealing away the rest of the treasure trove into crates, which were then loaded onto the train. The two lovers stared, mesmerized as the scene unfolded. There were five soldiers and twice that many MPs.

The mask was the last one to be moved.

Two men strained under the weight of the crate the mask was in and as they lifted it up onto the train it tumbled back, smashing on the ground. Among the splintered shards of timber lay the mask of the Medusa completely undamaged by the fall – its green eyes staring upward. Despite there not even being a mouth as part of the mask, Nadège thought she could see the damned thing forming a sinister smile.

As though the mask had planned its escape from the beginning.

One of the soldiers stopped and looked at it. He was a big guy, 250 pounds at least of solid muscle. Shaved head and plenty of tattoos. He looked like a total meathead. One glance at this guy and Nadège could tell he hadn't been conscripted. Here was a man who had volunteered at the first opportunity to go to war. Cruelty was in his blood.

The guy went to pick up the mask.

Someone else stopped him. It was an MP. He looked small compared to the first guy, but was probably big within his own right compared to most people. "Don't."

The big guy laughed. "Why not?"

"I don't know. MacCracken said not to. That thing's meant to be evil."

"Evil?" The big guy laughed again, as if to prove he wasn't superstitious or afraid. "How can an inanimate object be evil? It's just some stupid mask."

"Just don't…"

The big guy picked it up and placed it on his face. "Hey look, I'm a Medusa! Watch me turn all you guys to stone."

A few of the nearby soldiers backed away, their hands turned outward in a placating gesture. "Come on, man… that's not funny!"

The meathead asked, "What are you afraid of?"

"I don't know… there's something about that mask that gives me the creeps!"

"Hey, we just stormed Brest and took it from the Fallschirmjäger – the German paratroopers and most revered fighters. I think you can handle the curse of some stupid mask from ancient Egypt."

The MP laughed. "It's Greek you moron. The Medusa came from Greece, not Egypt!"

The big guy shrugged his shoulders. "What do I care? Its owner has been dead for thousands of years and so has its curse, so it can get stuffed! Who's with me, and who's afraid to even touch this thing?"

One of the other soldiers nodded, sheepishly. "You're right. Here, give that to me."

The big guy beamed. Like any bully, he seemed proud to have gotten his way. He passed the Medusa to the other soldier and said, "Good man."

The soldier took it, examined it, staring right into its glowing eyes and then handed it over to the next soldier.

Nadège watched on in horror as the scene of boyhood machoism played out, and each of the soldiered handled the mysterious mask with more confidence, until they eventually tired of the game, and resealed the hideous creature inside a crate, along with the rest of the artifacts.

A short while later, the big guy was the first to feel its wrath.

They watched the most horrific thing they had ever witnessed – throughout the entire war – unfold. There were screams of agony and the men who were playing with the mask just minutes earlier, died an agonizing death.

When it was all over, Nadège turned to Raphaël. "What the hell killed them?"

Raphaël shook his head. "I have no fucking idea."

*

The Bastille de Quilbignon, a medieval tower on a rocky motte beside the Penfeld River offered a vast panorama of the Brest Harbor with Château de Brest on the opposite bank. It was thought to have probably been built in the 14th century, during the Breton War of Succession. It was from these bomb-ravaged stone ramparts that Colonel Joe MacCracken looked out, staring at the men in green masks.

They wore M4 Lightweight Service Masks, as they went about the grizzly business. Only their eyes were visible behind the bug-shaped lenses. Their faces were covered with a green molded rubber facepiece, an anti-fogging nosecup, leading to a M10A1 filter canister via a long green pipe that looked like the snout of a small green elephant.

It was a deadly business, cleaning up one hell of a lethal mess. MacCracken shook his head. It was the first time since he landed on French soil that he'd felt truly afraid. Up until this point, he thought he was fighting for his life, for the outcome of the war, but now he realized this was bigger than all of that. If this got out, there would be no more world wars – there wouldn't be enough people left to fight in them.

Who could have imagined that in the middle of the Allied great push, that the Germans weren't the most dangerous threat to human life?

The soldiers handling the Medusa had all died that horrible death. Their bodies had been unceremoniously retrieved and packed into a large air-tight crate to be buried somewhere never to be seen again. The people who had helped move the bodies had died too. It was the third group who now wore gas-masks as they tried to contain this mess. They would need to find somewhere to bury the bodies, so that the curse could never escape.

MacCracken didn't envy the clean-up crew the task. It wasn't his job. His job was now to protect the Medusa. To make sure that it got to its intended destination where it could be destroyed permanently so its curse could never be released on the world once more. He knew that was what needed doing. No one would ever give him permission to do so, but that's what needed doing, and he was the man to make it happen.

A few minutes later, a young soldier greeted him. "The train's tender is loaded with coal and water. It's ready to depart."

"Thank you, son. I'll be there in a minute."

MacCracken had been given the task of taking charge of the German treasure trove, and seeing its safe delivery to Paris, where it could be professionally identified, valued, categorized, and maybe one day returned to its rightful owners. The mask of the Medusa was one such artifact, but he had little intention of ever letting it reach Paris. For that, he would most likely pay with his life, but that was a price he was more than willing to offer.

A few minutes later he stepped aboard the DRB 52 steam train. To him, it looked like a vicious monstrosity. The Deutsche Reichsbahn's Class 52 was a German steam locomotive built in large numbers during the Second World War. The large locomotive, the German steam engine, specifically built for its simplicity and economy of production during the war effort, was trailed by a fuel tender carrying coal and water, a designated armory and defense carriage, followed by an armored carriage, and finally trailed by a single flatbed carriage – upon which was a green 1932 Bugatti Type 53.

MacCracken glanced at Richardson. "Any idea who owns the Bugatti?"

"Not a clue. Probably some French Lord or Aristocrat." Richardson smiled. "Beautiful car though. I would love to have had the chance to drive it."

MacCracken nodded. "Me too."

He climbed onto the armored train and was introduced to an officer in charge of the train's security, and in command of roughly twenty soldiers who had been assigned to protect the priceless cargo. But it wasn't the priceless artifacts that interested MacCracken.

It was the Medusa.

He could imagine Hitler's interest in the ancient artifact. The man was known to be a believer in the occult sciences and something like the near mythical powers of the Medusa would have certainly appealed to him. As a weapon, it very likely could have shifted the outcome of the war, but then again, MacCracken guessed that the Nazis would have struggled to control its powers. Eventually, they must've resolved to leave the weapon alone.

MacCracken climbed on board. His task was to itemize, value, and catalogue the stolen Nazi treasures in Paris. He watched as a young man in heavily coal-stained overalls kissed his beautiful French girlfriend, before boarding the train too. MacCracken smiled as the two young lovers kissed, and the woman told him to make sure to come home. It was charming to see such strong love. But war was like that, he reflected. When life could be taken at any moment, people learned to determine what really mattered.

The locomotive engineer pulled on the pressure release, and steam whistled loudly. He shouted, "All aboard. Time to go."

The train pulled away, slowly picking up speed as it made its way across rural France. MacCracken met each of the guards, and was introduced to the engineer and Raphaël, the young French civilian, who manned the water pumps and shoveled coal at all the water stops. He then went and checked on the precious cargo. He looked through, making sure that everything was secure. On the small landing platform behind the armored carriage, he spotted the crate that held the Medusa.

He was horrified.

Why the hell wasn't it stored inside the armored carriage along with the rest of the precious artifacts?

He was quickly informed by one of the many guards that there wasn't room for it inside the carriage, and besides, the thing held no value, so there was no risk of it being stolen. MacCracken could have killed someone over such stupidity. If it was up to him, the entire train and its soldiers, would have been put at his disposal to protect the Medusa.

About three hours into the trip, the German armored train slowed, before eventually coming to a stop at Le Mans. Raphaël, the kid, jumped out to work the water pipes. He swung out the spigot arm over the water tender and began refueling the train.

The entire process seemed to be taking longer than MacCracken would have liked. He felt unsafe and trapped with the train at rest. With it moving along the tracks, he felt his precious cargo was safe. A couple hundred tons of steel cruising down the tracks at speed is a difficult thing to stop, no matter what you do.

MacCracken checked his watch. It had been nearly thirty minutes. He didn't know how long it should take to refuel, but he felt it was taking longer than it should. He stepped out on the track. The love-struck kid was high up, some thirty or more feet above, on the water tower. He tried to gesture to the blond-haired boy, but either the kid couldn't hear him, or as a French civilian, he couldn't speak much, if any, English. MacCracken didn't have the time or patience to wait.

He began to climb the wooden ladder to the top of the tower and clambered over the railing to question the young man.

MacCracken greeted the kid. "It's Raphaël isn't it?"

"Yes." The kid answered in English.

"What's taking so long?"

Raphaël gestured toward the train's water tender. "It's a big tank. Lots of water."

"All right, all right. Will it be much longer?"

"Not long. Almost finished and we can go."

"Good."

MacCracken drew a deep breath and slowly exhaled. He pictured the train underway and felt better.

A second later, that image was destroyed by the sound of machinegun fire.

*

MacCracken dropped to the floor.

He shielded himself in the hidden compartment at the top of the water tower and withdrew his M1917 Revolver service pistol. The weapon carried six .45 ACP full metal jacket rounds. The revolver was powerful enough to penetrate light body armor, but the downside was it was a bitch to reload. And although he couldn't see who attacked the train, it was obvious there were more than six of them.

It was a bloody firefight and there was no way of knowing who was winning. He peaked through a crack in the water tower, and stared down in horror. The robbers had taken their losses, but they had taken control of the engineer's cab and were already in the process of starting the train moving again.

MacCracken stood up.

Raphaël placed a hand on his shoulder to stop him. "Please don't."

MacCracken's face was lined with pain. "We have to help."

"I know, but there's nothing we can do. Let them take the damned Nazi treasure."

"It's not the treasure I'm worried about."

Understanding struck Raphaël's intelligent blue eyes. "You're worried about that hideous mask?"

"Yes! What do you know about the mask?"

"Nothing. My girlfriend and I saw what it did to the soldiers who touched it. That's all."

"Ah, so you know what will happen if its evil is allowed to spread?"

"You mean, you don't just have to touch the mask to die?"

"I mean the whole fucking world could get killed by this thing…" MacCracken gritted his teeth. "Unless we stop it."

"But how?"

"Come with me. The crate carrying the mask is stored on the landing platform behind the armored carriage. They'll be more concerned about protecting the treasure and probably won't have a clue about the Medusa."

Raphaël looked torn and undecided.

It was a terrible decision. One squeezed between what was right and had to be done for humanity, and the horrible cost of such honor would most likely result in his death. A life unable to be lived and a beautiful girl he'd never see again.

Steam hissed as it was released from the train's brake system.

MacCracken pushed past him. "Time's up. I'm going. Are you coming with me?"

Raphaël nodded. "I'm with you."

"Good man!" MacCracken said, with the sudden fervor of a man knowing that he's about to share his death with another noble individual because he knew with utmost certainty that it was what needed to be done for the greater good of the world. "Do you have a weapon?"

Raphaël gripped the iron rod used to pry open the water locks. "Just this." It was solid and heavy, but a poor weapon against machinegun fire. Still, it was better than nothing.

MacCracken nodded. "It will have to do until we can get you something better."

The malevolent steam engine rolled by the water tower.

Thick smoke billowed from its smokestack like a fire-breathing dragon exhaling pure malevolence. At the back of the train, the shooting seemed to die down, as though one side had either surrendered or finally lost.

When the coal and water tender lined up with the water tower, MacCracken and Raphaël jumped.

*

MacCracken landed hard on the pile of coal.

He held the revolver in his hand, ready to fire. His heart raced and adrenaline surged through his veins as he moved quickly, climbing down into the engineer's compartment. A worried frown creased his brow. The cab seemed abandoned. MacCracken didn't know how much was needed to keep the train going, but guessed that whoever started it moving, must have joined the fight.

Behind him, he heard someone say, "Where did you come from?"

MacCracken raised his hands slowly above his head, still holding the edge of the revolver's hilt. Holding his breath, waiting for death to arrive, he turned to face the man who had confronted him. He wore plain brown overalls and a blue, long-sleeved shirt with a V-neck – similar to what a French farmer might wear. The man spoke English with a slightly European accent that MacCracken couldn't place.

The robber aimed his pistol. "Are you on your own?"

Raphaël swung his iron bar as hard as he could. He was a skinny kid, but shoveling coal day in day out had made his arms as powerful as pistons. The bar connected with the back of the man's head. Skin and skull gave way to iron with a horrific crunch.

The man fell to the ground.

Dead.

Raphaël quickly picked up his pistol.

MacCracken exhaled slowly. "Thanks. I owe you one."

The kid examined the weapon.

"You ever fired one of those?" MacCracken asked.

"No. Is there anything I should know?"

"Not really. Point and shoot by squeezing the trigger."

MacCracken glanced at the pistol. The sight of the firearm turned his veins to ice. It was an American Colt M1911A1 service pistol. A better weapon than the revolver he'd been issued in his opinion.

Had they been betrayed by another American?

"Anything else?"

"There's a grip safety lever at the back of the hand grip and it becomes automatically depressed when you hold the pistol. There's also a manual safety lever at the rear of the slide." MacCracken reached forward and turned it to off. "You're good to fire."

The train was now moving at speed.

Silently, they made their way along the top of the water and coal tender. Wind whooshed by as they stood up. At the end of the tender, they looked down at the massacre beside the armored carriage. There were maimed bodies everywhere and so much blood that it was hard to tell whose side anyone had been on.

The victors were inside the armored carriage, most likely examining their spoils of war.

MacCracken and Raphaël climbed down from the coal tender into the forward platform of the armored carriage. They split up, climbing on opposite sides in a hope that by doing so, if one of them got caught the other might still have a chance to reach the Medusa.

MacCracken moved quickly. His long arms and legs allowed him to swing across giant gaps between various protruding pieces of armored steel along the carriage that he used as handgrips like the rungs of a ladder.

He reached the opposite side quickly and found the crate carrying the Medusa. Beside the crate, another box appeared to hold spare ammunition. It appeared new. And he wondered if their attackers had brought the box with them in preparation of the next phase of their robbery perhaps? He opened the box to find it stacked with Stielhandgranates — those long, German, grenade sticks. MacCracken carefully put the lid back on.

He frowned.

Raphaël was missing.

There hadn't been any shots or yelling to suggest that he'd been caught, but still he wasn't there — and that could only mean one thing — he wasn't coming.

MacCracken stared at the crate containing the Medusa. It was big. Much too big for him to move on his own. Impossible to move the mask while it was inside the crate. There wasn't much time to waste. At any moment he could be spotted, executed, and the Medusa would be free to wreak its havoc on the world. A plan slowly formed in his mind, but it was abhorrent, despite its necessity, and he wanted more than anything to find another one. From the other side of the armored carriage, he heard a commotion, followed by more gunfire.

That sealed the decision for him.

It was now or never.

He opened the crate and retrieved the Medusa. The decision would kill him. There was no longer any more time for him, but just maybe, there would be enough for him to destroy the Medusa and save others. He then grabbed the box of Stielhandgranates, hoping it would be enough and made his way to the final trailing flat-bed carriage.

He reached the green 1932 Bugatti Type 53.

It was a beautiful car, and he cringed to think about what he was about to do to her. He put the box of Stielhandgranates in the passenger seat beside him. There was no room for a luggage trunk on the sports car, but a single, wheel shaped trunk housed the spare wheel. MacCracken opened it, removed the spare tire, and sealed the Medusa inside, feeling somewhat irrationally better as the wheel locker clicked together to form a seal.

He then climbed in and turned the key.

The ignition clicked and the powerful Type 50 303.4 cubic inch, straight-eight engine came alive – capable of producing 300 Horsepower. MacCracken applied a little bit of throttle and the engine's smooth supercharger whirred. The Bugatti Type 53 was the first race car in the world to ever benefit from four-wheel drive, and was hand made by Ettore Bugatti himself.

MacCracken gripped the steering wheel, released the park-brake and readied himself for the inevitably violent ride.

Behind him, Raphaël yelled, "Wait for me!"

*

Machinegun fire followed the stricken voice.

MacCracken didn't have time to look at his new passenger who clambered in, blithely placing the box of Stielhandgranates on his lap.

He planted his foot on the accelerator, and the all-wheel drive Bugatti, true to her form, lurched forward...

It flew through the air, landing with a crunch on the railway tracks. Its fender grinding – metal against metal – along the tracks, sending shards of sparks in every direction.

MacCracken swung the wheel to the right, and the car turned off the tracks down the lip of the mound upon which the railway line had been built.

The car fishtailed but recovered quickly.

A few seconds later, MacCracken was in control, heading down the dirt road at speed.

Beside him, Raphaël was cackling with laughter. "I can't believe we're alive!"

They reached a three-way intersection along a main road. A sign, recently erected since the Allied Forces had liberated Paris, pointed the way to Paris, Brest, and the Pyrenees Mountains. MacCracken swung the wheel to the right, heading due south in the direction toward the Pyrenees Mountains.

"Where are you going?" Raphaël looked alarmed. "Brest and Paris are in the opposite direction."

"To protect civilization from the greatest threat to its very existence!"

"I thought the Nazis were already losing…"

MacCracken cut him short with the raising of his hand… "Not the Nazis… the Medusa!"

Raphaël's face wore a bemused expression, but underneath was a mask of pure terror and incredulity.

"Where are you going?" he persisted.

"To make sure no one ever sees the Medusa ever again."

Over the course of the next few minutes, MacCracken explained the plan that was only just now formulating in his mind to Raphaël. It was going to all hinge on this one young man. He would never live long enough to see the plan reach fruition. The kid was young, but he seemed smart, and above all, he had a certain sense of duty and honor that would be enough to see it through.

When he was confident Raphaël had heard and understood the plan, he glanced at the kid and asked, "Can you drive?"

"Yes."

MacCracken looked incredulous. "Really?"

"Yeah. I've driven my dad's Berliet GLR. A fruit truck." He then hastily added, "Before the war of course."

"Okay. Good." McCracken pulled over and got out. "Get in the driver's seat."

"Holy shit!" the kid swore. "You're serious. You're going to let me drive the Bugatti?"

McCracken looked at him, the lines around his eyes suddenly deeper, more serious. "Show me that you can drive it!"

"I can drive it," the kid said, suddenly displaying the confidence of an older man.

He put it into first, accelerated, and the sports car slowly picked up speed with a bit of a jolt. He glanced at the American. "See."

McCracken cracked a smile. "Well, I don't know if I'd give you a license, but it will have to do."

"I can drive!" he repeated.

"Forget it." MacCracken dismissed his complaints with a wave of his hand. "Listen, I need you to pull over."

"All right," Raphaël pulled over, taking the car to a stop. Disappointment written on his face, as though he was going to have to relinquish the car.

MacCracken got out. "I'm afraid this is as far as I go."

"We don't know you're infected! Your eyes haven't changed color like the others. Maybe…"

MacCracken wouldn't hear it. "I am."

Raphaël said, "I'm sorry…"

"It's all right. I've had plenty of good times. I feel better knowing you know what to do." He leveled his gaze on Raphaël. "You do know what to do right?"

"I do. I promise. The Medusa will be safe."

"Good man." Then, feeling some sort of intrinsic human need to see love succeed and conquer all, he said, "I hope you marry that beautiful girl of yours."

Raphaël smiled. "Me too."

With that, MacCracken picked up the box of German hand grenades, nicknamed by American soldiers as "Potato Mashers" due to their strange similarity with the kitchen appliance. When he got a hundred yards away, he simply pulled the friction wire from one of the Stielhandgranates.

There were twelve to the box.

Each one exploded simultaneously.

It was powerful enough to destroy a tank. To the human body, it left nothing but dust. In an instant, Joe MacCracken was vaporized, along with the deadly virus within his veins.

Raphaël watched in horror. He promised himself that MacCracken's death and valor wouldn't be in vain. He would fulfill the crazy American's request, and he would go on to live the best life he was capable of.

With that thought, he put the Bugatti into gear.

In the far distance of the horizon, rose the snow-capped peaks of the Pyrenees Mountains.

Chapter One

Zanzibar Archipelago, Tanzania – Present Day

It was as close to paradise as can be found on Earth.

A deep cerulean blue sky stretched all the way to the horizon, broken only by the scattering of a few bare cumulus clouds, like giant white fluffy cotton balls, indicating a day of fair weather would follow. The temperature was a balmy 84 degrees Fahrenheit.

A light breeze drifted over the ocean, offering an idyllic and near perfect atmosphere for tourist and beachgoers. Sparkling turquoise waters with patches of azure blue and sea green spread out across the horizon interspersed with the powder-white sandy beaches of the Mnemba Atoll. The crystal-clear water, itself, fell into that magical place, where it was refreshingly cool, yet simultaneously soothingly warm.

Two dhows – traditional East African sailing boats – with their long thin, narrow hulls and single masts sailed by with their linen settee sails opened fully to catch the light, eastern breeze. Dolphins played in the water, jumping out, flipping and diving in again, for no apparent purpose other than their own entertainment.

The serenity was broken by the rumbling sound of a boat's engine slowing to an idle, followed by metal chain-links running along a stainless-steel wheel, as sixty feet of chain was fed to the ocean like some sort of offering to Neptune – the God of the seas.

Each chain made a loud clank-clank sound, suggesting the size of each metal link was substantial – the sort of thing used on a ship or a working vessel such as a tugboat or an oil exploration ship – nothing like the sort of small pleasure cruisers or traditional boats used to take tourists out to the atoll.

A few seconds later, the large Rocna stainless steel anchor landed softly in the seabed, where it drifted briefly, before biting and taking hold. The chain went taut under the strain, the Rocna bit deeply into the sand, and after a short game of tug-of-war, all became still. The idling engine turned silent, and Mnemba Atoll returned to its state of peace. A large green sea turtle surfaced. Its round, protruding eyes glanced out across the water as though with irritation, searching for the sudden interruption to its near perfect world.

When all was done, a dark ship rested malevolently at its anchor, forming a stark and jarring contrast to the Mnemba Atoll. Shaped like a bullet, with a long, black hull and narrow beam tapering in to a razor-sharp bow, she looked like one in the water, too. Her entire deck was flat with glossy smooth metal, mirroring the blue of the sky and giving the ship the appearance that it went on for infinity.

The deck was absolutely level, as though her designers had ruthlessly removed anything that wasn't vital in an attempt to streamline the ship. There were no railings, no windows, no hatches or stairwells, no wheelhouse or pilot house, no wheel for that matter – in fact, to the casual observer, it might look as though the engineers, having been so focused on creating a thing of such beauty and performance, had forgotten to add the necessities for humans to actually use the vessel. It was all perfectly flat – as though the ship had been constructed as a naval marvel, to be remotely controlled, and never enjoyed by people.

Across her gunmetal gray hull was the ship's name –
Tahila

Toward her aft deck, there was a flicker of movement across her otherwise perfectly level deck. It was soon followed by a larger section amidships, where the deck began to rise to reveal a hidden elevator large enough to house a helicopter and a few small watercraft. Simultaneously, a small railing rose from the outer edge of the entire hull, and in under a minute, the space-aged, futuristic vessel, began to take the shape of a large pleasure cruiser.

The elevator came to a stop after rising more than a dozen feet above the infinity deck. A couple of seconds later, two men stepped out. One was unusually tall, the other just a little above average. Both accustomed to an active lifestyle, they wore board shorts and SCUBA gear, revealing wiry and heavily muscled arms and chests which tapered into slim waists. In one hand they carried their tanks, and in the other, a yellow diver propulsion vehicle.

They were followed by a dog – a golden retriever – its nose down, and its tail wagging with a mind of its own, like a powerful windshield wiper, it appeared to be eagerly pursuing the myriad of scents the outside world offered, taking little interest in the two men.

Sam Reilly stepped onto the deck. The warm sun touched his skin, and he recalled why he loved tropical diving so much. He began to assemble his dive equipment, and test its gauges. He switched on his diver propulsion vehicle. A little green light flashed from what could only be described as the dashboard of the handlebars of a motorcycle, indicating the device had a full battery. The device was basically a caged propeller attached to a pair of handlebars. It weighed just eighteen pounds, but could propel him at six knots through the water.

The light flickered across his ocean blue eyes. He stared out into the still water. His eyes narrowed, but all he saw was still water all the way to the horizon.

He turned to Tom Bower. "Do you see them?"

Tom shook his head. "Nothing yet."

Sam picked up his full-faced dive mask. Inside was a built-in microphone and radio. "Do you see anything, Elise?"

She was in the command center within the bowels of the *Tahila*, keeping her eyes fixed across an array of oceanography displays. Right now, her gaze was fixed on the sonar. Her voice was calm, authoritative. "I have eyes on them."

Sam looked up, running his gaze across the water surface. It appeared still as a millpond. "Direction?"

"Due east," she said.

He turned that way.

Still nothing visible.

Sam secured his first stage of his regulator to his tank, and casually pulled his buoyancy control device over his shoulders, like a jacket. He clicked the straps into place, and looked at Tom. "Are you ready to go diving?"

Tom suppressed a grin. "Are you sure this is a good idea?"

"What could go wrong trying to digitally tag a nine-ton beast in the name of science?" Sam countered.

Tom arched his eyebrows. "What indeed?"

"It can't be any more dangerous than our usual line of work." Sam gave a devil-may-care sort of smile, and attached his full-faced mask.

"That's what I was afraid of," Tom replied, securing his full-faced dive mask into place.

A moment later, Sam placed his hand over his facemask, gripped his diver propulsion vehicle in his right hand, and stepped forward, into the crystal-clear waters surrounding the Mnemba Atoll.

Chapter Two

Both men hit the water simultaneously, like synchronized divers.

Unlike their Olympic counterparts, the resultant splash was enormous. Sam watched as the white blur of bubbles cascaded across his face mask. Seconds later, they dissipated, revealing the crystal-clear waters of which Mnemba Atoll was well renowned. He let himself sink several feet below the surface, before leveling out, and checking his dive gauges.

Happy that everything was in order, he looked at Tom. "All good?" he asked, through the built-in radio, on the full-faced dive-mask.

"Great," Tom replied. "Thanks for introducing me to a genuinely new experience."

Sam suppressed a smile. "And that is?"

"Diving on a tropical atoll that might as well be paradise, instead of nearly getting killed trying to save the world."

"I thought you said you weren't sure diving with a nine-ton beast was a great idea?"

Tom shrugged. Holding out his arm to present the aquarium like view of their environment, inundated with tropical marine life. "On second thoughts, I was wrong. This is perfect. And as you said before, the beast is as safe as a school bus… as long as we don't get in its way."

Sam smiled, reassuringly. "Exactly."

He slowly turned around, running his eyes across the aquarium, really taking it in for the first time. Thousands of schooling fish, including snappers, sergeant fish, and Moorish idols roamed idly by. Sam cast his gaze to the sandy bottom some thirty feet below. The water's clarity and visibility so immense that it was easy to see the seabed, full of great coral bommies, leading to a spectacular plate of vibrant corals of a myriad of colors, where hundreds of nudibranchs of an equally spectacular array of colors, roamed.

Sam had always admired and loved the nudibranchs – the group of soft-bodied, marine gastropod molluscs that shed their shells after their larval stage – were noted for their often-extraordinary colors and striking forms. Although appearing helpless, they used a variety of chemical defenses to aid in protection, rendering them distasteful to any would-be predators.

A giant blue grouper, known as a Napoleon fish, nudged the sandy bottom in search of an unsuspecting meal of mollusk. Its large eyes meeting the two divers with the cursory indifference of a docile dog. Lots of reef fish such as angel fish, blue spotted rays, black snappers, red tooth triggers, flounders, octopus, leaf fish, scorpion fish, stone fish, frog fish and lots of trevallies came to feed on the reef. A single green sea turtle swam by, glancing at them, its giant eyes seemingly depicting recognition, as though it had seen these new strange creatures before, even though their large, noisy vessel was utterly unique to it.

Sam watched as a pod of dolphins swam by, playfully checking them out, intrigued by their diver propulsion vehicles.

His peaceful reverie was interrupted by Elise's voice on the radio. "Are you two going to stay around and stare at the wonders of the aquarium all day, or are you going to get some work done? Where do you think you are, on vacation?"

"We are on vacation!" Sam countered.

She laughed. "You don't do vacations!"

"Okay, well... it is a working one," Sam admitted.

Tom's deep voice joined the banter. "Hey, diving in the tropics of Zanzibar is as close to one as Sam will ever let us get for taking leave. So as far as I'm concerned, this is a vacation."

"Yeah, I'm with Tom on this one. Perspective's everything." Sam grinned. "Besides, this really isn't work. This is a favor to an old friend who's a marine biologist trying to get answers... the real work starts tomorrow when we go to Zanzibar and start our search for the final resting place of the African Slave Ship, *Midas*."

"And her infinite Spanish treasures!" Tom pointed out.

"Of course," Sam agreed.

"You're chasing a pipe dream," Elise said.

"Finding a lost shipwreck, nearly three thousand miles from where it was last seen two centuries ago and nowhere near where it belongs... how difficult can it be?"

She laughed. "How difficult, indeed?"

Sam said, "I'll bet you a week's pay on a tropical island that we'll find it."

"It's a deal," Elise replied. "But I don't just want a week on a deserted island. I want to block your number so you can't contact me for that time, too."

"All right, you're on," Sam said. Then, returning to the task in hand, he said, "Have you got a direction for me, Elise?"

"They're on a bearing north-east of your position. Six hundred yards away."

Sam set the digital compass on the diver propulsion vehicle to a bearing of 45 degrees. Shifting the throttle to full the little propeller hummed, and he surged forward with a jolt.

Tom, following beside him, yelled, "Yeehaw, let's go get em!"

"We're going to find the *Midas*," Sam said with a grin. "But first, we'll tag these whale sharks."

Chapter Three

The twin diver propulsion vehicles whirred.

Up ahead, Sam spotted a blurred movement in the distance. The first sign of several whale sharks. The pod of dolphins joined them on the hunt, as though it were a game, happily swimming in and out between the two diver propulsion vehicles.

Whale sharks are, ordinarily, masters of conserving effort. The stereotypical tropical ocean – warm, blue and clear – is a biological desert. Warmer water carries a lower oxygen content, and tropical waters are typically low in vital nutrients. Together, that means less phytoplankton, the tiny ocean plants that form the base of the food web.

The system can only support a few large animals.

Whale sharks are ectothermic, meaning that they don't have to burn energy maintaining a constant body temperature. Instead, their internal temperature naturally varies with the environment. A whale shark's metabolism is far slower than a whale of the same size.

Nevertheless, a giant shark still needs a lot of food. Whale sharks seem to be less concerned about what they're specifically eating, and more focused on how much. That's why whale sharks migrate in most areas. They travel vast distances to take advantage of short-lived explosions of productivity, whether that be plankton blooms, fish spawning events, or schooling baitfish.

It was just such an explosion of schooling baitfish, coinciding with Sam's arrival in Zanzibar that had attracted him to make this minor detour and do his part in the aid of these beautiful creatures by tagging them for science.

The wall of silvery bait fish came into view like a giant tornado.

Beside it, Sam caught his first vision of a whale shark.

Covered in white polka dots and roughly the length of a bus, the whale shark glided through the water. A docile filter-feeder, the whale shark challenges the stereotype of sharks as giant, toothy predators. Its 300 rows of teeth are microscopic, it moves through the water at a relatively plodding pace and has been known to allow phalanxes of other fish to hitch a ride.

Sam watched as the first 9-ton beast swam past.

The whale sharks' heads are flattened and have a blunt snout above its mouth. Short barbels – whisker-like sensory organs like catfish have – protrude from their nostrils. Their backs and sides are gray to brown with white spots and pale stripes. Their bellies are white. Sam stared at the whale shark's spots. They formed a pattern like a constellation, and served as each shark's own unique identifier, much like human fingerprints.

Sam looked at Tom, "Ready to do this?"

Tom held the first of several tags. "Let's do it."

Whale sharks are so placid that anyone, including snorkelers and SCUBA divers, can safely enter the water and swim with them. Their gentle nature has made the whale shark a popular focus of marine wildlife tourism. Sadly, these same qualities, coupled with valuable fins and meat, have resulted in people hunting whale sharks around the world. Major fisheries have operated in India, the Philippines and Taiwan, and are still ongoing in mainland China.

Sam adjusted the throttle, and the diver propulsion vehicle whirred, as he set a speed to match, coming in alongside the whale shark. Together, with Tom, they attached the first multi-sensor 'behavioral' tags. Over the course of the hour, they managed to tag eight whale sharks. The tags were temporarily affixed to the dorsal fins of each of the sharks. These tags used a battery of recording devices, including accelerometers, gyroscopes and pressure sensors, to reconstruct the shark's three-dimensional movements over hours to a few days, which Sam's friend was hoping would allow them to gain better knowledge of the spectacular beast's movements.

They reached the *Tahila* with ample air to spare in their tanks. The hull of the *Tahila* rose and fell gently in the calm waters.

Sam hung onto the boarding ladder and passed up his fins to Genevieve who greeted him on the deck, followed by his diver propulsion vehicle, before climbing up.

Genevieve was employed as the ship's general factotum, who performed a variety of tasks on the *Tahila*, ranging from cooking, through to diving and setting up gear. She originally came to be part of the crew after running from her original post as an enforcer in the Russian mafia – a job that didn't believe in ever letting its staff leave. With this background, she'd taken on the role of impromptu security officer on board. It was a large set of skill hats, but she juggled them well.

Tom passed his gear up to Sam, and then climbed the ladder in two swift movements. Instead of taking a seat beside the elevator to doff the rest of his diving gear, he stopped, and greeted his girlfriend, Genevieve.

"Nice dive?" she asked.

"Beautiful," he replied, bending down to kiss her.

She kissed him back happily and then pushed his chest back after a few seconds with a teasing smile. "Hey, you're all wet!"

Tom shrugged. "Sorry."

"That's all right…" she said, her eyes lingering on his muscular body. "You're lucky we're in the tropics."

Sam half-heartedly dried himself with a towel. Like so many men that were still boys at heart, it was a cursory attempt at drying, rather than anything serious. He toweled himself with a couple of quick pats, before throwing the towel onto the chair where it at least could dry. He then opened his drink bottle and took a long swig of water. There was something about breathing compressed air that had a way of drying the mouth and dehydrating people, and that was before one was diving in the warmth of the tropics.

He turned to Tom, who was already talking animatedly with Genevieve about the dive. "Well Tom, what do you think?"

"It was good fun," Tom replied with a grin. "Now, you want to tell me why we just spent the last hour tagging a bunch of whale sharks like a couple of cowboys?"

Chapter Four

Sam stood up and stared at the whale sharks in the distance.

His eyes were distant and his voice somber, as though he were speaking from the heart. "Half of the world's whale shark population has been killed since the 1980s. They were classified as a globally endangered species in 2016. Yet, despite the urgency of this disaster, marine biologists know next to nothing about these spectacular creatures including its breeding habits."

Tom asked, "How can you have an informed conservation plan for an animal if you don't know how, when or where it breeds?"

"Exactly," Sam said. "Scientists are now locked in a race against time. In the wild, once whale sharks are born, little is known about the first years of their lives, he says."

Tom stood next to Sam watching the whale sharks feast on silvery bait fish. "How much time are we talking about?"

"There's a number of lost years between when they're born until they've grown to about sixteen feet long. That period and in between those ages, we have no idea where they are."

"Any idea how old they are at sixteen feet?"

Sam shook his head. "None."

"We don't even know how old a sixteen-foot-long whale shark is?"

"No. Whale shark childbirth has never been witnessed." Sam drew a breath. "Tantalizing clues have turned up around the world, but never the real deal. In fact, for years marine biologists have debated whether or not they're viviparous."

Tom arched an eyebrow. "Viviparous?"

"It means the baby is developed in-uterus, and the mother gives birth to a live baby."

"Right... as opposed to what... eggs?"

"Yeah."

A large school of flying fish jumped out of the water, making a splash as they re-entered it a few seconds later. Three fish didn't take into account the *Tahila* within their calculations, and landed on the side of the dive deck. Caliburn barked happily and came over to investigate. Unfortunately for the fish, Golden Retrievers investigated with their mouths and their stomachs.

Sam chuckled at Caliburn's antics for a few moments. Then, returning to the subject of whale sharks he said, "Some creatures just don't get a break."

"No," Tom agreed. "How did they work that out without having ever witnessed a birth?"

Sam nodded. "A pregnant female harpooned by a commercial fishing vessel in Taiwan in 1995 was found to be carrying more than 300 pups in different stages of development. Analyses carried out years later allowed researchers to determine that 29 pups still remaining from the litter all had the same father, suggesting whale sharks mate once, store the sperm and fertilize their own eggs as needed."

"Holy shit! 300 pups? And they're monogamous?"

"It's a possibility, but unlikely. Whale sharks are notorious loners. Although, as we saw today, when there's a feeding bloom, they're more than happy to share their meal with other whale sharks. But, like today though, even if we do see groups of them together, they're all of the same sex never co-ed."

Tom asked, "So what do we know about whale sharks?"

"They're the largest fish in the world. Technically they're not whales, they are sharks. They have a lot in common with whales, though. For example, they are massive like whales and they feed more like whales than a typical shark.

"Plankton are their main food source, but they also eat shrimp, algae and other marine plant material, sardines, anchovies, mackerels, squid, tuna and albacore. They wait until the creatures reach a large mass, and then eat the entire school in their giant mouths."

Tom suppressed a laugh. "That sounds a little mean somehow."

Caliburn, right on cue, devoured the last of the flying fish on the deck. His tail wagging vigorously.

Sam shrugged. "The ocean's a cruel place."

"Anything else?" Tom asked. "I mean, anything else we understand about them?"

"The key is to understand that whale sharks are highly food-motivated. They're basically oceanic Labradors."

Caliburn ears pricked up at the mention of a Labrador.

The dog was quiet now, watching Sam talk about the whale sharks incuriously with his head resting on his front paws.

"For example, they love to eat fish eggs. There have been some cases where whale sharks have been recorded waiting as long as fourteen hours for fish to spawn on reefs. Then, they swoop in and eat the eggs. Somehow, they know where fish will spawn, and are happy to travel thousands of miles to find it."

"They're smart, and patient…" Tom reflected. "And devious despite their docile nature."

"Yeah, like most sharks, they have the time to be patient."

"Really? How long do they live?"

"No one knows for certain, but there are estimates of at least 150 years, but it could be longer."

Tom squinted his eyes against the reflection of the blistering sun. "You mean those sharks we tagged today are going to outlive us?"

"By a long shot. Particularly given the way we live!"

"Hey! It's the way you live, I'm happy to play marine biologist and tag passive sea creatures, but inevitably I have to put my neck out trying to save your backside. You know that, right Sam?"

"I do," Sam admitted. "And I appreciate it."

"Do sharks in general live long lives?"

"Most large shark species are long-lived and slow-growing. Greenland sharks, living in the cool Arctic and deep waters, grow less than one inch per year and can be over 2- foot at full size. A 15-foot female was estimated to be 392 years old."

"Incredible. So now what?"

"My friend will hopefully be able to monitor these whale sharks for the foreseeable future, and hopefully gain valuable information about their movements and breeding habits."

Sam grinned. "And we're going to go find the wreckage of the *Midas*."

Chapter Five

The *Tahila* motored slowly toward the island of Zanzibar.

Sam sat by himself at the Round Table in the Mission Room. The Round Table was taken from the Arthurian ideal, that all members of the team share an equal voice, and capability in achieving the team's goal. He had always enjoyed the symbolism of the concept. But that's where the Round Table's similarities to its Arthurian predecessor ceased.

The table itself was a three-dimensional touch-screen projector, which allowed them to bring up 3D images, expand those images, and search through in-depth 3D renditions of buildings, ships, locations, mine tunnels, and anything else the human mind could imagine, and engineers might have once built. The room itself was full of futuristic technology that one would expect to find at the heart of multi-billion-dollar tech companies, and most navies would kill to possess.

A huge bag of opened Fritos on his lap, Sam absently chewed, while staring at the 19th century oil painting he'd recently acquired.

It hung at the far end of the Mission Room, behind the Round Table – a stark contrast to the rest of the room, which was so modern that most people were unaware such high-tech even existed. Sam was pensive, his ocean blue eyes staring aimlessly at the painting, as though it might reveal some sort of hidden truth to him, if he were to just look at it long enough.

It was simply an oil painting.

The quality, along with the artist's skill, wasn't anything out of the ordinary. Not that Sam cared even a little about the artistic abilities of its painter. It was the subject of the painting, and its location that had caught his attention.

It depicted a Spanish slave ship anchored at the entrance to an ox-bow lake. An oxbow lake was a U-shaped Lake that formed when a wide meander of a river is cut off, creating a free-standing body of water.

There were a variety of wild animals depicted behind the ship, on the bank of the river. There were three elephants, a couple leopards, a lion, and several crocodiles lying in wait to feast on their unsuspecting prey. It looked like something out of the wildlife channel or a tourism advertisement for jungle tours. A pod of buffalo with their giant, leathery bodies, played in the water to the south of the *Midas*, indifferent to the apex predators that surrounded them.

Sam wondered if the animals were an actual image of the location, or if the artist had simply included them as a tribute to the wild beasts they had come across along their journey up the river? At the bottom of the right-hand corner, the location was marked as the *Save River, Africa* and the date on the painting was *16th June, 1834*.

The painting had been tested by two different specialists to determine its veracity, age, and authenticity. Both experts were satisfied the painting was legit. One of the specialists was a conservator-restorer, a professional responsible for the preservation of artistic and cultural artifacts, also known as cultural heritage.

Conservators possess the expertise to preserve cultural heritage in a way that retains the integrity of the object. Understanding the process, and observing evidence of deterioration, they analyze and assess, then carry out conservation treatments. A conservator's job is to ensure that the objects in a museum's collection are kept in the best possible condition.

To Sam's untrained eyes, the painting had looked both centuries old and original.

The specialist, a French conservator-restorer named Pierre, explained to Sam that he could tell just as much, if not more from the back of a painting than the front. Studying the other side of the canvas, he'd shown Sam the darkened tell-tale signs of oxidation expected from a painting dating 180-220 years old. Irrespective of whether the painting was a fake or not, the original canvas used was at least in the right ballpark.

Sam, more interested in the painting's value as a potential key in the search for the Midas, allowed Pierre to remove a part of the frame, and radio-carbon date the wood. The forthcoming report was conclusive. The frame was made 195 years ago plus or minus a decade, ending any doubt in Sam's mind about the veracity of the painting.

Even if the painting was legitimate, the date the right time, the question still remained, where was that location along the Save River?

And more importantly, where did the *Midas* go afterward?

Sam shook his head. It was all still one giant "if."

Tom stepped into the meeting room, grabbing a handful of corn chips from Sam's bag. With a grin, he said, "Still staring at that thing?"

Sam nodded. "Yeah…"

"Can't let it go?"

"No."

Like his friend, Tom took a moment to chew and stare at the painting. "What do you think our chances are of finding much about her final location in Zanzibar?"

Sam arched an eyebrow. "You mean the final resting place of the *Midas*?"

"Yeah."

The lines in Sam's face deepened as he paused to mull it over. "It's hard to say. I've contacted *Berlusconi's*. That's where we'll start.

"Berlusconi's?" Tom frowned. "I thought we were going to Zanzibar?"

"We are. It's in Zanzibar. A man named Tony Berlusconi owns a warehouse full of exotic and not so exotic paintings, artifacts, and junk there. It was in his humble shop where this work of art was first discovered and picked up by a representative of Christies' auction house. I'm hoping someone there might be able to find out where the painting came from."

Tom's hand snaked down to take another handful of chips, but before he could, Sam's gaze still on the painting, he handed him the whole bag.

Tom began crunching in earnest. "That's a tenuous lead at best," he said skeptically.

"Some of the best ones are." Sam shrugged. "Failing that, there's a historian on the island. He's agreed to meet with me tonight and go over a few things. Maybe he'll have some suggestions. At the very least, he can have a look at the painting and hopefully point us in some direction about where the river and location the *Midas* was at, when someone went to the effort to paint her."

"And failing that?"

Sam suppressed a grin. "You think we're going to strike out with two far-fetched chances?"

"It's a strong possibility."

Sam laughed. "Yeah, well, in that case, we'll just have to get lucky."

"How so?"

Sam looked wistful. "I have no idea. But something will just turn up. It generally does."

It was Tom's turn to look wistful. "No, bad guys who try and kill us generally turn up."

Sam shrugged. "That will be nice if they do."

"Really? Why?"

Sam's voice raised in brazen defiance. "Because that will confirm we're on the right track."

Chapter Six

Siktyakh, Siberia

The Mil Mi-38 transport helicopter flew northeast, along the Lena River.

The twin Klimov TVA-3000 turboshaft engines hummed stoically, each one producing 1,838 kW, driving the 69 foot, 3inch main rotor blade that made a defiant *whoop, whoop* sound as it beat the cold air of the Siberian morning into a frenzy capable of maintaining enough lift to overcome the helicopter's 13,000-pound payload. The large transport helicopter raced above the green-blue canopy of Siberian pine at roughly 150 knots. The powerful Russian designed and built machine was painted in carmine red and emblazoned with the company's name in a rich gold along both sides of its fuselage.

Precision Exploration.

The entire process of gold mining could be broken down roughly into four steps: prospecting, mining, extracting and refining. Early discoveries of gold relied on the blind luck of someone spotting a yellow glint in a stream or in a crack between rocks. But the search today is more systematic and precise.

It was the first of these steps, that *Precision Exploration* concentrated on. The company had made a fortune establishing drilling exploratory samples and then selling the geological data of profitable sites to mining companies. Geologists know that gold is present in almost all rocks and soil, but the grains are so small that they're invisible. Only in a few areas is the gold concentrated enough to be mined profitably.

Scientists search for these deposits. This is known as prospecting. Sometimes, these deposits contain pure gold. In most deposits, however, gold is combined with silver or another metal. After finding indications of gold, scientists drill to obtain samples from below the surface, which they analyze for their gold content. If there's enough gold in the deposit, the mining company may set up a large-scale mining operation.

Gold most commonly occurs as a native metal but will form compounds with tellurium, sulfur or selenium. The gold-bearing minerals that contain tellurium are called, tellurides. One particularly valuable telluride is a gold rich mineral called calaverite. It has a specific gravity of 9.35 and a hardness of 2.5. meaning that the calaverite could be dissolved in concentrated sulfuric acid.

In hot sulfuric acid the mineral dissolves, leaving a spongy mass of gold in a red solution of tellurium. It was this deposit of calaverite recently discovered along the banks of the Lena River that had the executives of the company so excited. Several deep drills had been planted in the nearby region in an expanding search grid in order to take core samples to determine just how large the deposit of calaverite extended. As with a lot of mining geology, it required extensive research. Determining the profitability of a site, was less of a science and more of an art – and a whole lot of gambling.

That's where Dr. Lev Preobrazhensky came into it.

Lev was a 42-year-old geology professor from Moscow University, who had recently been poached by *Precision Exploration* as they offered greater financial rewards than academia ever could. He had thick blond hair, and intelligent blue eyes. There was something about him that gave the impression of an erudite professor, but he was far from the image of an old, disheveled academic who only cared about ratifying a research paper. Lev was handsome. A little over six foot, he had a healthy physique, a warm smile, and boyish good looks.

He rode in the back of the loudly whirring twin Klimov, along with several other specialists and a few executives who had been brought in to expedite the process. The valuable discovery was rapidly shaping up to be the most profitable find in the company's decade long history.

Lev stared out the starboard window of the helicopter at the ground not so far below them. He was a bad flyer. Equally afraid of dying and a natural predisposition to motion sickness, the smell of machine oil and bacon the others had eaten wasn't helping. He'd taken a concoction of antiemetics before his flight as a precaution and skipped breakfast. It seemed to have worked, but that didn't mean his stomach wasn't churning. To make matters worse, he was new to the company, and this was a big project.

It would either make or break him, so they say.

The helicopter had left Mezhdunarodnyy Airport Yakutsk two hours earlier and before that, Lev had spent nearly eighteen hours on board an even more uncomfortable 18-hour flight from Moscow on board one of the company's old Antonov 28s, which leap-frogged between multiple locations on the way. He had only slept intermittently, in broken sets of thirty or so minutes, since he'd left Moscow.

His eyes traced the river, as it carved its way through the Siberian wilderness. A grizzly bear with two cubs came into view on the outskirts of the forest and the crumbling stone bank of the Lena. To the west of the river steep pillared cliffs and spires of rock rose in a series of monumental belts of limestone and dolerite karst.

Lev's geologist's mind perked with interest as he studied the rare rock formations for which eastern Siberia were famous. These are the fossilized remains of a very large Cambrian reef, comparable to the present-day Great Barrier Reef, which preserves the evolutionary record during the Cambrian explosion of life of a wide range of skeletal and soft-bodied fossils of very high quality, with extensive examples of karstic weathering in permafrost.

The fascinating geological monument seemed to waken him, like a magic trick that might tease a child's inner curiosity. He studied the formation with the joy of a child in a theme park, and for the first time in hours forgot that he was defying several of Newton's Laws in a veritable death-trap, of which Siberia was well renowned.

They passed over a small mountain range and began their descent into the valley far below, the pilot setting up an approach to land upon a makeshift helipad. The place was as remote as one could get – even in Siberia – which was really saying something. The V-shaped valley opened up at the far end and a tributary of the Lena flowed. The nearby river formed a serpentine course as it raced toward an ocean thousands of miles away. The place was remote all right. It would be a nightmare to set up a full-scale mining production in such wilderness, but Lev knew that if the concentrations of gold were high enough, mining companies were literally capable of moving mountains to obtain it.

A strange anomaly in the otherwise dense forest caught Lev's attention.

To the east, he spotted a noticeable irregularity in the vegetation. Something had damaged hundreds upon hundreds of trees. They weren't dead. Their growth was more stunted than anything else, or the trees were younger.

Lev studied the anomaly for a couple minutes with a scientist's eye. The lines were too regular and far too straight for them to be explained by the random growth of a wild forest. It made him wonder if the region had ever been mined previously... perhaps a hundred or more years ago, but the dossier on the site had made no mention of it.

The helicopter suddenly dropped its altitude and began to hover just above a landing zone. Up ahead, the forest gave way to a clearing. Two small aluminum buildings had been erected to house the workers. They looked like something out of a space-mission and were set in a strange geometric shape, rigidly hexagonal and designed to maintain heat in the Siberian winters, which could reach minus 60 or more degrees Fahrenheit.

The buildings set a jarring contrast with the otherwise green foliage of the ubiquitous carpet of Siberian pines that flooded the entire region. The buildings looked impressive, but Lev knew they weren't much more than expensive tents, and no more permanent. A couple exploratory technicians, upon hearing the sound of the helicopter, opened the door, and watched as the helicopter came in to land.

The Mil Mi-38's skids touched the ground, and the helicopter became firmly grounded once more. Time was money, so they say, and in the world of gold exploration, money meant everything. So, no one waited for the massive blade to stop spinning. The rotor was nearly fifteen feet above the ground – far too high to be dangerous to anyone. One of the technicians from outside opened the sliding door to the fuselage, while the pilot went about his business of shutting down the twin Klimov TVA-3000 turboshaft engines.

Lev was the first out of the helicopter.

It felt great to step onto the ground and know that he would be there for a few days at the very least. He stomped his feet just because it felt good to move and rubbed his hands together against the cool air.

He was greeted by a blonde woman in a pair of jeans, boots, and a thick jacket. "Doctor Preobrazhensky?"

"That's me," he said, offering his hand. His voice was deep and resonant. "You can call me Lev if you like?"

She took it. Her handshake was firm and authoritative. "Okay, Lev. I'm Anya Gorbachev."

"Excuse me, Madam Gorbachev. I didn't expect such a high-ranking member of the company to be here."

She smiled kindly, as though she'd expected him to be surprised by her appearance. "That's okay. You can call me Anya… we're not too big on formalities out here in the middle of nowhere."

Lev felt the familiar sense of fear and discomfort of flying rise in his throat like bile at his blunder. He'd expected to be met by a simple geological surveyor, a drill technician. Instead, they had sent the Vice President of the company, Anya Gorbachev. He recalled that she was some distant relation of the eighth and last leader of the Soviet Union and General Secretary of the Communist Party, Mikhail Gorbachev.

He'd never met her before but took her in with a glance. Her face was striking, but it was her compelling blue eyes that drew him in. With her long blade of a nose, Anya could not be called a beauty, yet she was striking in both countenance and personality. He had no doubt that those who met her never forgot her.

The VP was already on the ground.

That surprised him. The calaverite discovery must be bigger than he realized. Or he'd been told a lie and brought here urgently. Either way, someone knew something he didn't, if Gorbachev had made the uncomfortable trip out here to greet him.

His eyes landed on hers for a little longer than they should have. Embarrassed, he turned his attention toward those trees he'd spotted from the air. On the ground they weren't quite as obvious, but still, he could just make out that they appeared smaller and less vibrant. It was as though their roots had never been allowed to penetrate the ground below.

She seemed to follow his distraction, realizing that he was looking at the trees. He focused his gaze back on her face. There was something uniquely attractive about it, but he couldn't quite place the cause. She was beautiful, not so much in a traditional sense. After a while, he decided it was the composition of her flaws that somehow made her face appear unique and attractive to him. It was a distraction. At forty-two years of age, he thought he was beyond being so easily distracted by a woman. Obviously, that was naive. He just hadn't met anyone as attractive as Anya.

Anya said, "You're wondering what caused the strange changes in the tree lines?"

Like an anxious schoolboy some twenty years younger than he was, he drew in a deep breath, and once more met her eyes. His heart nearly stopped. Butterflies fluttered in his stomach. She was rich, intelligent, beautiful – and above all things, powerful. He smiled. "Yes, I was curious."

A group of men in khaki uniforms began unloading the helicopter, including the personal and professional items he brought. "This way," she said, walking toward one of the larger structures. "The trees were felled to make way for a train-line during the war."

Walking side by side with her, Lev didn't need to ask which war. He knew all about the Siberian Labor Camps. After the Russian Revolution, the labor camps in Siberia were closed down. These were later reopened by Joseph Stalin and opponents of his regime were sent to what became known as the Glavnoye Upravleniye Lagere – or the Gulag. It had been estimated that around 50 million perished in Soviet gulags during this period. In direct contrast with Anya's prestigious heritage, Lev's grandfather had once been a dissident, who had spent the best years of his life toiling in just such a gulag. It was a secret, his mother had worked hard to conceal, changing their family name before Lev was born.

Lev glanced around at the infinite expanse of Siberian wilderness. "Where in the world were they headed? I didn't think anyone had ever mined this region before?"

"They tried, but the permafrost made it too difficult to reap any rewards. Of course, that didn't stop Stalin trying. In the end, my guess is they found a better use for the laborers, and the project was scrapped."

"Are there any open mine shafts still accessible?" he asked. "I'd like to take a look underground. It might give me a unique insight into what we're looking at."

"Afraid not. My guess is they never got far enough. Or if they did, it wasn't deep enough to still exist."

Lev suppressed a smile.

Anya caught him. Her voice firm but interested. "What?"

He shrugged. "I don't know. You've read the preliminary geologist reports from the drilling sites." It was a statement, not a question.

"Yeah, there's a higher concentration of gold here than anyone could have ever predicted." She smiled. "Still, that didn't change the fact that in the 1940s, the permafrost would have made it nearly impossible to obtain."

Lev sighed. "Yeah, thank God for climate change."

She turned the palms of her hands up and outward. "Hey, we didn't cause it. But that doesn't mean the company shouldn't be opportunistic about its secondary benefits. Don't you think?"

Her voice was calm, but there was a distinctive challenge in the words, and Lev had to remind himself that he was speaking to the company's VP.

He smiled politely. "Of course."

Chapter Seven

Siberia, in the north of Russia, was one of the coldest, harshest places on earth. Famed for its inhospitable climate, it was also mineral-wealthy and unexploited – a true frontier region. Although it had attracted mining companies for decades, the challenging landscape and conditions have meant they have only just begun to scratch the surface of the area's potential.

This could now be changing as climate change leads to warmer temperatures, ice and permafrost were melting and potentially easing the mining process. The mining sector was the *second* largest contributor to the economy in Russia. An energy superpower, its biggest contributor is gas, oil, and coal.

Mining in Siberia grew exponentially during the 20th century, as successive governments and leaders sought to take advantage of it. The Siberian region was rich in minerals including coal, gold, diamond and iron ore. Coal was largely extracted from Kemerovo, Krasnoyarsk Krai, Sakha. Gold originates mainly from Krasnoyarsk Krai and Irkutsk Oblast.

Lev was fully aware that Siberian mining was "heating up" (no pun intended).

The effects of climate change were being felt around the world and were particularly evident in the frozen north of the world. This could be seen in the rate at which Arctic Sea ice was shrinking annually and was also being seen in mining operations in Canada, where work had been hampered by the melting of ice roads previously relied on for transportation.

Siberia was one of the coldest places on earth, with temperatures dropping as low as -76°F in the winter. But here too, warmer temperatures have begun to affect the landscape. Forest fires, which annually sweep the boreal forest and tundra to the south of Siberia, burned at a rate unheard of for 10,000 years in 2017. NASA assessments of the area show that there the temperature has been 7°F above average.

Large areas of Siberia are formed by permafrost, perennially frozen ground. As the climate warms, the superficial layers of the permafrost are melting and microbial activity in the soil rises exponentially. Climate data from Siberia show an increase of average temperatures in the last decade.

As permafrost thaws, microbes begin decomposing this material. This process releases greenhouse gases like carbon dioxide and methane to the atmosphere. When permafrost thaws, so do ancient bacteria and viruses in the ice and soil. These newly unfrozen microbes could make humans and animals very sick.

Lev was surprised when they passed the structure. "We're not going inside?"

"Do you need to?"

He shrugged. "Not really."

"Good as there is work to be done," Anya said. "This thing's going to be big."

"We won't know until we get down there…" Lev warned.

She smiled. "Exactly…"

He turned his arms outward. "Exactly what?"

She began to bring him up to speed. "As you know the ground below us and along this entire area is surrounded by karst."

He nodded, seeing where she was headed.

Karst is a topography formed from the dissolution of soluble rocks such as limestone, dolomite, and gypsum. It is characterized by underground drainage systems with sinkholes and caves. It has also been documented for more weathering-resistant rocks, such as quartzite, given the right conditions. Subterranean drainage may limit surface water, with few to no rivers or lakes. However, in regions where the dissolved bedrock is covered – perhaps by debris – or confined by one or more superimposed non-soluble rock strata, distinctive karst features may occur only at subsurface levels and can be totally missing above ground. Karst landscape underlain by limestone which has been eroded by dissolution, producing ridges, towers, fissures, sinkholes and other characteristic landforms.

Lev smiled. "You've found underground caverns?"

She nodded. "Several."

"Can we get eyes down there?"

"Soon. Ground penetrating radar shows a long cavern some twenty feet below the surface. It appears to be a natural cavern. We've sent down a snake."

His heart picked up its pace. The company did know something about the discovery he didn't. The electronic snake was a type of modular digital video camera, capable of being fed through narrow holes, and manipulated into otherwise impossible to visualize places. "What did it show?"

"The first cave is huge and laden with the metallic crystals of calaverite."

He felt she was withholding something. "What else?"

She met his eyes and smiled. There was something impish, and mischievous about her expression. If he didn't know better, he'd almost say she was flirting with him. "There's one giant gold seam."

"You think one of your technicians landed on the motherlode… or is this just the beginning?"

She nodded. "You didn't think we paid all that money to entice you out here, just because you're pretty, Dr. Preobrazhensky," she said, reverting to his surname.

He suppressed a grin. She was flirting with him, but he was used to it. He wasn't vain, but nor did he possess some sort of misplaced modesty. He knew he was good looking. He ate well, exercised moderately, but at the end of the day, it was just in his genes. He was born with that sort of look that women seemed to find attractive. What did surprise him, though, was just how much he was enjoying being attracted to Anya.

"How long will it take to drill an opening large enough to climb down?"

"We're just about there. One of the technicians is in the process of running our largest drill through the top. This will make a tunnel big enough to drop a wire ladder."

"Great. I'll go down and let you know what we have."

"Sounds good. I'll come with you."

It was the second time in as many minutes that he was surprised. "You'll descend into the chamber with me?"

"Of course. Why not?" She looked up and held his gaze. Her voice was soft, but there was a challenge in her tone. "You don't think I rose to the top of a mining exploration company being afraid of the dark, do you?"

He shook his head, "Of course not."

Instead, he thought, *You rose to the top of Precision Exploration because your grandfather used to be the leader of the Soviet Union.*

Chapter Eight

After a quick inspection of the entry site, Lev had a hot drink, used the facilities, and dressed for caving. His well thought out backpack covered every possible contingency. Shortly after, he and Anya made their descent into the cold, dark, earth.

The drilled tunnel was narrow. Barely wide enough for his shoulders to squeeze through. After dropping a wire ladder down the boring hole, they slowly climbed – one at a time – down to the bottom of the open cavern below.

They both wore hard hats with LED headlights.

At the bottom of the ladder, he called up to Anya that he was off the ladder, and she could come down. He kept some weight on the bottom rung, supporting it by adding pressure with his hands to stop the ladder from swinging too much. As Anya reached the void of the open chamber, he switched off his flashlight to prevent her being blinded by the light while she climbed down.

When she reached the bottom, she said, "What do you think?"

"I don't know," he admitted. "I thought I'd wait for you before I took a look."

"Good man," she said, appreciatively.

"Are you ready?"

"Yeah."

Lev left his helmet light off and switched on the brighter hand flashlight. Once he did, Anya turned her headlight off too.

The flashlight filled the cavern with a warm glow.

They both gasped simultaneously as soon as the beam shined through the chamber.

Calverite crystals lined every inch of the walls as far as the light traveled. The mineral often has a metallic luster, and its color may range from a silvery white to a brassy yellow. Normally even large amounts of gold cannot be seen with the naked eye, but not in this chamber. Here it was clearly visible running along the walls in traditional veins of gold.

Exhilaration and an innate sense of greed made his heart race.

So much gold! Everywhere the light shined sparkled like diamonds. Sometimes occurring in narrow lines in rock, these veins of the lustrous precious metal were thicker than Lev had ever seen. It was beyond anything he has ever even heard about, and seemed to be growing richer as they moved farther along. The seam meandered in an eastern direction, before disappearing into a solid wall of limestone. He fixed his flashlight on the last point, where the concentration of gold appeared to be at its highest. There was an opening just below it, where water had once seeped through, to form a sort of keyhole.

Lev kneeled down so he could get a better look.

He was greeted with pitch darkness. He shifted his position, shining the beam of his flashlight through the opening.

Something metallic reflected the glare of the light back at him.

"That's odd," he said, remembering the story of the disused train railway track from WWII.

"What is it?" Anya asked, kneeling beside him.

"There's a railway track here."

"Get out!" Her voice came across as playful, but there was a certain restraint mixed in with it too. "There's no record of a mine anywhere near here. Just some open pits where people have tried to penetrate the permafrost but found the gold too hard to be won."

Lev's mind began to churn over the situation. "Okay, now I'm *really* excited!"

"Only now?" Anya's tone was incredulous. "You're excited about a train line in an area we already knew was once toiled by those imprisoned in the Gulag?"

He began to chip away at the keyhole with his pickaxe as he spoke. "Help me with this, we don't need to move much, and I think we'll be able to slide through."

She shrugged and began to help him pull away a large chunk of limestone. "Sure. What are you thinking?"

Lev kept working on expanding the keyhole while he talked. "Look. There's nothing around for hundreds of miles, and yet someone went to the extreme trouble to build a railway line into the place."

"Not someone. Forced labor from Gulag concentration camps."

"Yeah, but why bother?"

"From what I hear, the purpose of the Gulag was for punishment as much as production."

Lev shook his head. "No. At the end of the day, there was a war on. Stalin needed material and supplies. He wasn't going to waste free labor building a railway to nowhere."

She arched a well-manicured eyebrow. "Well, what do you think he had in mind?"

Lev answered her question with another one. "What did Germany do when they became concerned that they might actually lose the war?"

"Surrender?"

"No. Before that?"

"Die? Starve like the rest of us?"

"What about the rich Germans or the ones who had gone around stealing priceless artifacts and a hoard of gold and silver during their war crimes?"

"They buried it."

"Exactly."

Anya wasn't convinced. "Lev…"

"Yeah?"

"We never lost the war."

He paused, thinking that through as he studied the opening. It was probably almost big enough to slide himself through. "No, but that doesn't mean we didn't commit plenty of war crimes of our own."

"So?"

A large chunk of limestone broke free and Lev pushed it through, making the opening large enough for them both to enter. "I think someone has stolen something they probably shouldn't have. Maybe large amounts of gold. A secret treasure cache. Whatever it is, it was too big to move by car. Maybe too cumbersome to shift. Instead, they brought it here by train."

She didn't even bother trying to conceal her skepticism. "Into the middle of Siberia?"

"Hey, no one's ever going to come looking for it this far away."

"Okay. So then what?"

"They bury it inside a tunnel, seal off the entrance, and rip up the trainline."

"Naturally." She drew in a big, theatrical, disbelieving breath. "To what purpose?"

He shrugged, making a gesture as though it were obvious. "So that whoever it was could come back here and retrieve the gold at the end of the day?"

Anya held his gaze. "Having ripped up the remnants of the railway line used to get it here?"

"Hey, I just come up with the ideas… I didn't say that they had to make sense." Lev got on his tummy, ready to pull himself through. He turned his head to meet her gaze. "You coming?"

"Of course," she laughed. "You don't think I'd leave all that treasure to you, do you?"

Lev slid into the hole first, using his hands to pull himself through. Standing on his feet, he then gripped Anya's hands, and pulled her through next. They shifted the beams of their flashlights in a long, wide arc. A cursory glance confirmed that there was indeed a railway line. It was a standard 5-foot gauge track, quite different to the narrow three-foot gauge tracks used in the Siberian mines by Gulags.

Lev scanned the tunnel with his flashlight. The beam landed on the end of the line, where the tracks were buried in a pile of rubble. He kept his light fixed there and said, "That looks like where they sealed it off to keep their secret hidden."

Attempting to pat dust off her clothes, Anya wasn't convinced about the treasure. "Or this is just a normal mine that ended with a cave in?"

"I doubt it."

"Why?"

"These tracks are a standard five-foot gauge."

Her eyes narrowed. "So?"

Lev smiled like a poker player who just won a winning hand. "Siberian gold mines worked by those in the Gulag throughout WWII all used 3-foot gauge tracks, whereas the standard five-foot gauge, was used throughout most of the Soviet Union."

The implication seemed to hit her. "Holy shit! There really is a treasure train hidden in this mountain!"

"I think so." Lev took her hand and said, "Come on, let's go find out."

She released his hand a few seconds later and together they purposefully strode down the tunnel, following the tracks.

They walked a good ten minutes before the tracks petered out, but there, at the end of the line, was a German Steam train. It was a Deutsche Reichsbahn's Class 52 – with a single armored carriage attached to the WWII locomotive.

Chapter Nine

Lev kept the beam of the flashlight on the WWII German locomotive.

It looked gloomy and malevolent somehow. Painted entirely black, there was additional armored plating to protect the boiler and engineering cab. Similar to a pillbox bunker, the iron embrasures had horizontal arced slits from which to shoot. These lined the engineer cabin that was otherwise entirely protected from external fire. Two anti-aircraft gun turrets rose from the armored roof of the engineer cabin and the coal tender.

Lev could imagine the powerful locomotive making an unstoppable force as it rolled across Europe. He turned to Anya. His heart thumping hard in his chest. A broad smile spread across his lips. "Well, what do you think?"

Astounded, she shook her head in disbelief. "I think we might just be about to become rich beyond our dreams!"

A split second later, she spontaneously jumped up to straddle him, almost knocking him over in the process. Lev took her weight with ease, supporting her back with his hand, as she turned to greet him and kissed him hard on the lips. The kiss started as an exuberant congratulatory peck at the discovery of the German treasure, but quickly changed. He felt her lips, supple and eager on his. Lev was more than willing. He opened his mouth to hers and felt the flick of her tongue exploring his, reveling hungrily in each other's desire before they broke apart.

Anya pulled back, a curious expression on her face, as though she wasn't quite sure what to make of her own reaction. Lev was contemplative about the sudden turn of events, but sensed she was okay. She wore an impish smile of triumph, as though she wasn't sure until that very moment that Lev would share her sentiment.

He said, "Are you okay?"

She nodded. "More than okay. You?"

"Sure." He squeezed her hand. "Come on, shall we go see what we've found?"

"Sounds like a plan."

They kept walking toward the train.

Lev still didn't quite know what to make of the sudden change in their relationship. *Was she interested in him, or had it been a spontaneous release as a result of what they had found?* Something about the excitement that surrounded the discovery of treasure that made people do strange things. It was the same in mining. There were few things that held so much power over people than the luster of gold fever.

The door to the engineer's cabin consisted of thick steel. Lev tried it and frowned. "It's locked."

Anya said, "Any chance you can break it open?"

Glancing at the pickaxe in his hand, he didn't even need to think about it. "No way. That door was designed to take a beating from machinegun fire. I could chip away at it all week without any luck. We'd have to go topside and return with some drilling or welding gear to get in."

Not to be beaten so easily, Anya kept going, walking around the other side. "Come on, maybe there's another way."

"Maybe," Lev agreed.

He followed Anya, the beams of their flashlights flickering across the limestone walls and wrapped around the WWII relic like a cloak. Whoever had dug the tunnel didn't expend any effort trying to widen it any more than they had to. It narrowly hugged the train. Anya slid between the train and tunnel with ease, but Lev had to turn sidewise and try not to take any deep breaths. His back rasped across the limestone wall and after about ten seconds of discomfort, he was rewarded with another door.

It appeared to be identical to the armored door on the opposite side of the engineer's cab, but instead of being locked, this one had been left fully open. The door was on a sliding rail but had long since rusted and fused in the open position.

Anya climbed up and Lev followed right after.

A rich smell of coal and grease wafted through his nostrils, the scent as strong as he imagined it might have been if the train had only just run along the tracks today. Lev swept the beam of his flashlight in a slow arc across the cabin. It was barren, revealing little, if anything of its previous owners or the people who worked her engine. At a glance, he could tell they would find nothing of value inside.

He saw all the normal things Lev guessed were common in a steam engine. A series of pressure gauges, dials, and levers that an engineer had once orchestrated to achieve locomotion, dominated the forward wall of the cabin, along with the small opening to the firebox, through which coal was fed. To the aft was a coal chute coming from the fuel tender, which carried coal and water was visible, along with a series of pipes and gauges. Two metal gunner's chairs were suspended from the ceiling, revealing the shooting positions of the twin anti-aircraft gun turrets.

If anything, the place reminded him more of what he pictured the inside of a battle tank would feel like than the engineering cabin of a train. Somehow feeling inspired, Lev clambered up into the gunner's seat. He stared out along the metal crosshairs into the darkness above, and like a child, imagined what it would have been like to be sitting there as British Supermarine Spitfires attacked. He could hear the smooth roar of Rolls Royce Merlin engines screaming as the pilots dived, raking the German locomotive with their deadly Browning .303 machineguns. He closed one of his eyes and concentrated on an imaginary target through the crosshairs and squeezed the trigger.

As expected, nothing happened, but Lev began making a *Pew, Pew...* sound like a child playing.

Anya glanced at him with an amused expression on her face. "Did you hit them?"

Lev climbed out of the gunner's chair. He faked an embarrassed smile, as though he hadn't noticed her paying attention, before his usual confidence returned, and he said, "Of course I hit them. Not just one fighter plane, but two!"

"Well done!" Then, climbing down from the cabin, she said, "The suspense is killing me, let's go check out the trailing carriage. Whatever was hidden here all that time ago, it must have been important."

"Agreed."

They walked around the train until they reached the last carriage. This one was armored, but unlike the rest of the locomotive, there were no iron embrasures through which to shoot. Instead, it looked like one giant safe.

Lev had a bad feeling that the previous owners of whatever treasures might lay inside, were unlikely to have left the door open. After a minute or two they reached what appeared to be the carriage's only door. It was made of steel with large, iron hinges. A steel latch was set in the downward – locked position – and then connected to a steel strut with a padlock.

Anya fixed the beam of her flashlight on it.

Lev felt his heart skip a beat. The key padlock was made of brass, measuring roughly 6 inches long and 3.5 wide with one central skeleton keyhole, over which a metal cover rested. The German Third Reich was marked on the top of the padlock. Below the talon of the Reichsadler – the heraldic eagle, derived from the Roman eagle standard, used by the Holy Roman Emperors and in modern coats of arms of Germany, including those of the Second German Empire, the Weimar Republic and Nazi Germany – the padlock was stamped with the acronym D.R.G.M. which stood for Deutsches Reichsgebrauchsmuster, meaning that the design or function of the item was officially registered inside all of the Germany states.

Anya said, "What do you think?"

Lev drew a breath. "I'm no historian, but one thing's for certain… whatever's inside this carriage, it was placed there by someone from the Third Reich." A warm smile crept along his lips. "I'd love to know how Nazi Germans managed to sneak one of their war locomotives across the Soviet Union, all the way into the outskirts of wild Siberia – and then hide it for nearly eight decades!"

"I have no idea, but I can tell you now, whatever is inside this thing… it's going to be valuable."

"Let's find out."

With that, Lev lifted the pickaxe and brought the point down on the old, dilapidated padlock. The brass gave way on impact, splintering into multiple pieces.

Lev exhaled with relief. He met Anya's eyes and gripped the steel latch. "Are you ready?"

"Yes!" she said, touching him affectionately on his arm. "No more waiting... I want to know what's inside!"

"All right, all right!"

Lev pulled on the latch. The internal locking mechanism was an iron swivel shaped latch and thankfully the freezing conditions had prevented it from rusting solid. It made a metallic rasping sound as steel slid across steel.

He pushed hard, and the door swung open.

Two sets of flashlight beams instantly drew toward the interior of the armored carriage. The carriage was empty with the exception of a single wooden crate. This one was big. Roughly ten feet long by four feet wide. A heavy chain had been wrapped around the entire box like a sinister shroud, with each end attached to a single brass padlock on the top.

Upon each side of the crate, including the top, there was a message written in English, German, French, and Russian.

Lev stared at the Russian message.

Danger! Do not open! The contents of this box will bring death to all.

Chapter Ten

Lev lifted his pickaxe, ready to break the lock as he did with the first one.

Anya placed a hand on his arm. "Do you think that's wise?"

Lev laughed. "Yeah, why not? It worked with the last one."

"Sure, but the last padlock didn't have a warning, '*The contents of this box will bring death to all.*'"

He nodded. Suppressing a condescending grin. "Okay, I'll admit that does have a kind of creepy ring to it."

"But you're not worried?"

"Nah. It's probably just a ruse. Like a final checkpoint to prevent would-be thieves from stealing whatever's inside."

She arched an eyebrow. "And if you're wrong?"

"Wrong?" He shrugged. "How far wrong can I be? What do you think they've hidden in here for nearly eighty years that could still be dangerous?"

"It might be a weapon?" She thought about that for a moment. "Or maybe a bomb?"

"I doubt it." Lev shook his head dismissively. "Why go to all this trouble to bury a bomb?"

"It might have been an early atomic bomb or something?"

"Hey, if Germany had managed to build an atomic bomb, I don't think they would have had the need to bury it in Siberia..." He met her gaze with a reassuring smile that suggested he was working hard not to make fun of how stupid that sounded. "No, whatever's inside, it will be valuable."

He met her eye, drew a breath, and held it.

Anya broke. "All right, all right. Open the damned thing."

It was all the confirmation he needed.

Lev used his pickaxe. He took a good swing and brought the blade down straight and true. It was well placed, and the rusty old padlock split into two pieces. He dropped the pickaxe and quickly removed the chains. The wooden lid had been nailed down long ago. The nails were frail and the wood rotten, but still the box remained firmly shut. He frowned, picked up the pickaxe once more and used its head to pry open the lid without further ado.

The lid resisted for a moment, before the seal gave way to Lev's force. He slid the axe head along the side of the gap, forcing each of the nailed sections to break free as he slowly worked his way around the entire top of the box.

Beside him, Anya involuntarily held her breath.

When the entire lid had been freed from its constraints, Lev and Anya lifted it together, slowly shifting it to the side.

Lev said, "Moment of truth."

"Moment of truth," Anya agreed, and fixed the beam of her flashlight on the internal contents of the crate.

She gasped at the sight.

Lev cursed. His eyes narrowing, trying to make sense of what he was seeing. The little cogs in his mind crunching over all the possibilities, like a computer attempting to make an equation work despite being fed conflicting data.

Anya shook her head. Disappointment, more than fear, reflected across her face. "I don't get it… they're just dead soldiers?"

"I don't get it either." He stared at them. They wore military camouflage uniforms, but their bodies had been mummified over time, giving them an unnatural appearance reminiscent of the over-the-top horror films of the 1980s. "What the hell happened to them? They look like they belong in an Egyptian temple."

"I don't know," she said, with genuine curiosity. "I've never seen anything like it."

Lev had never seen a dead body, let alone, one that had been trapped in a steel carriage in the harsh, cold environment, of Siberia – but he didn't think they were mummified. He might be wrong. There was something about them that looked strange.

Anya kept moving. She examined the bodies with more of a medical doctor's curiosity, trying to imagine where they had come from and how they had died. None of them seemed to have any visible injuries at all. If it was a mass grave from Nazi war crimes, one would have expected them to have evidence of bullet wounds somewhere, but there were none. The uniforms were intact. It was a mystery within a mystery. None of it made any sense. Just like so much of the rest of life.

She fixed the beam of her flashlight on the shoulder of one of the soldiers. "Here look at this!"

Lev took a look where she was pointing. It was a flag. "Hey, they're Americans."

"All of them?" she asked.

He ran his eyes across the small pile of human bodies. All the bodies seemed to have an American flag on their right shoulder. There were no other nationalities that he could see. "Seems like it."

She locked the light onto something and asked, "What's this one?"

Lev stared at it in silence.

The lines of his face deepened as his face crunched up with confusion. It looked like some sort of military insignia. It was originally concealed by a small flap of camouflaged material, but due to the position of the body, the material had fallen away to reveal a very distinctive stitching of an insignia that most likely represented the men's specialized unit. It had a ghost in white, on a black background, and from the left hand, three bolts of red lightning were expelled.

He shrugged. "Beats me. I guess they were all part of some type of specialized unit, but I've never heard of one that used a ghost as an emblem."

Anya turned and stepped away.

Lev followed. "Are you okay?"

"Yeah fine... I've seen enough. Let's go."

She couldn't hide the disappointment in her voice.

They both thought they had found the motherlode of Nazi treasure, but in the end, it was just another dozen seemingly irrelevant deaths out of the millions upon millions who had lost their lives during WWII. Maybe the authorities might one day reach out to their relatives and provide answers, but what did that matter in the scheme of things?

After all, none of the soldiers' loved ones would still be alive so what good would it do? As for their distant relatives, children, and grandchildren… they already knew their fathers and grandfathers had died in the war, only now they got to know that they were ignobly buried beneath a deserted mountain in Siberia. The entire thing seemed stupidly pointless to him.

They slowly retraced their steps to the surface.

Before they got there, Lev asked, "Are you really disappointed?"

"Aren't you?" she countered.

He shrugged. "I was never going to see the rewards of that treasure anyhow. After all, it would have had to have been assessed by archeologists and historians, and would eventually be turned over to National Trust, a museum, or even returned to its original owners. Even if it was deemed finders keepers, we both know *Precision Exploration* would have got it, not us, given that they funded the drilling in the first place. So, no, I'm okay with what we found. It was still exciting while it happened."

She stopped, placed her hands on his chest, and turned her head up to look at him. She wore an impish grin. "You weren't even a little tempted to steal it?"

"No." He laughed.

Anya looked at him inquisitively, as though she were trying to assess whether he was really telling the truth or just being polite and responsible. A warm smile broke through, and he guessed she figured he was being honest. "You're serious, aren't you?"

"Yeah, why not?" His shrug of indifference was genuine, but standing next to a beautiful woman, he could afford not to care. He was healthy, and happily employed in a profession he liked. "Besides, I can't believe we're really negotiating whether or not to steal hidden Nazi treasure that didn't even exist in the end."

"I know, it's silly." She kissed him gently. "You're a good man, Lev. A very good man."

"Thank you," he said, squeezing her hands affectionately, thinking, *I found something much better than treasure today.* "Come on. We're going to have to make a report. The company's not going to be impressed that the sale of this extraordinarily profitable mine might be delayed with bureaucratic red tape."

They traced the large seam of gold back to the main chamber, where the narrow, aluminum electron caving ladder dangled from the small, cylindrical opening high above. The ladder could only be climbed one at a time.

Lev waved his hand toward the ladder. "After you."

Anya had a wistful look about her, as she ran her eyes across the large seam of gold once more. "You go first. I want to spend another minute down here and just enjoy the view."

"Okay," he said, leaning in to kiss her once more.

Their lips touched gently. Chemistry was in the air. They shared a mutual desire and restraint, before desire won out, and their lips parted. It was only a brief kiss, but it was really nice.

She said, "Go on… get going… otherwise they'll begin to wonder what we've been doing down here."

Lev smiled. "I'll just tell them it was a rewarding experience."

She suppressed a grin. "Don't you dare!"

With that, Lev quickly climbed the thirty odd feet to the surface. As he clambered up the ladder, he had the odd feeling something big had happened. As though, this was going to be the luckiest day of his life. He felt a little out of breath by the time he reached daylight. That too, was to be expected, after all, he was forty-two years old and not as fit as he once was for field work.

He was greeted by a few technicians who asked him how it went. Lev told them to wait for Anya, who would fill them in on their discovery. As he waited, he turned around slowly, really taking in the beauty of his environment for the first time since arriving.

Sky high Siberian pines lined the valley. Nearby, a large eagle could be seen feeding its chicks. He walked toward the river that ran north to south as it cut its way through the valley. It was a parallel tributary of the Lena and made a striking setting as it carved its way through karst. He knelt down and filled his drink bottle with the pristine water. One of the off-duty technicians, who had been standing in the middle trying his hand at flyfishing, pulled in the largest Hucho taimen – the trophy of Siberian trout – he'd ever seen in his life. He gave a congratulatory wave to the amateur fisherman and returned to the opening to wait for Anya.

One of the technician's there caught his gaze. "What is it?"

"Sorry?" Lev asked.

"You had a pensive look about you. I was just trying to get an idea what was on your mind. You look like you've just found a gold nugget..." The technician said teasingly, "or maybe like someone in love?"

"Oh?" Lev was caught by the technician's surprisingly accurate perception. "I was just noticing how beautiful this place is...that's all."

"Right... I understand," the technician said, in a way that suggested he didn't.

A couple minutes later, Anya climbed out of the opening. She seemed to be huffing and puffing even more than he had been.

Lev asked, "Are you all right?"

"Yeah, yeah... just a bit out of breath."

She leaned over, placed her hands on her knees, clearly having difficulty breathing.

Lev studied her. It wasn't just that she was out of breath. Her paleness, her fatigue... something seemed off. She didn't look all right to him at all. "Are you sure you're feeling all right?"

Anya nodded. "I'm just a bit thirsty, that's all."

Lev offered her his water bottle.

"Thanks," she said, taking it.

Anya took a long, slow, drink from the bottle until it was entirely empty.

Lev laughed. "You really were thirsty."

She looked desperate for more, and a little scared. "You have no idea."

Chapter Eleven

Stone Town, Zanzibar

It was early afternoon when the *Tahila* motored past Kendwa Beach, a ritzy tourist town, to the north of Zanzibar. The water looked like an ocean of blue marble set against a backdrop of beaches made from the whitest sands on earth, surrounded by a dark forest of rich greens.

Several traditional sailing dhows lined the shore. The dhows were everywhere. Most local people didn't own cars or even bikes, but everyone seemed to have a dhow. Just off the beach, a couple of tourists looked like they were having fun trying their hand at kiteboarding. A fair-haired girl in her twenties was grinning at a dark-skinned man, with a muscular physique, and happy-go-lucky smile. The girl seemed to be getting the hang of it, but the man appeared to be struggling with the watersport.

The *Tahila* continued southwest, rounding Tombatu Island, before eventually coming to a stop along the western coast of Unguja, the main island of the Zanzibar Archipelago, and anchoring in the shallow waters off the coast of Stone Town.

Stone Town of Zanzibar, also known as Mji Mkongwe in Swahili, was the oldest part of Zanzibar City, the main city of Zanzibar, in Tanzania. The newer portion of the city is known as Ng'ambo, Swahili for, "the other side."

After lowering a Zodiac into the calm waters, Sam, Tom, Genevieve, and Elise used it to motor to the shore. Tom and Genevieve pulled it ashore above the waterline and Sam paid a local street vendor to keep an eye on it. Elise and Genevieve headed off to check out the town and local museums, arguing, that if this was the closest thing they were going to be seeing to a vacation for a while, they might as well take advantage of it.

They left the seafront promenade, enjoying their last gaze at the turquoise Indian Ocean, before entering the old city, where their senses were greeted and enveloped by a cacophony of tastes, smells, and sounds. The smell of spiced tea and hot grilling chapattis wafted through the air. In the distance, the call to prayer echoed out from the nearest mosque.

Zanzibar's main industries were spices, raffia, and tourism. In particular, the islands produced cloves, nutmeg, cinnamon, and black pepper. For this reason, the Zanzibar Archipelago, together with Tanzania's Mafia Island, were sometimes referred to locally as the "Spice Islands." As Sam walked through the narrow streets, it was easy to see, or more specifically, smell, why.

They headed past the remains of the Boma la Kale la Zanzibar, known as the Old Fort, the oldest building and original fortress in Stone Town, the capital of Zanzibar. They walked past the House of Wonders, once the former palace of the Sultan of Zanzibar and now a museum. The entire façade, including the clocktower had collapsed in December 2020, and a small army of construction workers were beginning to set up scaffolding to finally make the repairs.

The two parties split up, with Elise and Genevieve heading down a lane to get happily lost in the maze of Stone Town, while Sam and Tom headed toward the main part of the old city, in search of *Berlusconi's*, where Sam hoped to find answers to the origins of his unique oil painting.

Stone Town's architecture is a fusion of Arabic, Indian, European and African influences. Arab buildings are often square, with two or three stories. Rooms line the outer walls, allowing space for an inner courtyard and verandas, and cooling air circulation. Indian buildings, also several stories high, generally include a shop on the ground floor and living quarters above, with ornate facades and balconies. A common feature is the baraza, a stone bench facing onto the street that serves as a focal point around which townspeople meet and chat.

The most famous feature of Zanzibari architecture is the carved wooden door, a symbol of wealth and status, and often the first part of a house to be built – or sometimes older than the house, having been moved from a previous location.

Generally, Arabian-styled doors have a square frame with a geometrical shape, and "newer" doors – many of which were built toward the end of the 19th century and incorporate Indian influences – often have semicircular tops and intricate floral decorations. Doors may be decorated with carvings of passages from the Quran, and other commonly seen motifs include images representing items desired in the household, such as a fish (expressing the hope for many children) or the date tree (a symbol of prosperity). Some doors have large brass spikes, which are a tradition from India, where spikes protected doors from being battered down by elephants.

They passed the entrance to the Slave Market Museum, a sobering tourist attraction that exhibited details of Zanzibar's once rich slave trade. Sam headed south, into the maze of narrow streets and alleyways. A donkey passed them, pulling a cart. Its owner, greeting them with a warm, friendly, wave. On their left, they saw the Old Dispensary, a three story, colonial building with a distinctive teal façade. Once a prominent hospital, the building is little more than a decorative tribute to the island's rich colonial past.

Stone Town's amazing mix of cultures jostling peacefully alongside each other and becoming all the richer for it. In their short stroll, they had come across an array of different religious buildings, from Anglican Churches to Hindu Temples and Islamic Mosques echoing with the call to prayer, reflecting Zanzibar's melting pot of cultural history dating all the way back to the 9th Century, when Swahili merchants on Zanzibar operated as brokers for long-distance traders from both the hinterland and Indian Ocean world.

Persian, Indian, and Arab traders frequented Zanzibar to acquire East African goods like gold, ivory, and ambergris and then shipped them overseas to Asia. Similarly, caravan traders from the African Great Lakes and Zambezian Region came to the coast to trade for imported goods, especially Indian cloth. Before the Portuguese arrival, the southern towns of Unguja Ukuu and Kizimkazi and the northern town of Tumbatu were the dominant centers of exchange. Zanzibar was just one of the many autonomous city-states that dotted the East African littoral. These towns grew in wealth as the Swahili people served as intermediaries and facilitators to merchants and traders.

This interaction between Central African and Indian Ocean cultures contributed in part to the evolution of the Swahili culture, which developed an Arabic-script literary tradition. Although a Bantu language, the Swahili language consequently today includes some borrowed elements, particularly loanwords from Arabic, though this was mostly a 19th-century phenomenon with the growth of Omani hegemony.

Many foreign traders from Africa and Asia married into wealthy patrician families on Zanzibar. Particularly Asian men, who "wintered" on the coast for up to six months because of the prevailing monsoon wind patterns, and then married East African women. Since most Asian traders were Muslim, their children inherited their paternal ethnic identity, though East African matrilineal traditions remained key.

Sam and Tom entered a particularly narrow section of the Stone City.

Sam stopped and checked the map he'd bought off a street vendor, wondering if there was any resemblance between the map and the complex maze of ancient buildings in which he was almost certainly lost.

Tom laughed. "You can navigate through the Sahara with little more than the sun and the stars to guide you... hell, you can navigate through ancient tunnels beneath the Saharan desert using your instinct for natural watercourses alone... but I'm pretty certain we've just made our third circuit of this place."

Sam turned the map around the other way, trying to look at it from a different angle. "We'll get there eventually."

None of it was really matching up.

In the end, he turned to a local street merchant and asked if the man knew how to get to *Berlusconi's*. The merchant smiled. He nodded reassuringly, and pointed down another narrow street. Sam thanked him and headed in the direction the merchant had pointed. Several school children wearing their traditional dress, weaved in and out of a couple donkeys. Sam smiled, enjoying the day, and kept walking through the convoluted array of narrow streets, where ancient carved doorways sat slightly ajar, their secrets just out of reach...

The strong scent of spices became blocked for the first time since arriving on the island. It happened so quickly, that Sam didn't even recognize the cause. It just seemed to hit them, like a rock, with its jarring change. Something about it triggered the primitive part of Sam's brain into action. His heart picked up its pace.

Tom stopped. His eyes narrowed. "What is that?"

Sam swallowed, fighting down the sense of impending danger. "The street's filling with smoke!"

"Any idea where the fire is?"

Sam glanced toward a big building at the end of the row of shopfronts. Crimson anger arose from the burning blaze. The glowing embers leaped and twirled in a fiery dance, twinkling like stars in the hot swirling air before cascading to earth like gleeful fire fiends, setting alight the tinder of the building next door.

Local people, along with professional firefighters were running back and forth with buckets and hoses, trying in vain to put it out.

Sam and Tom ran to join the other volunteers.

They worked for the next half an hour to contain the fire. The firefighters succeeded in stopping the spread to the other buildings, but the original one had been lost.

Sam looked up, glanced at the smoldering remains, and cursed.

Beneath the fiery remains he could just make out the outline of a sign –

Berlusconi's Fine Wares

Chapter Twelve

The fire chief told the not-so-small group of volunteers that everything of value was destroyed in the warehouse, and it would be safer to let it burn now and concentrate on ensuring the adjacent buildings weren't destroyed.

Sam watched as they got control of the fire, confining it to the lone building to burn free.

Once the fire chief appeared to hand over to his deputy, and grab a drink, Sam went to see him. "I was supposed to be meeting the owner. I don't suppose you've contacted him yet. I assume he'll want to come down and see the damage with his own eyes."

The fire chief frowned. "That would be Tony Berlusconi?"

"That's him."

"I'm sorry to inform you, he was killed in the fire."

Sam glanced at the raging inferno and wondered how anyone could tell who was still inside. "Are you sure it was him?"

"Certain. I knew the man personally. He would have been the only one in the warehouse today. His body was found inside. As you can imagine, it's pretty charred up... but at a glance, I'm sure it's him."

Sam nodded. "I'm sorry to hear that."

They walked away from the disaster.

At a loss, Tom's face crunched up tight. Neither of them knew the man, but all the same it seemed like a terrible way to go. "I'm sorry, Sam."

"It's all right. I didn't even know the guy, but yeah... it's incredibly bad luck."

"What will you do now?"

Sam arched an eyebrow. "You mean, will I keep searching for the *Midas*?"

"Will you?"

"Of course." Sam picked up his cell phone. "I mean, it might seem disrespectful to Tony Berlusconi, but at the end of the day, we came here to find the *Midas*. His unfortunate death shouldn't prevent us from continuing with our quest."

"Good for you," Tom said, his voice soft and understanding. "I'm meeting Genevieve for dinner, but I'll be around if you need me."

"Okay, thanks," Sam said. "I should be fine. I'm just chatting to a local historian. I should be able to handle that on my own. Enjoy your date night and I'll see you when I get back onboard the *Tahila* tonight."

Sam found the contact number for the local historian. The man had grown up in Zimbabwe and gone on to become a prominent expert in Eastern African history and artifacts. The expert had agreed to meet up and talk about the painting with the *Midas*. He'd sounded incredulous about the theory of a lost slave ship finding its way up the Save River in Mozambique but had said he was interested to hear the story and review the painting and any other data Sam had gathered.

He pressed the green call button.

A man answered immediately. His voice was a deep baritone. Irritation at the disturbance of an unknown number was thinly veiled. "Hello?"

Sam suppressed a grin. "Greg Lamont?"

"Yeah. What do you want?"

"My name's Sam Reilly."

There was a long pause, as though the Lamont had never heard of him, and was trying to rack his brain for the connection.

Sam said, "We spoke a week ago."

"Ah... the boat guy. You're looking for some Atlantic slave ship." The guy tapped his pen on a desk as though trying to recall the conversation. "They were on a Portuguese slaver, having been picked up along the African West Coast... Sierra Leone or somewhere?"

"That's right. It was called Mendiland back then."

"Right. And the slavers... they were all Mendi?"

"That's right."

Lamont said, "I'm still finding it hard to believe that freed slaves from West Africa would choose to, let alone succeed, in sailing south around the Cape, and then up along the East Coast, before making their way inland."

Sam had had a disappointing day, he reflected. Dispirited he said, "Look, I was keen on getting your view on the location along the Save River, based on this painting of the slave ship, *Midas*. I know it's a long shot, but you never know. If you're too busy, I'll leave you be."

"No, no…" the man seemed to change his tone. "I'm interested I am. The story has me intrigued. I do remember you, Mr. Sam Reilly, it's just you called earlier than I expected. I thought you were going to Tony Berlusconi's?"

"I tried, but the place had burned down."

The phone went silent as Lamont digested that new information. "I'm very sorry to hear that. I didn't know Berlusconi very well, but I had met him. In my line of work, we kind of traveled in the same circles. I hope, for him, that it was a quick death."

Sam swallowed hard. "Yeah, me too."

Quick to recover. Lamont asked, "Have you eaten yet, Mr. Reilly?"

Sam checked his watch. It was only six p.m. "Not yet."

"Good. I'll have a place set up for you. You can show me your photos and we can talk about the lost treasure of the *Midas* and all the wonderful legends that might surround her."

"That's great. Where do you want to meet for dinner?"

"Why, Mr. Reilly… there's only one place to go for dinner in Zanzibar!"

Sam grinned. "And that would be?"

"The Forodhani Night Markets."

Chapter Thirteen

Forodhani Gardens – Stone Town

The bruised sky twisted into shades of red, purple, and ochre as the sun turned from orange to gold, before finally settling across the horizon on the Indian Ocean. Sam hurriedly walked through the busy park, discovering that, at sunset, Stone Town's Forodhani Gardens transformed into an open-air food market like no other.

He found himself lost as he walked through the marketplace full of delight. Where tourists had basked in the Zanzibar sun along the open grounds just hours earlier, makeshift tables, propane tanks, and grills now filled the entire area. The aroma of fresh fish, meat, shrimp and kebabs wafted through the air. His eyes feasted on Zanzibar pizzas, and limitless choices of grilled seafood, fresh tropical fruit salads, and an assorted array of sugar cane juices with ginger and lime. A vendor selling urojo, a thick mango-and-tamarind soup served alongside chickpea fritters, boiled potatoes, cassava flakes, chutney, and as much hot sauce as you dare, tried to tempt him.

Before he could politely decline, he was greeted by a short, corpulent man with massive shoulders. His tanned features were carved in lines of aggression and brutality, while beneath his morbidly obese exterior, he was solid. As though once incredibly active and muscular, he moved like a boxer. The man was immense - 400 plus pounds at least.

The man looked at him with the scrutiny of a fighter, sizing him up. "Sam Reilly?"

Sam nodded. "Greg Lamont?"

Lamont greeted him with a firm handshake and a surprisingly warm smile. "I have a table set up for us at the end of the park, so we can talk in private."

"Thank you," Sam said, following him, and taking a seat.

There was an arrogant aspect about Lamont that Sam didn't like at face value, but he couldn't quite place it. His dinner companion ordered everyone around, as though he felt he owned everything and everyone around him. Judging by the way the locals treated him, that probably wasn't far off from the truth, Sam thought. Not that it mattered, he didn't have to like the guy. He needed answers. Lamont was intrinsically well positioned and extremely knowledgeable.

Lamont took a seat opposite and two freshly opened, cold beers were placed on the table without being asked if he wanted a drink. Sam picked up one and glanced at the label. The brand was Kilimanjaro, a pale lager, with 4.5% alcohol. Lamont didn't wait for him, quickly taking a draught.

Sam had his own swig and smiled. It was dry and surprisingly refreshing. "This is good."

"The best," Lamont said, with what Sam could see was the man's habitual confidence. "It is Tanzania's most known and sold beer, loved by both locals and tourists. And for good reason."

"Cheers." Sam clinked the heads of their bottles together, before taking another sip.

Lamont's eyes narrowed, locking on Sam's. He spoke convivially, but there was a hardness to it too, as though he was judging Sam somehow with his answer. "So tell me, how are you finding our fine island of Zanzibar?"

"It's beautiful," Sam said, both dutifully, and honestly.

"I love it here," Lamont said, seemingly happy to hear his own voice again.

Sam had trouble placing the thick accent. Although Sam assumed it betrayed Lamont's upper-class, European ancestry in Zimbabwe – a mixture of British English, South African, and what was once called Rhodesian. Sam recalled that affluent, upper middle class and highly educated Zimbabweans were influenced by older forms of southern British English, especially the now archaic Rhodesian English.

"Have you always lived in Zanzibar?"

"No, no... of course not. I'm Rhodesian through and through," Lamont said, in such a way that suggested the country had never changed back to Zimbabwe in 1979. Without missing a beat, he went on. "Africa is part of my blood. My great, great, grandfather worked in the Cape Colony with Cecil Rhodes. I will always be Rhodesian... but Zanzibar... ah, Zanzibar with its tropical climate, pristine beaches, and nightlife? It's a much nicer place to live and relax."

One of the many cooks brought food out to them, some of it still alight. The table quickly filled with an exotic assortment of traditional Zanzibar cuisines. Lamont, proud of what he now considered HIS island, talked Sam through each one as it arrived.

Lamont pointed to the first plate. "This is Sorpotel, originally from Portuguese-Indian Goan origin, it is mostly boiled meat, consisting of a mixture of tongue, heart and liver. It's cooked with masala along with tamarind and vinegar."

Sam's mouth began to salivate as the rich aromas filled the air. "It looks good."

Next came Boko-boko, a sort of stew of meat cooked in maize, ginger, cumin, chili, tomato and onion and served with date and hazelnut bread. It was traditionally used to celebrate the end of Ramadhan, but Lamont mentioned that it goes very well with everything.

Another dish arrived. "This is Pilau meat."

Sam nodded, helping himself to a serving. "Looks good. What's Pilau meat?"

"Goose. It is sometimes made of calf or cow, but I assure you, this one is goose... cooked with potatoes, onions, spices, coconut milk, and rice."

Sam wasn't quite sure how they were going to eat half of the food that kept coming, but then a glance at Lamont and it was easy to see how much he enjoyed eating. And still more came. Pepper shark was the next thing to arrive. It was apparently a Zanzibar delicacy. Alongside it, was Pweza wa nazi, which in Swahili meant "octopus and coconut." It was served in a coconut curry, cinnamon, cardamom, garlic and lime juice.

When they had finished the main meal, an assortment of spice cakes was placed in front of them. Lamont explained the spice cakes were a typical dessert in Zanzibari cuisine. Sam tried one. It was made of a pastry with a mix of cinnamon, clove, nutmeg and chocolate and tasted delicious.

One of the cooks approached. "Anything else we can bring you, Mr. 360?"

Lamont turned to Sam without looking at the man. "You want anything else?"

Sam placed his hands on his somewhat protruding tummy. "I couldn't eat another thing."

Lamont nodded, dismissing the cook with the wave of his hand.

"Very good, Mr. 360," the cook said, and went away.

Sam waited, letting the name hang in silence for a moment. When Lamont didn't offer any explanation, he said, "Okay, I'll bite."

A puzzled frown creased Lamont's lips. "What?"

Sam suppressed a grin. "Why do they call you Mr. 360?"

The guy arched an eyebrow and shrugged. He was already chuckling. "Really? You need to ask?"

"Sure."

"It's because I look like a circle."

Sam frowned as though he didn't get the joke. Then, seeing Lamont look disappointed, he said, "Technically, you're more like a sphere."

Lamont laughed at that. It was big and boisterous and matched his size perfectly. Just the sort of laugh you'd expect of a guy who looked like him. When he'd finished, he said, "So, tell me about this painting."

Chapter Fourteen

Sam handed Lamont his dossier regarding the *Midas*, including several good quality photos of the original oil painting he'd acquired.

Lamont studied the photos in silence for several minutes.

When he was finished, he handed the dossier back and said, "Any chance the painting's a fake?"

"It's always possible, but I've had the painting assessed by professionals, and they don't think so."

Lamont gave a half-shrug. It almost seemed condescending to Sam. "You can never be sure about these things."

Sam said, "Two conservator-restorers have assessed it."

Lamont arched an eyebrow. "Their estimates are only as good as their skill."

"Both are experts in analyzing and assessing the condition of cultural property. One works for the Louvre, the other, the British Museum. I take their estimates as facts."

"Suit yourself." Lamont shrugged, picking up the original photo of the oil painting once more. It did look authentic. He frowned. "Any chance it's a Giclée?"

A Giclée was a form of fine-art 3D printing, usually archival, printed by inkjet. It was often used by artists, galleries, and print shops to suggest high quality printing, but is an unregulated word with no associated warranty of quality – and was notoriously renowned for its ability to create almost indistinguishable fakes.

Sam shook his head. "If it is, it's a very good one."

"I've seen some brilliant Giclées over the years," Lamont said as though he was helping Sam to accept the truth.

Sam turned the palms of his hands outward. "The frame has been radio-carbon dated to the 1830s plus or minus five to ten years."

"So, the forger has used a legitimate painting from that era and then printed over it with the image of the *Midas*?" Lamont spread his arms in an apologetic gesture that suggested it was better to know the truth than not know. "I have seen it done before."

Sam drew a breath. "You may be right. But given what the two experts I employed to assess the painting have told me, I'm going to keep working on the premise that the painting's genuine."

Lamont lifted a hand to stop Sam continuing, and with the other, he picked up a picture of the original image, and looked at it. "Okay. Let's work on the model that accepts the painting is authentic and does depict the Spanish slaver…"

Sam waited for a few minutes while Lamont digested the scenery and image of the *Midas* in the painting. In case Lamont didn't see the name at the bottom right-hand corner, he said, "It has a name of the river, just there… but I haven't been able to find the location of the river to match it."

Lamont continued staring at the image, then he began speaking without any indication that he cared whether Sam was listening or not. "The river's proper name is Mutsave or Save, "pronounced Sah-veh." It has played a major role in the history of the area.

"The Save River flows through Zimbabwe and Mozambique, rising south of Harare and flows southeast from the Zimbabwean highveld to its confluence with the Odzi. It then turns farther south, drops over the Chivirira, known as the "Place of Boiling" Falls, and is joined by the Lundi at the Mozambique border. The river continues as the Save, following an east-northeasterly course to its mouth near Mambone on the Mozambique Channel of the Indian Ocean."

Sam stopped him. "The Zimbabwean highveld?"

"It's Afrikaans. The Highveld means "high-field," a portion of the South African inland plateau which has an altitude above roughly 4500 feet, but below 6000 feet, thus excluding the Lesotho mountain regions to the south-east of the Highveld."

"Obviously," Sam said, although he'd never heard of the term before.

Lamont persisted. "The Save River was the route for the transport of gold from the interior centered on Great Zimbabwe to the Indian Ocean port town of Sofala, in Mozambique. As Sofala lies only about 60 miles north of where the Save River enters the sea. It developed into the most important gold-trading center between the coast and the hinterland occupied by the civilization of Great Zimbabwe in the 13th and 14th centuries AD.

"Sofala was founded about the year 700. Sometime in the 10th century, Sofala emerged as a small trading post erected by Somali merchants from Mogadishu – that's modern-day Somalia's capital to you by the way – to trade cotton cloth for gold and ivory. In the 1180s, Sultan Suleiman Hassan of Kilwa – in present-day Tanzania – seized control of Sofala and the Swahili strengthened its trading capacity by having, among other things, river-going dhows ply the Buzi and Save Rivers to ferry the gold extracted in the hinterlands to the coast.

"Sofala's gold trade proved a windfall for the Sultans of Kilwa, although ivory, iron tools, tortoiseshell, cloth, salt, and handcrafts were also traded and allowed them to finance the expansion of their commercial empire all along the East African coast and Sofala itself became the most dominant coastal city south of Kilwa itself. Sofala benefited not only from the gold trade into modern day Zimbabwe along the Sabi River, but via a land route directly with Chipangura (present-day Manica) the capital of the Manica kingdom and the site of a gold fair and along the Limpopo River valley with Mapungubwe."

Somewhere along the lines, Sam realized Lamont was waffling. He suddenly knew how it felt when he, himself, went on and on about useless information regarding historical sites. It interested him sometimes but not others.

When he couldn't take it anymore, Sam stopped him. "Can you tell me where this location is?"

Lamont shook his head. "No, but I can tell you where it is not."

Sam's eyes narrowed. "Go on."

"It's not anywhere along the Save River."

"Why are you so certain?"

"Well, for starters, in 1831, the Save River was known as the Sabi River. So that makes this painting an anachronism. Either the ship arrived here a hundred years too early, or the painter had the most remarkable foresight to predict the river's future name."

Sam's lips curled into a smile. "You knew it was a fake from the moment you set eyes on the painting?"

Lamont nodded. An unabashed and lop-sided grin forming on his lips. "Indeed, I did."

"And yet you still went on to tell me the whole damned history of the Save River?"

"Yes."

"Why?"

"Because you wouldn't listen when I suggested the painting was a fake." Lamont laughed hard, as though it was one of the funniest jokes he'd enjoyed all day. "So I figured if I couldn't enlighten you about the painting, I might at least do so regarding the Save River."

Sam let him go for a while. When the big man had finally stopped laughing, Sam asked, "Any guesses what river this might have been?"

Lamont suppressed a smile. "I could tell you what river it is… in fact, I could tell you the exact location, but it won't do you much good."

Sam felt an uneasy feeling rise in his gut, as though he was about to be hit with another dead end. "Why?"

Lamont's voice became solemn. "That's the Upper Zambezi."

Sam frowned. "In Zambia?"

"Yeah."

"So we need to be searching the Upper Zambezi."

Lamont shook his head. "No need to search it."

"Why not?"

"Because there's no way the *Midas* was ever there."

"Really?"

"No."

"You're certain?"

"Hundred percent."

"Why?"

"Unless they worked out a way to carry the *Midas* more than a hundred feet vertical… it would have never made it above Victoria Falls."

"Which means this thing's a fake."

Lamont spread his arms in an apologetic gesture. "Looks like it."

Sam frowned. "It seems I've come a long way seeking a wild goose."

Lamont patted him on the back, a big grin on his face. "No, my friend. You've come a long way to Zanzibar to discover the glorious delights of the Forodhani Gardens."

Chapter Fifteen

Sam tried to pay for dinner, but Lamont wouldn't hear of it.

Instead, he insisted that given all the distance that Sam had traveled to reach the place, it was only fair that he should pick up the bill. Lamont told Sam he would walk him back to the promenade where his ship was waiting. For the most part, Stone Town was safe for tourists, but after dark it could sometimes become problematic for foreigners.

Sam gave a half-shrug as though this, too, seemed fair.

They walked back via the Old Fortress, before cutting through a series of narrow, dark, alleyways of which Stone Town were so renowned on their way to Livingston's Beach. Lamont had kept drinking his Kilimanjaro lagers throughout the evening. Consequently, he was much closer to the drunk end of the inebriation scale, but appeared to be happy about that. He laughed, joked some more, and then laughed at his own jokes – some of which, were obviously being told in the man's head.

It was a warm night, and Sam was comfortable in a pair of day shorts and a polo shirt. They were taking a short cut, which meant little to the mental mind map created in his head, but that didn't bother him. He'd enjoyed the night and even a couple of the Kilimanjaros, so he was happy to wander aimlessly and get lost in the ancient city.

He glanced in wonder at Lamont. Intoxicated or not, and despite the endless maze of the narrow streets, the man seemed to know where he was going. His ability would have impressed even a disoriented M.C. Escher.

In front of them, the narrow street reached a sudden dead end.

Its passages splitting into two perpendicular directions. Both of which, were barred by fully loaded donkey carts. A puzzled frown creased Lamont's mulish face. Despite his intoxication, he seemed to awaken, his posture no longer slumped, his eyes alert.

Something was wrong.

Directly in front of them, an ancient carved doorway stood, like so many others in Stone Town, slightly ajar. It was an Arab-styled entrance, with a square frame and geometrical shape, decorated with multiple carvings of passages from the Quran.

Lamont's instincts had been well founded. He turned, and mouthed the words, "Run!"

The door opened.

And a man stepped out.

He looked Asian. Possibly Chinese if Sam had to guess. There was something disturbing about the man's posture.

Before Sam could react, his adversary drew a long blade – more like a traditional sword than a knife – and drove it firmly into Lamont's chest. It was a swift, well-practiced movement, placed with the precision of an expert assassin. The tip pierced Lamont's heart, killing him in seconds. Lamont glanced down at the wound, his face filled with surprise more than fear, as the realization that it was a mortal wound, hit him.

Sam turned to run but was stopped by two more Asian thugs.

He was trapped.

His eyes darted between the man with the blade and two men who stood with their arms out, ready to prevent him from running. Sam considered his chances of pushing through the two men. It was low, but probably better than winning an unarmed fight with a professional with a sword.

Sam chose the two thugs.

Carrying nothing except a small backpack containing the dossier for his researching on the *Midas*, and nothing else of value, he looked for something he might use as a weapon. Yet there was absolutely nothing nearby.

If this was a normal mugging where thieves were looking to steal something of value, he would have thrown the backpack, but he doubted the men were after his wallet.

Sam launched himself at the closest one.

Neither of the thugs were particularly big. Sam thought his chances were better than fifty-fifty. He had at least fifty pounds on either man, and despite approaching forty, he had the athletic, muscular build of someone who'd spent his life outdoors.

Sprinting forward like an offensive tackle in American football, Sam struck the man with his shoulder.

And bounced.

It had felt like hitting solid rock. Sam was thrown to the ground. Quickly rolling back onto his feet, he was ready to try again.

The man with the sword lifted the weapon, ready to deliver a lethal blow. His countenance twisted in a malicious expression of authority. "Sam Reilly?"

Sam drew a breath and nodded. "Yeah."

"Do exactly as I say, or I'll cut off your head."

Chapter Sixteen

Sam became statue rigid. He then lifted his hands slowly, in a placating gesture.

The guy with the sword nodded. "Good man."

Sam examined his adversary. He was almost certainly of Chinese heritage, but he spoke English without a trace of an accent, indicating he'd either studied abroad, or more likely had been raised in western society.

Eyes subtly darting everywhere, Sam tried to determine his next play. There weren't many left. It was late at night, and he was trapped in a deserted, dead-end street in Stone Town. His crew, unaware of his peril, were back on board the *Tahila*, safe and sound.

The man with the sword asked, "What do you know about the *Midas*?"

So that was what this was about. They were after treasure. At least that much made sense to him, although how they came to know about it, he couldn't have guessed.

He decided to buy some time. "A couple months ago, I bought an oil painting that was sold here on the island. The painting depicted an old Atlantic Slave ship, bearing an exact likeness of the *Midas*, a Portuguese Guineamen at anchor along an oxbow lake on an African River. There were dozens of wild African animals along the bank, crocodiles in the water, and a pod of hippos. At the bottom of the painting was a name and date. The location was the Save River, and the date 1934."

An incredulous expression crossed the swordsman's face. "You came out here because of the painting of a boat in Africa?"

Sam gave a half-shrug. "It was a tenuous lead at best, but you'd never believe how many times I've gotten lucky with those."

The guy was disinterested in his colorful past. He lowered the point of the sword until its bloodied tip rested on Sam's chest. "This is a razor-sharp blade. With the slightest push, my sword will travel through your heart."

It was a statement. No question about it and Sam decided to remain silent.

The guy shook his head. "What do you know about the crew of the *Midas*?"

Sam was puzzled. But answered, "They were all slaves originally from Mendiland, taken prisoner by Spanish slavers in 1829 and shipped to the Americas as part of the Atlantic Slave trade. Somewhere along the way the slaves rebelled and took control of the ship. They set about taking other vessels, pirating the highly treasured Caribbean, as other ships – Spanish, English, French, Dutch, Portuguese – you name it, passed through their waters. Sometime after 1831 the ship disappeared, never to be seen again. That is, until this painting turned up suggesting that her crew, instead of sailing to Sierra Leone, headed farther south, rounding the Cape, and making their way up the East African coast, before heading inland via one of the rivers."

"But what were they doing there?"

Sam was taken aback by the question. "The Portuguese Guineamen was transporting slaves from Mendiland to the Spanish ruled Caribbean. As you know, the Treaty of Tordesillas did not allow Spanish ships in African ports and thus, Spain had to rely on Portuguese ships and sailors to bring slaves across the Atlantic."

The swordsman pushed the blade against his shirt, as though threatening him to tell the truth. "Why were they in East Africa?"

Feeling the tip pierce his skin, Sam said, "Whoah! I don't know, I was wondering the same thing myself."

"You don't know?" the man's voice dripped with skeptical distrust.

Sam closed his eyes and drew a breath. "I honestly don't know what you're asking."

"Why are you so interested in finding the *Midas*?" The man was yelling now.

Sam gave a happy-go-lucky smile. It said he'd accepted his life was no longer in his own hands. "Does anyone need a good reason to go looking for a lost ship loaded with Spanish treasure?"

The swordsman persisted. "Just tell us if you know whether the *Midas* reached it?"

Sam asked, "Reached what?"

The man held Sam's gaze, genuine surprise emanating from his dark eyes. "You don't know the truth, do you?"

"What truth?"

"You're just some dumb ass treasure hunter." The swordsman shook his head, like a crazy man, but calm. He held his weapon… ready to execute Sam. "You just stumbled on the *Midas*… and never really knew what she was doing here or what she was trying to achieve?"

Sam turned the palms of his hands outward. "Okay, now I'm completely lost…"

The two thugs came in behind him and removed his backpack, taking out the dossier on the *Midas*. One of them flicked through the pages. "It's all here. The painting. The location along the Upper Zambezi River… all of it."

The swordsman said, "Thank you my friend. You have saved us a lot of trouble."

"I don't understand!" Sam said, "Where was the *Midas* headed?"

The swordsman nodded at his men. Instantly, the two thugs pushed Sam to the ground, holding him on his knees with his head forward, so the sword could slice through his neck.

"I am truly sorry, Mr. Reilly." The swordsman raised the blade high, ready for a quick slicing motion. "I'm afraid you've stumbled upon a secret we've protected for more than 2,000 years, and now, you too, will have to keep it, with your life."

Sam felt a unique peace wash over him like a warm blanket on a cold night. He had played his last hand and lost. There were no hard feelings. He'd had a good life. Plenty of good luck, but as with anything, he'd danced with death one too many times. He closed his eyes and exhaled, ready to meet his maker.

A second later, he heard the crisp sound of pistol fire.

Chapter Seventeen

Genevieve acted on instinct.

Her steady hand moved with the muscle memory of a lifetime of training. In a fraction of a second, her weapon was aimed at the swordsman's head, her fingers clasped around the hilt of the Glock 23, and she gently squeezed the trigger – twice.

Two rounds fired.

Both 9mm parabellums flew true, landing neatly on the swordsman's forehead. A red mist appeared to explode from the not-so-neat looking exit wound at the back of his head. The ancient looking Asian style sword fell to the floor, making a metallic clanking sound as it hit the stone pavement. The swordsman's body, like a puppet with its strings cut, lay beside his sword.

The two thugs reacted before the dead man hit the ground. Moving with such a speed that she couldn't help but feel impressed, as one dedicated killer to another professional might. Instead of turning to fight or trying to surrender, they pushed forward – past the swordsman and Sam – disappearing through the ancient carved doorway.

Genevieve's heart thrummed in her chest like a lethal crescendo. She could hear the surge of blood hammering in the back of her ears as instinct kicked in. As though a ravenous predator in pursuit of its next meal, there was something primitive about her response. Reason disappeared as she shot after her prey. There was no way she was going to let those two men escape.

In her periphery, she heard Tom rushing to check on Sam, but didn't give them a second glance. Instead, she gave chase.

She ran past Sam and Tom, through the Arab-styled door. It opened to a storage facility for a shop that specialized in spices. The room was dark, with just a single lit candle providing light. The flame flickered, sending shadows dancing across the walls of the small building, while the scent of vanilla, cinnamon, and nutmeg filled the air. Giant traditionally woven baskets, filled with exotic spices lined the room, and hallway, and a stairway at the back of the room that appeared to crisscross and lead to the roof three stories above.

On the top of the second set of stairs, she spotted the distant whirr of one of the thugs climbing toward the top. Genevieve paused for just a second, her professional impulses reigning in her primitive hunter desires, giving her time to run her eyes across the room. There was no telling whether or not the second thug was lying in wait for her. Besides, there was no reason to think they were unarmed. Unable to spot him, she kept going – pushing forward. Climbing the stairs.

Halfway up the stairs, one of the men pushed a basket of spice behind him. The basket rolled down the stairs. She turned her shoulder to take the brunt of the force as the basket landed on her, sending a plume of turmeric everywhere.

Genevieve brushed it off and kept going.

At the top of the stairs, she gripped the door handle, but it wouldn't turn. She kicked the door hard. Unlike the Arab-styled, ancient door at the front of the building, which would have taken a small bulldozer to push through, this one was made from local bamboo, More ornamental than structural. Her foot went straight through the door, ripping it free from its hinges.

She pushed the door aside and stepped out onto the roof. The buildings were all made of coral-stone, like the majority of those within the city, for which Stone Town achieved its name. Her eyes darted left and right. The adjoining buildings were all connected higgledy-piggledy, and the roof tops glowed silver in the light of the crescent moon.

There was no sign of anyone.

She held her breath, waiting to hear a sound.

In the distance, at the far end of the building, she heard the heavy breathing of two people. She aimed her pistol toward the sound.

The two people made their move.

Splitting in opposite directions, they began to bolt across the roofs, flashing by with the speed and grace that would have impressed parkour. She turned, aimed at the one moving to the left. The man was fast. Really fast. He jumped across a small gap between the buildings. She drew a breath. She didn't believe in warning shots.

These men had already crossed the line when they tried to kill Sam.

The man, still running hard, leaped across a giant gap.

She squeezed off a single round.

The bullet hit her target in the back.

He flew through the air, slamming into the wall on the opposite side of the building, before, his limp body fell, crashing onto the cobbled stone street far below with a sickening crunch. If the bullet hadn't killed him, the fall, almost certainly would have.

Genevieve didn't look to see.

Instead, she turned her attention on the second guy. This one was carrying Sam's backpack – presumable with the dossier on the *Midas* – inside. She kept running, following him across a narrow ledge.

The man moved fast, and with a head start, was quickly outpacing her.

Undaunted, she pursued him ruthlessly.

Genevieve watched him make a large jump – crossing a gap of at least seven feet – before disappearing off into the distance.

She stopped just short of the gap.

Her eyes fell all the way to the ground far below, and the sound of the guy she'd shot crunching as he hit the stone street, echoed in her memories. She tucked her Glock into the back of her shorts, drew a breath, backed up to the end of the roof, and then sprinted. She planted the ball of her foot at the very edge of the roof, launching herself across the void.

She cleared the gap.

Her hands gripped the roof as her body slammed into the building. The impact winded her badly, but there was enough adrenaline surging through her veins, and the fear of falling to her death was enough to keep her going. She gritted her teeth and pulled herself up the wall, and onto the roof.

Everything hurt.

Looking around, she was unable to see the man.

Genevieve walked to the opposite end of the building, just in time to catch sight of the thug. He performed some sort of Spiderman-esk stunt, bounding between the walls of two adjacent stone buildings, before safely reaching the ground far below.

Cursing in her native Russian, she thought about trying to follow. At the thought of her almost certain death, she decided it wasn't worth the risk. Not for the safe return of Sam's dossier. Disappointed, and ready to retrace her steps back to Sam and Tom, she backtracked only to realize, she would need to jump the seven odd foot gap.

She looked up and stared at the gap.

The roof she'd launched from was actually a few feet higher than the one she was now standing on. It made everything moot. Even if she could muster the energy to hazard a jump, she would never be able to leap across and vertically anywhere near high enough to clear it.

Sam and Tom, following at a jog, came to a stop at the gap.

Genevieve saw relief wash across Tom's eyes when he saw that she was all right.

Sam's eyes meandered from one side of the gap to the other, before landing square on her shoulders, locking eyes with her. He smiled appreciatively. "You jumped this?"

"Yeah," she said, in a voice that suggested it was one of those stupid things she might do when she got fired up enough in the thrill of the chase, and now just realized how dangerous it had been. "Not much good it did for me. The guy got away, anyway."

Sam shrugged as though it didn't matter. "Thanks for saving my life."

"That's all right," she said. "Tom was going to do it, but I thought I'd beat him to the honor this time around."

"I'm serious, Genevieve. I owe you one."

"No problem." She turned and looked around the building. It must have been the only damned free-standing building in Stone Town. "If you want to repay me, can you go to the ground entrance, and wake up whoever lives below so they can let me down… it appears I'm a little trapped."

"No problem," Sam said. "Glad to help."

Ten minutes later, Sam had found the owners, and convinced them to let Genevieve use their internal stairs.

The police arrived shortly after.

Sam filled them in with the events. The authorities promised to look into it, but so far, all three bodies – the two Chinese assassins, and Greg Lamont's – had all disappeared. Whoever was involved in this thing, they weren't taking any chances.

They headed back to the *Tahila*.

On the way, Sam said, "This wasn't just a simple robbery. These people knew we were looking for the *Midas*. They wanted to know how close we were to finding it."

Tom frowned. "They knew about the *Midas*?"

"More than that. In fact, there was something else, too…"

"What?"

"They wanted to know if I knew whether or not the *Midas* reached it?"

"Reached what?"

"I have no idea," Sam admitted. "But whatever it was, they seemed certain the *Midas* was on a quest to do something or arrive somewhere. It must have been important for someone else to be still searching for it all these years later."

Genevieve said, "The question is what?"

"According to the guy you just shot, it was something more valuable than all the gold the *Midas* might have been carrying…" Sam's voice trailed off, hard and solemn. "… and far more dangerous."

Chapter Eighteen

On Board the *Tahila*

Sam placed the Chinese sword on the Round Table.

The Round Table was both the symbolic and physical heart of the ship. Sitting around the table, the entire crew of the *Tahila* planned their next move. Tom, Sam's director of operations, Matthew, the ship's skipper, Veyron, the ship's submersible engineer, Elise, a computer whiz, and Genevieve, a retired Russian assassin whose unique skill set had been appropriated for the team. As Sam took a seat, their resident dog, a Golden Retriever named Caliburn, lifted his head and wagged his tail without getting up.

"It's called a Dao," Sam said, gently running his hand along the single sided blade. "It's designed to slice through things, like a saber does."

"Like your neck," Genevieve pointed out.

Tom suppressed a laugh. "You stole his sword?"

Sam shrugged. "Hey, the guy's dead. I didn't think he'd need it."

"Or that the local police would be interested?" she chided.

"Hey, they're in way over their heads with this one. Besides, I don't think it has anything to do with their turf. These people came here because I started asking questions about the *Midas*. Those deaths, and this battle is for me. So, I'm going to take the responsibility to find out who's responsible and make things right."

Genevieve asked what was on everyone's mind. "Why did an assassin bring an ancient weapon to a modern-day fight?"

Sam opened his arms. "That's a good question. One that Elise has a theory on. It's an ancient Chinese weapon and the sword of choice used by the Youxia."

A puzzled look crossed Tom's face. "The Youxia?"

"Yeah…" Sam said, "I'm going to let Elise take this one. Elise?"

Elise said, "The Youxia was a type of ancient Chinese warrior folk hero celebrated in classical Chinese poetry and fictional literature. It literally means wandering vigilante, but is commonly translated as knight-errant, adventurer, soldier of fortune, or underworld stalwart."

Sam said, "But we weren't talking about any folk hero here to be celebrated in classical Chinese literature. These guys were real and they're deadly, professional assassins?"

"Right," Elise confirmed. "At its most basic level, a Youxia warrior is someone with the means and power to help others in need. The term refers to the way these men solely traveled the land using physical force or political influence to right wrongs done to the common people by the powers that be, often judged by their personal codes of chivalry."

Tom patted Sam on the shoulder. "Hey, it's you and me! We're Youxia warriors!"

"Sure, we are," Sam agreed.

Elise went on. "The Youxia didn't come from any social class in particular. Various historical documents, wuxia novels and folktales describe them as being princes, government officials, poets, musicians, physicians, professional soldiers, merchants, monks and even humble farmers and butchers. Some were just as handy with a calligraphy brush as others were with swords and spears.

"The Youxia were associated with the Mohist ideology, which stressed the importance of equality. At the end of the Warring States Period, former Shi knights who did not transition into scholar-officials became Xia as Mohist defenders of the weak. The 16th and 17th century saw a great revival in the Xia culture of using martial arts to right wrongs. Some of these were recruited to serve in the Ming resistance against the Qing."

"So what the hell were these so called do gooders doing trying to kill me in Zanzibar?" Sam said, "I mean, I know they were after the information on the *Midas*, but why? What would a bunch of altruistic warriors want with hidden treasure?"

Elise said, "I think the key is to look at their purpose throughout history and try and link that to the Midas. You said the swordsman seemed to believe that the *Midas* was carrying something dangerous, a secret, or a weapon that needed to be protected?"

"Yes, he said the crew of the *Midas* had wanted to reveal a secret that his people had been trying to protect for thousands of years."

Elise nodded. "You see, the eight common attributes of the Xia are listed as benevolence, justice, individualism, loyalty, courage, truthfulness, disregard for wealth, and desire for glory. With the exception of individualism, they match Confucian values identically."

"Okay, you can count me out," Tom said. "I'm good with the rest of it, but I'm not interested in the disregard for wealth thing."

Genevieve knew Tom didn't chase wealth. He had no intention of hoarding away more than he could ever spend. She smiled at him. "Really?"

Tom shrugged. "Hey, I'm just trying to keep up with my friends."

That gave everyone a laugh. They all knew Sam came from a family loaded with money. It's what made everything possible. They could concentrate on these side projects because Sam didn't have to worry about making a living.

Elise continued. "The Yuxia follow a certain code that emphasizes the importance of repaying benefactors after having received deeds from others, as well as seeking vengeance to bring villains to justice. However, the importance of vengeance is controversial, as the Yuxia's code also stresses Buddhist ideals, which include forgiveness, compassion and a prohibition on killing."

Sam said, "I guess they missed the memo for the last one."

Genevieve smiled. "Why Sam… I don't think I've ever seen you hold a grudge before!"

"That's because you haven't seen someone try and hack my head off with a medieval sword."

"Technically, it's an ancient weapon," Elise corrected him.

Sam waved a dismissive hand. "All right, enough. Let's bring this back to the original question. If these people were a part of this ancient group of altruistic warriors, what the hell were they doing searching for a 19th century Portuguese slave ship?"

A faint smile tugged at Elise's lips. "Beats me. I just provide the data, it's your job to make sense of the stuff – or if you're Genevieve, simply eliminate it."

Genevieve sat up, a cross look washing over her face. Suppressing a quick retort she thought about Elise's statement. With a smirk and a nod, she finally said, "Yeah, that's me."

Tom asked, "Any chance something was stolen from the Chinese emperor back around 1829?"

"By the pirate crew of the *Midas*?" Sam recalled what he knew about Chinese maritime history and considered the possibilities. "Unlikely. The Qing Dynasty ruled during that period, concentrating exclusively on land defenses. Their navy was neglected, and their period of exploration stalled into non-existence."

Tom asked, "Then what interest could Chinese Nationals have in the *Midas*?"

"I have no idea." Sam said, "I've spoken with Zanzibar's Chief of Police, who tells me whoever they are, they got into and out of the country undetected by customs or quarantine." He paused. "One thing's for sure, we haven't seen the last of them."

Tom frowned. "Why do you say that?"

"They stole my dossier with all my information on the *Midas*."

"That's good, right?" Tom said, his knuckles knocking the table with finality. "Now they know the entire thing was a hoax."

Sam shook his head. "But is it? They clearly don't think so." With a frustrated sigh he added, "It makes me wonder... what do they know that we don't?"

Tom patted him on the back. "You're not going to let this one go, are you?"

"Not by a longshot." There was a hard set to Sam's jaw. His cell rang then, and he picked up. "Sam Reilly," he answered, and his friends were treated to a one-sided conversation. "Uh-huh. Yes? Yes. I see. Okay. Thank you." Sam slipped his phone back in his jeans.

Tom asked, "Who was that?"

"The Zanzibar Chief of Police."

"And?"

"He says according to CCTV footage, an unknown group of Chinese nationals illegally arrived twenty-four hours ago... presumably by boat or seaplane. They were caught on camera heading into Tony Berlusconi's warehouse this morning. That was the last time Tony was seen alive."

"Did he confirm that the body inside Berlusconi's was in fact Tony's?"

"Yeah. He did more than that. He said Berlusconi wasn't killed by the fire."

"He wasn't?"

"No. This gang, if we're going to call them that... the Yuxia gang spoke to him, and now he has two bullets in the back of his head. Death by execution."

"Why would anyone kill Berlusconi?"

"Or Lamont?"

"Especially if the photo of the *Midas* was a fake?"

"Maybe they're not looking for the *Midas*."

"What then?"

"We're going about this all wrong."

"How so?"

"They're not looking for the *Midas,* they're doing their very best to maintain her secrets."

"We don't even know what those secrets are!"

Sam looked at his friends, his expression fierce. "No, but so far two people I know have died because I picked up the phone to ask questions. Now I intend to find out why."

Chapter Nineteen

Sam stepped out of the Mission Room, up onto the deck of the *Tahila*.

There was a lot to do, but no more leads to follow. Elise was trying to track down any of the members of the Yuxia, using the photos captured of them by local CCTV footage in Zanzibar. But trying to match up three Chinese Nationals based on photo recognition software with a database of more than 1 billion people in China, she didn't exactly exude confidence.

His cell phone rang.

He picked it up and spoke animatedly for a couple minutes.

When he was finished, Tom, who had followed him up onto the deck, asked, "What is it?"

"You're never going to believe this, but do you remember all those digital tags we placed on those whale sharks?"

Tom kept staring at him, unsure if he was being rhetorical. When Sam didn't go on, he said, "Of course I remember diving with a bunch of 9-ton beasts. What about them?"

"Every one of those tags we placed imploded."

Tom caught his breath. "They imploded? Weren't they rated to six thousand feet or something?"

"Eight!"

"Why would a sea creature that spends nearly its entire life on the top twenty feet of the ocean's surface feeding on plankton – that floats on the surface – feel the need to dive to greater than eight thousand feet?"

Sam shook his head. "I have no idea, but I can't wait to find out."

"You have any theories?"

"Not really… well, one actually, but it's more the type of thing you would expect to read about in a book co-written by Stephen King and Michael Crichton."

Tom grinned. "A nice combination. I've read a book by the two of them."

"Yeah, me too!"

Tom persisted. "So what's your theory?"

"No one has ever seen whale sharks mate or give birth, even though we know they are viviparous."

"Right," Tom said, trying to follow.

A look of wonder crept across Sam's face. His eyes wide. "Imagine if whale sharks exist in a sort of collective hive arrangement!"

"Come again?"

"Think about it. What if they work like the hive of a bee or a colony of ants?"

"Okay, now I'm really not following."

"What if there's a queen – or this case, a king whale shark – that lives at depths? A really, really deep depth by the way. Maybe the whale shark king doesn't ever leave its nest to eat. Instead, all its worker whale sharks go out and source the food. Then, when they're full, they return to the king. This is where they mate. What do you think?"

"I think that's a really long shot."

"I know, but I can't wait to find out what the truth is!"

Tom asked, "What about the *Midas*?"

Sam shrugged. "What about her?"

"I thought you were fired up to find out who these people are that are so keen to protect whatever secrets the *Midas* has kept concealed all these years?"

"I am, but I don't have any leads. So, we may as well keep working out what's going on with these whale sharks, while we're exploring other avenues to work this thing out with the *Midas*."

"Okay, I'm in." Tom said, "So what do we do, head back to the Mnemba Atoll and retag the whale sharks?"

"No. According to my friend who's a marine biologist, they'll be gone by now."

"Then where are we headed?"

"Apparently whale sharks are constantly migrating in search of a better food bowl."

"Any idea where that is?"

"Yeah." Sam grinned. "According to my friend, we're headed for Nosy Be, Madagascar."

Chapter Twenty

Siktyakh, Siberia

The Albino wore a blue, tailor-made Dräger CPS 7900 fully encapsulated biohazard suit. The gas-tight suit was designed to provide protection against an array of industrial chemicals, biological agents, and other toxic substances. Its impervious material was so tough it worked equally well in explosive areas and for handling cryogenic substances. Beneath the suit, he wore top of the range Self Contained Breathing Apparatus (SCBA).

The Albino looked at the two bodies at the entrance to the mine.

A woman and a man. The man seemed to be embracing the woman somehow in a lover's tendril. The last thing they ever did. It kind of reminded him of the people from Pompeii, whose bodies were immortalized by the pyroclastic flow that hit them, when Mount Vesuvius erupted. It was a fleeting thought, and his attention quickly returned to the task at hand. He glanced at the corpses.

They looked mummified.

Behind the clear face-shield of the biohazard suit, his eyes went wide at the sight. He had a rare genetic disorder that made the pupils of his eyes each develop into different colors. One was a dark green and the other a deep blue like a galaxy. Despite the anomaly, they looked severe and intense as he examined the bodies. There was a small pool of frozen liquid beside the bodies. He stepped back from it, slightly repulsed and equally enthralled by the sight.

The Albino turned and spoke to one of the assistants. "Where are the rest of them?"

"There was a total of eight other surface workers – mostly geologists and technicians – on the ground. The first ones tried to render assistance, offering some sort of first aid, but…" the assistant's eyes, behind the fully encapsulated biohazard suit, drifted toward the mummified bodies. "As you can imagine, there wasn't a lot first aid was going to do for these people."

"So where are these technicians now?"

"Mostly scattered around the forest, having tried to escape the contagion."

"All dead?"

"Yes. All bar one. There was an off-duty technician who was fishing at the time. Said he witnessed what happened and ran."

"Good. What happened to him?"

"He called the company, who fortunately called us. They asked us to take care of him after we're finished here."

"Did he talk to anyone?"

"Just his boss at the company."

"Good. And the company won't talk?"

"Not a chance. They're worried about all the legal ramifications. They're much happier to make the whole thing disappear permanently."

"Good." The Albino arched his pale, blond, eyebrow. "You took care of the fisherman?"

"Yes sir. A single shot to the head."

The Albino carefully inserted a large needle into the large jugular vein in the male's neck. What blood was left was so hard it would be impossible to withdraw. He knew this would be the case and came prepared. He attached a 10cc syringe to the intravenous needle. It was pre-loaded with plasmin, an anticoagulant, and formaldehyde, an embalming agent. He injected the whole lot. Waited a few minutes, and then pulled back on the syringe.

A dark liquid that barely looked like blood came out, filling the syringe.

There wasn't a lot of blood in there. But it would be enough for what he needed. He then completed the same process with the woman's body.

When he was done, he said, "Is everything ready to go?"

"Yeah, the explosives are set up to bury this place for good."

"Right. Give me a hand and we'll drop these bodies down the well," he said, referring to the boring hole.

When the bodies were removed, the Albino asked, "Any sign of the Medusa?"

"No." The guy shrugged. "What does it matter? We've already got the bodies. Isn't that enough to work with?"

"It will have to do. It would have been nice to have the original source, that's all."

The guy shrugged. "Who cares? This will do the job. Look at what happened to all these geologists. I can only imagine what it would do if this virus was released upon the rest of the world!"

The Albino drew in a breath, as he knew exactly what it would do to an unsuspecting world.

Chapter Twenty-One

Nosy Be, Madagascar

If the Mnemba Atoll in Zanzibar was paradise on Earth, then Nosy Be was a very close relative. Its name meant, Big Island, in the local Malagasy language. Laying just five miles off the coast of Madagascar in the Mozambique Channel, it was the largest of a small cluster of islands, made up of eleven volcanic craters. The island itself was lush with greenery, and renowned for its chameleons and the Stumpffia pygmaea – the world's smallest frog.

The *Tahila* motored past Hell-Ville, the island's capital city. With its rich French colonial buildings, and stunning beaches, the place looked like it couldn't be any farther from Hell. The ship slowed before coming to rest at its anchor off Mahazandry Bay, a large volcanic crater that rose straight out of crystal-clear turquoise waters, surrounded by impossibly white sandy beaches.

Sam and Tom dropped into the waters with their diver propulsion vehicles, armed with another set of behavioral tags for the whale sharks. This time, Veyron, had devised a new housing method for the tags, that made them capable of withstanding the most extreme depths of the ocean. So long as the whale sharks didn't manage to knock the tags off their dorsal fins, they were going to find out once and for all, the reason why the giant fish dived to such incredible depths.

They got through the dive in a little under an hour, having developed an easy technique for it a week earlier when they first tagged the whale sharks in the Mnemba Atoll. Finishing up, they climbed back on board the *Tahila* feeling good about the world.

On the deck, Sam and Tom were greeted by the entire crew of the *Tahila*, their faces a somber mixture of fear and dismay.

Sam's brows drew down. "What did we miss?"

Chapter Twenty-Two

Sam dried himself as he and Tom made their way down to the Mission Room.

Elise pressed play, and a recording from CCTV came into view on the overhead projector. It depicted the surveillance outside an ATM at the Musée d'Art Moderne in Paris, with the Seine in the background, and the Eiffel Tower rising proudly in the distance. A young Parisian woman in a striking yellow dress, high-heels, and looking like the quintessential height of French fashion, withdrew several hundred Euros from the ATM.

As she was leaving, her face distorted into a mask of urgency, coupled with embarrassment. She took the Euros, placing them in her handbag, and then stepped back. Her right hand went to her tummy, as if guarding against some sort of internal pain or discomfort. She tried to take another step, but something stopped her.

She held her breath and tried to cross her legs.

Her young, dignified, and extremely attractive face revealed abject horror, aligned with dismay. A moment later, unable to restrain herself anymore, she appeared to let go, and urinated on the pavement, wetting her dress.

The liquid gushed uncontrollably.

Sam's eyes narrowed, as he began to realize what he was witnessing.

The woman screamed.

It was blood curdling. Not the whimper of someone embarrassed about an accident. This was the terror of the dying.

And still the liquid kept coming.

She tried to jam her hands between her legs, as though she were capable of somehow stemming the ongoing disaster.

The scream changed its pitch to a shriek.

Her previously soft, glowing, skin became sunken and shriveled, like one would expect of someone who suddenly aged several decades in the blink of an eye.

Abruptly, the scream mercifully came to a stop.

Sam stared at the woman in the video. She was no longer breathing. How could she be? Every drop of liquid had been expelled from her body.

Leaving her body mummified.

Chapter Twenty-Three

Sam swallowed hard. "What the hell did we just witness?"

Voicing Sam's thoughts, Tom said, "Did she just become a mummy?"

"I suppose it's too much to ask for it to be just a hoax?"

"I'm afraid it's not a joke. That's actual footage." Elise's face hardened. "A bizarre virus appears to be spreading around the world."

"A pandemic?"

"We don't know yet."

"They've locked down Paris to contain this thing. I wouldn't worry too much. It'll burn itself out soon enough. Historically, the worse a virus tends to be the faster it burns, and the quicker it ends. Just look at Ebola. It was deadly, but it tended to kill its hosts so quickly that the disease was unable to spread globally."

Elise said, "Unfortunately, the same horror scene has unfolded in Paris, New York, London, Dubai, and Singapore today."

Sam swallowed. "They're all central cities. Millions of people coming in, traveling from all over the world."

Elise nodded. "Yes. You know what this means, don't you?"

"This isn't an accident. Someone weaponized this virus, releasing it in locations most capable of spreading the disease. The world is under attack."

Tom asked what was on everyone's mind. "What do you want to do, Sam?"

"There's nothing much I think we can do. I mean, we're not epidemiologists or microbiologists. This isn't our war. I'll contact the Secretary of Defense and see if there's anything we can offer, but realistically, I don't think there's anything we can do."

Tom said, "Then where do you want to head from here?"

"It's up to the rest of you but given there aren't any cases on the African continent, I don't see why we can't continue our project and keep searching for the *Midas*. If the world ends up needing to shut down, this is probably as safe a place as any to isolate." Sam looked at the faces of his crew. There was a fear that he hadn't seen before. These people had all fought innumerable battles and worked in some of the most remote and inhospitable regions on Earth, but this was different. This was an invisible virus. Something that could kill them without being seen. "What do you say?"

There was a unanimous agreement that they'd rather keep working on the current project while it was possible until this thing burned itself out.

"Good." Sam slowly exhaled. Then, to Elise, he said, "Okay, contact the WHO and the CDC and see if you find out any more about this thing."

"Will do," she said.

Sam stood up. "Oh, one more thing…"

"Yes?"

"Do they have a name for this virus yet?"

"Its scientific designation is H5X7-2021."

Sam considered the name, but it didn't mean anything to him. He said, "H5X7-2021."

Elise said, "But non-scientists are calling it something else."

"Someone's decided to give it a nickname?"

"It happens. Normally there's a scientific name. For example, H1N1 was called Swine Flu because it originated in pigs, Zaire ebolavirus was shortened to Ebola, H5N1 was called Bird Flu because…"

Sam waved a dismissive hand. "What are they calling this one?"

Elise sighed. "They're calling it the Medusa's Curse."

Chapter Twenty-Four

Sam brought up an image of the Greek Medusa.

Perfectly proportioned with a symmetrical, porcelain face and emerald eyes, she was captivating. At first glance, her hair was blonde and full of ringlets. It was only on a second, deeper, inspection, that one noticed the faintest outline of serpent heads from the ends of her hair. It was on this second inspection, that one might notice that the large lips, were subtly twisted in some sort of sinister sneer.

Sam said, "In Greek mythology, the Medusa turned all who looked at her into stone."

Tom took a drink from his water bottle. "See, now there's an advertisement for the fact that it matters more what's on the inside than the outside."

Genevieve touched his hand affectionately. "Wouldn't you still love me if I could turn you into stone?"

Tom shrugged. "Ah, to be honest, you're capable of killing me with your bare hands, so you're really no less lethal than a Medusa." He smirked. "I'm surprisingly good with it."

Sam continued, "The petrifying image of Medusa is an instantly recognizable image in popular culture. Medusa has been featured in several works of fiction, including video games, movies, cartoons and books. In particular, the designer Versace's symbol is reflected through the Medusa-head symbol. It was chosen because she represents beauty, art, and philosophy."

Tom asked, "Was there any historical evidence she existed?"

"Not really, plenty of Greek imagery associated with the mythology, but the ancient Greeks liked their mythological stories."

"You want to tell us the story?"

Sam shrugged. "I was afraid you wouldn't ask."

"Go on." Tom waved his hand in an 'after you' motion. "I give you permission."

Sam said, "In Greek mythology, the Medusa was a monster, a Gorgon, generally described as a winged human female with living venomous snakes in place of hair. Those who gazed upon her face would turn to stone. Despite her fame, she was one of three sisters, all of whom possessed the power to turn people to stone.

"The three Gorgon sisters – Medusa, Stheno, and Euryale – were children of the ancient sea gods, Phorcys and Ceto, chthonic monsters from an archaic world. Strangely, they had three more sisters who weren't Gorgons, called the Graeae – Grey Women – who were prominent in Aeschylus' story of Prometheus Bound, who all shared a single eye, and one tooth."

Sam shrugged apologetically when Tom rolled his eyes. "Hey, I didn't write the story."

He continued, "In most versions of the story, Medusa was beheaded by the hero Perseus, who was sent to fetch her head by King Polydectes of Seriphus because Polydectes wanted to marry his mother."

"Obviously," Tom said, with a scoffing chuckle.

Sam said, "Well aware of the problem, the Gods gave Perseus help in the form of a mirrored shield from Athena; gold, winged sandals from Hermes; a sword from Hephaestus; and Hades's helm of invisibility. Since Medusa was the only one of the three Gorgons who was mortal, Perseus was able to slay her while looking at the reflection from the mirrored shield he received from Athena. During that time, Medusa was pregnant by Poseidon. When Perseus beheaded her, Pegasus, a winged horse, and Chrysaor, a giant wielding a golden sword, sprang from her body."

Tom asked, "What happened to Perseus?"

"After he beheaded the Medusa, Perseus thereafter used her head, which retained its ability to turn onlookers to stone, as a weapon until he gave it to the goddess Athena to place on her shield. In classical antiquity the image of the head of Medusa appeared in the evil-averting device known as the Gorgoneion."

"That's some seriously screwed up story." Tom grimaced in distaste. "Who comes up with these sorts of stories?"

"I don't know. Who understands the minds of fiction writers?" Sam asked. "In my opinion, they're the worst of the worst."

"Writers?"

"Yeah, they don't *do* anything except write!"

"I agree," Tom said. "So clearly this virus has nothing to do with the Greek mythology."

"I guess not," Sam said, "But you must admit, having watched that horrifying CCTV video, the similarities seem uncanny."

"Yeah, I don't know. I guess we will just have to let the Medusa's Curse run its course." Tom looked at Sam. "Where does that leave us?"

Sam thought about it for a moment, and grinned. "Trying to work out where the *Midas* actually went."

Chapter Twenty-Five

Sitting at the Round Table, Sam and Tom worked their way through a series of maps of river systems along the East Coast of the African Continent.

The four major rivers in Africa are the Nile, the Zambezi, the Congo, and the Niger. The Nile is one of the longest rivers in the world. Sam ran his fingers along the ocean navigable portions of each of them. None of them brought them very far inland.

Tom said, "Why are there so few navigable rivers in Africa?"

"I know. It seems crazy given how solid these rivers are. Internally, the rivers of Africa are easily navigable throughout the continent, but very few of them can be accessed from the sea. The Congo and Niger rivers are important, navigable waterways."

"Why is that?"

Sam said, "A few mllion years ago, the tectonic plate where most of Africa lies, was lifted up a few hundred feet. The big rivers that flowed into the sea kept flowing, but developed huge waterfalls at their mouths. After many years, erosion has done away with the steepest falls, but there are still rapids at the mouths of the rivers.

"Most dramatically, this is seen at the mouth of the Congo river. The river is navigable from the sea for a short distance, up to the port of Matadi. Then the rapids block the way for any ship. After that, the river is easily navigable for a few thousand miles."

"Really?" Tom said. "Couldn't they just build a ramp or a series of water locks, like they did in the Panama Canal?"

"They could now. But at the time they couldn't. This made the exploration of Africa difficult. When Sir Henry Morton Stanley discovered how the Congo river ran, the Belgian king Leopold II took over the whole Congo basin. He had a 250 mile railway built to circumvent the rapids, and from there navigation along the river was very easy."

Tom stared at the oil painting that had started it all. "Didn't Lamont tell you he knew where the image of the *Midas* on the river was actually set?"

"Sure, the Upper Zambezi, but that doesn't help us much."

"Why not?" Tom grinned. "Why don't we simply follow the Zambezi upriver?"

Sam laughed out loud. "Well that solves that..."

"What's so funny?"

"Well, it's unlikely the *Midas* sailed the upper Zambezi."

"Why not?"

"It's impossible, unless those slaves managed to somehow free the *Midas* of its earthly confines and fly over Victoria Falls."

Tom laughed...

Sam asked, "What's so funny?"

Tom paused. "What if they did?"

Sam's upturned lips flattened into a hard line. "That's impossible."

"Maybe, maybe not..." Tom agreed. "But, hypothetically, if they could have gotten past Victoria Falls, how far inland could they have traveled along the Zambezi?"

Sam grinned. "If they somehow overcame Victoria Falls, they could then have sailed uninterrupted... all the way into the heart of Africa."

Chapter Twenty-Six

Sam brought up a 3D image of the Zambezi River.

A spectacular, moody waterway that passed through six countries on its path toward the Indian Ocean, the Zambezi was the fourth-longest river in Africa, after the Nile, Congo and Niger rivers. The river is uniquely changeable – in some places, it's wide and lazy, averaging a width of up to three miles. In others, it's thrilling, passing through narrow, deep gorges. In every part, the river is endowed with amazing floral and faunal biodiversity that's threatened by development.

A wide variety of animals – including giraffe, lion and leopard – have access to the river from surrounding areas. Elephant and buffalo are common on the banks of the Zambezi River. The river is teeming with hippo and crocodile while the park has a good number of resident antelopes, including waterbuck and bushbuck.

The river has three distinct stretches: the Upper Zambezi, which flows from its source to Victoria Falls; the Middle Zambezi, which flows from Victoria Falls to the upper reaches of Cahora Bassa reservoir; and the Lower Zambezi, which flows through Cahora Bassa to the Zambezi Delta.

The undammed Upper Zambezi, where the Lozi live, remains a pristine wonderland with its vast floodplains and vibrant fishing culture. This stretch of the river is home to artisanal fishing, sport fishing safaris and angling tournaments. Anglers from all over the world are drawn for game fishing of the fighting tigerfish.

The Middle Zambezi, which forms the border between Zambia and Zimbabwe, is the ragged part of the river, and it's marked by a plethora of gorges, falls and rapids. This is the section that famously challenged David Livingstone's ambition to navigate the mighty river. It's home to the magnificent Victoria Falls, the world's largest waterfall and a UNESCO World Heritage site.

The falls are followed by the Batoka Gorge, a zig-zagged gorge cut deep into the earth that offers one of the world's most revered sites for whitewater rafting. Batoka Gorge attracts huge amounts of tourism for both Zambia and Zimbabwe, contributing significantly to the GDP of both countries.

Sam asked, "What are you thinking?"

"I'm thinking we take the *Tahila* up the Zambezi as far as she's navigable and take a look how far we can go."

Sam brought up a series of digital reproductions of old paper charts on the table. "I can tell you right now we can reach this point, here about two miles back from Victoria Falls and go no farther."

"Good, then that's where we'll go."

A wry smile played out across Sam's lips. "What?"

"Do you remember the Mahogany Ship?"

Sam laughed. He and his father had been obsessed with the legend of the shipwreck. Sam and Tom had finally found it a few years back. The massive ship had been carried inland, its thousand plus strong crew, literally dragging the ship overland in an attempt to avoid the southern waters off Australia.

"Yeah, I remember the Mahogany Ship."

"Good. Because I have an idea if the freed slaves aboard the Midas were anywhere near as defiant as I'm guessing they were, they might just have had the same level of conviction to pull it off."

Sam shook his head. "They never would have had enough people to do so."

"No, but the history books say the area was populated with Bantu tribes. They might have helped."

Sam thought about that. "It's not impossible. Still, the question is, why would the crew of the Midas have gone to the trouble?"

"Why would they have skipped their home port of Mendiland and sailed south, around the Cape of Good Hope and all the way to East Africa?" Tom countered.

"They might have gotten lost."

"No way, any seafarer capable of surviving such a journey knew enough to know where they were. If they headed up the Zambezi, they were looking for something specifically. Searching for something."

"If they created a portage or a system to elevate the Midas beyond Victoria Falls, there would have been some sort of evidence left there…"

Sam stopped talking. Realization of where Tom was going suddenly hitting home.

Tom smiled. "What do you think I'm planning on looking for as we take the *Tahila* up the Zambezi?"

Chapter Twenty-Seven

Kwibisa Plains, Zambia

Freya Capel moved quickly through the African wilderness.

Breathing hard, she worked her way up the small mountain that stood out like a jagged scar on the plains, to a peak of 1,500 feet. It wasn't a tall mountain, but the gradient was steep, and she had to watch her footing to avoid falling to her death.

She maintained a constant speed.

Freya was on her own but had made the journey many times in the past six months since she'd arrived in the country. At first, she had tried to match the locals who had shown her the remarkable vantage point, and then, surpassing it to set her own pace. She was tall and lithesome, moving with the assertive gait of an athlete, and the wary gaze of a hunter. Even in shapeless clothing, she had a willowy elegance about her as she climbed.

Freya was in a race against time.

She needed to reach the top in time to watch the animals come to the lake to drink at dusk. She carried a Holland & Holland Royal Double Rifle. Loaded with .577 Nitro Express, the weapon was capable of stopping even the largest animals in Africa. The weapon was an anachronism. Nearly eighty years old, it was hand crafted for her grandfather, who had used it to hunt big game after the War.

Freya had never used it to hunt, although she was an excellent shot when she needed to be. She had no interest in shooting anything in Africa, but nor did she feel the need to get killed. She carried it whenever she was out and about in the wilderness. Because of its caliber, the weapon was considered a 'charge stopper.' One well-placed round had large or dangerous game dropping on the spot.

She neared the crest of the small mountain, where giant sandstone boulders rose out of the top, like the turrets of some sort of medieval castle. She ducked through a narrow gap between two, and then – slinging her rifle across her shoulder – she clambered up the opposite side of the boulder, progressively gaining altitude as she jumped from one to the next until she reached the largest slab of sandstone of them all, and the best vantage point in all of Zambia.

Her heart was pounding from the effort. She drew a breath and smiled, revealing a set of white, evenly spaced teeth. She felt the same sort of exuberance every time she reached the summit. It reminded her of that scene from the Lion King, where Simba was able to overlook his entire kingdom. That's how she felt. In a very small way, this was her kingdom, and she was responsible for the safety of all who lived wherever the light touched.

The sun was lying low on the plains.

She removed her rifle and laid down on the summit, using the scope at the top of the weapon to get a better look at the wildlife.

Her eyes traced the outline of the Zambezi River. It snaked lazily along the flat Kwibisa plains, before opening up into an oxbow lake. Once, a long time ago, the river formed a U-shaped bend. Time ate away at the banks of the river, eventually cutting it open, and forming a large area of water for the animals of Africa, both large and small. At the center of the lake, two massive boulders rose out of the water, like giant elephants greeting one another.

The place looked like something out of an African wildlife show. Her eyes narrowed on the crosshairs of the scope, trying to identify the animals. There were sable, zebra, and hartebeest. All tentative and wary of the nearby crocodiles that waited for their prey to become sloppy. Farther downstream, a pod of hippos mingled, indifferent to the ongoing battle of prey and predators that was played out throughout the African Continent. A tower of giraffes drank from the nearby waterhole. There was smaller game, too. Including duiker, reedbuck, tsessebe, and even a solitary bushpig. And a whole flock of birds, the names of which, she was yet to discover.

The sun began to set on the distant horizon. Freya removed the rifle, sitting cross-legged, and simply enjoyed the view with her naked eyes. The sight filled her with so much joy. Her parents were Dutch, and she had grown up in Australia, but there was something about Africa that had pulled at her heart strings from childhood. An unexplained yearning. An invisible force that drove her to return. And when she was there, she felt at home. She stood up, ready to make the journey down the hill, and back to the clinic, before it became fully dark.

Freya was strikingly beautiful.

Standing roughly 5"9' with a strong physique. She was neither skinny nor fat. She wore thick leather boots. They appeared rugged and well-worn rather than fashionable. She wore gray cargo shorts, revealing a long pair of muscular legs, toned from years of traveling by foot across some of the most isolated and inhospitable regions on Earth where her work had taken her. She wore a purple tank top. Her blonde hair windswept, tied behind her in a casual braid with indifference. A couple wisps of blonde hair escaped, cascading across her face. She ran the fingers of her left hand across her forehead, tucking the strands behind her ear.

It was her eyes that startled people. They flickered between blue and green depending on the light, giving her a piercing, almost mesmerizing gaze. Behind which thrived a mischievous and daring soul. Her eyes were almond shaped, with long lashes. Her face, slightly oval, with a sharp nose, noticeably high cheekbones, and a long neck.

She had full lips with a small scar on her lower lip. It somehow enhanced her appearance rather than detracting from it. There was something sultry and sexy about those lips. There was kindness and something else too – a sort of unbidden, and wild mischievousness, barely suppressed – as though life was just one hell of a wild ride to be lived to the fullest.

Behind her, she was startled to hear someone cry her name.

"Freya!"

She stood up to greet the messenger. Her blue-green eyes flashed like cut emeralds in the fading sunlight. Turning, she spotted Amakusana, a young woman with dark skin and expressive blue eyes who worked at the same hospital clinic as her. She was carrying a medical backpack. It was Freya's and held the basic equipment needed in an emergency.

Freya frowned. "Amakusana! What is it?"

"Oh Freya, you must come quickly!"

Freya was already making her way down the sandstone outcrop. "Of course, what's happened?"

"There's an emergency."

"What's happened?" Freya asked again, following her quickly down the hill.

"A local woman is in labor."

A puzzled expression washed over Freya's face. Women were always having babies. More often than not in Zambia, they were delivered naturally at home without complication. "What's wrong?"

"The baby is breech."

A breech birth was where the baby delivered bottom down, instead of headfirst. It was more dangerous than a normal birth, but still, in Freya's experience, many breech births delivered without incident.

Freya persisted with the questioning. "What's wrong with the mother?"

Amakusana met her eye. There was fear in her look. "The baby is stuck."

Chapter Twenty-Eight

Freya felt a shadow of fear. "Take me to her – as quickly as you can!"

Freya now urged Amakusana on. A breech birth that fails to progress naturally on its own can be fatal if left untreated.

She was a midwife with Médecins Sans Frontières – AKA Doctors Without Borders. Six months ago, she arrived in the small community of Kwibisa to set up a small clinic for women's health. It was a small project, but something she believed in, and she felt her purpose was to drastically improve the lives of some of the poorest women on Earth. In doing so, she hoped to turn around the worst life-expectancies on the continent, along with infant and childhood mortality rates that were unfathomable in the modern world. There wasn't a lot of funding, and a lot of her work looked at education and promoting basic health care initiatives. Most women delivered at home and only brought their babies to the clinic for routine assessments and vaccinations, but sometimes she was still called upon to deliver babies when there were complications.

After twenty minutes, Freya and Amakusana reached the woman's house. It was a traditional Zambian home, constructed with mud-brick walls and sheet metal roofing. Beside it, was a thatch insaka – a type of shared kitchen – used by the community.

Outside the home was a large Biglobosa tree, its branches covered in big red seed pods. Lying in the shade beneath it, on a hand-woven ratan mat, a pregnant woman was moaning quietly in pain. The woman wore a brightly colored shirt, and her lower body was covered with a light blanket.

Children played nearby, while a single woman sat with her offering some support.

"Hello, Mulubwa," Freya said. Her voice was calm, empathetic, but above all, confident and controlled. In her experience, reassurance, beat medication more often than not. She smiled warmly. "My name's Freya. I'm a midwife with the clinic. Did I say your name right?"

The woman nodded and kept breathing hard. "Yes."

"Amakasuna tells me your baby is coming out bottom first. Is that right?"

"Yes."

Freya's lips curled into a smile. She was surprised. She was the only midwife in the area, and she hadn't heard of the woman, so she wondered how she knew the baby was breech. "Have you seen someone from the clinic?"

"No," she responded through intermittent episodes of panting.

"Have you seen a traditional healer?" Freya asked. Traditional healers were often the first line of care in Zambia, helping to fill the gaps in a public health system suffering chronic drug shortages and a lack of skilled staff.

She shook her head. "No."

Freya nodded. "I'm curious, how did you know your baby is coming bottom first?"

"This is my fifth baby. I know something is wrong. I feel it. It's very different. That is how I knew that I was in trouble."

"Five babies. Did you have any complications with the other ones?"

"No. All come very fast."

"Except this one." Freya made a reassuring smile. "That's okay. At least we know your body can do it."

"Yes."

Freya said, "Now tell me, is any part of the baby showing?"

"I don't think so."

Freya smiled. "Okay, do you mind if I have a look?"

"Yes..." she gasped as another contraction came on. "Please... I want the baby to come!"

Freya assessed her patient, observing full labor, with regular contractions, coming every few minutes apart. She pulled back the blanket. There was no sign of the baby. More importantly, no sign of a breech birth, with a footling or umbilical cord coming first. It was a good sign.

Freya felt her heart settle.

A true breech delivery could be dangerous in a western hospital with copious resources, including an anesthesiologist and obstetrician if the baby needed to be delivered surgically. Out in the remote wilderness of Kwibisa plains it could be a death sentence for mother and child.

She put on a pair of latex gloves, and asked, "When did your waters break?"

A worried look creased Mulubwa's face, and she didn't answer.

Freya thought there might have been some confusion in the translation. There were seven official vernacular languages in Zambia – Bemba, Nyanja, Lozi, Tonga, Luvale, Lunda, and Kaonde. Freya had learned some basic words in each. Mulubwa spoke Bemba. She asked a phrase she'd memorized in all seven languages. "The water that comes before the baby?"

Mulubwa frowned. "It hasn't."

Freya looked at Amakusana, who spoke both languages fluently. "See if you can find out when her waters broke."

The two Zambian women broke into a fast exchange of words in Bemba. When they were finished, Amakusana looked at Freya, with her arms open, she said, "Mulubwa says her waters definitely haven't broken yet."

Freya nodded. Looked at Mulubwa with a warm smile. "That's okay."

A few seconds later, Mulubwa began to pant heavily. She reverted to Bemba and cried out. Freya glanced at Amakusana, who translated, "She says, she's ready to push now."

"Okay..." Freya held Mulubwa's hand. "You're in control. If you feel like you can push, go for it."

Nothing happened.

Then, uncomfortably, Mulubwa stood up.

Amakusana tried to prevent her, but Freya stopped her with the wave of her hand. "It's okay, let her find the position that's best for her."

A moment later, Mulubwa screamed.

Freya moved to support the baby that was now coming into the world fast. Probably a little too fast. She moved quickly to catch the baby.

And in an instant, the entire baby, still cocooned in its amniotic sac greeted her hand.

She caught the sac fully intact.

Both Amakusana and Mulubwa screamed at the sight.

Freya had tears in her eyes, she was so moved by the experience. It was called an en caul birth, and was an extremely rare and beautiful event, occurring in less than 1 in 80,000 births. As with many extraordinary circumstances, some cultures believe that en caul births are spiritual or even magical. Being born en caul is seen as a sign of good luck for both baby and parents.

A moment later, the squirming baby broke open the amniotic sac, just like a chick hatching.

It was a girl.

Freya placed the girl on the skin of her mom's chest. The baby cried. It was pink. Well. And safe. Freya drew a breath and exhaled gently.

Mulubwa looked startled and scared.

Freya said, "It's okay. Your baby is fine. Better than fine. She is very fortunate."

"It is good luck?" Mulubwa asked, wrapping her arms around the newborn.

"The very best of luck." Freya nodded with a smile. "It's called an en caul birth. They say a baby born like this can never drown."

Mulubwa made a prayer of thanks in her own language.

Then, Freya said, "But just in case, don't test that drowning thing out, okay?"

About half an hour later, Freya and Amakusana left the new mom and daughter, and made their way back to the clinic. It was after twilight, and Freya gripped her double barrel rifle, wary of predators in the dark.

On the way, Amakusana asked her about this strange virus that was apparently spreading around the world – the Medusa's Curse. As far as Freya was concerned, it was the least of Zambia's problems. In a world where approximately 2,000 children under the age of 5 die on a yearly basis, and more than 3,500 new-born babies died from infections that were linked to contaminated water in Zambia, some distant virus seemed like the least of their worries.

Amakusana said, "Do you think it's real?"

Freya stopped, met the girl's eyes. "The Medusa's Curse?"

"Yeah."

Not sure if it was real news or just some horrible hoax. Freya shook her head. "I've no idea. I'm a midwife. Virology isn't really my thing." She sighed. "Either way, it hasn't reached the African continent yet, and even if it does, it's unlikely to reach this far into Zambia."

Reassured, Amakusana flashed her a bright smile. "Thank you."

"We'll be all right," Freya said. "If anything, I think if the pandemic really does spread, the heart of Africa is probably the safest place on Earth."

Chapter Twenty-Nine

The Zambezi River is the fourth-longest river in Africa.

Somewhere along the river's 1600 miles of waterways, lay the wreckage of the Portuguese Slave Ship, *Midas*. The river rises in Zambia and flows through eastern Angola, along the north-eastern border of Namibia and the northern border of Botswana, then along the border between Zambia and Zimbabwe to Mozambique, where it crosses the country to empty into the Indian Ocean.

It was a lot of water to cover. Enough that a lifetime dragging specialist underwater research equipment, and bathymetric mapping sonar buoys, would likely fail to deliver any results. That meant they needed to get lucky, or better yet, find a way to narrow their search area down considerably.

The *Tahila* navigated from the Zambezi River's delta that opened onto the Indian Ocean, following it inland and westerly until they reached the lakes at Cahora Bassa. Over the course of multiple days, they worked their way through the narrow gorges and various rocky impediments until they eventually reached Lake Kariba, where the Kariba Hydroelectric Dam prevented them from navigating any farther up the Zambezi on board the *Tahila*.

On the back of the *Tahila*, the Eurocopter was brought out from its storage hold below decks. Sam and Tom loaded the helicopter up with nearly a ton of bathymetric mapping equipment. With Genevieve at the controls, they took off, heading to Livingstone Island where they had rented a motorboat to base themselves for the next few weeks as they searched and mapped parts of the Upper Zambezi.

The Eurocopter took off, flying low through the Batoka Gorge, where the Zambezi cut a two-hundred-foot perpendicular wall through the basalt landscape. Far below, several white-water rafts navigated the rapids – some of the best grades rafting in the world – where the Zambezi flowed swiftly through the gorge.

Genevieve flew toward Victoria Falls. The mile-wide waterfall marked the boundary between the upper and middle Zambezi, while the falling water created a cloud of spray that could be seen from more than 30 miles away. The world's largest sheet of falling water, its cliffs are more than twice as high as Niagara Falls as it crashes down the 345-foot-deep precipice on the Zambia–Zimbabwe border.

At the end of the Batoka Gorge, Genevieve brought the helicopter up and over the Victoria Falls, where everyone on board simultaneously gasped in delight. The stunning shock of the panoramic display touched them. All of them were speechless, while more than half of them were moved nearly to tears.

What everyone on board the Eurocopter saw was a stunning rainbow against a blue, blue sky, and a backdrop of Victoria Falls rainforest. The woodland jungle was vibrant green with ferns, palms, and fruit trees nourished by the constant droplets of water.

"I've never seen anything like it," Tom said reverently.

"Worth the price of admission," Sam agreed.

They flew north-east across the top of the falls, where several tourists posed for an Instagram-worthy shot of Devil's Pool, a natural infinity pool that formed along the lip of Victoria Falls. Determined to enjoy the full experience, Genevieve banked the helicopter north, taking them over the top of Livingstone Island, before coming in to land on a jetty that doubled as a helipad for some of the more privileged tourists.

There they were greeted by a river guide they'd hired named Wakhumelo, a wiry Zambian who was six foot-five at least, with a polite and laidback attitude to the world. The man helped them unload their dive equipment, bathymetric mapping sonars, and other equipment they might need for the next few weeks. Tom kissed Genevieve goodbye, and they watched the Eurocopter take off, as she made the return journey to the *Tahila*. Wakhumelo led them to the powerboat they had hired, an Aquila 36 Sports Cruiser, aptly named, *Zambezi Runner*.

The sun was setting over the Zambezi River, and Sam, Tom, and Wakhumelo sat down at the luxurious dinette on board the Sports Cruiser, drinking three cold beers. They were Kilimanjaros, which Sam discovered were appreciated in Zambia as much as Zanzibar. They discussed their plans and goals, and showed maps of various places, that might match with the image from the oil painting.

As the night wore on, Wakhumelo said, "Rest well tonight, gentlemen. Tomorrow, I will make all of your dreams come true."

Chapter Thirty

Livingstone Island, Zambia

They untied the *Zambezi Runner's* bow lines at six a.m.

Wakhumelo, standing at the helm, gently opened up the throttle and the Aquila's powerful twin Mercury 350 Horsepower engines gave a smooth, throaty sound, and the Sports Cruiser began its eastern journey up the Zambezi.

It was a two-day journey to the first location the guide recommended.

The three of them took turns at the wheel. It was slow going. The river was shallow in parts and filled with dangerous reefs, and an array of dangerous impediments – not the least of which, were the omnipresent hippos that seemed to rest with their heads just above the surface of the water, while their massive bodies remained unseen and as deadly as an iceberg. Sam felt like he was on a real-life Jungle Cruise in Disneyland where wild African animals abound, and everything had the ability to either sink their boat or kill them.

When they reached the Sesheke Plain, the river widened, and a large herd of elephants meandered along the riverbanks. There were dozens of different types of game animals, too, including buffalo, eland, sable, roan, kudu, waterbuck, impala, duiker, bushbuck, reedbuck, bushpig, and warthogs – all warily drinking from the river, always watchful of the many predators. In the water, crocodiles picked off their choice of meals, while on land lions and leopards ruled.

The river widened into an oxbow lake, and Sam imagined the location matching the scene from the oil painting, with the *Midas* at anchor. The Zambezi, he discovered was riddled with oxbow lakes, and Wakhumelo informed him that some of these come and go depending on whether or not it was the wet or dry season.

They spent the next week dragging sonar buoys in a grid-search pattern but came up with nothing. Wakhumelo wasn't hopeful they would find anything. Not because he didn't believe they were in the right place, just that with the seasonal flooding of the river, he doubted very much that had the *Midas* sunk in the region, anything of its wreckage would still be in the river.

A part of Sam tended to agree with him, then again, sometimes you never know what you might find when you start to search a riverbed. The majority of the Portuguese ship's hull would have rotted away a century ago, given that it was fresh water without the protection of seawater found in ocean wreckage. But that said, it depended on what the *Midas* was carrying. There were plenty of parts on a ship that were metal – a bell, a cooking pot, weapons. All they needed was to find one of those and it would confirm the presence of the ship in the river.

At the start of the second week, they moved farther east, to another place that matched the oil painting. A couple of river dhows sailed across the river. The locals were in the process of using dynamite to widen the river, and remove some unwanted underwater reefs that were a hazard to the river's small shipping cargo fleets.

The whole set up seemed careless and disorganized. Someone was going to have body parts blown off.

Sam cringed, as he watched them working. Anywhere else in the world and work safety authorities would have had a field day shutting the operation down. But Zambia was a world unto itself, and still several decades away from introducing occupational health and safety laws.

On the third week, they hit paydirt.

It was a region of narrow, meandering river, some twenty miles east of the Kwibisa Plains.

A couple round objects came up on the bathymetric imaging display. They were so small that Sam almost missed it.

They circled back and got a better look.

On the second run, it became obvious that a trio of spheres were in their sights. Yet there was nothing in Africa that naturally formed a perfectly spherical ball, much less three of them. Each one spaced out by five or six feet.

Sam grinned. "Gentlemen, if I had to guess, I'd say we just found the remains of cannon balls."

Chapter Thirty-One

Sam and Tom geared up quickly.

The water was shallow. Just ten feet. It was clear enough they could see the riverbed from the deck of the pleasure cruiser. They were diving with a single tank, buoyancy control device, regulator, mask and fins. The water was warm, they didn't need wetsuits. They had inflatable lift bags, which were basically empty balloons with a pair of hooks at the bottom. The idea was to use the regulators to inflate the bags with air, and then use those to lift the cannon balls.

They would be in and out within fifteen minutes.

It was the middle of the day a time when most land predators were asleep trying to conserve energy during the tortuous heat of the day. Even so, Sam gave a not-so-cursory sweep of the nearby shore, searching for dangerous animals.

There didn't appear to be anything nearby.

Just a few miles back, he'd seen several local kids swimming in the water. If it was safe for them, he figured this part of the river must have been okay for him and Tom. A couple hundred yards upriver he spotted a lone hippo basking in the water. Only its head was visible, and a couple oxpeckers with their distinctive yellow beaks were standing on its head, like a little deserted island in the middle of the river. The birds shared a symbiotic relationship with several large African mammals, feeding on ectoparasites, particularly ticks, as well as insects infesting wounds and the flesh and blood of some wounds as well.

Sam stared at the hippo.

Then turned and exchanged a glance with Wakhumelo.

The guide laughed. "That hippo won't cause you any trouble unless you disturb it."

"You're sure?"

"Certain." Wakhumelo grinned. "Besides, I'll be here on the deck to keep an eye out just for you. I assure you, losing rich American tourist... is very bad for business."

"That's very reassuring." Sam exchanged a glance with Tom. "You happy?"

"Sure. Diving in an African river. What could go wrong?"

They jumped into the water.

Sam turned around to look back at the boat.

Wakhumelo had disappeared into the pilothouse. Sam frowned. He wanted the reassurance there was nothing about to come and eat him and Tom before he dived. A moment later, the guide returned to the deck carrying a large bore rifle.

Sam cursed. "I hope that's not to be used to protect us against crocodiles?"

"No, of course not. Just a warning against hippos or elephants. They generally don't mean to harm you, but if they get spooked, they can charge and that ends as well as can be expected when you hit a bus."

"Oh, right," Sam said, feeling better. "I was afraid you were going to say you were going to use it to defend us against crocodiles."

Wakhumelo laughed and shook his head. "No. Of course not. Crocodiles are too fast. By the time you see one, it is too late to stop them."

Sam didn't know if the guide was joking or not. In the end, he didn't wait around to find out. To Tom, he said, "Quick. Let's get this over and done with."

They dived swiftly.

The water was clear and teaming with life. Small schools of yellow fish, bream, and tilapia filled the river. He imagined crocodiles were so well fed they would never even consider going after a pair of SCUBA divers.

They worked together, securing a harness around each of the cannon balls, before attaching a lift bag. Sam used a tether to link all three lift bags together, and Tom controlled the lot of them like a kid at a theme park with a few hot air balloons. Sam exchanged a couple hand gestures with Tom, acknowledging they were ready to head to the surface.

Halfway up, Sam spotted it.

It looked like a log sticking out of the edge of the river's sandbar.

His heart jolted, thinking it was a crocodile.

It wasn't.

His eyes narrowed. He pointed two fingers to his eyes and then back to the thing sticking out the edge of the sandbar. Tom picked up on the hand gesture, and followed his gaze.

It looked like the tip of cannon.

Together, they brought the three balls to the surface, and Wakhumelo helped lift them up from the back deck, before offering to take Sam and Tom's fins.

Sam shook his head. "I think we found something."

They returned to the sandbar, and went to work removing sand, and freeing the remnants of a cannon. It took longer this time to secure several lift bags, but with the last of the air in their tanks, they inflated the lift bags and rose to the surface.

Wakhumelo had the robotic crane arm hanging out the back of the pleasure cruiser. The crane was used for loading the boat and also for hauling in large fish. Sam secured the nylon lift straps from the cannon to the crane, and it was slowly maneuvered onto the deck.

Sam and Tom passed their fins to Wakhumelo and climbed the ladder onto the deck. Out of the water, and without even cleaning the metal object, Sam knew exactly what he was looking at – a 32 Pounder Carronade – typical of Portuguese warships and merchants of the time the *Midas* was captured by uprising African slaves.

They spent the next two days dragging the sonar buoys in a crisscross search grid, but despite their best efforts, a single 32 Pounder Carronade and three iron balls were the only treasure the river yielded.

On sunset of the third day, Sam said, "So now that we know the ship was here, the question is, what do we do now?"

"There's no treasure," Tom said. "My guess is that the crew ran aground and took their treasure with them."

"Agreed." Sam frowned. "But the question is, where would they have taken it?"

Tom shrugged, "Who knows?"

Sam said, "We need to talk to the locals. I wonder, Wakhumelo, are there any people native to this area? People who've lived off the land for centuries, and who might have heard of a story of a ship that didn't belong here?"

Wakhumelo shook his head. "The San people have lived in this region since the dawn of man. If anyone knew about such a story, it would be one of them."

The San people of the Kalahari Desert were once called Bushmen. This came from the Dutch term, 'bossiesman', which meant 'bandit' or 'outlaw,' a name with negative overtones. A friendly, creative, and peaceful people, the San had never developed weapons of war, and have lived in harmony with their natural environment for at least 20, 000 years. Something western society is still trying to do.

Sam's breath caught with hope and excitement. "I don't suppose you happen to know someone we might talk with?"

Wakhumelo grinned proudly. "Actually, I know just the person you need to meet."

Chapter Thirty-Two

It took them nearly three weeks to track the man down.

They hired a Toyota Landcruiser at Mongu and Wakhumelo went through the painstakingly difficult, and time-consuming task, of locating him. It wasn't that he didn't want to be found, but that the man traveled constantly, and was utterly indifferent to the schedules or locations of westerners. And why should he be? His world had no use for money or anything civilization could offer.

The Bushmen of the Kalahari Desert, also known as the San peoples, are among the oldest cultures on Earth, and are thought to be descended from the first inhabitants of what is now Botswana and South Africa. The presence of the San in Botswana is particularly evident in northern Botswana's Tsodilo Hills region. San were traditionally semi-nomadic, moving seasonally within certain defined areas based on the availability of resources such as water, game animals, and edible plants.

San kinship is comparable to Eskimo kinship, with the same set of terms as in European cultures, but also uses a name rule and an age rule. The age rule resolves any confusion arising from kinship terms, as the older of two people always decides what to call the younger. Relatively few names circulate – approximately 35 names per sex – and each child is named after a grandparent or another relative.

Children have no social duties besides playing, and leisure is very important to San of all ages. Large amounts of time are spent in conversation, joking, music, and sacred dances. Women have a high status in San society, are greatly respected, and may be leaders of their own family groups. They make important family and group decisions and claim ownership of water holes and foraging areas. Women are mainly involved in the gathering of food, but may also take part in hunting.

Water was important in San life. the Kalahari droughts may last many months and traditional waterholes may dry up. When this happened, traditionally the Bushmen used to either use hollow grass straws to extract water trapped in the crooks of tree branches or dig sip wells.

To create a sip well, a Bushman will dig a deep hole, down to where the sand is damp. Into this hole he will pack a bundle of dried grass and insert a long hollow grass stem. Afterward, the hole is back-filled to create a vacuum. By sucking hard, he can get the moisture from the damp sand to condense on the grass and eventually yield water. An empty ostrich egg is used to collect the water. Water is sucked into the straw from the sand, into the mouth, and then travels down another straw into the ostrich egg.

Historical evidence shows that certain San communities have always lived in the desert regions of the Kalahari; however, eventually nearly all other San communities in southern Africa were forced into this region. The Kalahari San remained in poverty where their richer neighbors denied them rights to the land. Before long, in both Botswana and Namibia, they found their territory drastically reduced.

Wakhumelo introduced them. "Sam, this is Kxoma. His people have lived in this region longer than most humans have lived anywhere else on Earth."

"It's nice to meet you," Sam said, with genuine pleasure, locking onto the man's intelligent brown eyes. Barely five foot tall, he was copper skinned, delicately formed and in prefect proportion. Sam had always been interested in the San and their unique way of life, ever since he was a child and had the good fortune to read, Laurens van der Post's two novels, *A Story Like The Wind* and its sequel, *A Far Off Place*.

Kxoma smiled back at him and began speaking to Wakhumelo in his own tongue. Sam watched with avid fascination as the two men conversed. Words crackled like electricity from their lips, as nearly every other consonant in the San People's language was a clicking sound of some kind.

When the two were finished, Wakhumelo said, "He says he's happy to help you."

"Tell him that's very kind."

"What do you want to know?"

Sam told Kxoma the story of the *Midas* and sinking along the Zambezi River a very long time ago, a time when our ancestors still walked the Earth. Wakhumelo translated everything between the two of them.

When Sam was finished, Kxoma said, "I know of this very large boat."

Sam was blown away. Of all their threads regarding the Midas, this seemed to be the weakest. How could he have possibly heard about the ship after so many years? Especially as his tribe had no written language.

He said, "How do you remember a story from so long ago?"

Kxoma smiled, revealing big white. "A story like this is like the sands of the Kalahari Desert, it cannot be forgotten."

"What story?" Sam asked, his interest piqued now.

"The story of the walking Gods."

Sam frowned as it sounded like a creation myth common to native cultures. He'd almost believed the man for a moment there. But it appeared to be for nothing. He listened politely as Kxoma's story was translated.

"The Gods came in a big boat – much, much bigger than the largest canoes his people had ever seen at the time. They carried weapons that made loud bangs and lots of smoke."

Sam nodded. "Like the rifles used by people to hunt animals?"

Kxoma shook his head. "No. These people who came on this ship, had the power to split mountains, cause earthquakes, and tear the world apart. But the Gods didn't know how to use their strange powers, and in the end, it destroyed their ship."

"So the Gods died?"

Kxoma shook his head again. "No. They were Gods and Gods cannot drown." The way he said it suggested that everyone knew that. He went on. "The Gods survived the shipwreck, carrying their most sacred possession to a secret cave…"

Sam waited for him to continue. When he didn't, Sam asked, "Where's the cave?"

"I don't know."

Sam arched an eyebrow. "But you know that the treasure of the Gods was taken to a cave?"

"Yes."

"To be protected and stored for the future?"

"Yes."

Sam exhaled slowly. "How do you know this? I mean, how do your people know about the existence of this secret cave?"

"One of the Gods survived... only he was weak by the time my ancestors reached him, but by the time the man died, he had painted a rudimentary map of the location where his treasure had been buried and said that if more people came, and if these people asked, they should be shown the map..."

Sam asked, "Did anyone else ever come looking for the treasure?"

"Never. No others from his ship came. Then, all was forgotten."

"Do you know where this cave is?"

"Yes, of course."

Sam grinned. "Can you take me?"

Kxoma smiled, realizing that this was what the strange white man wanted all along. "Yes, I will take you to the cave."

Chapter Thirty-Three

The cave was on the outskirts of the Liuwa Plain National Park. It took a day to drive out there and nearly four hours on foot, following Kxoma as he carefully found the way of his ancestors. It amazed Sam that the story of the *Midas*, having been passed on via word of mouth, like legends and myths, was so detailed that Kxoma, having never been to this ancient cave, was retracing his ancestors' steps to find it.

By the time the blistering sun was directly overhead, the native gentleman had led them down a hill toward a small series of sandstone boulders, where water pooled. At the edge of the water, there was a natural spring, used by San People for thousands of years.

Behind it, there was a small gap, only just large enough for a fully grown man to slide through. The opening was hidden in plain sight, and only really visible to those who were looking for it. If Sam had been wandering through and collecting water from the spring, he would have simply assumed it was a fracture in the sandstone. Or possibly the remnants of a wild animal's long since discarded burrow.

Kxoma pointed and indicated that Sam and Tom should go first. Sam was doubtful that the cave was large enough to fit all of them, but his new friend insisted. Sam switched on his flashlight, and slowly slid through the opening into the cavern on the opposite side.

It was large enough to stand inside.

He spread the beam of his flashlight in a wide arc to reveal an enormous cave. Big enough to fit thirty or more people comfortably. He was shortly greeted by Tom, Kxoma, and Wakhumelo who followed him inside. There were several ancient markings on the walls, but Kxoma brought him to the one depicting the River Gods.

Sam fixed the beam on the cave painting, and grinned.

It seemed almost too easy!

The cave depicted a strange geological formation. Three granite stones high up on a sandy beach, surrounded by a U-shaped bend in a river. It wasn't too dissimilar to the location where the oil painting had most likely been made, although the cave paintings didn't show any African wildlife.

Sam studied the granite stones.

The geology seemed wrong for some reason, but that didn't mean there was no granite anywhere along the Zambezi.

Two of the stones were almost identical in size. They were massive and rounded, almost like the outline of a pair of giant elephants. The third one was about a quarter of the size, more like a baby elephant following its parents. The three stones fell upon each other, to form a small, hollowed section at its base, and presumably an opening to the secret cave of the Gods.

Kxoma said what Sam was thinking. "Find those three stones and you will find the cave."

Sam took a photo.

It was like a damned treasure map.

All he needed to do was put the image into a database of known geological formations in the region and hopefully the location would jump out at him.

Below the image of the three elephant stones, was a series of carved markings. They were even, and although Sam didn't have a clue what they meant, he could guess that they were written in the Mende Kikakui script, a syllabary used for writing the Mende language of Sierra Leone. He took a photo of the script, making a mental note to send it to Elise as soon as he could so that she could find someone to have it translated.

Sam said to Kxoma, "This is the first time you have told this story?"

"No, no. This is a story passed on throughout the generations." He looked proud as he spoke. "I have told it many times."

Sam nodded. "But we are the first white people to ask about it?"

"No, no… in fact, you're not even the second person to come here recently looking for this. There have been two others."

Sam swallowed. "Others?"

"Yes. One a couple of years ago. And another one just four weeks ago."

"Four weeks!" Sam thought back. To Tom he said, "That was only a week after I was attacked in Zanzibar."

Tom frowned. "You don't think the Yuxia found Kxoma through the photos in the dossier?"

Sam turned to Kxoma. "These people who asked these questions... what did they look like?"

Kxoma frowned, confused.

Sam tried to clarify. "Did they have copper colored skin like you, or dark skin like Wakhumelo?"

"No."

"Pale skin like the tourists who come on a safari?"

Kxoma shook his head. "No."

Sam's eyes narrowed. "Somewhere in between?"

"Yes."

Sam brought up a photo of the men who attacked him in Zanzibar. It was taken from the CCTV footage provided by the Chief of Police. "Did they look like this?"

Kxoma studied the photo. "Yes."

"And you took them to the cave?"

"Yes," he said, once again, his voice coming across proudly.

Sam turned to Tom. "So once again, we're on a race against the Yuxia."

"It would appear so," Tom agreed.

Sam said, "Kxoma, do you remember the person who came to visit, asking these questions, two years ago?"

"Yes."

"Do you remember what he or she looked like?"

This time their new friend answered with a definite yes.

A wry grin formed on Sam's lips. He picked up a stick. "I'm going to draw three shapes in the sand. Can you tell me which one looks closest to the man you saw?"

Kxoma nodded.

Sam drew a triangle, square, and circle.

He then handed the stick to Kxoma. "Now you show me which one came to visit."

Sam grinned.

Because the Bushman drew a line down the middle of the circle. Only it wasn't a circle, it was a sphere, and the man's name wasn't really 360, it was Greg Lamont. Which meant the man had lied to him about everything.

As soon as he was outside the cave and in the open air, he opened his satellite phone and texted Elise the image of the script.

Can you confirm this is Mende Kikakui script?

If so, can you please have it translated for me ASAP?

Thanks.

On their way back to the four-wheel drive, Sam thought about the image in the cave.

The image was like a treasure map...

Sam pictured it. The *Midas* being destroyed, and its treasure being secured by her survivors and hidden inside some cave.

They reached the Toyota Landcruiser.

Sam's satellite phone flashed with an incoming message.

He clicked the receive button and Elise's message came up.

Yes, it's Mendi Kikakui script.

It reads as follows:

Here lies the greatest treasure of all,

Too powerful for mortals,

Death befalls all who seek its riches.

Some secrets are best left buried.

Sam read it out loud and wondered what it could possibly mean.

He turned to Kxoma and asked, "Have you ever seen the three stone elephants?"

The man shook his head, and spoke in rapid fire clicking sounds to Wakhumelo.

Sam turned to their guide and translator. "What does he say?"

Wakhumelo spread his arms open. "He says, the picture in this cave is just a dream. It doesn't exist."

Chapter Thirty-Four

Onboard the Tahila

Sam brought the rest of the crew up to speed on the search for the *Midas*.

Afterward, he said, "So now we know the *Midas* sank somewhere along the Zambezi or one of her tributaries. Her precious and potentially dangerous cargo was then taken to a cave, between these two rocks," he paused, then added, "somewhere along the edge of a river."

"And no one knows where that place is?" Elise asked.

Sam shrugged. "According to Kxoma, the San tribesman who spoke of the legend, the painting in the cave is just a dream."

She arched an eyebrow. "But you doubt it?"

"It's not unusual for people to get killed over a legend, but I think there's too much involved in this complex series of events for it to simply be that. No, I think this place exists. We just need to find it."

Elise nodded. "Okay, I'll take those photos you took of the three elephant shaped boulders a couple hundred yards from the river's bank at the bend in a river. Then I'll run them through a program that compares images to known landscapes or photos on social media. If it's so unique, someone will have taken a photo of it and put it on the internet somewhere. And if they have, I'll find it."

"Thanks." Sam closed that part of the meeting and said, "All right, now, do you want to bring me up to date with the progress of the Medusa's Curse?"

Pushing her hair back from her face, Elise said, "The news is all bad, I'm sorry to say."

"What do we know?" Sam asked. "I've never heard of a virus mummifying someone before."

"No. I think this brings a whole new meaning to the term, 'novel' virus. Elise brought up an image of the human body. It was a 3D projection on the round table, split into multiple sections like an anatomical figure in a medical textbook. "Doctors are still working around the clock to come up with a cause and solution, but they have a theory that the virus triggers a positive feedback mechanism in the kidneys."

Sam frowned. "You want to tell me what that means in English?"

"The body has two sorts of feedback mechanisms that control most things. The most common one is the negative feedback system. For example, a person's blood pressure gets a little high. Specially designed receptors in the carotid arteries and aortic arch called baro-receptors identify this and signal to the body to lower the blood pressure."

"Okay, and a positive feedback mechanism?"

"Positive feedback mechanisms are a little trickier. Basically, the body gets a trigger that tells the body to keep going, stronger and harder until a certain objective is achieved. For example, during childbirth a baby pushes against the cervix, causing it to stretch. This in turn, causes nerve impulses to be sent to the brain, which triggers the posterior pituitary to release oxytocin. This causes the smooth muscle lining of the uterus to contract, thus pushing the baby against the cervix, which then continues to strengthen the loop."

"Until the baby is born."

"Right. Unless something goes wrong, and then this sort of positive feedback loop becomes deadly."

Sam drew a breath. "It doesn't stop on its own?"

"Not unless it achieved the original goal of childbirth."

"Right, and so the doctors are hypothesizing that a similar action is happening in the kidneys?"

Elise nodded. "Yeah. There's a diagram over here of what they believe is happening. They just haven't worked out how to stop it."

She swiped the original holographic diagram away with her left hand and brought up a new one with her right. This one showed the anatomical outline of the kidneys and a diagram showing the natural pathway that the body used to maintain fluid homeostasis – or equilibrium.

"That," Elise said, pointing to the diagram labeled, *Loop of Henle*, "is where the magic occurs."

Sam stared at the model. "Okay."

"The long U-shaped portion of the tubule conducts urine within each nephron of the kidney of reptiles, birds, and mammals. ... This function allows production of urine that is far more concentrated than blood, limiting the amount of water needed as intake for survival."

Sam concentrated hard. "In English please?"

"The Loop of Henle determines whether to remove more or less fluid from the blood. A whole class of highly successful diuretics work by increasing the elimination of sodium chloride – that's salt by the way – and in doing so, the drawing of more fluid out of the blood via osmosis..."

Sam dismissed the science lesson with the wave of his hand. "Okay. So basically, the virus tricks this Loop of Henle to go into overdrive and the body excretes all liquid from the body?"

Elise considered that. "Yes. Basically, the person's own body causes it to become mummified."

Sam thought about that. "And turning them to stone as though they looked into the eyes of the Medusa?"

"Yeah, I guess."

The mental cogs in Sam's brain worked like a computer, trying to jam solutions together that were neither medical or based on science. Just looking outside the box, and as far as boxes were concerned this virus was the mother of all of them. "Why can't they simply drink more water?"

"It doesn't happen slowly. From what the doctors are worried about, the patients have been infected for some time... possibly a month or more. It has a long incubation period. Most people don't even know that they're infected, and from that point on they're a ticking timebomb. The virus builds up in the kidneys and eventually triggers this thing."

"Right. When it explodes, their kidneys dump everything and within minutes they're turned to stone."

"So the world could be heading for a deadly pandemic?"

"Not heading in, it IS in the deadliest pandemic our species have ever faced." Elise sighed. "They don't know how transmissible the virus is. It has a long incubation period, so that heightens the risk, because it means the otherwise healthy host has plenty of time to transfer the virus to other hosts."

"Scary stuff. I wonder if we should head back to the US?"

"Right now, there are no cases on the African continent."

"That won't last long given the number of international flights," Sam warned.

Elise said, "All international flights have been shut down."

"Everything?"

"Yeah. This thing's real. Just like that… someone flicked off the switch and the human society was no longer global."

"Is there any way of knowing that you've been infected?" Sam asked, glancing at the rest of the crew. "I mean, if this thing has an incubation period of 28 days, who's to say none of us have it?"

Elise nodded. "They believe there's three phases in the virus's cycle. First phase, the person exhibits no signs of infection, and are a very low risk of transmission. That would be the first day, few minutes, or week after exposure… we don't really know."

"And then?"

Elise lifted her hand as if to say, bear with me on this one. "Then their eyes turn green."

"Come again?"

"Strange I know. But something about the way the virus binds with the copper that's carried in the blood. Normally most of the copper in your blood is carried by a protein called ceruloplasmin. Adults have 50 to 120 milligrams of copper in their body, mostly in muscle and the liver. Copper helps make melanin, bone, and connective tissue."

"And what, this copper tends to bind with the virus?"

Elise nodded. "Yes, and once it's connected to the virus' protein, it can be seen anywhere blood may be spotted. The most noticeable place for this to occur in normal times is a person's eyes. For example, the sclera can appear blue due to thinned areas that allow the vascular area below it to show through. A blue color is also observed when there is a build-up of silver in the tissue. And of course, there is the yellow color of a jaundiced eye."

Sam said, "And in people infected by the Medusa's Curse?"

Elise's brought up an image of a person infected by the strange virus. She let the image sit there in silence for a few seconds, expelled a deep breath, and said, "A greenish hue of a resolving subconjunctival hemorrhage develops. It's similar to a bruise on the skin, only instead of the blue-purple of a bruise, the sclera becomes a luminescent green."

Chapter Thirty-Five

Kalahari Desert, Botswana

North of the Kalahari Desert, a yellow tent made of impervious materials stood at the base of a sand dune that was as old as time itself. To the east were the Tsodilo Hills, a small area of massive quartzite rock formations that rose from ancient sand dunes. The rocky outcrop had a small freshwater spring, supplied by an underground water basin. These caves had provided shelter and protection for more than 100,000 years.

With one of the highest concentrations of rock art in the world, Tsodilo has been called the "Louvre of the Desert." Over 4,500 paintings were preserved in a seven miles squared portion of the Kalahari Desert. The archaeological record of the area gives a chronological account of human activities and environmental changes over at least 100,000 years. Local communities in this hostile environment respected Tsodilo as a place of worship frequented by their ancestral spirits. To the west, a dry fossil lakebed and the sands of the Kalahari Desert that stretched all the way to the Namibian border.

Despite the tent's modest appearance, the biolab housed one of the most advanced bio-research units in the world. It was because of the desert's profound dryness, and stifling heat – in which the virus struggled to survive – that the Albino had chosen just such a location to work.

It was here that he had led a small team of virologists to weaponize the Medusa virus. There was no question that the original virus was lethal. Incredibly so. The problem was that it was too deadly. It killed its hosts so quickly that there simply wasn't enough time for widespread distribution and contagion of the virus.

All viruses can be split into two classes.

DNA and RNA.

The Medusa strain was a DNA virus. Unlike RNA viruses, which are single-stranded, DNA were mostly double-stranded. This allowed it to be much more stable, and unlikely to mutate. This was one of the reasons the virus was allowed to lay dormant for so many years in a cave beneath the Siberian permafrost. Influenza A was an RNA virus which was why people needed annual booster shots if they were to maintain immunity to any mutations. Similarly, the modern coronavirus was RNA, which was why it was capable of mutating into multiple strains, each one more difficult to contain.

It was in this biolab that the Albino edited the virus, using futuristic gene-editing technologies paired with viral vectors. Like a surgeon, he operated on the virus genome, tweaking it, using a tool called, Clustered Regularly Interspaced Short Palindromic Repeats, or CRISPR for short. It was within the genome's capsid, that he'd found so much success in weaponizing the Medusa strain. In fact, in the end, it had been relatively simple.

A capsid was basically a protein shell of a virus that enclosed its genetic material. It consisted of several oligomeric – that meant, repeating – structural subunits made of protein called protomers. The delivery of the genome into the host occurs when the capsid began to disassemble and thus, release the genome into the host's cytoplasm, or by ejection of the genome through a specialized portal structure directly into the host cell nucleus.

The virus may lay dormant in the host's body, but until the capsid disassembled, the active virus was unable to affect the host. It was after this occurred, that Medusa triggered the fatal positive feedback mechanism in the kidneys, killing the host within minutes. And all it took was to adjust the time for capsid degradation to occur, using CRISPR – just like setting the countdown clock on a timebomb.

After some trial and error, he settled on a timeframe rate of 28 days.

The Albino watched the news.

He was both enthralled and horrified by what he had created. It was the culmination of a collective dream he'd shared for as long as he could remember, but now as he reaped its rewards, he felt a certain sense of loss.

For the first time, he questioned if he'd been on the right side of good and evil? Suddenly, he thought about all those who had betrayed his people for so many years and wondered whether such a terrible wrong, might make the world right again?

Or had he simply introduced new malevolence on an already wretched world?

The biolab's phone rang.

The Albino answered it.

A familiar voice greeted him. "Have you seen the news?"

The Albino nodded. "Yes. It is a terrible thing we have done."

"It's horrifying, yet equally wonderful, isn't it?"

The Albino was not so sure. "There's still time to alter the genome again. Make it slightly less deadly. Perhaps we have gone too far?"

The man laughed. "Are you kidding me? This is exactly what we wanted to achieve. Forget double guessing your actions. You opened Pandora's Box, now there is nothing you or I can do to put its beauty back again."

The Albino said, "I still have the data. The genomic codes here. That means there will always be a way to return this plague firmly back inside Pandora's Box."

There was silence on the line.

After several seconds, the familiar voice returned. Although it sounded harder, more emphatic. "Are you sure that's how you feel?"

"I'm not sure how I feel. But it has to be an option."

There was something somber about the way the man spoke, a certain type of finality to his voice. "I was afraid that was how you would feel. I'm sorry. We will never forget your service. But we can't let you stop this thing. Goodbye, my friend."

The Albino looked around the room.

There were hundreds of things he would have liked to take, but there was no time for any of that. He'd known the man on the other end of the line since he was a child, and the man didn't make idle threats. He didn't say, "We'll see how this goes." He had said goodbye. And in this organization, that was a euphemism for eradication.

The Albino grabbed his water bottle. It was a half-gallon, a little over two-thirds full. It wasn't much, but it would have to do. He would have liked to warn the rest of the team. But there wasn't time. He opened the fridge, and retrieved a small, black canister that was small enough to fit in the palm of his hand. Inside, it contained six of the vials of the deadliest substance on Earth.

He glanced back at the office that had been his home for the past few weeks, pulled his keffiyeh over his face to protect his skin from the scorching heat, and stepped out into the rolling sand dunes of the Kalahari Desert.

The Albino got three minutes away, before the bomb exploded.

He clambered over the crest of the sand dune, taking shelter from the imminent blast wave. It had been a significant explosive device. His master and friend must have concealed the ordinance within the lab as a fail-safe before they had arrived. Or the Albino unknowingly carried the bomb with him when the team first set up the biolab.

He wondered why his friend bothered to pass on a warning?

Not that it mattered. They had been dropped off after hours of flight by helicopter. The albino was surrounded by hundreds of miles of desert in the middle of summer.

It didn't matter the bomb had missed him.

He was already a dead man walking.

Chapter Thirty-Six

Not since the black plague had the world ever seen such an event. The Medusa virus had 100% mortality rate.

193 countries in the world had simultaneously shut its borders, restricting all but utmost essential travel. As for essential, we're not talking about making movies, or business meetings. We're talking about bringing in specialist scientists capable of making vaccines or treating the virus. The economy ground to a halt, people boarded up their homes and prepared to survive on the most basic of food rations until this thing blew over.

Something had changed since this whole thing began. The deadly virus had mutated faster than anyone could have imagined, and now it took 28 days for the host to die. That meant people were walking around with a deadly timebomb ticking inside their own immune system, spreading the terrible disease wherever they went.

As Sam read the report, and witnessed the satellite images from around the world that depicted a dark New York City, Paris without lights, Argentina without color, he was amazed by how rapidly the world had mobilized into pure isolation. Unlike smoking cigarettes, which killed people after decades, here was an invisible threat with a 100 percent mortality rate. No one got out alive once infected. People could see that. Everyone knew of, or had heard of someone mummified. The hundreds of CCTV footages that captured the horror, gave justice to the idea that it was a terrifying death.

The people didn't need a big stick or their governments to tell them what to do. It was human instinct. No. Cross that. It was the most primitive animal need and strongest desire on Earth – the will to survive. Single people locked themselves away. Family grouped together. Resources were buried, hoarded, and protected with people's lives.

On board the *Tahila*, Sam was contacted by the US Secretary of Defense.

He picked up his cell phone.

She spoke first. "How are you enjoying your African safari?"

"It hasn't been uneventful."

That was enough preamble for her. "Good. The vacation's over."

The outer lips of Sam's mouth curled upward. "Why does everyone think we're on vacation?"

She didn't respond to that. Instead, she said, "I need you to fly an unauthorized secret mission into Botswana."

Sam's smile turned into a hard line. "Botswana," he repeated the name to make sure he got it right. "What's in Botswana?"

"Nothing. At least, nothing anymore."

She paused and Sam waited.

The Secretary of Defense got like this sometimes. She started handing out mission assignments and orders, and there was nothing really stopping her. Instead, you just needed to let her get her train of thought out in her own due time. Sometimes she filled in the gaps, sometimes she didn't. What Sam knew, but few others did, was that she didn't do this by accident.

If the Secretary of Defense left out vital details, it was intentional.

Sam didn't take the bait. Instead, he said, "What can I do for you in Botswana, Madam Secretary?"

"Until a few days ago, satellite images show a building in the northern parts of the Kalahari Desert. Indications are its a temporary biolab, and it became operational a week before we were introduced to Medusa patient zero. We believe a terrorist organization set up an advanced gene-editing lab in the isolated safety of the desert to weaponize the original virus, increasing the duration between infection and death, and subsequently snowballing the period of contagion."

Sam asked, "What makes you think this was the tent where this horrific thing was weaponized?"

"We're pretty certain."

"Why?"

"The people there had the capabilities to do so."

"Surely there are thousands of people with the skills?"

"Not thousands. Less than twenty."

"So, it could be any of them?"

"No. We keep tabs on people with these sorts of skills. For this exact reason. Most of them work for us. Some of them don't. Either way, we've kept track on all of them. And only one man in particular was in that tent in Africa for the past six weeks."

"Where is he now?"

"Dead. Most probably."

"How?"

"The biolab was destroyed. We believe the terrorists set up an explosive device to clear all evidence of the bioweapon's development."

"You think he was forced to do this?"

"Maybe, maybe not. His father was killed during the Afghanistan – Soviet Union war during the 1980s. He and his family tried to take refuge in our embassy in Kabul. Unfortunately, it was the day the embassy was attacked. His mother and two sisters were killed."

Sam drew a breath. "If that's not a reason to become radicalized, I don't know what one is. If that's the case though, it doesn't explain why they killed him?"

Sam felt his heart race. "Why would a terrorist organization want to kill everyone on the planet?"

"There's several theories we're working on, but only time will tell. You can't help me on that score, so forget about it and concentrate on what I do need from you."

It was an order, not a question. "Yes, ma'am."

"Good. Now, to make a treatment for the virus, we need to gain access to the original strain – the one before its genome was edited…"

Sam interrupted. "Why?"

"I haven't got a clue. I'm not a microbiologist or virologist. But the experts who have advised the Administration are telling us that it will take time to make a vaccine, but that time can be shortened if we have the original strain."

"Okay. You want me to go in and get a sample?"

"Yes." Her voice was cold as she spoke. "We believe part of the reason the biolab was burned was to destroy all the research developments, and thus prevent us from getting a head start. There's a water source that originates beneath the dunes where the biolab was destroyed. That water source comes out in the form of a natural spring in Tsodilo Hills along with several wells in the region. We're hoping that a small sample of the virus might have washed through."

"Okay. You want us to fly in and take as many samples as we can?"

"No. Just you. I can get someone who flies a local tourist helicopter that deals with African Safaris and sightseeing, to come get you. The world is highly unstable at the moment. Our normal chain of international relations is shattered. Therefore, this needs to be a ghost mission. You go in and come out. If something goes wrong, we're going to deny we ever had anything to do with it."

Sam said, "I understand. When will the helicopter be here to pick me up?"

"It will be overhead in about five minutes."

"Right," Sam said, without surprise. He was never being 'asked' to perform a ghost mission. It was always going to be an order he couldn't refuse.

The Secretary of Defense said, "We'll send you an update with everything we know about this virus and its transmission, but in the meantime, I suggest you bring a biohazard suit – and a weapon, just in case."

"I understand, ma'am."

"And Sam…"

"Yes, ma'am?"

There was an almost motherly warmth in her voice. "Good luck. The world's counting on you."

Chapter Thirty-Seven

Kwibisa Plains, Zambia

Freya glanced up at the sky. A large white helicopter flew overhead. It looked corporate, like a JetRanger or an Airbus. Not small like the Robinson 44s the Rangers used to fly surveillance to protect the wildlife from poachers. The helicopter banked, and headed due south, revealing a large picture of African animals, and the words, *Hwange National Park Adventure Sightseeing*. She frowned. It was the third time she'd seen the same helicopter in the past few days. It didn't make sense. And it made her mad. Over the top, irrationally angry. The world was in lockdown, yet some sort of rich asshole still wanted to enjoy their African safari.

The clinic was empty now.

Nobody wanted to get caught up in this thing. Somehow the local Zambia people knew the best action to take was to return to their remote communities and stay away from the external world. The sight of the helicopter, a small beacon of civilization and other human beings, hit her. For a moment, Freya allowed herself the freedom to acknowledge her emotions, which, until that point, she had worked hard to suppress.

Freya was isolated, lonely, and somewhat despondent at the thought of spending weeks, if not months on her own.

Originally, she had planned to stay behind to keep the clinic running. After all, she was here to provide basic health care to some of the poorest people in the world. Why should a global pandemic take that away from them? But as she watched all the local people retreat into the wild, she began to wonder, why bother? Then she tried to book a flight, assuming there would be a grace period, for stranded travelers to reach home. There wasn't. This thing was too serious for any gaps to slip through.

Now she was trapped in a foreign country, in the middle of the African wilderness, and all on her own.

At first, she was motivated. She loved the wild of Africa. This was what she had dreamed of. The giant game animals, the isolation, everything – so why not make the most of it? She would read some of her favorite books. It would be one of those cathartic episodes in her life, full of self-reflection. But now, not more than a few weeks into it, and she already felt a deep-rooted sense of despair.

A sound interrupted her thoughts of self-pity.

She looked up at the long grass in the distance. It was moving. Her first thought was to reach for her rifle. It was kept at the same place she stored the valuable drugs needed in medical emergencies. She was inside, so it was unlikely to be an animal. Something about it, alarmed her. Suddenly the thought of another human approaching the clinic, was a bad thing. Her heart thumped in her chest, and she chided herself for getting spooked like a child.

Freya jumped to her feet, striding purposefully toward the rifle, conscious of her need to keep everything she could control safe. Settled.

And a second later, she heard the familiar voice of her assistant, Amakusana. "Freya!"

She stepped out onto the front porch and drew a breath. The sight of her friend made her feel so instantly happy, she nearly burst into tears. She stepped forward and threw her arms around Amakusana's shoulders, pulling her into a heart-felt embrace. The generous welcome went on a bit longer than she planned.

Amakusana hugged her, soothingly patted her back, then pulled away. Meeting her eyes, she asked, "Are you okay, Freya?"

Eyes stinging, she nodded. "Yes. I'm sorry. I just got a little scared out here on my own."

"Ah, I understand…" Amakusana said these words in such a way that it made Freya feel she really didn't.

Freya said, "What are you doing back here? Is everything all right?"

The young girl looked surprised by the question. "Yes, nobody is hurt. I just came to collect that book I started reading. I figure I might as well keep learning."

Freya had lent her a textbook on Women's Health. A lot of it was above her level of English, but she was slowly working her way through it and would most likely take over from Freya when she eventually returned to Australia.

Amakusana grabbed her book, talked to Freya for a bit, and then hugged her again before leaving. A helicopter flew by once more, and she spotted Freya's reaction.

The young girl asked, "What is it my friend?"

"Nothing, it's just that helicopter. I've heard it a few times lately. It just seems odd, that's all."

Amakusana tilted her chin up, gazing indifferently at the airborne machine. It was a common enough sight in the region. "Why?"

The helicopter banked toward the south and kept flying.

Freya said, "Look at that. It's for tourists."

"So?"

Freya frowned. "The world's suffering the deadliest pandemic in its history. Everyone and everything is shut down. Even North Korea wasn't able to keep this virus out. People are locking themselves in their own homes."

Amakusana shrugged. Then, with a puzzled expression on her face, she said, "North Korea?"

"Don't worry about it." Freya shook her head. "It's just that it's an antisocial country in normal times, so I was surprised to hear the virus had reached it."

"Oh."

"The point is, why would anyone be running tours of the Game Park right now?"

"I don't know."

They embraced once more, wished each other luck, and then Amakusana disappeared into the Kwibisa Plains where her family lived.

Freya decided to pick up a good book and sat on the deck, overlooking the wild plains. After her friend's visit, the prospect for her day was already looking up. In her experience, perception was everything. It was a big one.

Taking up her novel, she read, *World Without End*, by Ken Follet. The book was a tome that might give her a week's worth of satisfaction. It was set in Medieval Europe during the Black Plague. There was something poetic – or ironic – reading about other silly buggers suffering the trials of the Bubonic Plague while being trapped during a pandemic.

She had barely gotten through the prologue when she heard the sound of an approaching car. It was moving fast. Her aid work instincts kicked in. Generally, when this happened someone had been shot, or badly injured by an animal.

Instead of being frightened, she stepped out onto the road to greet them.

It was a big Ford F Series Pickup.

The driver jammed on the brakes, and the big wheels skidded to a stop in the unpaved clinic driveway. She swallowed and prepared herself to help. There were people in the open tray and the back. They looked alive and worried. She moved to the back of the truck, expecting to find the injured person in there.

She wasn't too worried about Medusa.

Some cases had reached the African Continent, but none as far inland as Zambia. The likelihood of them being infected was remote.

Freya reached the back of the flatbed. "What's happened?"

A man with a rifle stood up to greet her. Wearing a twisted, malicious grin he pointed the weapon at her. "Hello. You're coming with us."

Chapter Thirty-Eight

They made her sit at the back of the pickup.

There were five men in total. Two rode up front with the driver, and two sat at the front of the tray bed. All carried guns. Mostly old rifles. Nothing expensive. If there was only one of them, she might even consider jumping out and taking her chance that the weapon would misfire, giving her precious seconds to escape. But against five, her odds of surviving were non-existent.

She looked at her kidnappers. They shared the same intensely dark skin of most Zambians, but they spoke a different language to the local people of Kwibisa, who predominantly spoke Bemba. There were seven official languages in Zambia. She could pick a few words in each language. Most of them medical words. If she had to guess, these men spoke Kaonde.

None of them talked to her or told her where they were heading as they drove south. The man who pointed a rifle at her spoke English, but there was no way to know if the others did until one of them tried. They had ransacked the clinic, stealing her precious drugs and the rifle that she should have kept on her. No one spoke to her or told her where they were going or what they wanted her to do. It was the not knowing that scared her the most. It must be some sort of primitive function of the mind to imagine the worst-case scenario. She considered multiple scenarios, and all of them were really bad.

They drove for hours.

Her mind fluctuated between thinking, *"I am so dead!"* and *"Well… they haven't killed me, or threatened to rape me, so I might just get out of this alive."* Maybe they were just kidnapping her for a ransom. Everyone in the area knew that she had come from Australia. Her family were far from rich, but that wouldn't stop them being able to round up the equivalent of a small fortune to get her back alive and unharmed.

She couldn't even hate them for it.

Freya had worked in Zambia long enough to know just how much pain and suffering extreme poverty scars a person, and what a starving person with a family of malnourished children will happily do to ease the hurt.

She tried to communicate with the two men in the back of the pickup. "My name's Freya. I'm here with *Doctors Without Borders*. I'm here to help. Can you tell me what you want with me?"

The men looked at her, but said nothing.

"Look. You must want something from me? What is it? I'm sure you know that I'm frightened, but I don't blame you. You're just doing what you have to do. And so am I. Can you just tell me what I can do to help?"

Still nothing.

"What do you need?"

She wanted to scream at their silence, but restrained from showing her weakness.

Freya kept an eye on the road trying to keep track of where they were. If she ever escaped, she would fare better, if she knew where she was. To her right, she spotted Ngonye Falls. It was near the town of Sioma. She felt rewarded and pitifully grateful for the knowledge.

The pickup slowed, crossing the Zambezi River on a concrete bridge, and headed southwest, passing over the border into Botswana. Freya saw a couple of hippopotami in the tall rushes and reeds below, feeding on lush grasses. She wished she were down there with them. They were dangerous, but not as deadly as these five men.

After another hour or so, the truck slowed to a stop. In the distance, she spotted several large quartzite boulder formations. She drew a breath and relaxed a little. At least she recognized the location.

They were at the Tsodilo Hills, Botswana.

The driver climbed out of the cab, and offered his hand to help her down. She rejected it, jumping down with ease.

The man shrugged and said, in reasonable English. "Suit yourself."

Her eyes darted between the five men and the nearby rock formation at Tsodilo Hills.

The man laughed. "Thinking about running hey?"

Freya forced herself to smile. "The thought did cross my mind."

"Well, you'd better uncross it," he snarled. "For what we want from you, we don't need you alive, so my men won't hesitate to shoot you, understand?"

Fear wrapped its ugly hands around her chest like steel bands. Something about the way the man said it without emotion made her heart thump against her ribcage.

She nodded. "I understand."

"Good."

They walked her along the trail toward the caves.

It was getting late. The sun was low on the horizon, causing the western cliffs of the Tsodilo Hills to radiate a glowing light that could be seen for miles. This was known locally as the Copper Bracelet of the Evening.

Several paintings in red lined a nearby boulder. It made her remember when she had visited the historic site after she first arrived at the clinic. Strangely, the paintings brought back a whole gamut of vivid memories of that trip.

It was called the Louvre of the Desert, for the thousands of paintings found throughout the caves, spanning more than a hundred thousand years of human evolution within the region. She still remembered some of the paintings. It seemed strange that her mind should think about ancient history at a time like this.

The man brought her into a large cave.

Someone had set it up as a makeshift hospital. There was a small table, bottles of various cleaning products, and an array of surgical tools.

The driver said, "Hello Doctor. This is Freya Capel."

The doctor was a white man with dark hair, roughly forty-five years old. He had a kind, clean shaven face. If she met him in vastly different circumstances, she would have probably considered him quite handsome. He spoke with a European accent. "Hello... Miss Capel, is it?"

"Freya. I think we're probably past formalities."

"You're right. I'm Lukas." He spread out his hand, gesturing toward the bed. "Take a seat. Get comfortable. This won't take long."

"What the hell do you want with me?"

The doctor seemed not to notice what she asked. Instead, picked up her medical kit, and scanned through the drugs within it. A serious expression crossed his face, like he was trying to work out some complex equation.

He picked up two separate glass drug ampoules. Looking at her, he spoke like one would to a medical colleague. He looked her in the eye and smiled politely. "Tell me, would you prefer the morphine or the ketamine?"

Freya's mouth opened in a silent scream.

He nodded and smiled. "Yes, what am I thinking... the ketamine will be best."

Chapter Thirty-Nine

Freya fought like a fiery fiend.

She kicked with her legs, and swung her arms. Adrenaline raged through her veins, and she put everything she had into it. The doctor hadn't said what he wanted to do to her, but ketamine was a sedative and a powerful anesthetic. If the doctor got a chance to inject it into her, there was no doubt in her mind that she was never going to wake up again.

Two men grabbed her arms, pulling them behind her back. The doctor approached with an intravenous cannula. His lips curled into a condescending and somewhat disappointed smile, as though she was being childish trying to avoid the inevitable. The best thing for all concerned would be if she just sat down like a good girl and took her medicine.

She yielded to the stronger men holding her, leaning back hard into them until they were taking all of her weight. Then, abruptly and unexpectedly, she kicked the doctor with her feet.

It was a decent hit, landing both of her booted feet square on his jaw.

The doctor fell backward. The blow wasn't powerful enough to knock him out, but it was enough to rattle his brain a little.

He shook his head, trying to regain his composure.

The driver was the first to react. He didn't speak. Instead, he just stepped forward and punched Freya hard in the gut. The fist connected with her solar plexus, sending a wave of pain through her chest. Her diaphragm became paralyzed by the blow.

She opened her mouth to scream but no sound would come out.

The driver stepped toward her again, but the European doctor reached out to stop him. "No! Don't! I can't have them damaged."

"The stupid bitch…"

The doctor grabbed the driver by the front of his shirt. "What did you expect her to do? Go willingly under the knife?"

The driver turned to her. "I'll kill you if you hit the doctor again. Do you understand?"

She nodded, but she was thinking, *you'll kill me if I don't*.

The doctor wiped away the blood that was dripping from his nose. "Now, hold her down on the bed."

It took four people to get her on the table. One on each arm and leg, they pinned her down. She struggled at first, but all she was doing was wasting what precious energy she had left. Freya knew this was the time to fight, but all the fighting in the world wouldn't allow her to break free from four big men.

She needed to wait.

There *had* to be one more chance left. Somewhere. Somehow.

The doctor prepared an intravenous cannula and inserted it into the large vein in the bend of her elbow, known as the cubital fossa region. He secured the needle with a couple pieces of tape and injected a full 10 ccs of normal saline to make sure it was where it belonged in the vein. The saline pushed easily, confirming the needle was in the right place.

The surgeon prepared a freezer box, the sort of thing one uses for organ transplants. Then he arranged an array of surgical instruments, including different sized scalpels. Freya could hardly believe it as the man fucking whistled a happy tune as he worked, like some sort of Dr Jekyll and Mr. Hyde psychopath.

Which, Freya thought, made sense given that was exactly what he was.

He stopped whistling, brought up some Ringer's Lactate solution – a bag of fluid commonly used to treat low blood pressure during times of significant blood loss. He held it up. "Do you want to double check the name and expiry date of this for me?"

Freya was too stunned to respond.

He shrugged. Attaching the cannula, he then placed it back on the hook above. He turned it off, so it would be ready later in the operation no doubt. "All right, suit yourself. It's always good to double check. You wouldn't want me to make a medication error. I'd hate for you to have a complication because we weren't thorough or diligent enough with our procedures."

The surgeon laughed at his own joke.

Freya wanted to puke.

Instead, she worked to change the position of the IV tube at the bend in her elbow. Not enough to be noticeable, but enough to do what she needed to do. She *had* to get the needle of the cannula to move back just slightly. Not enough to be noticeably dislodged, but enough that any drug the doctor might inject would end up being dispersed harmlessly into the interstitial space, not into her vein. The drug would eventually reach her body, but it would take a while, and probably wouldn't be effective enough to knock her out by the time it did.

She could feel the needle wiggling inside her arm as she moved. The problem was, there was no way to tell if the intravenous cannula had tissued or not.

The surgeon drew up an ampoule of the sedative ketamine. He smirked with psycho glee. "Okay, darling. Say good night."

Freya remained silent.

The surgeon made a tsk, tsk sound. "Ah Freya, I thought we were friends. No last words before you go off to sleep?"

She looked at him. Her eyes locking vehemently as she spoke. "Just a promise?"

"Oh yeah?" He smiled revealing a creepy, yet really good set of teeth. The sort of teeth a dentist would be proud of. "I like hearing what sort of thoughts enter my patient's mind as they're going to sleep. So, what sort of promise would you like to make me?"

The obstinate knot of fear in her belly gave way to the serenity of cold, unrestrained hatred. "If you inject that in my arm, I'll fucking kill you."

The surgeon laughed at that. "Oh, you will, will you?"

Freya didn't say anything else.

The driver said, "Can we get a move on, please? Some of us have places to be."

The surgeon attached the needle with the ketamine and pushed it into her cannula.

And Freya inwardly smiled.

Because she felt the cool liquid disperse into the interstitial space in her skin instead of her arm, which meant she might just still have a shot.

Chapter Forty

Intravenous ketamine worked within seconds.

Her nerves ragged and on edge, Freya intentionally made her speech slurred. "You're a really bad doctor…"

Lukas clasped his hands together. "I'm actually a very good surgeon."

She was swaying, as though she was trying to fight to remain conscious. She fixed her eyes on him and said, "You're just a bad person… you know what I…"

She didn't finish the sentence. Instead, she let her eyes roll back in her head, and she tried to relax her whole body. She gave a few disrupted breaths the way someone naturally being anesthetized might, before holding her breath completely to give the appearance of apnea.

The surgeon shrugged. "I'm sorry. I missed that last bit. I guess we'll never hear now."

The driver said, "Are you all right with her on your own now Doc? We want to go shoot some dinner."

His voice came back confidently. "I think I can manage a young unconscious woman on my own."

"You're sure, because she looked like she got you pretty good back there?"

"I'm fine."

The surgeon went back to whistling. He turned to finish setting up his equipment. Freya stretched out and grabbed a scalpel from the table, concealing it in her hand.

Lukas stared at her.

The whistling stopped.

"You, my darling, are really quite something. Want to know a secret? It has been a long time since I've looked upon anyone as beautiful as you." He made a theatrical sigh. "What a waste."

Freya's eyes opened.

She tried to speak... but there wasn't enough strength to make much sound.

The doctor said, "Oh my... you're still awake?"

Her words came out as an inaudible whisper.

"It's okay, my darling... don't overexert yourself. I'll come to you."

He leaned in, turning his head so that his left ear was right next to her lips. "What was that you wanted to say?"

She whispered...

He said, "I'm sorry, I just can't hear you... try a little harder. I'm quite curious. What's the last thing you want to say?"

Freya snarled, "Fuck you!"

Then she jammed the scalpel into his throat at the point of his right common carotid artery. Then she heaved the blade to the right – severing his windpipe, and slicing through the tissues, tendons, and ligaments of his neck before finally carving right through his left common carotid artery.

The surgeon's eyes dilated. His face twisted into a mask of primal fury mixed with fear. His right hand reached for his throat to stem the bleeding. Blood spurted between the gaps in his fingers. In that instant he knew, anyone would – especially a surgeon – that she had inflicted a mortal wound.

The surgeon's eyes fixed on hers. Blood bubbled from his mouth, but his lips moved coldly. Insubstantially. It was as if a ghost was speaking, but Freya clearly read the last words on his lips just before he fell on her.

"You... are... amazing!"

Pushing his slumped and bloody body to the side, she rolled him off her onto the ground. His corpse made a thud as it hit the rocks. Freya forced back a wave of nausea, stood unsteadily and looked at the lifeless body of the monster she'd just killed.

There was no regret.

It was kill or be killed.

But she didn't allow herself to wallow in the ecstasy of her triumph. In the distance, she could hear the men who had kidnapped her shooting some wild animal. They would be back soon. She ran her eyes along the landscape. Besides the giant pillars of quartzite stone that formed the caves of the Tsodilo Hills, the entire region was barren. She was in the heart of the desert.

Freya fought back the urge to run.

If she followed her instinct and ran into the desert, she would be recaptured and killed very quickly. She was worthless to these people now that the doctor was dead, and they had no way to retrieve whatever organs they wanted.

Her mind changed mental gears.

She needed a new plan. Her heart pounding in her ears, she searched for a weapon. The scalpel was about as good as there was, and it was woefully inadequate against rifles. Freya's eyes caught on her medical kit. There were a few pre-filled syringes with anesthetic drugs. She opened the pouch and retrieved one labelled "Rocuronium." It was a neuromuscular blocker – AKA paralyzing agent – with an incredibly fast onset rate, even for intramuscular injections.

A series of short, crisp rifle shots echoed from the direction of where the pickup had been parked. It was followed by the shouting and more shooting.

Freya stood still listening.

Then she heard someone shout in English, "Hey, go see if the Doc wants some dinner before we go."

Oh shit! she swore.

Freya's timeline for escape was just cut short.

Chapter Forty-One

Freya ran silently deeper into the rocky outcrop of the Tsodilo Hills.

Behind her, she heard the shouts of her captors reporting the death of the doctor, and telling each other to spread out and find her. Abject terror started to hit her like heavy raindrops. Big thuds of non-stop fear. She was trapped within a small outcrop of rocks with limited hiding places, and was being hunted by four men with rifles.

The men screamed and shouted, making no attempt to approach her by stealth. Instead, they sounded like a group of baying hounds on the chase, and she was the fox. Trapped. With nothing worth mentioning to defend herself.

She kept running, trying to place as much distance between her and her pursuers. There were a couple shallow caves on her left. They weren't deep or dark enough and would be the first place her attackers would have looked. On her right, she spotted a well-worn path to a natural spring, where crystal clear water spilled into the otherwise dry landscape.

Freya turned left, and began to climb the rocks. An overhung cave, covered in red paintings depicting various African animals led to a narrow ledge with a fifty-foot drop on the side. Huffing and puffing, she kept going, forcing herself to run her hand along the inward wall instead of looking at the potential life-ending fall on the other side. It was less than a foot wide, but broad enough to move along with ease.

Too narrow for four men to climb together, she hoped.

Freya rounded the corner. There the ledge she was on abruptly opened into a large chamber. It was a dead end. She just prayed this wasn't going to be *her* dead ending! She turned around to see if she could backtrack. Already, she could hear the sound of someone beginning to climb out onto the ledge. Pulling herself back from the corner, she hoped to hell that her pursuer hadn't spotted her.

She looked around the chamber.

The entire thing dipped steadily inward. There was a small boulder above, one she might be able to hide behin, or at least buy herself time to run. The odds were really poor. But it was all that she had. Taking a deep breath, she decided to go for it.

Freya carefully climbed the ten feet, squatted down behind the boulder.

It wasn't much but it would have to do. Yet as she waited, a wickedly simple plan hatched in her mind. Freya withdrew the pre-filled syringe of "rocuronium" and waited in silence.

Her attacker was whistling as he came around the rocky ledge.

Freya resolved not to look, but he must've stopped inside the cavern as he called cheerfully. "Come out, come out wherever you are little girl."

Freya mused, what is it with bad guys and whistling? And then, strangely given the circumstance she thought, I'm 38 years old. Since when has someone considered me a little girl? It was an odd notion, given the fact that she was in all likelihood going to die in the next few minutes.

The man came around the corner.

Deciding to peek, she watched him give a cursory sweep of the large chamber. Holding a rifle in his hand, a puzzled frown swept across his face. He lifted the rifle up and aimed it at the darkness within the cave. But in the darkness, he couldn't see her!

Freya crept from her hiding place.

With the syringe in her hand, ready to inject, she jumped onto his back. She hit him with a loud thud. The force alone was enough to wind him. Simultaneously, she jammed the needle into the big muscles of his right shoulder, injecting the full contents of the syringe.

He yelled and fired off a single shot.

Before dropping the rifle in the altercation. She locked her arms around him in a giant bear hug, gripping with all her might. He was at his most dangerous for the next ten to fifteen seconds. Like a wounded animal he threw himself around, trying to remove her, slamming his back – with her on it – into the nearby rock wall.

Then his arms became shaky. His movements stilted. And a few seconds later, one by one, each of his muscles failed him until he was paralyzed, and collapsed on the floor. His chest heaved a few last, weak breaths, before the muscles of his intercostal spaces of his ribcage, and diaphragm, too ceased to function.

His pupils dilated in extreme terror.

Rocuronium blocked muscles from functioning, but did nothing to sedate a person or anesthetize their pain.

Injected with the powerful tranquilizer, Freya's attacker was now paralyzed, yet still entirely awake – suffering a condition known as locked in syndrome. He felt everything. Especially the urge to breathe, but was powerless to do anything about it.

Freya saw the pain deep in his eyes.

She exhaled slowly, and said, "I'm sorry."

Then, without waiting to watch his life end, she picked up his rifle and turned to greet her next attacker.

Chapter Forty-Two

It was a Ruger Hawkeye African.

She knew the weapon well, being a popular big game rifle. It was drilled and tapped for scope mounting, but also fitted with adjustable open sights, and chambered for the most classic of all dangerous-game cartridges – .416 Ruger. With a ballistic performance similar to the best big game rifles, it threw a 400-grain pill at 2400 feet per second with over 5,000-foot pounds of force. That was enough to stop a raging elephant dead in its tracks, let alone a hundred- and eighty-pound man.

She checked the weapon over. Beneath the action there was a three-round capacity box magazine with a metal floor plate and a latch, unobtrusively concealed in the trigger guard.

Flicking it open, she found two shots left.

It would have to do. She stepped to the edge. Someone, having heard the original shot, was running to greet her. The man spotted her, and kept coming. She stepped back around the corner, backing into the dead end to wait. She stood, aiming the rifle at the gap in the corner – the only place anyone but spiderman would have to come – and then she waited.

Freya had never been interested in hunting.

But shooting was different. She'd been around guns all her life. Her father was an avid hunter, and so the two of them met in the middle with both enjoying shooting. She'd developed a natural aim and a steady arm. After a lifetime of practice, she was an expert markswoman.

The man didn't seem to realize she had a weapon.

He walked slowly around the corner.

She squeezed the trigger and fired a single shot. At this range, she could have put the bullet into the back of a blowfly. It flew true, hitting mid-torso. The .416 Ruger round was designed to take down big game animals. When it slammed into the man, it just about took part of his chest clean off, throwing the man backward, and off the edge of the cliff.

A third person came running.

She didn't wait for this one to come around the corner. Instead, she lined up the sight, and fired – picking him off as he stepped onto the ledge. His body fell inward, hitting the overhung cave, before ricocheting off the cliff.

Inwardly she cursed her stupidity for not waiting long enough to shoot him somewhere where his body wouldn't fall off the cliff. Or more specifically, where she wouldn't lose his weapon. Freya was out of rounds.

The question was, did the last of her pursuers know that?

She didn't have to wait long to find out.

The driver, the horrible dickhead who seemed to be in charge of everything, stepped out confidently on the ledge. "Well, well… little miss. Aren't you a dangerous, pretty little girl?"

There was nothing to be gained by entering an exchange of banter with him, so she kept silent.

When she heard him approach the narrow ledge, she stepped out just enough for him to see she was armed with the Ruger Hawkeye African rifle.

"That's close enough," she said. "I'm armed, and I have the protected higher ground. I'm willing to bet I'm a much better markswoman than you."

Pointing a finger at her, he began to laugh. "Ah, yes. You are an excellent shot," he mocked. "I'll give you that. But a far worse gambler and a terrible bluffer."

A shadow of fear crossed over her like death. "Not another step forward. This rifle can take the head off of a lion. If you take another step, I'll shoot and there won't be anything left of you."

"No, you won't."

"I killed the doctor and three of your men. Don't bet I won't kill you too!"

He nodded and took another, albeit tentative, step closer. "But you and I know that the Ruger Hawkeye African is designed to take three rounds of the powerful .416 Ruger shot. Now, by my account, my friend wasted one when you first killed him – how did you kill him by the way?" He lifted a hand as if to stop her answering. "Don't worry, it doesn't matter. Then you killed two of my men with the single shots. I admit, mathematics was not my strong point, but even I feel pretty confident, that's three shots fired out of a possible three shots."

"Take another step forward, and let's find out if you're right."

The driver paused.

It was hard for him to dismiss the fact that this weak, foreign woman had already killed four people. But numbers don't lie. Yet she was out of ammo, and he was still armed with three rounds. No. He could keep going.

Freya turned and broke into a run.

Panic gripped her, as she struggled to find a way out of the chamber. She glanced at the edge of the cliff. It was impossible to climb around, even if she had been a good rock climber, which she wasn't.

She already knew it, but now she really *felt* it. She was trapped.

Freya moved the scalpel from her pocket, and slid it gently up the sleeve of her shirt. There was just enough give in her loose-fitting, long-sleeved shirt that she could reach it using her thumb and forefinger. She waited, still holding the rifle in her hands and stood her ground at the back of the chamber.

The driver came around the corner.

He shook his head. "See, your luck's run out."

She gave him a hostile, 'just-try-it' type of smile. "Or maybe I'm waiting for a shot I couldn't possibly miss?"

"No," he was quick to dismiss her challenge. "You are an expert marksperson. Otherwise, you wouldn't have outshot two of my men."

She threw the butt of her rifle at him.

It was a futile show of resistance and he dodged it easily enough.

The driver laughed.

Swallowing hard, she raised her hands in a gesture of meek supplication.

"You're not so dangerous now," he said, putting his rifle down.

Her gaze locked on the weapon. It wasn't his rifle. It was the Holland and Holland Royal Double Rifle, loaded with .577 Nitro Express, making it probably the deadliest rifle on the continent. And it belonged to her.

The driver's eyes darted between the weapon and her, meeting her gaze with a steadfast resolve. "You're wondering if you could reach your rifle somehow?"

Freya shrugged, gave a 'you-got-me-there' kind of smile. "The thought crossed my mind."

"Well, you can entertain the idea, but I don't think it will work out so well for you," he said, pulling out a traditionally styled Machete, known locally as a Panga. It was a broad blade with an upswept point. Essentially an oversized knife, it was deadly.

"Okay..." she said, with a slight lilt in her voice, suggesting submission. "What do you want?"

"Your organs are no longer valuable to me, given you killed my damned surgeon – useless prick that he was – but perhaps, all is for the better. As I said, you're a beautiful woman, perhaps you are worth more to me alive?"

There was lust in his eyes.

Freya attempted to bolt, running past him.

The driver was too big and too fast for her. He hit her once in the gut, and the force knocked her to the ground. The muscles of her abdomen spasmed, and the pain shot up through her spine like tiny jolts of electricity. She was temporarily paralyzed.

In seconds he was on top of her.

"You may be a very dangerous girl," he said, pinning her forcefully to the rocky ground by her wrists, hard enough that it hurt her back, while simultaneously bruising and abrasing the soft skin on her wrists where he gripped her.

She tried to squirm out of it, not giving him the satisfaction of hearing her scream.

The driver's eyes met hers, and he said, "But you're still a very beautiful little girl."

"Oh no," she gasped. "You've got the wrong idea, boy!"

"Look," he smirked, grunting with the effort of holding her struggling body down. "We can do this your way, where I'll probably break your jaw. Or we can do it my way."

"Trust me," she too grunted with effort. "You don't want to go there," she said pugnaciously. "Believe me, this is going to end so badly for you."

"I doubt it. But I applaud your confidence."

Momentarily stopping all efforts to escape, she smiled. "And also, since when am I a little girl?"

"Since you no longer have a gun to protect you."

Freya reached for the scalpel she'd tucked in her sleeve. She couldn't reach it. He had both her wrists restrained behind her head, in his hands. She tried to shift her position. But he was too strong for her. She squirmed once more, as though she were trying to escape, while all the time she was concentrating on gaining those extra few inches to reach the hilt of the scalpel.

She moaned and it excited him enough to relax some of the pressure on her wrist.

It was all that she needed.

She grabbed the scalpel.

Freya stopped squirming. Ice poured into her veins and she hardened her resolve for what must be done. Where she was taut, fighting for dear life, resisting his every move a moment ago, her body was now relaxed. Submissive.

Her blue-green eyes suddenly locked seductively on his. "Maybe you're right? I'm sure I could be capable of finding a way to be more valuable to you alive."

His face filled with lust.

"That's more like it."

He moved to kiss her.

She lifted her long neck, tilting her chin, to meet his lips.

In that moment she made her move.

But it was too early.

The driver spotted the scalpel in her hand.

He reacted a hell of a lot faster than the surgeon. His hand beside her wrist squeezed tight, like a vice. It was hard enough that the tendons that controlled her fingers inadvertently spasmed, and she dropped the scalpel.

He then slammed her wrist into the rocky ground so that the scalpel was knocked out of reach.

Now she was fucking scared.

The driver laughed. The sight of primal fear in her eyes triggered an equally primitive desire in his loins. He began to rip off her clothing. It was harder than he imagined. Her clothes were all working clothes, designed for the harsh conditions in which she worked and traveled, rather than for their aesthetics. They didn't rip easily. And he was too filled with unrestrained lust to take the time to unbutton them.

Adrenaline surged in her body.

Time slowed.

Behind the driver, she saw the ghost of a shadow move.

It was a man in a yellow fully encapsulated biohazard suit. The stranger moved in complete silence. There was no warning about what he intended to do. He offered no chance for the driver to negotiate or compromise. The man acted on some deep altruistic instinct to right a wrong. As a witness to the horror, his body moved as judge, jury, and executioner.

The stranger picked up the rifle, pressed the barrel to the side of the driver's head, and squeezed the trigger.

The .577 Nitro Express obliterated the driver's skull.

She rolled another dead body off her, for a second time that day.

Freya stood up, looked at the man in the yellow biohazard suit, smiled graciously, and said, "Thank you for saving my life."

"You're welcome."

Her anxiety receded, and she smiled. "I'm Freya. Can I ask your name?"

"I'm Sam Reilly." Inside the clear plastic, she saw him smile. "Please, follow me."

Chapter Forty-Three

They stepped into another cave.

It was no more than fifteen minutes away by walking in the red dust and dirt.

Sam Reilly had set up a makeshift safety zone earlier, with a shower and protective, impervious bags to seal the exposure suit. He first showered while still in his suit and then unzipped the back of it, carefully placing the yellow protective equipment in a large bag, before sealing that up once more.

He was still wearing SCBA – that's SCUBA without the underwater part, she recalled. That too, he soon removed. It was the first time she got a good look at his face. He had a handsome, kindly face, with brown hair, blue eyes, and a genuine smile, with a nice set of teeth. She didn't believe you could always judge a person by their looks, but there was something about this man that was hard not to like.

His face simply read – honor, duty, trust. You are safe with me.

Her eyes dropped a little, and for the first time, she realized he was just wearing a pair of underwear. Her throat went dry. He had the strong and athletic figure that suggested he was anything but a lab geek – not that she had anything against lab geeks – with broad shoulders, muscular arms, and a torso that tapered nicely into a narrow waist, with just the hint of an outline of a sixpack. He didn't have the fully ripped appearance of a weightlifter or exercise enthusiast. Instead, his physique looked naturally acquired, as though his lifestyle or work drove his strength. One of those forms taking on the shape required to function, rather than the other way around.

Sam smiled. "You want to throw me that bar of soap?"

She spotted it beside the rest of the cleaning gear. Picking it up in her left hand, she tossed it his way. "Catch."

He snatched it from the air with his right hand. "Thanks."

A moment later, he spun around, removed his underwear and washed without shame. She turned her face away, surprisingly embarrassed. He washed quickly, dried himself and got dressed. He then went about the business of packing everything up into a large duffel bag. Freya half-expected him to explain why he was in the middle of nowhere in a biohazard suit, but he seemed happy to go about his business without voicing any explanation.

At least he wasn't whistling.

Finally, her curiosity got the better of her. She said, "Why were you wearing a biohazard suit?"

He smiled. "I was taking water samples."

"Obviously," she said, in such a way that suggested it was anything but. "Should I be worried?"

He shook his head. "I don't think so. It doesn't look like the virus has reached here yet."

She made a face. "Well, duh... I mean, we're in the middle of nowhere and the virus needs a host to spread. That means people, and there aren't many people around here for hundreds of miles."

He looked at her, opened his mouth as though he was going to try and explain, and then, having thought better of it given their circumstances, said, "What about you? Should I be worried about any more of your unwanted lovers?"

"No. I mean, I don't think so. There were four of them. I killed three, you killed one, so I think we're good now."

"Right." Sam looked at her with piercing blue eyes that reminded her of the ocean. He was sizing her up, trying to understand if she was capable of doing what she'd just said. Instead of working it out, he seemed to accept her at her word. Turning to humor, he said, "Just three? What stopped you killing the last one?"

"I was getting around to it."

"Oh, right. I'm sorry, I wouldn't have intervened if I knew you had it under control."

Freya choked out a laugh. "That's all right. I appreciate your help anyway."

"No problem." Having finished packing up his gear, he pulled the massive bag over his shoulder, tightening his waist strap to take some of the load. "Shall we go?"

Her eyes narrowed. "Where?"

"I have a ship waiting for me down the Zambezi."

"In Zambia?"

"No. Down from Victoria Falls, inside Zimbabwe." He paused. He still hadn't asked her what had happened, where she was from, or where she wanted to go. "I mean, I just assumed you'd want a lift somewhere. Unless you want to stay here?"

She appreciated that he didn't push her to tell him everything. She wasn't sure if she was ready to yet, anyway. Not that she knew why. She didn't have anything to feel guilty about. It wasn't like she'd come to Africa to kill four desperately impoverished men.

Freya met his eye. "I'll come with you if it's okay."

"No problem," he said, beginning to walk down the Tsodilo Hills. "Where do you want me to drop you off?"

She considered that for a second. "To be honest, I don't know."

He gave her an empathetic look. "Well… where do you live?"

"I'm Australian, but for the past six months I've been running a women's health clinic in Kwibisa Plains, Zambia."

Sam said, "That's easy enough. I can drop you off there on my way through."

She frowned. "I missed the last flights out of the country when the world went into lockdown. At first I was happy to stay and look after the clinic, but now everyone else has left, so I'm on my own. I wouldn't ordinarily mind, given that I had a purpose. But now, no one will use the clinic. And with the world in turmoil, and uncertainty even more rife than usual in Zambia, it's become a dangerous place for anyone – let alone a single woman – to stay."

Sam's face mirrored her concern. He gave her a warm, reassuring smile that said, whatever happens, I'm not letting go of you until you're safe. "It's all right, you can come with us."

A wry and incredulous grin formed on her lips. "Are you going to Australia?"

"No. But I'll find you a way to get there if that's where you want to go. I might warn you though, it may be a while until we get you on a flight."

She drew a breath, feeling a sudden sense of ease wash over her that she hadn't felt since the pandemic had begun. It seemed foreign to her. She'd lived anything but a sheltered life, and certainly didn't need a man to take care of her. But right now, in this instance, she was happy to never leave Sam Reilly's side.

"I'll take my chances and come with you." She laughed. "Where are you going by the way?"

Sam shrugged. "To be honest, I have no idea," he paused, grinned. "Not yet."

Freya stared at him, still in wonder, trying to judge how serious he was. She covered her mouth with her hand. "Omgosh… you're serious, aren't you?"

"Afraid so." He turned the palms of his hands skyward. "Still want to join me?"

Smiling, she replied with absolute certainty. "Yes."

Chapter Forty-Four

Sam didn't quite know what to make of his new acquaintance.

Over the course of the next twenty minutes, she had filled him in on the rough details of her kidnapping. Even making room for any modest hyperbole of the narrative, she was undoubtedly one of the most extraordinary women he'd met in a long time – and he was surrounded by extraordinary women.

Freya walked with the Holland & Holland double rifle in her hands. She carried the weapon with the ease and comfort of someone who'd grown up with guns. He could imagine her taking on the dangerous men she spoke of, but found it difficult to reconcile that inner menace with the person he had just met.

He found that he had to work to contain, or at least suppress some of his feelings toward her. Much of which, were too strong for someone he didn't know. It was a unique experience killing someone to save another person's life. He had no regrets. The man was a rabid dog that needed to be put down. There were no doubts in his mind and he had no qualms with doing so. Yet now he and Freya shared a strange connection. It was a type of emotional bond, almost palpable. Even so, he wasn't sure how he felt about her.

She was strikingly beautiful.

At first, he had judged her to be quite pretty, but now that he had time to look at her, he realized that description had been entirely flawed, and "pretty" was woefully understated. Freya was a stunner. There was a strong European cast to her bone structure, a high jaw line, and a long neck that suggested Dutch ancestry. He saw strength of character in her face, too. Her wide mouth was sexy, but also determined, and there seemed to be an iron purpose in those blue-green eyes.

It would be the easiest thing on Earth to fall in love with her.

They kept walking through the maze of boulders that formed the Tsodilo Hills. In harsh contrast to the otherwise barren landscape of Botswana, the rocks stuck out like a jagged scar. Up ahead, they entered a long, protracted cave. At the far end, were the remnants of what could only be described as the most basic of field hospitals or a makeshift surgical facility – although that was probably stretching it. All the equipment had been knocked over and damaged.

On the ground was the body of a male corpse.

Its throat had been sliced through, and a small pool of blood had filled the otherwise dry ground. It was a gruesome death. Whoever the assassin was, had most likely been large and extremely strong, given the amount of strength required to inflict such damage.

He exchanged a glance with Freya. "Do you know this guy?"

"Afraid so."

"Who is… I mean, who was he?"

"His name's Lukas." She spoke matter-of-factly, without any emotion whatsoever. "He's a German surgeon and he was going to kill me to harvest my organs."

Sam drew an inaudible breath. "You killed him, as well?"

She nodded, her expression just a little sheepish. "Guilty."

His eyes narrowed, taking in the scene. "What were they trying to do?"

For the first time since this began, she actually considered what their goal was. "Hmm." She frowned with concentration. "That's a very good question. Were they after my organs? If not, what were they trying to do to me?"

Sam mentally traced the outline of the events. The four local kidnappers, the European surgeon. The icebox. Somehow it all of a sudden made sense to him.

He licked his lips.

His face grimaced with distaste, and deeply lined with concern. "They were going for your kidneys."

She felt the sense of fear rise in her throat like bile. "My kidneys. Why?"

"Yeah... you know how this virus triggers the kidneys to go into overdrive?"

Freya nodded. As a registered nurse and midwife, she knew a lot more than most about the human body. "It triggers a positive feedback mechanism in the kidneys that causes the body to literally excrete all liquid."

"That's right," Sam nodded. "And from what I've been told, this system lays dormant for a matter of weeks before triggering."

"28 days is what I hear." Freya closed her eyes, made a silent prayer and said, "What a nightmare. Imagine knowing that you have a ticking time bomb in you, just waiting to explode, and there's nothing you can do about it."

"That's right, except rich people don't accept that."

Freya shook her head. "Death is the big equalizer in life. Rich and poor. In this case, they both die. There's no known cure yet."

Sam met her eyes. "But death is never equal when you compare the rich and the poor."

Freya nodded, sitting down on an overturned crate. She had seen first-hand the disparity between the haves and the have nots in Zambia. In reality, nowhere was the great divide of wealth more apparent than in health outcomes and life expectancies. "Still, what does this have to do with my kidneys?"

"There's no known cure for Medusa's Curse yet, but there is a systemic treatment."

"A kidney transplant!" she cried out, suddenly realizing it was so obvious. A puzzled frown creased her brow. "But that doesn't make any sense?"

Sam turned his arms outward. "Why not?"

"The virus doesn't only live in the kidneys. It's still circulating in the body. So, after the transplant... the newly transplanted kidneys would become infected!"

Sam nodded. "And in another 28 days someone else would need to die so that Mr. or Mrs. Rich gets to live another 28 days."

Freya felt like she was going to be sick. "It's hard to imagine."

"That there's people willing to kill you to sell your kidneys?"

"No." Freya sighed, her eyes distant, not really focused on anything. "Those are just desperate people trying to survive. It's that some people are willing to kill others to steal their organs. It's hard to imagine that such evil exists in the world."

The sky had turned from gray to dark, and the seemingly millions of stars spread across the horizon. It was time to go and they walked on without talking.

A moment later, their silent reverie was broken.

An explosion rocked their world.

And in the distance, one could just make out the warm glow of a burning helicopter.

Chapter Forty-Five

Sam said, "Come on... we need to go!"

"What the hell was that?" Freya asked, gripping her rifle, ready for another fight.

He was already running in the direction of the explosion. "I think we just lost our ride."

"Our ride?" she asked, trying to keep up with him.

"That's our helicopter!"

"Where are you running to?"

He didn't appear to hear her, and if he did, he wasn't listening. Sam kept running until he reached the wreckage of the Eurocopter. He opened up his bag, grabbed his SCBA and covered his face with the mask. He pushed through the dark shroud of burning smoke, howling and billowing black like an unbidden wraith rising to the sky. He tried to reach the cockpit, but the resonating heat from the inferno was too much.

Even with SCBA, it was impossible.

One glance, and he knew that even had his pilot still been alive in there, he would be so horrifically burned by now that he wished that he wasn't.

Sam backed away and removed the mask of his SCBA.

Freya was screaming at him. "What the hell is wrong with you?"

He heard her, but the words were meaningless.

His concentration was fixed, looking for the person responsible. Further down the path, he spotted someone running toward a Ford Pickup. Sam reached into his already open backpack and withdrew a Heckler & Koch MP5 submachinegun.

Freya's eyes went wide. "Holy shit! Who are you?"

Sam left his backpack there, and made chase.

Freya followed with her double rifle.

The man jumped into the driver's seat, and the pickup sped off down the dirt road. Sam aimed the MP5 submachinegun. It was a long shot. The car was probably out of reach. He aimed at the driver and squeezed the trigger.

Firing three short bursts.

The rounds ripped into the back of the cabin.

And the driver kept driving...

Sam swore.

He watched the taillights fade into the darkness. Just when they disappeared entirely, there was a flash of bright light that filled the nearby sand dunes. The explosion echoed.

Sam looked at Freya, knowing full well from experience that gasoline tanks only tended to explode in the movies. "What the hell was that?"

She shrugged, the glint of a smile in her green eyes. "I think I have an idea."

"Really?" Sam really looked at her, seeing her for the first time since the explosion on the helicopter, and the adrenaline had taken over. A wry grin on his face. "You do?"

"Yeah. When I was in the pickup, I noticed there was a box of Molotov Cocktails."

"That would explain what he used to set the helicopter on fire. Aviation fuel is just about as high octane as one can produce. It wouldn't have taken much for it to explode."

"I'm sorry about the pilot."

"Yeah, me too."

"Were you close?"

"No. I only met him today. Someone sent him out to pick me up. We barely chatted on the flight, but I know he was scared about this virus. It seems like such a terrible loss to die the way he did. But that's life for you. People don't usually get to choose."

Freya looked like she had more to say on the topic of life and death, but didn't quite know where to start, so he left her to her silence. As he waited for her to find her voice, he looked into the sky.

It was a particularly clear and beautiful starry night. The Milky Way was a broad river, a foaming swath of stars. He searched for the Crux, the constellation that centered on four stars in the southern sky in the brightest portion of the Milky Way. The Southern Cross had been used by Polynesian mariners to navigate for thousands of years.

Sam looked at his watch and sighed. "Okay."

Freya suppressed a smile at his quirkiness. "Okay what?"

Sam said, "Okay, so I'm guessing the Ford Pickup was your ride here?"

"Yeah, although I don't know where that murdering arsonist came from. Maybe there was a fifth bad guy with the doctor or something. I don't know. Either way, he must have gotten it in his head that you were on the other team or something. The only way to stop the good guys from coming after him, was to destroy your helicopter."

"The good guys." Sam smirked. "I like it, and your theory is solid. It sort of makes sense."

She grimaced. "So we're stuck smack dab in the desert without a ride?"

"I guess we'll have to do it the old fashioned way."

Freya arched an eyebrow. "Old fashioned way?"

He brought out a map and showed where the *Tahila* was waiting for him. "We walk."

She laughed out loud at that. Then, she gasped, placing her hand across her mouth. "Oh shit..."

Sam smiled. "What?"

She swallowed. "You're serious."

"Sure. Why not?"

"You may not have noticed, but Africa's a little wild."

"No other choice." Sam opened the map the pilot had given him and pursed his lips. "Okay, we're here at Tsodilo Hills," he said, pointing to their position.

Glancing at the map, Freya gained her bearings. Most of the places she recognized and could instinctively visualize distances on foot. "Right."

Sam indicated the Zambezi River north of them. "We head northeast to the Zambezi. Find a boat and sail all the way down to the dam at Lake Karabita, where my ship is waiting for me. Easy."

Freya laughed at his optimism. "That seems doable. Except…"

"Except what?"

"It's a little over a hundred miles walk to reach the Zambezi."

"Okay, so it will take a few days."

"And you do know we have to walk through Chobe National Park?"

"What is it full of scary animals?"

"Yeah, something like that."

Sam lifted the Heckler and Koch MP5 submachinegun. "I'm not really afraid of wild animals."

She laughed at that. There was something about it that made him think he could get used to hearing that sound. When she stopped, her voice became serious again. "That thing fires 9 mm Parabellums. What do you think that's going to do to the King of the African Jungle, when you shoot it?"

"I think I could kill a lion if I had to."

She laughed again. "You think a lion's the most dangerous predator in Africa?"

Sam frowned. "It isn't?"

"No, not by a long shot. It's a common misnomer though, so I'll forgive you. In fact, I think even Disney made a movie out of the concept. I can't remember what it was called?"

Sam suppressed a grin. "The Lion King?"

Freya's voice rose a notch. "See, they were pushing the lie. And let's face it, lions look great. Probably better than any number of other animals that are way more likely to kill you out in the Game Park."

"Great. So, what do we need to watch out for?"

"Everything. It's the African jungle! Everything will kill you."

"But not lions?"

"No. Lions will kill you too. I'm just saying they're not the King."

Sam took the bait. "So what is?"

"Hippos, Elephants, and the Nile Crocodile – in that order."

"Really?"

"Hippos kill upward of three thousand people a year. Lions, less than two hundred."

Sam nodded. "Okay, so we'll stay away from those three."

"Oh, and don't get bitten by any mosquitos."

"Yeah… that I've heard about. Some of them carry diseases?"

She expelled a breath. "Not just some diseases. All of them. But, Yellow Fever, Zika virus, West Nile virus, Dengue Fever, and of course Malaria will all potentially kill you."

"Okay, but if we get past all that, we should be all right?"

"Sure. Of course, there's a lot of gangs working the river because of the pandemic. But they're mostly disorganized and desperate people, trying to survive. We should be able to avoid them."

Sam nodded. "Okay, it's agreed. When do you want to make a start?"

Freya glanced at the sky. "Well… night's only just fallen, and we're still in the Kalahari Desert, so I suggest we start now. We'll sleep tomorrow, when the sun comes up and it becomes too hot to keep walking. How does that sound to you?"

Sam looked at the stars, leading all the way out to the horizon.

Then he shot her a boyish grin. "It's a date."

Chapter Forty-Six

Chobe National Park, Botswana

They talked a lot through the night.

They gathered what supplies they might need, and packed them into Sam's large backpack, leaving anything that wasn't completely necessary. There was three gallons of water between them. It wasn't much for a journey of some forty miles through desert.

There was little wind, and as they walked, they became accustomed to the unique sounds of the African bush. Once a lion roared – thankfully it seemed far away. Freya told him which sounds were of an owl, a night plover, or the howl of a hyena. They could see quite well as their vision became accustomed to the night. Besides, the sky seemed to be bursting at the seams with the weight of the stars.

Sam enjoyed the walk.

Or was it just the company?

He heard all about how Freya ended up setting up a Women's Health clinic in Kwibisa Plains, and that she had originally worked in Luapula, also in Zambia. After implementing a project to improve infant mortality rates in the region became too much for her mental health, she needed something different. Something less stressful where she still had a chance to make a real difference.

He asked, "How is Zambia progressing with primary healthcare and infant rates of survival?"

"It's actually a success story. The infant mortality rate in Zambia has been on the decline since the 1970s. It's been a long, slow, journey – and there's way more to go to bring it up to western standards of survivability rates – but it's good."

Sam concentrated hard on what she was saying. "What's a good number?"

"In 1970 the infant mortality rate for Zambia was more than 108 deaths per 1,000 live births. Now it's only around 42 deaths per 1,000 live births."

"And you're helping keep it traveling in that direction?"

"Luapula's different." Freya's face hardened, her voice lowered, and despite all that was happening, Sam could see the pain that she was feeling – as though she took it personally. "Luapula's still bucking the trend. The current stats are over 89 per 1,000 live births. Just imagine nine out of every hundred children born doesn't make it!"

"Why is that number so shockingly high?"

"The big problem isn't so much HIV/AIDs, those rates of infection have remained mostly constant for more than two decades. It's the rise in tuberculosis that runs wild in those already immunocompromised by HIV."

"What are they doing about the problem?"

"There's not much they can do. The health system is underfunded, understaffed, and basic necessities just aren't available."

"That's sad."

"Yeah, it really is."

"Is that why you moved to a remote clinic in the Kwibisa Plains?"

"Uh-huh. It's a small clinic where I make a real difference to the lives of the women who live out there."

The next day they took shelter under a small rocky outcrop, before sleeping during the hottest parts of the day, then waking a couple hours before sunset.

Sam spotted a large tortoise crawling down a red sand dune with a mixture of black and orange spots all over its shell.

He shook his head. "What the hell is it doing here in the Botswana desert?"

Freya shrugged. "Maybe he got kidnapped? Then his ride got destroyed..."

Sam chuckled at her joke, then his forehead furrowed. "I mean, we've got to be miles from any water?"

She laughed. "That's a Leopard Tortoise."

"Don't tortoises live in water?"

She shook her head. "They're land creatures. They can't even swim."

"Go figure." Sam smiled wistfully as he walked. "What else can you tell me, Miss Attenborough?"

She looked affronted. "Hey, I love David Attenborough as much as the next girl and wanted to travel with him, but he's about a million years too old for me, don't you think?"

"Maybe I meant Miss Attenborough, his daughter..." he glanced at her face, saw he was still off, and said, "Granddaughter?"

She held his gaze, trying to determine if he was serious. Before eventually deciding that he was and said, "Okay, I could be his granddaughter."

Sam said, "So what else do you know?"

She arched a delicate eyebrow. "You want to hear some random bits of wildlife trivia?"

He laughed, happy for the interruption to the monotony of desert travel on foot. "Sure, what have you got?"

"What do you want to know?"

He shrugged. "Surprise me?"

"All right, let's talk about turtles... since you brought them up."

Sam was happy to play the game. "Okay, what do you know about turtles?"

"They, along with frogs, salamanders and sea snakes are capable of breathing out of their butts."

Sam said, "No way!"

She smiled, revealing a perfect set of evenly spaced, white teeth. The tip of her tongue touched her top lip as though she was trying hard not to break into laughter. "Technically the term is cloacal respiration, and it's not so much breathing as just diffusing oxygen in and carbon dioxide out, but the fact remains – when turtles hibernate, their main source of oxygen is through their butt."

"You're making this up!"

"No! I'm serious... it's true."

"It's a fairly common breathing process among amphibians and reptiles and is properly called cutaneous respiration. Besides the turtle butt-breathers, notable users of cutaneous respiration include frogs, salamanders and sea snakes." She laughed, evidently taking pleasure in his shock. "Frogs can breathe like many other vertebrates, with their lungs. But they can also absorb oxygen from water through their skin. Frog skin is covered in a mucus to stay moist, and the capillaries in the skin help absorb oxygen from the surrounding water."

Sam laughed.

Freya liked the sound of it. There was something genuine and unrestrained about Sam's laugh, and she realized early on that she could get used to hearing it more often.

Sam's laughter finally segued into mock seriousness. "How do you know all this stuff?"

Freya shrugged. "What can I say, I was that girl who never really got into the sitcoms of the 90s. Instead, I got hooked on all the wildlife documentaries. I suppose, even though I'm here for the children… what originally inspired me to learn about Africa was watching David Attenborough. Does that sound crazy?"

He met her gaze. Looking at her, seeing her. Really meeting her at some sort of emotional level. He shook his head. "That you should find yourself on the other side of the planet, helping provide basic health to children… because you watched some nature docos as a kid and became interested in Africa?"

"Yeah, I guess."

Sam thought about that for a moment. "No. I don't think so. I mean, there's no real rhyme or reason why we end up doing anything in life. It's just one giant jigsaw puzzle, with infinite experiences and choices, leading to another array of infinite choices and outcomes. Sometimes we make bad choices and they turn into good outcomes, sometimes we make good choices and they turn into bad outcomes. All we can do is try our best and see how life plays out."

She squeezed his hand. "I'm glad you get it."

He smiled. "Crazy is when your brother drowns at sea and you promise yourself that you'll never go on a boat again, but then become the director of a Global Maritime Salvage and Rescue company."

She put her hand on his chest and stopped him. "You're kidding me!"

"I wish I was, but its no word of a lie."

When she realized what he'd said she swallowed, and her hand covered her mouth. "I'm so sorry to hear about your brother."

"Yeah, me too. It was a long time ago and it changed my life. If there's ever a silver lining – and admittedly, this one's pretty damned thin – the fact is, death shapes a person. It drives you to be better. His passing made me realize that nothing's permanent. It's driven me to achieve what I want to achieve today, not wait for some imaginary future when everything comes together in perfect order. I've learned to make my decisions. If I don't like the consequences of my actions, I'll do what it takes to adjust the direction of my life."

Freya gave that some thought, then her lips turned upward in a warm smile. "I like that."

Chapter Forty-Seven

They crossed the large flood plains of the Okavango Delta.

The Chobe National Park was known for its large herds of elephants and Cape buffalo, which converge along the Chobe Riverfront in the dry months. Lions, antelopes and hippos inhabited the woods and lagoons around Linyanti Marsh. The floodable grasslands of the Savuti Marsh attracted numerous bird species, plus migrating zebras.

Freya said, "The animals are different since the pandemic."

"Really?" Sam was puzzled. "Why?"

"I don't know. I guess they somehow sense the people are missing from their world."

"In what way are they behaving differently?" he asked. "I mean, they look like wild animals to me."

"They're mixing in larger numbers. They're keeping away. Giving us more room than normal. As though they have an underlying fear that we might carry the sickness."

Sam's eyes narrowed. "You got all that from seeing them out here in the wild?"

She shrugged. "I go for a long walk every day, fifty miles north of here. You get to tell when the animals as a group seem off."

They kept their steady pace in silence. Sam began to notice that Freya kept intermittently glancing at him, almost to the point of staring at him.

He smiled. "What?"

Freya asked, "What does a director of a Global Maritime Salvage and Rescue company do for a living?"

Sam grinned. "To be honest, I'm sort of like an action hero-cum-star of a thriller series..."

"Really?" Her forehead furrowed as she half-heartedly attempted to suppress a laugh, there was a teasing and mischievous lilt to her voice. "That's what you're going with?"

Sam spread his arms and did a modest little twirl. "Hey, what can I say? If you heard the truth, you'd probably find it harder to believe."

A wry grin formed on her lips. A small scar on her lower lip somehow made it appear fuller, sexier. Curiosity and intrigue filled her intelligent blue-green eyes. "What do you really do?"

"There's not a lot to it. I work for my dad's company, predominantly on the maritime rescue and salvage arm of Global Shipping."

"But you're not here doing shipwreck salvage, are you?"

Sam glanced at the jungle. "No. This is a special case I got roped into."

"Why?"

"Coincidences and circumstances."

She paused a beat, waiting for him to elaborate. When he didn't, she said, "Such as?"

"I was researching the wreckage of the Portuguese Atlantic Slave ship called *Midas* that went missing in 1831."

Suppressing a grin, she ran her tongue across her teeth, then said, "In the Botswanan desert?"

"No. I was looking for it in the Zambezi conflux."

"Really? How did a Portuguese slave ship end up in the Upper Zambezi conflux?"

"We don't know that it did yet," Sam admitted. "We haven't found it, but we've followed the story from historical documents, and it's led us there." He paused. "The upshot is that I was diving the Zambezi, trying to find signs of it when this pandemic hit. We considered returning to the US, but eventually decided not to. After all, we had everything we needed on the ship, and what better place to quarantine than where we were, right? It would probably only last a couple of months at most."

"Only it didn't."

"Right. It fooled the world and became a much bigger threat than we could have ever imagined. Which brings me to how I came to be here in your delightful company."

Listening intently, her eyes narrowed. "Go on."

"Someone from the State Department contacted my people having heard that we were in the area. It's believed the original virus originated from a biolab nearby."

"Botswana?" It was clear she didn't believe it for a second. "There haven't been any cases reported anywhere near here since this thing began."

"No. The virus didn't originate here. We still have no idea where it came from, but we believe it was brought to a secret lab in the Kalahari Desert, where a team of biologists managed to weaponize it."

"And someone from the State Department asked you… a Maritime Rescue Specialist, to… what spy on the lab?"

"No. The lab was burned to the ground."

"When?"

"A week ago. But it was originally erected four weeks before patient zero arrived in Paris."

Freya was quiet for a few minutes. Her face registered a mixture of fascination, genuine interest, and melancholy, as she put it all together. "Someone planned this entire thing?"

"I'm afraid it looks like it."

"So what were you looking for?"

"Water samples. It's believed that in the process of weaponizing the original strain of the virus, some of it washed into the nearby water supply. I've collected samples and it's hoped that our people back home can reverse engineer an antibody if they have access to the original strain."

She stared at him for a while, taking him in, looking up at him, and really listening. Her face, unreadable. After a while she patted him on the shoulder. "So you sometimes do a little more than maritime rescue and salvage?"

"Sometimes…"

The air was dry and warm. Except for the occasional bird and insect sounds, the desert was quiet. They walked on in the silence for a while.

It wasn't an awkward silence. It was significant. Almost surreal. Both of them simply trying to put together what life was throwing at them.

Freya patted his left shoulder affectionately, her eyes distant, almost in a dream. "Tell me about the *Midas*."

"What do you want to know?"

"Why does anyone care where the shipwreck is after all these years?"

Sam shrugged. "Why not? Why does anyone care about any shipwreck after all these years?"

"Sure, but you know…"

Sam shook his head. "No, I don't know. What?"

"The *Midas* disappeared in 1831 it must have been what, one of about a million Trans-Atlantic Slave Ships during that time…"

"…so what makes it any more important than all those others?" he finished the sentence.

"Exactly."

Sam said, "The conditions were poor on Atlantic crossings in those days, but particularly bad for slaves. The slave cargo of the *Midas* originated from Mendiland – that's to the eastern tip of modern-day Sierra Leone by the way."

She smiled at his condescension. "I do know a little about African geography, by the way."

Sam let it pass. "The Mendi were a formidable people. Instead of dying of starvation and malnutrition during the voyage, they rebelled and killed the crew. Once they gained control of the ship, they became pirates. For nearly two years they attacked and stole from every French, Spanish, and Portuguese ship that went by."

"Where did all this happen?"

"The Caribbean."

She smiled. "Obviously."

Sam laughed. "Oh, why do you say that?"

"Well, you know…" she suppressed a smile. "The Pirates of the Caribbean and all that."

Sam shot her a boyish smile. "*Now* who's following Disney for their information?"

Holding his gaze, she frowned. "Are you saying my pal Walt got it wrong again?"

"No," Sam admitted. "In this case, Disney got it right. The Caribbean was full of pirates from the 16th Century onward. Especially after Queen Elizabeth introduced the Sea Dogs and offered "Letters of Marque" to merchant sailors, which made their plundering of Spanish ships legal under English Law."

Freya said, "Interesting. So what makes you think the *Midas* ended up in Zambia?"

"An oil painting was recently sold at a dealership in Zanzibar. The painting depicted an image of the *Midas* at anchor along the Zambezi, with a date – 1833."

She smiled. "That's it?"

"Yeah. That's it."

"What do you think your chances are of finding it?"

"I started with a fifty-fifty, but it's a bit higher now."

"How so?"

"A few weeks ago, we dragged a net of sonar buoys along the Upper Zambezi. Ten miles east of Kwibisa Plains, we struck paydirt."

"You found the ship?"

"No. Three cannonballs and a Portuguese cannon to be exact. It's not definitive, but it's pretty much as close to it as possible. The Spanish Atlantic Slave Ship sank somewhere on the Upper Zambezi."

Freya paused mid-stride. "Hang on a second. Spanish? I thought you said it was a Portuguese ship?"

"It was a Portuguese ship, on consignment to Spain, for the transport of African Slaves."

"Right. Obviously." She met his eye. "Was there a reason for Spain to hire a Portuguese ship? I thought the Spanish were tremendous sailors during that time? I mean, wasn't Christopher Columbus Spanish?"

"First off," Sam said. "Christopher Columbus was an Italian Explorer, who got commissioned to lead an expedition sponsored by King Ferdinand of Spain in 1492 to find a new route east, and in the process, discovered the New World. And second, the *Midas* being Portuguese had nothing to do with the Spanish ability or inability to sail."

"Okay, I'll bite. What did it have to do with?"

Sam said, "It had to do with the Treaty of Tordesillas which did not allow Spanish ships in African ports. Spain had to rely on Portuguese ships and sailors to bring slaves."

Freya frowned. "Sorry, my early history of the Americas is a bit rusty. The Treaty of Tordesillas?"

"Sorry. When the Spanish and Portuguese first began exploration of the Americas, the governments of Spain and Portugal agreed to the Treaty of Tordesillas, named for the city in Spain in which it was created. The Treaty of Tordesillas neatly divided the New World of the Americas between the two superpowers."

"Where did they draw the line?"

"Spain and Portugal split the New World by drawing a north-to-south line of demarcation in the Atlantic Ocean, about 100 leagues west of the Cape Verde Islands, off the coast of northwestern Africa and then controlled by Portugal. All lands east of that line were claimed by Portugal. All lands west of that line were claimed by Spain. Spain and Portugal adhered to the treaty without major conflict between the two, although the line of demarcation was moved an additional 270 leagues farther west in 1506, which enabled Portugal to claim the eastern coast of what is now Brazil."

"Interesting."

"The results of this treaty are still evident throughout the Americas today. For example, all Latin American nations are predominantly Spanish-speaking countries with the sole exception of Brazil where Portuguese is the national language. This is because the eastern tip of Brazil falls east of the line of demarcation settled upon in the Treaty of Tordesillas, and was where the majority of Portuguese colonization occurred."

Freya brought the conversation back to the hunt for the *Midas*. "What will you do now that you've found the cannon and balls in the Zambezi?"

"I thought we might have hit a dead end, but we tried our luck with a local San tribesman who knew of a legend regarding an enormous ship that sailed the Zambezi of his ancestors."

She was intrigued. "What did he say?"

Sam smiled. "That a bunch of Gods with the power to split the world and make earthquakes sailed on a ship. That they couldn't control their powers, and the ship was sunk as a result of them. And that the ship's precious cargo was taken to a secret cave, where it has been lost ever since."

"Any idea where the cave might be?"

"No idea. The San tribesman says it's just a dream, but I think it's real."

"Do you have a picture?"

"Yeah, back on the ship. Remind me, and I'll show it to you… maybe you've seen it around?"

"Maybe."

They walked at night, and slept curled up together for warmth at every sunrise. In the end, it took four days, but they finally reached the Zambezi River at Sesheke.

Chapter Forty-Eight

Sam found a traditional river dhow pulled up high along the riverbank.

It was roughly eighteen feet long with a mast and a single settee, a lateen sail with the front corner cut off, giving it a quadrilateral shape. Inside, there was a heavy wooden box. There was a sticker label on the box. It was orange with a fractured ball and blast symbols shooting out of it. Sam frowned. It was the universal hazard symbol for explosive chemicals. He recalled seeing the crew of a similar dhow on his way up, using dynamite to remove underwater obstacles to navigation.

He began to pull its long sleek hull toward the river.

Freya said, "You're just going to take it?"

"Do you want to walk the hundred and fifty miles along the banks of the Zambezi to my ship?" he countered.

"Hmm… Maybe if we get out of this alive, we'll return the boat or even a better one someday?"

"That sounds reasonable to me."

They pushed out into the river.

Sam hoisted the single sail, and then set a broad reach east along the river. It was a warm day, with a light breeze. At the nearby Sesheke Plain, the river widened, and a large herd of elephants meandered along the banks. There were dozens of different types of game animals, and several Nile crocodiles. After about an hour they passed a lone cheetah, a comparatively rare sighting along the river.

Several Natal Mahogany trees lined the river. The large riverine trees were covered with deep green leaves, and a characteristic, round canopy with low-reaching branches that shaded the river from the scorching African sun. A troop of baboons ate the tree's distinctive orange and black fruits. The dhow tacked as they rounded the bend and settled into a slow steady course.

Freya was stretched out on the opposite side of the hull, laying on her back with her feet up on the side of the boat. She had relaxed and settled into the journey. There was something about her face. She looked pensive and distant.

Sam studied her for a few seconds and then asked, "What are you thinking about?"

"Oh, it's nothing." Freya smiled, an attractive tinge of pink flushing to her cheeks.

"It's okay if it's something you don't want to talk about. I get it."

She brushed him aside. "No, I was simply thinking about life."

"Anything in particular?"

"Not really. Just how funny it is that I should have ended up here."

Sam waited for her to elaborate. When she didn't, he said, "How did you end up in Zambia?"

"I told you, I've always been drawn to the continent, and as a midwife rural Zambia was a good choice. It was where my skill set could provide the greatest good to local women."

Sam smiled. "No, I mean, why now?"

"What's wrong with now?"

"Nothing. Traditionally, I figured aid workers in Africa were really young… as in, straight out of college and full of youthful altruism or old, and, having seen some of the dark side of the world, feel the need to make a change."

"Not people in between?"

Sam shrugged. "I suppose so. Just an observation. And I was interested what changed in your life that made you decide to do it now."

Freya said, "As opposed to later?"

Sam shook his head. "As opposed to earlier. You mentioned you'd been drawn to Africa since you were a kid."

She stared at him. Judging him somehow. Her lovely face was animated, and enchanting as she spoke. "You're pretty intuitive, aren't you?"

"Just curious." Sam lifted a hand off the tiller, and said, "You don't have to tell me."

Freya spoke with the candor that was only possible of two people who had shared so much in such a short period of time. "I got divorced."

"And finally decided to do what you wanted to do?"

"Yeah, I had wanted to do this for a while." Hesitating for a long moment, she finally said, "I suppose, unintentionally, my husband's life got in the way. And that's no fault of his – really, he's a good man – we just were the wrong people for each other. Does that make sense?"

"Sure," Sam said, feeling that she hadn't gotten around to opening up to many people about this. He was surprised anyone would leave someone so lovely as her. "You left him, didn't you?"

"Yeah." She smiled. "Why did you say that?"

"How did I know you left him?"

"Yeah?"

Sam said, "Although I don't know much about you, what little I do know, tells me that you're an extraordinary woman, and I don't think there would be many men on Earth who would be dumb enough to let you go."

He was certainly enchanted by her.

She listened with interest, laughed a lot, and touched his arm often, as if issuing an invitation to be part of her world.

Freya was going to brush off his casual remark as flattery, but it seemed too trivial to do so. That wasn't the conversation they were having. Instead, she simply said, "Thank you."

"Hey, I could be wrong. Maybe you're a heinous…"

"Maybe?" she said with an amused expression on her face, before he could finish the statement. Then, eyeing him directly, she asked, "What do you know of love?"

"I know that love comes in many different forms, and it's a mistake to confuse them with one another."

Freya lifted an eyebrow. "There are so many different meanings of love?"

"Sure there is. There's the love of one's children that's unconditional. There is the love for another, where you want what is best for them, and will always be there for them. And there's the other."

Her brow furrowed slightly in a curious expression. "What's the other?"

"It's the sort of love that fairy-tales were supposed to be written about. Not the stupid, Cinderella meets a Prince, falls in love sort of stupidity, but something all the more special and equally as rare."

She arched a blonde, delicate eyebrow. "I'm listening."

"The other is when you just simply love a person. It's almost spiritual. Like two souls yearning for that same, intrinsic, emotional connection. When despite all reason and logic, you simply can't keep your hands off each other. You love each other's bodies without a thought about what their shape is or anything else. Simply, because it belongs to the other person. When two people simply make each other happy. Not because they're trying to please each other or change each other, but because they have broken the inexplicable, imaginarily impossible, odds of meeting someone who truly makes them happy. It's got nothing to do with what they do or say. Simply the person, at an almost cellular level, connects with you, and makes you happy." Sam laughed. "And of course, you simply can't keep your hands off each other."

"Can you have that love for someone and not have it reciprocated?" she asked, her voice curious and challenging.

"No. It doesn't work that way."

She was intrigued at his theory. "Why not? If love is all in our own heads, why can't you fall in love with someone who doesn't love you?"

"Because lovers at the very most basic level are mirrors. They see us as exactly who we are. If they see the good in us, we feel loved. If they see the bad in us, we feel bad. Love… real love… doesn't work one sided. You need to see and feel that it's reciprocal. Love cannot be one sided. That's infatuation, a very different experience, altogether very different to love."

Freya considered that. "I like it."

After several minutes of sailing in silence, she asked, "Have you ever been in love?"

"Sure…" His response seemed trivial, almost flippant, but there was a sudden sparkle in his blue eyes, that swirled, lost in the profound ocean of memories… "Yeah, I've been in love."

"What went wrong?"

He smiled at that. People liked to make things simple, provide neat little answers to life's greatest mysteries. Life was never like that. "Nothing."

"So why didn't you marry the girl?"

"Honestly?"

"Yeah."

"I don't know… I was never able to work that one out."

"Do you want to talk about it?"

"No."

"Come on. Why not?"

"It brings back the unanswered questions. And the might-have-beens. Few things, I assure you, will devastate like the might-have-beens. Most people believe the end of an incredible relationship is the cruelest thing of all. Not so. After a while, hope is a far more abusive mistress."

"Wow!" she said, her hand instinctively reaching for her mouth to suppress a laugh. "You were really in love, once?"

"Yeah." Sam met her eyes. "Memories, you see, hurt. The good ones most of all."

She seemed to intrinsically feel his pain. "Will you try again?"

Sam arched an eyebrow. "Am I capable of falling in love again?"

"Yeah." She placed a hand on his chest and held his gaze. There was an expression on her face, and a twinkle in her eye, that he couldn't quite read. Then she asked, "Are you?"

He met her with certainty. "You bet I am."

"Really?" The answer seemed to have surprised her. "Do you think it could ever live up to your expectations?"

Sam shrugged. "Look, people can go on and on about how it is better to have loved and lost than to never have loved at all. I don't think it applies to me."

Freya crossed her arms and suppressed a smile. "Oh, you don't, huh?"

Sam said, "You see, it's in our DNA to repeat the same mistakes, even after we know better."

She didn't have anything to say to that one, and they kept sailing in silence.

Up ahead, they approached Livingstone Island.

A small motorboat began to increase its throttle, racing toward them at full speed. As it got close, Sam realized there were several men on board, all carrying rifles. There was a flag he didn't recognize on the boat.

Before he could ask, Freya said, "That's not good. They're part of the same rebel gang that kidnapped me."

"How many rounds do you have?" Sam asked.

The hardened lines on Freya's face tensed. "Just two."

Sam glanced at his own weapon, did the math. "I have five left in my submachinegun. It's not going to be enough."

"We'll just have to make them count," she said, fiercely.

"You're certain they're not here to lend a hand?"

"No," she said, her voice full of certainty. "Hundred percent. They're with the rebels who wanted to sell my kidneys."

"All right. That's settled then."

"What's settled?" she asked, a worry crease on her forehead.

With a determined, no-nonsense grin, Sam ducked down and opened the box of dynamite. "We do it my way."

Chapter Forty-Nine

The motorboat pulled up alongside them.

There was a lot of hand waving and gestures with rifles. Sam and Freya played dumb, but it didn't get them very far.

One of the apparent leaders, said, "You are outgunned and outnumbered. I suggest you put down your weapons, and step aboard."

Sam slowly lowered his Heckler and Koch submachinegun.

In his head, he began to count.

Ten. Nine. Eight.

Freya was a little more reluctant to give up her weapon. In the end she threw it all the way to the river's bank. "You can go fetch."

The leader on the boat shrugged. "All aboard."

Sam held Freya's hand. He stepped onto their enemy's motorboat and made his way to the far end of the craft. Three guys held the two hulls of the two boats together, while two more men climbed aboard the dhow to search for anything of value.

Five.

Sam wrapped his arms protectively around Freya's waist.

Four.

Pushing through to the very back of the boat, they both jumped into the river.

Three.

The rebels started laughing.

After all, where were they going to escape to?

One.

The box of dynamite exploded.

Chapter Fifty

Sam and Freya's heads disappeared beneath the water.

They duck dived as the two boats exploded, sending a shockwave and a meteor storm of deadly debris high into the air. His ears rung with the sound of the detonation blast. Beside him, several underwater projectiles whizzed by, narrowly missing him and Freya. Bubbles whirred everywhere. Sam turned over, so that he could look straight up.

Above them, the water's surface was a wall of flame.

They needed to stay under long enough for the blast space and superheated air above to burn out. If they came up too soon, the water would be so hot it would burn their skin, and as soon as they took a breath, the superheated air would destroy their lungs.

Sam gripped Freya around her waist, his head next to hers, they met eye to eye. He stared at her blue-green eyes, and saw a mixture of fear, pain, and hope etched inside.

After thirty or so seconds, she began to fight to reach the surface.

Sam held her tight, knowing full well that if she surfaced, she would die a horrible death.

Fear turned to panic, and he knew that he was losing her. Sam pressed his mouth to hers. They created a perfect seal between their lips. It was an intimate embrace, involving a level of trust from another person that few people will ever experience in a lifetime. She breathed in slowly, as the two of them shared each other's exhaled breaths.

The panic faded.

It was an old Navy Diving technique known as pendulum breathing. The same, although much more efficient technique, was used in modern day closed-circuit rebreather SCUBA systems and modern ventilators. Atmospheric air holds roughly 21 percent oxygen. When you breathe in, your lungs utilize somewhere between four and five percent of that oxygen, and you exhale the rest. Thus, in theory, two people can "rebreathe" each other's exhaled air. It also served to calm the natural rise of panic that is triggered when the lungs aren't able to open and close, which in turn, reduced the amount of oxygen the body requires. The process allowed divers to extend their underwater time to nearly three minutes.

That was as far as Sam was willing to push it.

He slowly surfaced.

They both gasped a large breath of air. It was still hot to breathe, but not a lung-destroying temperature. They took in several breaths. The two boats were still burning in the distance. Hideously scorched bodies lined the surface.

Sam said, "Come on, we need to get out of the water!"

Freya nodded. "That's okay with me!"

Sam paddled toward the sandy bank of the Zambezi.

They nearly reached it, when one of the charred bodies drifting face up, came alive. The man's back was a blistering mess of burned skin.

The rebel screamed, launching himself at Freya, and grabbing her around her neck. There was panic in the man's shrill shriek, and it was hard to tell if he was trying to kill her, or simply use her buoyancy to prevent himself from drowning.

Sam swam forward, and punched the man in the face.

His knuckles collided with the bridge of the rebel's nose, shattering it with the sound of a violent crunch. It was enough to daze the murderer, but not quite enough to kill him.

The rebel's arms flailed wildly, as though trying to connect with Sam. It was the last-ditch efforts of a dying man, but that didn't make them any less dangerous.

In front of them, another predator approached.

This one had the unique body form that allowed the eyes, ears, and nostrils to be above the water's surface while most of the animal was hidden below. It had a wide, U-shaped mouth, lined with 68 jagged teeth. Its reptilian skin was thick and plated like an armored machine. Barely making a ripple in the water, it moved deceptively slowly. Yet, the big river predator would be impossible to outrun or outswim.

The most feared Nile Crocodile approached.

The rebel who had attacked Freya screamed. It triggered an instinctive attack reaction from the crocodile, which lurched toward them.

Sam grabbed hold of the man.

The crocodile swung its long and massive tail, launching itself right at Sam. He gripped the rebel's body, turned it in a quick movement, and pushed the man into the wide-open jaws of the Nile Crocodile.

The predator's jaws closed with a crunch.

The water turned a murky red as flesh was torn. The crocodile dragged the rebel underwater. Sam saw the man's body was still thrashing, but this time in death throes.

Sam and Freya didn't need any more encouragement to get out of the water. They quickly clambered up the steep muddy edge of the river and well up and onto the shore.

Lying roughly twelve feet up and out of the bank of the river, they both breathed hard, trying to catch their breath. Their hearts pounding in their chests, their bodies trembled from shock and a truckload of adrenaline. Sam wrapped his arms around Freya, in the happy embrace of two people who came as close as possible to being killed and yet survived.

A moment later, something else pushed out of the water.

It was big.

Much bigger than the first, another Nile crocodile charged its way out of the river and up the bank, coming straight for them.

Freya shouted, "Run!"

They split up, each running in opposite directions.

Freya ran left.

Sam ran right.

The crocodile went for Sam.

There was nothing but open ground nearby. No trees to climb. Nowhere to go. No possible way to protect himself from the crocodile.

He would have to outrun the monster.

And that was impossible.

The Nile crocodile could hit speeds of over 20 mph in the water and on land.

But it didn't stop Sam from trying. Adrenaline flooded his veins, and he sprinted as fast as humanly possible. The remnants of a small flood plain acacia tree was suddenly in front of him. But his legs were racing as fast as his heart. Not breaking his stride, Sam leapt.

Unfortunately, his right foot clipped the log.

Sam tumbled face down, *hard*. Hurriedly scrambling in the mud, he grabbed a branch and turned, to face his hunter.

The crocodile growled like something out of Jurassic Park.

It opened its massive mouth.

Sam got a good look at those razor-sharp teeth.

A whip-like "snap" cut across the bank of the river. Sam grinned. He knew that sound. It was the sonic boom that occurs as a projectile moved through the air at supersonic speeds. This one was caused by a .577 Nitro Express, a projectile weighing 650 grains and traveling 1,800 foot per second out the barrel of a Holland & Holland Royal Double Rifle.

The world seemed to move in super slo-mo as the bullet hit the crocodile between its ears.

Releasing 7,010-foot pound-force of pressure.

It was more than enough to blow the crocodile's massive head clean off.

The headless body kept moving for a few seconds more, the giant muscles of its limbs working from momentum, instead of neurological intention.

Sam swore, and rolled to the side, moving out of the way of the dismembered reptile.

He turned to Freya who was now walking toward him, still holding her grandfather's rifle. The very same type of weapon Ernest Hemingway had used on all of his adventures throughout the years.

Sam met her proud and lovely face. "Wow!" he said. "That's some really good shooting."

She smiled. It wasn't coy. She'd been telling him all along she was an awesome shot. "I told you I could shoot."

"Yeah, well you weren't exaggerating." Still raggedly breathing, Sam pushed to his feet. "Thanks for saving my life."

"No problem. I think we both owe each other our lives, more than once now." She shrugged. "But who's keeping score?"

"Indeed." Sam laughed. "That was good thinking throwing your rifle over here. I wished I'd thought of doing that with my machinegun. Now we're down to only one shot."

"If we need it, I'll just have to make sure it's a good one." Freya met his gaze. "Hopefully we won't need it."

"I'm with you on that." Sam studied the lifeless, headless crocodile that had nearly bitten off his head. It had to be twenty feet long and maybe 750lbs. Looking up, he then checked out the remnants of death and destruction he and Freya had left in their wake.

Frowning, Freya joined him in staring at the wrecked boat, the blood, and human carnage. "Well, that's about the most awful thing I've ever seen in my life," she observed.

"It was them or us," Sam said. "They didn't give us a choice. We had to use the dynamite."

"Them or us," Freya agreed.

"And you're right," Sam said. "That wasn't very nice at all." Licking dry lips, he suppressed a grin. "Hopefully the next people we meet will be nice. Otherwise, our body count is going to keep piling up."

Chapter Fifty-One

They followed the road down to Victoria Falls, crossed the bridge into Zimbabwe, and climbed the stairs down into the small bay where white water rafts pulled into the river at the bottom of the Batoka Gorge.

Freya, now accustomed to the theme of the day, said, "Shall we break into the white-water rafting store?"

"Sounds good. Are you any good as a rafter?"

"Good enough."

All in total, it took four hours to run the rapids of the Zambezi, through the Batoka Gorge. It seemed strange trying to guide a six-person raft with just two people, but it was the wet season, which meant there was more water in the river, and conversely less rapids.

They reached the Kariba dam where the *Tahila* was meant to be waiting for them by the early afternoon, and found the ship mysteriously gone.

Chapter Fifty-Two

Sam found and opened the survival kit from the raft.

Inside was a map of the area. He scanned the map, seeking the closest signs of civilization. They needed to reach a phone to contact the *Tahila*. There were any number of reasons the ship would need to be moved.

The most likely was that when he failed to return by helicopter on the first day, Elise would have used overhead satellites to take photos of the site. When those came back with images of a burned-out helicopter, they might have feared the worst. Even so, he would have expected them to fly out and check.

He dismissed the thought. First step was to make contact. Then they could work out an extraction point.

Freya studied the map from over his shoulder. "What are you looking for?"

"I need to find a phone." Sam ran his fingers across the chart, searching for somewhere big enough to have a phone line, but not necessarily too big they were going to run into trouble with more rebels. "If I can contact my ship, they'll be able to come get us."

Freya pointed to a place roughly twenty miles from where they were. "How about here?"

Sam frowned. "The Lion's Den, Hwange National Park?"

She nodded. "Yeah. There's a small ranger's outpost here. There's a permanent phone where they can report poachers."

"In the Lion's Den?"

"It's just the name of the area." She smiled. "And before you ask, yeah, it's because the place is packed with lions."

Sam sighed. "Well, at least you have one shot!"

"We'll be fine."

"Okay. We won't make it there tonight."

"No. I have an idea where we can sleep tonight, but we'd better get a move on."

They packed up the map, survival bag, and small, self-contained meal packs that Freya had found inside the rafting store, along with a couple bottles of water. Over the next two hours they moved quickly through grasslands and the mopane woods, home to large elephant herds, lions and African wild dogs.

The animals tended to give them a wide berth, instinctively aware that humans were dangerous. Or it could have been the sight of Freya carrying her grandfather's double rifle. How were they to know she only had one shot left?

The golden sun began to settle low on the horizon, casting long shadows across the plains. A tower of giraffes trailed off in succession, as though they too, were slowly following the sun to bed. The sounds across the African savannah changed in small, but noticeably different ways. Small insects came out to play, making unique noises. Birds flocked to their places of safety, and zebras – more active at night – began to graze.

Sam said, "We still need to find somewhere to go for the night."

Freya exchanged a playful glance with him, a wry smile on her parted lips. "Shall we see if the Ritz has any vacancies?"

"Very funny."

She touched his arm. "Too expensive?"

Sam said, "Hey, I'm happy to pay if you can find one."

Her eyes narrowed. "What about the Holiday Inn?"

"You choose. Whatever you like, Freya."

She looked up, staring at a huge tree in the distance. It looked like a giant up-side-down tree, with its thick branches like the roots growing toward the sky. "How about a baobab tree?"

Chapter Fifty-Three

The baobab was a majestic African tree.

Native to the African continent, it was commonly known as the upside-down-tree, a name originating from the myth that said they were once plucked from their roots, turned up-side-down and stuck back in the ground again.

They were a hardy and long-lived tree, with some speculation suggesting that they might survive in the order of 1,500 years. They have traditionally been valued as sources of food, water, health remedies or places of shelter and are steeped in legend and superstition. The local San tribesmen used the tree to identify underground water sources for thousands of years.

Some of them stretched upward of sixty feet in the air, but this one was just thirty. The lower trunk was wider than a medium-sized car, and roughly twenty feet high, before spreading out like an umbrella, providing a large platform upon which to rest. There were no branches on the lower trunk, but the bark was thick and strong, which created holds just big enough to grip and climb.

Sam watched Freya climb first, admiring the view.

Lighter than him, her body was slim, muscular, and lithe. Freya moved elegantly up the rugged landscape of the trunk, looking like a professional rock climber.

At the top, she turned around, lifted her arms up gracefully in the air, and said, "Ta-da!"

"Well done," Sam said, genuinely impressed by her feat.

She laughed. "Now your turn."

Sam swallowed. With each movement slow, and each hold tenuous, he found climbing the baobab harder than it looked. Where Freya seemed to fit her fingers nicely into each groove in the trunk, he found the holds too small for his thick fingers to comfortably reach inside. It was a delicate dance, but eventually he reached the top, and quickly climbed over the edge onto the small, platform-like top of the tree.

He glanced back, realizing just how high up they were, and turned back. His eyes flashed with vertigo, and he turned back to the outline of Freya's beautiful face to ground himself.

She suppressed a grin. "You're afraid of heights?"

"Just a little," he admitted. "Well, I have no idea how we're going to get down after this, but at least we're safe from lions."

Freya laughed. Her laugh turned to a chuckle, and segued into silence. "Oh, you think we're safe from lions up here?"

Sam frowned. "We're not?"

"Not even a little."

"Lions can climb trees?"

Freya's gaze leveled, her blue-green eyes landing on him. "They're cats. Have you ever heard of a cat that can't climb trees?"

"No... but a lion's what... 300 pounds?"

"Closer to 450 for an adult male," she said, like a grown-up telling the scary part of a story to a nervous child. "Obviously, it's a bit harder for a lion than a leopard to climb a tree. Their bodies just aren't quite as well adapted to it, but they get there, if they really want to."

Sam drew a breath. "Do they want to very much?"

"Sometimes. Strangely, it's becoming more common throughout the South Saharan Africa."

"Really?" Sam asked.

She nodded her head. "It's true."

"Why?"

"No one really knows. There are entire prides in the Serengeti that sleep in trees. Some say they've discovered that it's cooler in the tree than on the ground. Others suppose that it could be to avoid the wet ground and grass. Who likes wet feet?"

"Indeed," Sam said, in a voice that was unimpressed.

"Others still say that the behavior mimics that of a typical cat, which likes to have an elevated view of its surroundings. A few experts put forth that they climb to avoid the armies of insects that irritate them on the ground. They do seem annoyed by buzzing flies, to be fair. Failing any better theories, we must assume that all of these might be at least partially correct. It seems unlikely that a lion would climb a tree just for the fun of it. Even so, when they do climb, they will only venture onto the lowest and strongest branches. Like people, they're better at getting up a tree than down it."

Sam glanced over the edge of the tree. They were a long way up. "How do they get down?"

"They stumble and usually end up in a combination of falling and jumping when gravity inevitably pulls them down."

"So, tell me again why we're safer up here?"

"It's still easier to be eaten by a lion on the ground, there's less chance of elephants crushing us, and the crocodiles won't find us here... also, the fattails aren't as likely to be a problem."

"Fattails?"

"A local type of scorpion."

Sam grimaced. "Let me guess... its sting is deadly."

"Not always fatal. If you can get to a hospital within the first hour, you should survive."

Except that most hospitals, along with everything else in Africa and across the globe, had been shut months ago. The world was in crisis mode as people isolated in the hopes of staving off the Medusa's Curse. So far, it was shaping up to be the deadliest pandemic in history.

"All right, we'll stay in the trees."

Chapter Fifty-Four

There wasn't much room on the tree.

Sam found himself, by way of necessity, positioned close to Freya. He was sitting with his back against a large branch, with his legs set apart in a slight V-shape. She soon moved in front of him, at first trying to find a comfortable position apart, before, naturally easing her back onto his chest. His arms draped around her, and held her.

It was an intimate position.

Shared with someone who'd been a stranger to him just days ago, but whom, he now shared this incredibly intense connection and vulnerability in equal proportions. He suddenly found himself feeling very safe. The soft wind blew, the leaves of the trees danced, and he instinctively held her tighter in silence, enjoying the view. It was a surreal experience and better than anything he'd imagined for a very long time.

The sun began its nightly journey below the horizon.

As it did, the sky turned to beautiful smudges of coral, lavender, turquoise, and a fiery orange, all blended together to create a sight so astounding it threatened to sweep them away from all their worries. The purple and orange of sunset finally gave way to a polished pewter.

The tree's leaves began to rustle. Simultaneously, as if orchestrated by an invisible conductor, the hundred or more large, foot long flowers on their tree began to open. It was a magical sight. At dusk they opened, so quickly that the movement was visible by the naked eye. The large, old baobab carried hundreds of flower buds.

Not all the buds opened, but the ones which did open did so in perfect synchronization – as if the tree gave a silent sign. Whether a bud opens in the evening can be seen in the afternoon. No sooner had the buds opened to beautiful pink and white flowers, than the Zimbabwe rose beetles arrived to enjoy the nectar and to nibble on the white petals.

Freya leaned forward and opened the travel pack she'd taken from the rafting store. Inside was a bottle of red wine, two glasses, and an array of packed food. She poured the wine. A South African Papegaaiberg Merlot, with a soft, fruity aroma. She then picked a baobab fruit, still on the branch from last season. She cut through its hardened core, splitting it into two slices.

She handed it to him. "Here, try this."

"Thanks," he said, taking a bite.

Its velvety texture felt similar to a coconut in the flush of youth – minus the long hairs. Inside it looked similar to dark honey, but the taste was tart, more like lemon curd, its texture gritty like a tangy pear, or what he imagined sherbet might taste like if it were grown as fruit. His face crunched up tight with distaste.

Freya laughed. "What do you think?"

"I think it looks more appealing than it tastes." Then, seeing her open her mouth in complaint, he said, "Maybe I just need to get used to it?"

"No, that's about the general consensus by most people who try it," she said putting the fruit aside.

Sam asked, "Are you going to try some?"

"Hell no. The stuff taste terrible."

They both laughed and took a few bites from the lunch pack. Most things were sealed in plastic wrappers so popular a decade ago before most countries banned the sale of single use plastics. But the dried food was quite nice.

Freya lifted the glasses of wine. "To surviving life."

Sam clinked his glass with hers. "To surviving."

They both took a sip.

The merlot had a taste of sweet, berry tones, with a touch of oak. It was dry and soft, and perfectly matched to their evening.

In the distance, dark clouds rolled in.

They talked some more, and drank some more.

Sam could have listened to her voice, and looked into those beautiful blue-green eyes all night if she let him, and would have wanted nothing more out of life.

He looked at her for a long time.

Freya turned to face him, tilting her chin, so that their eyes met. He felt the warmth of her breath on his skin. She slowly wrapped her arms around his neck and kissed him.

It was a sweet moment. Her lips on his were soft and mobile. He closed his eyes for a second and inhaled the scent of her skin.

She pulled back, briefly.

Freya stared at him with her bewitching eyes. Her lips, supple, and sexy, set in an expression of restraint, as she examined him.

After a few seconds, restraint seemed to give way to desire, and she wrapped her arms around his neck and pulled him in tight. She had an impish and lascivious grin spread out across her parted lips, the tip of her tongue just touching the spacing between her white teeth. A moment later they surrendered to their every desire.

The wine bottle emptied and the first images of lightning began to register on the distant horizon, making the world outside flash. It was as though they were taking mental photographs of their perfect night, in the hope they would remember these feelings for the rest of their lives.

Chapter Fifty-Five

Sam lay awake beneath the myriad of stars.

Freya was curled up asleep with her head on his chest, and his arms wrapped protectively around her body. His mind reeling from what had just happened. At nearly forty years of age, he'd been fortunate enough to be in love twice. But if he wasn't careful, Freya might just make it a third time. If he was honest with himself, he was falling hard. He had some experience with love, even though he'd never been married.

Something was different here…

He thought about the way they made love.

Everyone was different in bed. Some people were submissive, some liked to take control, some were serious, angry, happy… Freya was all of these… but she was different… too…

There was another word for her…

Something that really lingered with Sam. Like something he'd always been missing but never even knew about. It played on his heartstrings and teased him.

He thought about the word… trying to find the right description… before finally landing on…

Playful.

Freya had a mischievous, almost wicked sparkle in her witchy eyes during sex. It teased him… almost daring him…

He opened his eyes.

To the east, the first faint light of morning had begun to consume the lowest stars on the horizon.

Freya stirred, rolling over to kiss him. Her lips were soft and responsive. It was a short, sweet, embrace, before she pulled away.

It was time to get going if they were to reach the ranger's outpost.

Chapter Fifty-Six

Hwange National Park, Zimbabwe

The Albino was dying.

He had been walking for weeks now. Living off the land, but his strength was leeching from his body with every day. He still hadn't reached civilization and what's worse yet, he didn't even know if there would be much civilization left by the time he reached it.

The doctor kept moving, but it now took so much effort just to take a step that the task of reaching the next waterhole seemed impossible, and much too onerous to achieve. The sun was gaining, and the sensitive skin of his face kept burning, despite the wrapping of his keffiyeh.

He paused and looked at the small, black case that held six vials of the deadly virus. It would be irrelevant by now. He imagined much of the world would already be infected. What was it that his leader had told him?

You can't put Pandora back into the Box.

He put the case away and kept it, just in case.

More time seemed to pass, given the movement of the sun across the horizon, and yet, he felt as though he hadn't moved at all.

After a few minutes, he felt ready to give up.

He pulled back at the delicate chain that held the medallion so that he could look at it for a millionth time.

It was an ancient tribal Afghan necklace with natural Afghan lapis lazuli and silver medallion.

He turned it over.

A series of numbers were engraved in its backing.

Despite his best efforts, he never discovered what those numbers meant.

And now, it was unlikely that he ever would.

He should have kept going. He wanted to. But his legs wouldn't listen.

The Albino stumbled.

The ground offered a comfort to his pained feet. He wanted to get up, but he couldn't. Instead, he lay there, the warmth of the sun burning his back.

After a while, a soft wind lulled him into a shallow sleep, and he dreamed of when he was a boy...

Chapter Fifty-Seven

Pul-e Khishti Bazaar, Kabul, Afghanistan – 1989
It was a bitterly cold morning.

A father and son walked through the ancient city. Their hurried breaths crystalizing into mist. The Afghan city of Kabul was situated some 5,900 feet above sea level in a narrow valley, wedged between the domineering Hindu Kush mountains. The gray sky of pre-dawn turned a vibrant shade of pink before edging toward purple and a few seconds later, the snow-covered mountains that shrouded the ancient city turned golden as the distant sun crept over the crest of the awe-inspiring peaks. The first splintered rays of warmth glistened tediously across the city, casting shadows along the banks of the Kabul River.

At just five years old, Firooz Sayyid already knew that he was very different from the other children – in every respect. The first light touched the delicate skin of his face. He instinctively pulled the keffiyeh across his young, innocent face to protect himself. He wore both a traditional Afghan woolen pakol, as a sign of respect, and the keffiyeh so that it could shield him from the imminent dangers the new day bore on his eyes and skin.

Out of habit, his gaze turned downward. He walked quickly. Dawn was breaking and it wouldn't be long before its heat would be too much for him.

Holding his hand, his father sped up, hurrying them along in a race against the rising sun. They walked across the Pul-e Khishti bridge, where its small bricks spanned the dried-up, garbage-strewn Kabul River, to the old city in the south bank. There, Afghan men gathered to smoke heroin, seeking a fleeting escape from poverty and war. To the west, the blue dome of the Pul-e Khishti Mosque rose majestically toward the sky. Twin minarets towered above, casting long, narrow shadows. The muezzin stepped out from the balcony of the one on the left, and began to recite the dawn adhan – the Islamic call to prayer.

They entered the Pul-e Khishti Bazaar open air marketplace.

Many of the buildings had been damaged by the Soviet-Afghanistan War, which had been going on longer than Firooz had been alive. According to his father, the war was fought between Afghanistan rebels called the Mujahideen and the Soviet supported Afghanistan government. The United States had supported the Afghanistan rebels – both financially, and with high quality military equipment and technology. The Americans wanted the communist government to be overthrown, thereby preventing the evil spread of communism.

Firooz was smart for his age, but he couldn't tell you the meaning of communism. He didn't have to, all he knew was that because of communism, war had ravaged his homeland, leaving his people in desperate poverty and at constant risk of starvation.

Pul-e Khishti Bazaar was Kabul's main open-air market.

Firooz always liked coming to the place. As soon as he entered, he was enveloped by a dissonance of sight, scent, and sound. Pul-e Khishti Bazaar, in the Old City, was regarded as not only one of the most ancient but also one of the most beautiful outdoor markets in the world – a jewel of a tourist attraction during Kabul's pre-war era, a happier time of outdoor cafés, treed streets, short skirts, and abundant hashish.

His father turned down a narrow alleyway into the bazaar, where slaughtered sheep and cattle hung upside down on heavy iron hooks. Off to the side, their skins lay in neat, folded squares beside decapitated heads. Internal organs – so vibrantly red they were almost neon – hung next to the carcasses that once cocooned them. One magnificent white ram with corkscrew horns, his crown of curls hennaed red, rested with its spindly legs tucked underneath, oblivious to the blood miasma of his slaughtered brethren.

Next to a lean-faced man selling fresh-brewed tea was another narrow wooden stall, its keeper a blue-turbaned Sikh spice trader. Bright yellow, orange, and bronze spices such as turmeric and saffron, as well as rose petals used in perfume making, were displayed out front in utilitarian metal containers. One famous fragrance, *7 Virtues,* used the perfumes from Afghanistan orange blossom oils and rose oils. Its signature scent, the *Noble Rose of Afghanistan,* was made from the essence of 178 hand-picked rose petals from the province of Jalalabad.

Near the carnage of meat were carts piled high with harvest vegetables. There were corpulent purple eggplants, striped pale-green melons piled like boulders, jade clusters of grapes, and plump, perfectly complexioned apples like the sunburned cheeks of children. Emerald-green cilantro and mint were stacked in sheaves, the scent as startling as perfume. Indeed, this is increasingly what Afghanistan mint is being used for. French perfumers are buying it in bulk to distill for use in their scents.

At the end of the Ka Farushi bazaar, his father stopped outside an unobtrusive and heavily dilapidated concrete building, riddled with deep scars of shell blasts and bullet holes. In abject contrast, the façade was adorned with bright colored fabric, strings, and intricately carved wooden spools.

They had reached the kite shop.

Flying kites was a national pastime in Afghanistan. At the peak of this tradition was the kite fight. The objective of the kite fight was to slice the other flier's string with your own, sending the vanquished aircraft to the ground.

Kite flying in Afghanistan is a pastime, but "kite fighting," was a competition.

A kite fight consists of two expert kite flyers who fly their kites and then try to cut loose the other party's kite in the air. And for this purpose, they need a kite string that can cut well, therefore they prepare a type of string that is glass coated "cutting" line called Tar in the Afghan language. They coat the string of the kite with powdered glass to increase its cutting ability. Any kite that is cut loose is a free kite and whoever catches it, owns it.

Afghan fighter kites are similar to the Indian Fighters in that they are made from tissue paper and bamboo. The biggest difference is that they are much larger than the typical Indian fighters. The wingspan on an average Afghan fighter kite is 3.5 feet long, some even up to a 5-foot wingspan. Because of the kite's size, the line is usually 9 lbs or more, and they think nothing of using all 1000 ft. when fighting, sometimes they even tie on more line while they are flying.

Rules in an Afghan fighter competition...

THERE ARE NO RULES!

Everyone puts up his kite – this is strictly a Male dominated event and the fighter usually has an assistant to help with the line and spool. There can be over 25 kites in the air at any given time, all fighting. These large kites have quite a pull to them when up in the air, but most of the fighting is done with Release cutting which requires a lot of patience. The young kids on the ground have a great time trying to capture the cut kites, and can compile quite a collection by the end of the day.

Firooz was one of the very best pilots in the country.

And today, he was going to compete against the very best in the game.

His father had gone to great lengths to have the very best fighting kite made for him. His father paid the craftsman and the storekeeper handed Firooz the kite.

Firooz thanked the storekeeper.

He pulled back his keffiyeh and the sight of his face, caused the man to draw a breath.

Even at five years of age, Firooz was used to the reaction.

It was because of his eyes.

They were a rare mixture of dark, vibrant blue in one eye, and a deep green in the other. It gave him a striking, yet unnatural appearance, like some sort of distant galaxy, beneath long, pale eyelashes – making a jarring contrast against his ghost-white skin.

His father, an educated man, had gone to some lengths to discover that the cause of such an appearance was the result of two separate genetic disorders. One being albinism and the other sectoral heterochromia. The former, a condition that reduced the amount of melanin pigment in his skin, eyes, and hair, while the latter caused a difference in coloration of the iris.

The combination of the two conditions were so rare that few had ever seen it, and no one in Kabul had ever been exposed to it. As a result, people often reserved a mixture of fear, superstition and awe when they met him.

God, in his wise, yet perverse wisdom, had gifted him with an equally rare mind. His memory was exceptional, but his ability to learn and comprehend new information unmatched. Already, he'd learned to read and write in 3 different languages, including English, which his father had insisted upon, telling him that if he were to ever use his gifts, he would need to first escape Afghanistan.

They took the new kite to the flying ground.

Firooz loved his new kite, and flew it gallantly. He was one of the best fighters in Kabul, and today he had been lucky. He won the competition, personally destroying five other kites in the battle. When the game was over, he reeled his spool in and his father grabbed the kite.

It was the best day of his life.

On their way home, his father was met by a man neither of them knew. The stranger asked his father something Firooz couldn't understand about a place he'd never heard of. Without waiting for his father's response, the stranger withdrew a Pesh-kabz – a traditional Afghan knife, commonly used by tribesmen along the Khyber Pass.

Then he stabbed his father in the chest.

The assailant ran off.

It was only a small wound, but the blade had pierced the vital organs near his father's heart. Even at such a young age, he knew without any doubt that his father had been delivered a mortal wound.

Chapter Fifty-Eight

Firooz hugged his father.

There were tears streaming down his eyes.

His father said, "You are special Firooz. Very special. Your brain is incredible, and you are going to do amazing things. God, in his wisdom has chosen you for a great purpose."

"Father! Don't go…"

He whispered, "I am dying son…"

"No!" It came out as an emphatic whimper.

His father lifted a single hand to get his son's attention. He removed a medallion from where it hung around his neck, sitting at his chest, and handed it to Firooz. "Take this."

Firooz gripped it and tried to speak, but his father stopped him.

"Go find your mother and your sister. Take them to the American Embassy. Give one of the soldiers that medallion and they will take you away. They will take you away from this terrible place… promise me you will do that!"

"I promise," he said, obediently.

"Good. Now go. While I make peace with my maker."

Firooz ran all the way home to his mother.

There were tears streaming down his face. An awful, guttural sob forced its way up from deep in his lungs and out through his lips. He quickly told her the news, and what his father had commanded that they do. Without delay, they made their way to the American Embassy.

At the base, Firooz handed a soldier the medallion.

He looked surprised.

Turning so his back was to them, he used his radio to contact one of his superiors. But as the soldier turned around, a stray bullet whizzed past their heads. It struck the American soldier in the jaw. The second bullet went a little higher, and the man was dead before his legs gave way.

Firooz and his family took cover.

Soldiers protecting the embassy, opened fire.

When the monstrous sound of machinegun fire finally died down, Firooz stood up to run. But beside him, his mother, and sister did not move. He tried to cajole them on. But then he saw the stream of dark fluid running down their backs.

And in that instant, he knew he was now all alone in the world.

Firooz kept running until he was far away.

Cold, hungry, and suffering from indescribable grief, a kind man spotted him. The man said that he came from the mountains, and that the boy could come with him.

Without too much effort, Firooz agreed.

The man grasped his hand, and offered him food, shelter, and the true meaning of Islam…

Chapter Fifty-Nine

Hindu Kush – 1990

The Hindu Kush commonly understood to mean Killer of the Hindus, was a 500-mile mountain range that stretched through Afghanistan, from its center to Northern Pakistan and into Tajikistan. The range forms the western section of the Hindu Kush Himalayan Region and is the westernmost extension of the Pamir Mountains, the Karakoram and the Himalayas.

It divides the valley of the Amu Darya to the north from the Indus River valley to the south. The range has numerous high snow-capped peaks, with the highest point being Tirich Mir or Terichmir at 25,289 feet in the Chitral District of Khyber Pakhtunkhwa, Pakistan. To the north, near its northeastern end, the Hindu Kush buttresses the Pamir Mountains near the point where the borders of China, Pakistan and Afghanistan meet, after which it runs southwest through Pakistan and into Afghanistan near their border. The eastern end of the Hindu Kush in the north merges with the Karakoram Range. Toward its southern end, it connects with the Spin Ghar Range near the Kabul River.

Firooz sat inside the mountain cave.

It was a stronghold where young Islamic men learned to become Mujahideen. At the back of the cave, were a series of armory supplies, in an assortment of boxes. These included more than a dozen FIM-92 Stingers – man-portable air-defense system, known as MANPADS, that operated as an infrared homing surface-to-air missile (SAM) from infantry shoulders. From inside the cavern, he had a clear view of the valley leading to the Karakoram Range.

Gunfire erupted, and everyone took cover, retreating to the well protected depths of the cave system. It was a veritable maze that would take their Soviet attackers' years to flush out. At the sound of gunfire, everyone ran for safety inside.

All except, Firooz.

He would not cower in fear of the Soviets.

The little Albino stepped out to the edge of the cave and peered outside. Several men were making their way along the pass. They released their pack animals, and took shelter. He recognized the sound of AK-47s. The travelers were shooting, but Firooz couldn't yet spot their prey.

A few seconds later, the entire region erupted in the downward whoop, whoop, of an Mi-24D helicopter gunship. It was the most feared predator in the Hindu Kush, used by the Soviets to enforce their control throughout Afghanistan.

Like a colony of ants swarming to take down a large insect, his soldier brothers bravely focused their attack on the gunship. The helicopter banked, and quickly began to exert its greater firepower. It focused its deadly Gryazev-Shipunov GSh-23 twin-barreled 23 mm autocannon.

One by one, the travelers were killed.

Yet one man at the front of the group kept running.

The Soviet helicopter banked again in a large U-shaped direction, and took up the chase. The Albino couldn't stand by and watch any longer. He stepped back into the cavern, picking up one of the prized American FIM-92 Stingers Surface to Air Missiles.

Running back to the entrance of the cave, he placed the MANPAD on his shoulder, looked through the simple sighting mechanism, and aimed at the Soviet helicopter gunship.

He pressed the trigger.

And the FIM-92 Stinger fired, leaving a trail of flame in its wake.

The shot struck the Mi-24D on its fuselage.

The gunship exploded.

For a few split seconds, the massive rotary blade at the top of the helicopter kept spinning, as burning wreckage of the Soviet aircraft stayed frozen in the air, as if in defiance of gravity. Then the magic wore off, and the helicopter plummeted to the earth.

The helicopter and those inside her smashed into the ground, obliterating whatever parts of the structure had survived the original explosion.

The man who outran his compatriots survived. He casually glanced up at the mountain area, quickly ascertaining the location of the shot. Seeing the Albino, he waved.

The fortunate traveler approached the cave.

As the man got closer, the Albino realized he recognized him. And why wouldn't he? After all, it was this man who had saved him from a life of almost certain starvation back in Kabul. It made a balanced kind of sense. His friend had rescued him when he was a child. Now that he was grown, he had saved the life of his friend.

The man smiled at him. "Well, my little Albino friend, I always knew God had great plans for you. From this day forward, you shall be known as The White Tiger."

Chapter Sixty

London – 2021

It was the setting sun that woke the Albino.

Firooz used block-out curtains, but still a certain amount of light always seemed to escape. It didn't bother him when he slept, but somehow, its absence suddenly lifted him out of his unconsciousness, notifying that primitive part of his brain, that it was time to start his day.

He was an anomaly to his colleagues. He lived alone and worked permanent night shift. A world without harsh lights. He was an excellent doctor, devoutly religious, and believed in the genuine goodness of all people. He volunteered his time in third world countries with *Doctors Without Borders*, had a PhD in biochemistry and was an Intensive Care Consultant, in charge of the night shift at The Royal London Hospital.

Firooz sat down to eat breakfast of a bowl of oats with soymilk. No sugar or honey. He looked after himself and ate for nutrition, not pleasure. He wasn't one of those doctors who didn't take his own advice, who went against medical recommendations and smoked or were overweight.

His cell phone began to ring.

It was one of those original standard phone sounds. Nothing cute. No modern music or something that younger people liked to download in order to personalize their cell tones. Just the standard sound of a phone ringing. The sort of thing one has heard more than a thousand times by the time they're five years old.

Yet something so plainly innocuous, set Firooz's heart into a flutter. He jumped to his feet, immediately on edge. He only knew his work colleagues, and they considered him aloof and antisocial. Outside of the work environment, he had no friends. He knew he was a social outcast, possibly related to his strange albinism. Yes, Firooz had a cell phone, but very few people had its number. Nobody rang for social reasons. In truth, no one rang at all.

Firooz frowned. And let it keep ringing.

He didn't have voice mail, and the phone kept ringing.

Firooz glanced at the security monitors that displayed the image of the front door, side of his apartment, and driveway. As well as being somewhat eccentric, he was beyond neurotic on the subject of security. His whole family had been killed. He had seen many people die, and he didn't want to be one of them.

The phone kept ringing.

Who was calling and what did they want? But Firooz feared he knew the answer to those questions. Closing the blinds, he drew a deep breath, and pressed the green answer button.

"Hello?"

A man with a deep voice said, "It's time."

A shadow of terror crossed his face. He felt as though the temperature of the room chilled a few degrees. Firooz tried not to move. To quieten his breath. Anything so as not to disturb the man who was calling.

"Okay." He knew exactly what they expected of him.

"Good. I've been told it was time to tell the White Tiger that we found the Medusa's strain..."

Firooz was silent.

The caller said, "You know what that means?"

"Yes."

"Good. You must leave immediately."

Firooz panicked. "I have a shift at The Royal starting in thirty minutes."

"Cancel it."

"I can't cancel it. I'm the Staff Specialist in charge of the Intensive Care Unit for the night!"

"It doesn't matter."

"Of course, it matters!"

"No. It doesn't! If you fulfill your part, the death of every patient in that unit will become irrelevant sidenotes in the annals of a long-lost newspaper, discussing the evils of a civilization no longer in existence. So, cancel your shift. Say it's a family emergency and do your fucking job."

The Albino submissively lowered his eyes. "Yes, of course. I'm sorry. Where do I go?"

"Transport has been arranged. They will pick you up in fifteen minutes."

"That soon?" Firooz asked. "How do you expect me to pack so quickly?"

The man sighed. "Living among them has made you soft, White Tiger. But that's okay. Everything you need will be provided."

Chapter Sixty-One

Hwange National Park, Zimbabwe

Sam and Freya reached the Ranger's outpost by midday.

Most things had been destroyed or taken by rebels since the pandemic had shut the world down. Yet they found the phone, and fortunately the line was still intact.

Sam contacted the *Tahila*.

Elise answered the ship's phone. "Hello?"

Sam said, "Hello Elise."

"Sam!" There was a short hesitation, and a tap of keys. "What are you doing in a Ranger outpost in Hwange?"

"It's a long story." Sam expected more of a surprise from her about being alive. He was going to ask how she knew where he was, but he'd long since stopped asking how she performed her technological magic. "Want to send Tom or Genevieve to come get us?"

"Sorry, we can't."

"Why not?"

"The *Tahila's* been moved."

"I noticed," Sam said. "Where are you?"

"The Arabian Sea."

"Oh, obviously." Sam paused. Elise wasn't feeling in a mood to be forthcoming with much information. "What are you doing in the Arabian Sea?"

"The Secretary of Defense asked Genevieve to retrieve a blood sample from an old friend of hers who's working as a mercenary in Pakistan."

Sam frowned. "Why?"

"The Mujahideen in the Afghan mountains appear to be immune to the virus. They have left their strongholds and are in the process of reclaiming parts of Afghanistan attacked during the 1980 Soviet-Afghan war while the rest of the world reels from this disaster."

The reality of the news hit him. "The people of Afghanistan are immune to the virus?"

"Not all of them. Just the Mujahideen. The Islamic rebels from the mountains."

It was starting to make sense. But how the hell did Afghanistan manage to produce such an advanced viral weapon?

"One of Genevieve's colleagues has captured a Mujahideen soldier. They've taken a blood sample to see if they can reproduce the antibodies to create a vaccine."

"That's the idea."

"Why didn't the Secretary of Defense send her own team of SEALs in after the blood sample?"

"International relations are at an all-time low. They can't be seen to be getting involved in local skirmishes or taking sides."

"Why the hell not?" Sam asked exasperated. "That's what we do!"

"Not anymore. Our resources are a little tied up with the pandemic."

Sam sighed. "All right. Well, I'm glad to see you weren't too worried that I had died out here in the African jungle."

"Oh, we knew you were all right."

"You did?"

"Yeah, the satellite photos caught an image of you leaving Botswana's Tsodilo Hills."

Sam's eyes flashed anger, and he fought to suppress the fury that was boiling in him. "You knew I was alive."

"Of course, we did."

"Then why the hell didn't you send a helicopter to extract me?"

"Priorities," she said, noncommittally. "Saving the world from a deadly virus kind of trumps saving your life. Besides, we figured you'd get yourself out soon enough. It's not like you were in any real danger."

"In the African jungle?"

"Hey, you had your Heckler and Koch MP5 submachinegun. I'm sure if the King of the Jungle picked a fight you'd come out the winner. I mean, with a submachinegun, even you could probably hit a lion."

"Elise. Do you realize there are much bigger, more dangerous animals in Africa than lions?"

That seemed to rock her usual ironclad poise and confidence. "The lion's not the King?"

Sam drew a breath. "Not even close, apparently."

"But Disney did a movie about it!"

"I know, right?" Sam said, glad even Elise shared his sentiment of betrayal.

She took it well. "Oh well, no harm no foul. You're alive, aren't you?"

"Thanks." Sam glanced at the sun, slowly creeping overhead. It was going to be another scorching day. "So do you have a plan for an extraction point?"

"Yeah, there's an airport about three miles to the east of you. If you get going now, you should be able to reach it just in time."

Sam asked, "In time for what?"

"Tom will be landing the Gulfstream there in about an hour. If you hurry, he won't have to wait around for you."

Sam shook his head. "You're happy to send me through lions, leopards, hippos, scorpions, and crocs on my own, irrespective of how many days or weeks it takes for me to literally walk out of the jungle. But with Tom, you're worried about making him wait an hour?"

"You know as well as I do, we have no idea what sort of reception Tom might get when he arrives. If it isn't a warm one, he's not going to be able to wait around for you, and then you're on your own. Good luck, Sam." Elise laughed. "If it makes you feel better, I lost the bet. I predicted you would have reached us a day ago. You disappointed me, but I'm glad you're alive, all the same."

"Much better," Sam said. "Goodbye, Elise."

Freya looked at Sam's face. "What's the story?"

Sam picked up his backpack. "There's going to be a jet waiting for us at Hwange airport within the hour."

Chapter Sixty-Two

Sam and Freya climbed down from the Ranger's outpost. Glancing at the sun, he set an eastern course.

Freya stopped. "Omgosh! Look at this!"

At the bottom of the outpost, there was a large termite mound. Beside which, a swarm of large black ants appeared to be raiding the smaller termites.

Sam tensed, wary of what large predator might be approaching. Seeing nothing, he asked, "Ah, the ants?"

"Not just any ants. These are Matabele ants."

"Okay."

Seeing a clear lack of recognition on his eyes, Freya said, "AKA Paramedic ants."

"Right... okay." Sam made a concerted effort to look at them for about a minute and then said, "We have a plane to catch. Shall we?"

"Sure."

They kept walking.

Sam asked, "So what's the story with Paramedic ants, Miss Attenborough?"

Freya suppressed a grin. "Matabele ants, native to sub-Saharan Africa, lay siege to the termite colonies they eat by the hundreds, braving the potentially life-threatening bites of large soldier termites that defend them. When an ant is injured, the ant's mandibular releases a chemical trigger to alert the nearby "Paramedic" to take them back to the nest. The injured ant even rolls up into a ball to make it easier to be carried."

Sam's eyes narrowed. "What do they do, bring them back to a hospital?"

"You're not far off. It turns out their battlefield rescues are just part of the story. Back in the nest, ants take turns caring for their injured comrades, gently holding the hurt limb in place with their mandibles and front legs while intensely "licking" the wound for up to four minutes at a time."

"They treat them with "licks?""

"Yeah. Their saliva excretes a type of anti-bacterial agent, that prevents infection, and they have a 90 percent survival rate on ants that would have otherwise died of their battle wounds."

"That's crazy!" Sam got an evil look on his face. "Do you want to go back and jump on some ants?"

"Sam! That's terrible!"

"I'm joking!"

She looked at him, judging if he was serious or not. "All right, I believe you."

Up ahead, a couple white-backed vultures circled in the sky, before landing beside a carcass. Tensing, Freya raised a hand to stop Sam from walking farther. She aimed the rifle, ready to shoot if need be.

Sam waited in silence.

After a good minute, he asked, "What is it?"

"I don't know? There's a carcass on the ground up there."

"I guess if its dead, it probably won't hurt us."

She shook her head. "I'm not worried about the carcass. It's the other predators I'm concerned about."

They scanned the nearby landscape, but there wasn't anything they could see.

The vultures approached the dead animal. A second later, they backed away. Then flew several feet away. They looked frightened.

And on the ground, a man started to moan loudly.

Chapter Sixty-Three

Freya said, "He's alive!"

Sam stopped her. "Careful. We don't know if he has the virus."

She glanced at the body. The man was covered in clothing, but even from a distance she could tell he wasn't mummified. "That's not the virus."

They approached carefully.

Freya said, "Hello?"

The man didn't respond.

"Hello. My name's Freya and this is Sam. We're here to help, if you want it?"

The man began to speak, but it came out as an inaudible ramble.

Freya said, "He's confused. Probably severely dehydrated."

"Dehydration," Sam said, "Not the Medusa Virus?"

Freya shook her head. "No. Look at his eyes."

The guy was staring vacantly right at them.

Sam said, "One's green and one's blue. Do you think that means the virus is taking over his body?"

"No." She spoke with the confidence of someone who'd looked after people for the better part of their life. "That's part of his albinism. He's not infected."

"You're sure?"

She thought about that for a moment. There was no way to know for certain. "Yeah, I'm pretty certain that's just normal dehydration."

They sat him up and gave him some water.

He was a little incoherent, but happily drank the water as it was poured into his mouth.

He kept taking it until Freya took the bottle from Sam. "We'll make him sick if we keep pumping him with fluid so quickly."

"But he looks like he might need it?"

She gave him a direct look that without speech clearly said in a mocking tone, "Have you been a nurse for eighteen years?"

Sam nodded. "All right. I'll go with what you think."

"How magnanimous of you," she said, condescendingly.

The stranger soon began to come around.

His eyes went wide.

Sam recognized the rush of adrenaline in his dilated pupils. The man was bordering on insane.

He grabbed Sam with surprisingly strong hands.

Sam tried to gently placate him. The man was no threat to him in his current condition.

They locked eyes.

Sam said, "It's okay, we're here to help you."

"I'm sorry! I'm so sorry!" The Albino said, his voice husky. "It's all my fault!"

Sam's brow furrowed with confusion. "What is? What's your fault?"

The Albino seemed to appear to reach a moment of lucidity.

He met Sam's eyes, there was plenty of intelligence in there. The man's voice was somber and clear. "Everything! I created the Medusa's Curse."

Chapter Sixty-Four

Sam looked at the stranger.

His eyes were wide, but the lucidity seemed to be returning. The man's comment about the Medusa's Curse was so farfetched, he couldn't take it seriously.

Even so, he asked, "Why did you create the Medusa's Curse?"

The stranger said, "I'm sorry, what?"

"You said you created the Medusa's Curse. I'm asking why?"

"I'm sorry. I don't know what I was thinking…" A moment later, he seemed to drift back to sleep.

Sam paused. He exchanged a glance with Freya. "Do you think that was meant to be that he doesn't know what he was thinking when he made the Medusa's Curse, or he had no idea what he was thinking when he told us that?"

She shrugged. "I don't know. But I can't imagine the monster who created that virus would be lost, traipsing through the Hwange National Park in Zimbabwe. Just a thought."

"I agree."

They gave him some more water, and sat him up.

Freya firmly gripped and twisted a portion of his trapezius muscle in his shoulder, performing a test more commonly used to wake up drunks and people having drug overdoses. When done correctly, it caused a highly painful, but non-physically damaging response – unlike a sternal rub, which left bruising.

The stranger sat bolt-upright. "Ouch! That really hurt!"

Freya smiled in such a way, that offered reassurance, but also suggested he'd left her with no other choice, but to apply pain to wake him. "I'm sorry. You need to wake up enough to drink. Otherwise, you won't wake up at all."

"All right, all right. I'll drink."

She said, "Good man."

When he'd consumed a good portion of Sam's bottle of water, they stood him up. Sam said, "Come on, we need to get going."

A puzzled expression swept across his face. "Where?"

"Does it matter?" Sam asked. "We can't stay in the jungle."

"You're right. I'll come wherever you two are going. Out of curiosity, where are we going?"

"There's a flight coming to pick us up in about thirty minutes."

"Great. Where's it taking us?"

Sam sighed. "To be honest, I don't know."

They started walking.

Sam asked, "Did you create the virus?"

"What virus?"

"The Medusa. Why? How many viruses have you created?"

"To be honest, thousands."

He seemed lost for the time being.

Freya looked at Sam. "You know he's still delirious, right?"

"I know. I don't think he created the virus. All the same, I'd like to know who he is."

"Good point, let's ask that," she said. "Maybe something a little easier on his brain."

Sam said, "What's your name?"

The man looked back at him. Fear and curiosity plastered across his face. "Mike Haddock."

"What are you doing here, Mike?" Sam persisted.

"I don't really remember."

"What's the last thing you do remember?" Freya asked, helpfully.

"I was here on assignment. I'm a virologist, specializing in DNA genome editing. I normally work at London University Hospital, but six weeks of the year, during my vacation period, I work with Médecins Sans Frontières."

"That's very noble of you," Freya said. "I work for Doctors Without Borders too."

"You're a doctor?" he asked, and Sam thought he saw his eyes flash with fear. Then, as though resorting to humor, he said, "No wonder your trapezius squeeze was so painful. I'm lucky you didn't just do a sternal rub."

She laughed a little at that, stopping herself. "No. I'm a midwife. I was working to set up a Women's and Children's health clinic in Zambia."

Mike smiled at her. "That's very kind of you. You must be very popular. Everyone likes midwives."

She laughed. "No, they don't. But that's okay. The moms do."

Sam returned to the virus questions. "When you were a little delirious you mentioned it all being your fault."

"Yes. It was," Mike confirmed.

"How?"

"My job was to work out how to stop this virus entering the sub-Saharan Africa, where it would be difficult to manage given the nature of most people's employment in the region."

Freya said, "It slipped through, and you blame yourself?"

"Yes, I do."

Sam said, "How did you end up here?"

"My clinic was attacked by rebels. Most of the people I know were taken prisoner. I... cowardly escaped and saved my own life. I don't regret it. There was nothing I could have done to prevent my friends being taken prisoner. My conscience accepts that I did the only thing I could to survive."

"And then you ended up walking through the jungle searching for civilization?" Freya asked.

"Yeah. That just about sums it up."

They kept walking.

After a while, Sam asked, "Why are viruses so hard to kill?"

Mike said, "Well, the short answer is, it's complicated."

Sam smiled. "I gather."

"The fact that they are not alive means they don't have to play by the same rules that living things play by." The doctor stumbled, and Sam held onto his arm so that he could keep going. "Viruses have been among the biggest threats to humanity since the dawn of modern society, with the current pandemic showing how these pathogens can shut down countries, halt entire industries and cause untold human suffering as they spread through communities."

Sam said, "Viruses have also evolved in such a way that they are difficult to kill. What makes them, including the coronavirus, so tricky to cure?"

"Part of the problem is the nature of viruses themselves. They exist like freeloading zombies – not quite dead, yet certainly not alive."

"Really? Zombies?" Sam asked, thinking first we're dealing with an ancient Greek legend, now we're dealing in Zombies?

Mike said, "Viruses don't really do anything. They're effectively inert until they come into contact with a host cell, but as soon as that happens, they switch on and come to life."

"They switch on?"

"Yes. The odd makeup of these infectious agents is part of what makes them difficult to defeat. Compared to other pathogens, such as bacteria, viruses are minuscule. And because they have none of the hallmarks of living things – a metabolism or the ability to reproduce on their own, for example – they are harder to target with drugs."

Mike tried to talk, but his tongue caught on the dry coating in his mouth.

Sam handed him the drink bottle.

"Thanks," the doctor said, taking a swig and kept going. "Antibiotics, which are used to fight bacterial infections, attack the bacteria's cell walls, block protein production and stop bacteria from reproducing. But they aren't effective against viral infections, because viruses don't carry out any of those processes on their own. Rather, viruses need to invade and take over host cells to replicate.

"But a virus can't break into just any cell in the body. Instead, one of its proteins will bind to another protein – akin to a key fitting into a lock – which then allows the virus to hijack certain cells. With this outbreak, the Medusa's so-called spike protein primarily fits "locks" that are present in the eyes, which is why infection produces the tell-tale sign of the green hue around the otherwise white sclera.

"Once the invasion takes place, the cell in essence is transformed into a factory that churns out hundreds and hundreds of copies of the virus, based on instructions encoded in its genetic material – RNA, or ribonucleic acid, in the case of the Medusa."

Up ahead, they reached the airport.

They watched as a Gulfstream G280 came in to land.

On the far side of the airport, three Ford Pickups changed their direction to intercept the aircraft. The Gulfstream landed and taxied to their side of the runway, coming to a stop directly in front of them, turning around 180 degrees in preparation of a reciprocal takeoff.

Tom opened the side hatch, and a small set of stairs unfolded. A golden retriever greeted them with a bark.

Sam, Freya, and Mike all climbed in.

"Welcome aboard," Tom said, pulling the hatch closed. "Buckle up. We've got company. This might be a bumpy ride."

Chapter Sixty-Five

Sam jumped into the copilot seat in the cockpit.

In the distance, he spotted what Tom was worried about. Three Ford Pickups were racing toward the airport.

Tom folded his large frame into the pilot's chair. Pulling his seatbelt on, he pushed the twin throttles all the way forward.

He glanced at the pickups. "Friends of yours?"

"Not really."

"Didn't think so."

The Gulfstream G280 crept forward. Its two Honeywell HTF7250G engines purred smoothly, each one offering 7,624 pounds of thrust.

Tom did a mental calculation.

And predicted they were going to need every one of those pounds of thrust to takeoff before the rebels reached them.

The Gulfstream G280 slowly approached its takeoff speed. The Hwange National Park whipped past them through the windshield at 130 knots. Tom kept a little bit of forward pressure on the wheel, keeping them grounded until the very last minute.

In front of them, the Pickups drove through the wire fence and onto the runway, racing straight for them.

Someone started shooting.

The shots went woefully wide.

"It think that will do," Tom said, pulling the wheel back toward his chest.

The Gulfstream climbed with ease and Tom kept it steady at a rate of climb of 5,000 feet per minute, quickly taking them to a cruising altitude of 45,000 feet – just out of reach of most commercial airliners.

Sam said, "Where we headed?"

"At this stage, Dubai."

"What's in Dubai?"

"Nothing. It was just the closest place I could take off from. Why? Do you have another plan where to go?"

Sam shook his head. "I'm good." He unclipped his seatbelt, clasped his hand on Tom's shoulder and said, "Thanks for coming and getting me, Tom."

"You're welcome. Where's our guests?"

"One of them is most likely asleep by now. He's a doctor with *Doctors Without Borders*. Had some bad luck and nearly got himself killed."

Tom nodded sympathetically, and said, "And the girl?"

"Caliburn's entertaining Freya."

"He'll enjoy that no doubt."

"No doubt," Sam agreed. "I'm going to go check on our passengers, and then I'll come back."

"No problem." Tom said, "I'll bring us up to cruising, then put it on autopilot, and come join you."

Sam wandered back to the main cabin.

Caliburn was indeed entertaining Freya or vice-versa, Sam couldn't tell. She was teaching him tricks, and the dog was wagging his tail triumphantly, as he basked in her praise.

Freya looked at Sam. "Smart dog."

"You have no idea."

"I taught him to sit."

"Well done."

"Hey, I did! Want to watch? Caliburn, sit."

Caliburn didn't move.

Freya persisted. "Come on, you did it before… sit."

Caliburn rolled over.

Freya shook her head. "What's come over you? You followed all these things just minutes ago."

Sam waved a dismissive hand. "It's okay. I believe you."

"No, I'm serious. You should have seen it! Caliburn obeyed everything I asked him to do."

"Okay, now, that I don't believe. Caliburn rarely listens to anyone." He frowned. "Wait. No that's not true. He listens, but then chooses to do whatever he likes."

Freya tried again by lifting her palm. "Caliburn, can you shake hands?"

Caliburn crawled forward, looked at her and gave a single bark. It was curt and suggested that he was proud of what he'd done. His tail wagged enthusiastically.

"Ah… I don't care. I know you're smart," Freya said, patting him along his mane of thick, blond, hair.

"He should be, he's genetically engineered."

Freya glanced at Sam, trying to work out if he was serious. "Engineered? Why?"

"It was a secret military experiment. We rescued him." Sam smiled. "It brings a whole new meaning to the rescue dog, thing, doesn't it?"

Caliburn barked and nudged him in response.

"Yeah, we're all pretty fond of this old dog."

Caliburn barked again, playfully.

"All right, all right… you're not an old dog… but you are a genius."

Freya met Sam's eye. "Are you making this up?"

"No. I'll prove it to you."

"How?" she asked.

"Caliburn. Go get the Scrabble pieces."

Caliburn headed off to the back of the Gulfstream and returned about thirty seconds later. He stopped in front of Freya and dropped a bag of Scrabble pieces. Each one containing a single letter.

Sam said, "She doesn't think you're a genius."

The dog placed his head on his front paws, and mewled. His tail wagged, and if one could read anything by it, they would guess Caliburn didn't care what Freya thought.

Sam said, "Our guest thinks you're a smart dog, but doesn't believe you're a genetically engineered genius. Want to prove it to her?"

Caliburn barked. It sure looked like an affirmative.

"Good," Sam said, patting him. "Spell her name."

Caliburn pulled on the back of the pouch that held the Scrabble pieces. The entire packet fell out. The dog nudged them aimlessly, without spelling anything, and then barked. His big brown eyes darting between Sam and Freya, his tail wagged, as though he was expecting praise.

Freya laughed, and then, having thought better of it, she covered her mouth apologetically with her hand. "I'm sorry."

"Me too," Sam said. Then, to Caliburn, he said, "Hey, I can't believe you can't remember our guest's name. It's Freya. Got that?"

Caliburn barked.

The dog quickly set about moving the game pieces with his nose. When he was finished, he nudged them with his nose and then barked at Freya.

She laughed again, waiting to see what the trick was. Then she read it out loud. "F.R.E.Y.A!"

"See?" Sam said, "Smart dog."

The edges of her lips curled upward. She was incredibly beautiful when she smiled. "Yeah, smart dog. Nice trick."

Caliburn ignored that, and kept working on a set of words. This time it took a little longer. He had to keep nudging the pieces, as though searching for specific letters. When the dog was finished, he backed away.

Freya stared at the words left.

SEE HE TOLD YOU I WAS A GENIUS

Chapter Sixty-Six

Freya stared at the words.

Her eyes turned to Sam's. She placed a hand on his chest. There was a subtlety to the gesture, but no doubt about the affection. She smiled. "You're serious, aren't you?"

Sam nodded. "About Caliburn being a rescue dog from a military experiment?"

She nodded. "Yeah."

"Yes," he said.

"Wow. Amazing."

"How much does he understand?"

"About you?"

"Yeah, what I'm saying."

"Probably more than I do."

She laughed. "Amazing. Any other tricks I should know about?"

"Yeah, his hair changes colors just like a chameleon."

"Really?"

"Afraid so."

To prove it, Caliburn changed his color to perfectly match the leather seats, and mahogany armrest. Then, as if to say, 'Aren't you impressed with what I can do?' He gave a little woof and began wagging his tail like crazy.

"Okay, now I'm impressed." Freya gave him a good pat. Then, turning to Sam, she said, and I thought as an Attenborough girl, I had seen it all? How does it work?"

Sam said, "Caliburn was engineered with a mixture of DNA extracted from an octopus, among other things. He inherited from the octopus DNA a unique ability to camouflage its skin. The concept wasn't entirely rare in nature – albeit a little unusual for a dog – the defensive mechanism worked with chromatophores, or little sacs in an animal's skin and hair follicles, filled with pigmentation, that erupt in response to external impulses in its nervous system that allows its hair follicles to alter color as part of its intrinsic camouflage defense."

"That's amazing."

Sam asked, "How's the doctor?"

"Good. I think he's sleeping at the back of the plane. I'll go check on him."

"Okay, thanks."

Sam sat with Caliburn and poured himself a glass of water. He had a drink and patted the dog. Caliburn barked and nuzzled his nose into Sam's lap.

Sam said, "It's good to see you too."

Caliburn barked again.

Sam nodded. "Yeah, I like you too."

Freya returned a couple minutes later.

There was something deeply disturbing about the look on her face. An obstinate knot of fear twisted in his belly. It started to hit him like heavy raindrops.

Big thuds of fear.

"What is it?"

"I don't think the doctor is who he says he is."

The color drained from his face. It was as if the question had turned a spigot. His head swiveled toward the back of the jet.

"He's not Michael Haddock?" A puzzled frown formed on Sam's lips. "Who do you think he is?"

"I don't know." She placed a small, black container on the table beside him. Inside were six vials. Each one labeled Medusa Virus – version 1-6 – "But I found him holding these."

Chapter Sixty-Seven

Sam pulled up a laptop and passed it to Freya.

She connected to the internet and logged into her account with *Médecins Sans Frontières*. She found the staff page and list of medical volunteers, and typed in Michael Haddock. A name came up for an ED Staff Specialist, but the face was completely different to the man they had found in the Hwange wilderness.

Her eyes narrowed. "This confirms he's lying, but the question is, who is he?"

"I don't know. I can send a photo of his face to Elise, a computer whiz who works for me. She has access to some pretty secure databases around the world. She'll be able to find out who he is."

Behind them, they heard a man speak. His voice was hoarse, as though his throat had been damaged with dehydration. "That won't be necessary."

Sam looked at the stranger, who seemed to have improved remarkably in the short time on board. Sam wished he'd taken the time to search the man earlier. He now worried the man might be carrying a weapon. He suddenly felt vulnerable without a handgun.

In Sam's momentary pause, Freya lifted her double rifle and aimed it at the stranger. "Who are you?"

The Albino raised his hands. "My name is Firooz Sayyid and I am the man who created this terrible virus. I never intended for it to be used the way it has, and when I realized just how dangerous this thing was, I tried to tell my people it needed to be shut down. Instead, they released it upon the world. They also tried to kill me and my colleagues. I got away, but my fellow researchers did not. They also destroyed all the precious work we had done."

"The biolab in the Kalahari Desert."

"Yes, they demolished it with a hidden bomb, I had unwittingly carried myself."

Sam stared at the man. It was hard to believe he was looking at pure evil. He had a genuine, almost kindly face, filled with apology. Not the face of one of the worst mass-murderers in the history of the human race. The words escaped Sam's lips, slowly, and almost softly with a barely audible, question – "Why?"

Firooz said, "Why did I make the worst virus the world has ever seen?"

"Yes."

The Albino nodded. "To answer that, my friend, I must tell you a story."

Chapter Sixty-Eight

Over the course of the next thirty minutes, Firooz went through a heavily abridged version of his story. From his happy childhood, through to his father being murdered, the medallion being taken to the American Embassy.

Starving and being saved by the American backed Mujahideen rebels who lived in the Afghan mountains. Becoming what he figured Sam and Freya would consider, radicalized. Saving the leader's life by shooting down a Soviet Helicopter Gunship and becoming The White Tiger. Eventually, being sponsored to study medicine at Oxford, even working for *Médecins Sans Frontières* – that much wasn't entirely a lie – he'd worked all over the world providing aid to people in impoverished places. Going on to become a specialist in biochemistry, specializing in CRISPR, the new wonder technology for radically altering and editing DNA genomes, to make targeted cures – and eventually being called upon to create the Medusa's Curse.

When he was finished, Sam said, "I can understand some of the strange events that have shaped your life, but you must know, none of this makes what you've done right?"

Firooz nodded. "I understand that. I do. Sometimes we make mistakes that no amount of penance can make right. I assume that eventually, I will be handed over to the authorities, tried for my crimes against humanity, and most likely sentenced to death."

He spoke matter-of-factly, like someone who had already known the only outcome of a court case. It was impossible to imagine it going any other way, when the guilty party knows they're guilty. It seemed like such an insane waste. The man was clearly a genius. If things hadn't gone so terribly wrong in his life, he would have probably gone on to win a Nobel Prize for producing giant leaps in Science and Medicine.

Sam felt that inherently, Firooz was a good person, despite the horrors that he helped create. And as an intelligent man, he'd already reached the same inevitable conclusion that Sam had regarding the outcome of his life, which was that he would be tried and convicted in an archaic country that still believed in capital punishment, and eventually sentenced to death.

Out of curiosity, Sam said, "Did you ever find out why your father sent you to the American Embassy?"

Firooz shook his head. "I tried many times. But never found anything. You see, I have since learned that when my mother and sister were killed by the American soldiers, the American Embassy had been attacked. This was in January 1989. After the attack, the US government pulled its people out and closed the Embassy. Over the next two years, the CIA funneled 20 billion dollars' worth of American technology and weapons – mainly the prized FIM-92 Stingers – man-portable air-defense system, known as MANPADS, that operated as an infrared homing surface-to-air missile (SAM) from infantry shoulders to destroy the Soviet Mi-24D helicopter gunships into supporting the Mujahideen rebels."

Freya said, "Twenty billion dollars? That's a lot of money for the US to throw at some obscure war in Afghanistan, isn't it?"

Firooz shook his head. "As I understand it, the Americans were trying to prevent the spread of communism, and stave off the threat of a Third World War."

Sam had read the files. There were plenty of mistakes. Not to mention all these years later, those same, American made FIM-92 Stingers had been used on American Blackhawks and Humvees. But hindsight is a critical master. It is always easy to see what should have been done in retrospect. And he still believed that those in power at the time did what they thought was best – despite the unfortunate outcomes.

Sam said, "So with the American Embassy closed, you never got to find out why your father wanted to go there?"

"No."

"What about the medallion. Did it offer any hidden truth about your past?"

"No. Nothing. I have searched many times, hoping that perhaps it would lead to some secret that explained everything. But sometimes we search for answers or purpose, because, like a child, we feel the need to have everything explained to us, wrapped up in a nice package. But sometimes, there is no answer. Things just happen."

"Can I see the medallion?"

"Sure."

The Albino passed it to Sam.

It was an ancient tribal Afghan necklace with natural Afghan lapis lazuli and silver. The sort of thing one would expect to buy in a trinket shop. He turned it over. There was an alphanumerical number etched into the silver.

Sam asked, "Any idea what this number is?"

Firooz shook his head. "No. I've tried many times, but it doesn't match anything and there's no record of it anywhere. I've searched information about embassies, American and others, hoping that maybe there was a known code or filing system. Perhaps my father had tried to arrange a visa into the USA? I don't know. At the end of the day, whatever it was, it doesn't matter anymore. I've kept it all these years so that I can remember my father, nothing more."

Sam brought his phone up. "Do you mind if I take a photo of this? I have someone who works at the State Department. If this does mean anything, she might be able to help."

"Sure. But, as you and I both know, I'm awaiting a death sentence, so whatever you find is probably a little moot?"

"I know. It's just another mystery I'd like cleared." Sam returned to the task at hand. "There must be something we can do to stop this virus."

The Albino says, "I can make a vaccine."

"How?"

"Given enough time, I can make a vaccine from the current strain."

"How much time?"

"About a month."

"That's what it took last time. Of course, that's a vaccine, not a cure."

Sam said, "Afghanistan! You vaccinated the Mujahideen!"

"Yes. It was only so my brothers could take back the lands of our fathers. So that Afghanistan could be returned to those with whom the harsh lands belonged."

Sam was incredulous. "You destroyed the world to unite Afghanistan?"

"I never thought it would get so out of hand. The virus was supposed to be kept strictly within Afghanistan. Our people were supposed to have been vaccinated. They were supposed to reclaim our land while the pandemic raged and the unbelievers struggled to work out how to live with the Medusa's Curse... it was supposed to be a sign that God was on our side."

Sam didn't have time to play moral crusader or even look at right or wrong. The fact was, Firooz was the best person in the world to find a cure, not just a vaccine. Later, he could be prosecuted for the horrific crimes he'd partaken...

Sam said, "How long to make a cure?"

"And save those already infected?"

"Yeah. Is it possible?"

"A cure is always possible, but it will take time."

"How much time?"

"Months. Possibly a year. There will already be a lot of good people working on this."

"Any way to speed things up?"

"Yes."

"What?"

"I need the original virus."

"What do you mean the original virus?"

"The virus that's killing people around the world has been weaponized. The original virus was too deadly to be useful to us."

"Come again?" Sam said. "How can a virus be too deadly to be useful?"

"The original strain killed within thirty to forty minutes of infection. I tampered with its proteins, to increase the incubation period – that's when a person's infected and capable of transmitting the virus, but so far shows no signs or symptoms of the illness."

"Where could I find the original virus?"

"I have no idea."

Sam felt anger rise like bile. He controlled himself, as he knew he had to. Every second, let alone minute, counted here – for millions of people who were going to die around the globe. "Okay, where did you get the virus?"

"It was discovered in a mine in Siberia."

"Siberia?" Sam considered that. "The permafrost melted, revealing the virus?"

"No. A new bore hole was drilled in search of gold. They found gold all right, but also a secret Nazi steam train from World War II…"

"A Nazi train?" Sam arched an eyebrow. "What the hell was a Nazi train doing in Siberia?"

Firooz shut him down with the wave of his hand. "Who can say? The fact was, inside there were a number of American soldiers. Their bodies were mummified. An hour later, the geologists who found them were dead too – their bodies mummified."

Sam said, "They were infected with the Medusa's Curse?"

"Exactly."

"Okay. So where's this mine? We'll just fly straight to Siberia and find you a sample of the virus."

"It's not that easy."

"Why not?"

"The infected bodies were all removed and then the mine shaft was loaded with dynamite and the entire place imploded. It would take a month to reach the old train using a small army of digging machines."

"Okay. So how did the American soldiers get infected?"

"That's a good question. That I couldn't tell you. There's a theory."

"Go on."

"Have you heard of the Greek Medusa?"

"Sure. The Gorgon turned people to stone that looked into her green eyes."

Firooz said, "The green eyes belonged to a series of snakes that made a home in her hair."

"Obviously," Sam said with a little bit of sarcasm. "What about it?"

"According to legend, the Greek mask of this Medusa really existed. In fact, it was this mask that the American soldiers almost certainly found. If I had to guess, I think Hitler probably had access to the mask, and was trying to make a weapon, but the Allied Forces reached it before he had any luck making anything akin to a usable weapon. It is this mask that has the very original strain of the virus. If I can access it, it will change everything."

Sam was incredulous. "Why?"

"Do you have a doctorate in microbiology specializing in DNA genome editing?"

Sam withheld a smile. "No."

"Then it would take me a year to try and explain the reason. But suffice it to say, if I have the original strain, I can do something."

Sam said, "If I can find you this mask, could you make a cure?"

Firooz nodded. "Something that could be replicated and brought up to scale to save the millions already infected?"

Sam persisted. "Could you?"

Firooz didn't have to think about it. "Find me the mask and I'll get you a cure within a matter of days."

"Why can't you make the cure with the current strain of the virus?"

"It's too difficult. Everything's changed. I need the original strain – the one used before it had been weaponized." He stood and began to pace. "I need it, you see. To target the right proteins. That way I can isolate..." His mind seemed to wander as he continued speaking using medical and technical terms that only he could understand.

Sam lifted his hands to stop him as he was going over his head anyway. "But if I get the mask, you can find a cure."

"Absolutely."

"How can you be so sure?" Sam wasn't convinced. "I thought you said viruses are rarely curable, and that generally, treatment is in the production of vaccines?"

Firooz smiled.

It seemed somehow distant and forlorn.

Finally, when the Albino spoke, he said, "Because I already made one."

Chapter Sixty-Nine

Sam cursed. "You've already made a cure!"

Still pacing, Firooz stopped and threw his hands in the air. "Yes! Of course. We couldn't have this virus running unchecked throughout Afghanistan, could we?"

"Obviously. So why can't you just replicate your original findings?"

He shook his head. "It doesn't work like that."

"Why the hell not?"

"There are... complex equations. Things that we need to produce such an antiviral agent."

"So find them!" Sam countered.

Firooz shook his head. "Everything I've produced since this thing started was in that damned biolab in Botswana."

"And it was burned down."

"Yes."

"To prevent you from having a change in heart?"

"Exactly."

"And with it, humanity's hope of survival."

"If you can find that mask, I can replicate the antiviral agent that destroys the Medusa's Curse."

Sam thought about that for a second. "Okay. So we need to find out where those American soldiers had come from. Can you remember anything about them?"

"No."

Sam persisted. "Anything at all?"

"Wait... they were wearing camouflaged uniforms with an American flag on their right shoulder if I recall correctly."

"Okay. That's a start. American soldiers who came into contact with a Nazi train. Were there any German soldiers?"

Firooz thought about that for a few seconds. "No."

"You're certain?"

"Not really. Fact was, I couldn't care less who was there. I was only interested in the virus."

"Is there any chance the mask was still on that train? I mean hidden somewhere?"

Firooz said, "It's always a possibility. But I doubt it. I had a team that searched the entire area, looking specifically for the mask."

"Okay. We're going to have to work on the assumption the mask isn't in that train."

"I can't be certain though," Firooz warned.

"It doesn't matter."

"Why not?"

"Because if it is in the train, the point is moot as it would take too long to find. By that time, you could probably find the cure on your own. What else have you got for me?"

"Like what?"

"Anything. Can you remember what the soldiers looked like?"

"They were mummified."

"No, I mean an insignia or something that might suggest where they had come from."

"Of course!" Firooz said, hitting his forehead with his palm. "I remember now. There was a strange emblem on one of the soldier's jackets. It seemed odd, that's why it stuck with me. The thing looked like a ghost, with three bolts of red lightning shooting out of its hands.

Sam grinned. "The 23rd Headquarters Special Troops – AKA Ghost Army."

"Come again?"

"They were a tactical deception unit during World War II."

Firooz considered that. "They tricked the enemy by using deception? Dummy tanks, aircraft, fake noise?"

"That's the one. Unfortunately, they served in a lot of places. What's more, the Ghost Army recruited from a variety of professions, including artists, actors, and museum curators. In fact, one of the reasons these soldiers might have come into contact with the Medusa could have been specifically because they were specialists in art or artifacts."

"That makes sense." Firooz considered the ramifications. "Suppose some of the Allied Forces penetrated a German stronghold and come across Nazi treasure. Now suppose somewhere inside, they locate the Medusa. Perhaps even Hitler – a known believer in the occult – might have tried to use it to produce a bioweapon? Either way, having found the strange artifact, who would you turn to in order to determine its value or purpose?"

"Someone from the Ghost Army who had a degree in fine artifacts?"

"Exactly. Find that person. Find out where they went, and we might find the Medusa!"

"It's a long shot, but one we've got to take."

Sam left Firooz in the care of Freya and Caliburn. Freya was happy as long as she could keep her double rifle aimed at the man.

Sitting down in a makeshift office with his laptop, Sam contacted Elise. He brought her up to speed with everything and asked if she could track down any historical reference to the Medusa during the Allied Forces great push.

She did some sort of computer whiz magic to make it so that his computer mirrored hers, so that he could see what she was looking at and vice-versa. Sam could hear the sharp staccato of her fingers on the keyboard.

A few seconds later, she'd brought up a list of the names of those involved in the 1,100-man strong Ghost Army and where they had been during the war. It was an extensive list, and pooled alongside the multiple battles, it made the possible computations untenable.

She then included in the criterion, any reference, or story, or anything about a Medusa or something that turned people to stone and then put the search criterion dates five years either side of WWII.

Only one came back with a hit.

"Bingo!" she said.

Sam's heart raced. "What have you got?"

"A 96-year-old French woman named, Nadège Rousseau, in the city of Brest wrote an article about seeing just such an event during the Allied Forces liberation. Her story was dismissed as crazy and never taken seriously. She never repeated the story."

Sam sighed. "I don't suppose she's still alive?"

"Still alive. And what's more... I have the address."

Sam grinned. "Thank you. Where?"

Elise said, "She still lives with her daughter in the medieval city of Brest."

"That's great. Thanks."

"Anything else I can do for you?"

Sam thought about it for a second. "Actually, Firooz Sayyid says his father, an Afghani peasant, gave him a medallion when he died and told him to take it to the US embassy. He assured his son that once he was there, they would offer him and his family a visa to America."

"Okay, I remember the story. What do you want to know?"

"There's an alphanumerical number on the back of it." Sam sent the image to her. "Any idea what it could have been for?"

A moment later, having looked at it, she said, "Yeah. I've seen that. It's a CIA operative's bailout number."

"Come again?"

"Undercover CIA operatives used to carry a particular code that looked just like that. It was a kind of life insurance. It meant, if the agent was killed or something went wrong, their families could return the medallion to an embassy. That number would be accessed for instructions, which would result in agreed upon pre-death provisions made for the family."

"Like a will?"

"Yeah, but it was more than that. Sometimes the operative might want to keep a certain message or something as a backup. Like a safety break."

"How did it work?"

"You have to remember these were the days before the tremendous rise of computers and the internet. People couldn't keep digital safes. Instead, this code, opened a specific fireproof cabinet with a complex lock that was stored at the Pentagon. Neither the agent nor the CIA staffers knew which code belonged to which operative. Only the locked safe provided answers. It kept both sides safe."

"Okay, so what could Firooz's father have kept secret?"

"I don't know. Anything. Everything. Maybe who they were investigating and why. You have to remember, these operatives worked in a world filled with cloak and daggers, smoke screens, and mirrors. Quid-pro-quo was the name of the game and spies had things on each other."

Sam said, "I just had an idea."

"What?"

Sam drew a breath. "What if the information stored on that medallion was so valuable and dangerous that Firooz's father was killed to keep it secret? And what if when his son and family approached the US Embassy in Kabul it made them a target? In that case, someone attacked the Embassy that day in order to prevent those secrets from getting out."

Elise said, "It's a strong possibility. I'll contact the Secretary of Defense and make some quiet arrangements."

Sam said, "Thanks Elise. Let me know what you find."

Then he strode up to the cockpit to talk to his best friend, the pilot. Tom greeted him.

Sam said, "Change of plans. We're heading to Brest, France."

"Okay, what's in France?"

Sam grinned. "If we're lucky, the Head of the Medusa."

Chapter Seventy

Brest, France

The Gulfstream G280 landed at Brest Bretagne Airport at 9:15 a.m.

It was mostly deserted, but being an airport, security was surprisingly still intact. Sam and Tom left Freya and Caliburn on board to look after Firooz.

The *Tahila* had retrieved the samples of blood from one of the vaccinated Mujahideens and was en route to the Mediterranean Sea to rendezvous with the Italian navy. There a leading biotechnician would take ownership of the sample and reproduce it. The vaccine would prevent people worldwide from contracting the terrible Medusa virus but would do nothing to save those already infected.

For this, Firooz Sayyid, had promised to do his best to make amends by creating an antidote. It was a wild long shot, but he was probably the most qualified person in the world to take that shot. And besides, if he failed, the world was no worse off than if he'd never even tried. On board the *Tahila*, a secure room down below had been transformed into a makeshift biolab. The Italian navy had promised to secure all the supplies Sayyid had informed them he would need.

There was a car waiting for them at the airport.

A bright yellow Citroën 2CV. In Sam's opinion, the machine might just have been the ugliest car of all time.

Conceived by Citroën Vice-President Pierre Boulanger to help motorize the large number of farmers still using horses and carts in 1930s France, the 2CV had a combination of innovative engineering and straightforward, utilitarian bodywork, with extra thin panels, reinforced by corrugating the metal. It was often called "an umbrella on wheels," the fixed-profile convertible bodywork featured a full-width, canvas, roll-back sunroof, which accommodated oversized loads, and until 1955 even stretched to cover the car's trunk, reaching almost down to the car's rear bumper.

They drove the short distance from the airport to the harbor.

Brest is a port city in Brittany, in northwestern France, bisected by the Penfeld river. It's known for its rich maritime history and naval base. At the mouth of the Penfeld, overlooking the harbor, is the National Navy Museum, housed in the medieval Château de Brest. Across the river stands Tour Tanguy, a medieval tower. To the northeast are the National Botanical Conservatory and the Océanopolis aquarium.

They found the small stone cottage overlooking the back of the harbor. It was a quintessential rural French cottage.

They knocked on the door and were greeted by the woman Elise spoke to on the phone. The woman was in her sixties. She carefully looked at both Sam and Tom's eyes, ruling out the telltale sign of the green haze around the normally white sclera.

She nodded. "You're all right to go inside."

Sam thanked her in French.

The woman took them to meet her mother, Nadège Rousseau. They found her sitting in a recliner chair, reading the leatherbound book of a journal. She was a short, slim woman, with intense eyes, and almost serene expression on her face. At a glance Sam could see the flowing handwriting of the journal was of yesteryear, and he wondered if she had once written those words. The daughter introduced them in French, and then told Sam she would leave them to talk.

Tom, unable to speak much more than a few phrases in French, stood silently, allowing Sam and Nadège to talk. Sam showed her a printed version of the original story she had allegedly written. He then asked her about the mask of the Medusa, and if she had indeed been the author.

Nadège's eyes became instantly alive. "Yes."

Sam asked, "How did you know it was the Medusa?"

The woman gave an audible grunt. She shifted in her seat, like something didn't quite seem right to her. "I was there the night they found it."

Sam said, in a quiet voice. "Go on. What did you see?"

There was a long, drawn-out pause, as though she'd forgotten where she was, or perhaps she was looking into the past. Then, just before Sam was about to prompt her again, she began to talk. And when she spoke, she had the animated authority of a much younger woman.

"You must remember," she began, "most of those men in the Ghost Army... they were just kids. Some of them were older than most traditional soldiers, mind you, but idiotic children none the less. Even the professor was still a youngster. They were passing that damned mask around like it was some giant toy."

"What happened?"

"Well, as you probably already know, that mask – it was evil to its core." The old woman sighed. "That's why Hitler wanted it. That was what he yearned for to comprehend. The Medusa yielded an unseen power. It was a harbinger of death."

"What happened after everyone played with the mask?"

"They died, of course."

"How?"

"They turned to stone."

"All of them?"

"Every one of them that had been close to seeing the Medusa's eyes."

"There's no record of this?"

She gave a shrug and there was a mysterious twinkle in her eye. "There wouldn't be."

"Did you report what you had seen?" Sam asked.

"Of course, I did."

"And?"

"No one believed me. Yet that is what happened."

"It became a big secret?"

"That's right," she said. "The whole thing was swept under the rug. After all, when more than seven million Jews are killed, what is a dozen American academics who turned to stone?"

"Your daughter said you've never spoke about it to her or anyone else in all these years since you wrote that article."

"No. I did not wish anyone to think I was crazy."

Sam laughed. "I understand. What changed your mind?"

"You mean, why have I come forward after all these years and agree to talk to you?"

"Yes."

"It is this plague, of course."

"You think they're connected?"

"Non." The woman's face was set with hard determination. "I believe it is identical. As soon as I saw those bodies, it was like washing away 75 years of my life. How could I forget? I was a young woman with her young man, consummating our love for the first time. Minutes later, we watched those men turn to stone as if by magic. Mark my word, whatever virus the Medusa held, it's currently ravaging the world."

Sam said, "I need you to concentrate very hard."

"Yes?"

"Do you know where the mask was taken?"

"After the men were killed?"

"Yes."

Sam leaned in close, as though he was really interested – which he was – to hear what happened. He said, "Could you tell me?"

Nadège smiled. "It's a long story, but if you have the time, I'll tell you."

"Thank you. I would really appreciate hearing it."

She smiled again, there were almost tears in her eyes. "I'll tell you, but I must warn you. It is the story of the greatest love on earth."

Then, she told them.

Chapter Seventy-One

Having listened to the incredible story, Sam thanked her and went to speak to the woman's daughter.

Sam said, "Your mother's an interesting woman."

"Thank you. She has lived quite a life. I suppose she wasn't much help, but I'm sure you brightened her day. So thank you, too."

Sam frowned. "No, no... she was very helpful, although some of it, didn't quite match up."

"Like what?"

"She said her husband stole the Medusa and buried it somewhere no one would ever find it. But the problem is, she couldn't seem to tell me if her husband is still alive."

"Raphaël Labouchère is my father, and he is still alive."

Sam heard the different surname and remembered that when a woman marries in France, she doesn't change her surname to that of her husband. Instead, women retain their surname as their legal name, which is used on official documents, and adopt their husbands' surname as a "usage name."

"Is there a way I can contact him?"

"Certainly. He lives at Belcastel. I can get you the address if you like?"

"That would be great, thank you so much."

"You're welcome, but I can tell you now, he never found that mask my mum keeps going on about."

Sam felt all his elation at finding the link, coming crashing down. "He didn't?"

"No way."

Sam frowned. "Your mother said that he and the professor, a colonel and art historian from the Ghost Army, rescued the Medusa and buried it somewhere."

The daughter nodded knowingly. "Yeah, she says a lot of things that aren't true these days."

Sam went on, "Apparently, your father and the professor stole the medusa from a Nazi Treasure Train. They escaped driving a Bugatti Type 53. Your mum said she and your dad used to drive that car out to a nearby lookout and just watch the night go by."

The daughter put a hand up. "I'll stop you there."

"What's wrong?"

"My parents never owned a Bugatti."

Sam said, "Your mum seemed pretty convinced. When she spoke about it, her voice was wistful, her eyes distant, as though she were seeing a beautiful memory. She said, 'It was green and like the color, it was the envy of everyone around us. We used to go out and have the most magical dates in that thing.'"

The daughter said, "Yeah, that never happened."

"Are you sure?" Sam asked. "She seemed pretty convinced."

"Mr. Reilly..."

"Yes ma'am?"

"My mother has end stage dementia. Most days, she doesn't even know where she is or who she is, let alone what happened during the war."

"Dementia?" The word hit Sam like a slap in the face. "She seemed so with it to me."

"It happens. Some days are better than others. It looks like you had a pretty good day with her today, but the fact remains, most of what she told you is pure fantasy." The daughter sighed. "That's why my father doesn't live here anymore."

"She doesn't recognize him anymore?"

"Not usually. He stays at Belcastel, with a small commune of monks, spending most of his last days on earth in meditation and silent reflection. He still loves my mother more than anything else on earth, but on most days when he comes to visit, she just gets so angry at the disease that he knows he has to leave her."

The daughter poured some coffee. "Would you like some?"

Sam shook his head. "No, thank you."

She took a sip and continued with the story. "My mother doesn't recognize him at all anymore, but what's worse, is somewhere in the back of her primitive part of her brain, her soul recognizes him, it stirs, and it gets so angry that they are no longer together, and able to share this world. In the end, my mother lashes out, burns so much energy she ends up sedated and sleeping for a week. But every now and again, she has a good period. When that happens, my father will come and stay with her for as long as she can handle it. Yet it always ends the same way... her in a state of incognizant fury."

"That's terrible."

"Yeah. It sure is."

Sam said, "I'll still like to go see your father. You never know, perhaps he can shed some more light on this whole Medusa thing?"

"I doubt it, but you're welcome to try. I'd give you my father's phone number if he had one, but I'm afraid he doesn't carry anything anymore. Like my mother, he's distancing himself from the real world — only in his case, it's a choice, whereas, in hers, it was stolen from her by a vile disease. I'm just warning you, it's the dementia. My mother is convinced about a lot of things that aren't real anymore, so you're probably wasting your time."

Sam said, "I know, but I thought when people suffer with dementia, it's a cataloguing issue with new memories. Like data — the recording device is still working, but it's retrieval of the data they struggle with. Old memories, like those from the war, were catalogued correctly, and are easily accessible. She seemed sharp as they come when we were talking about the events of the war."

The daughter shrugged. "I don't know what to say. But I can tell you this, my parents never owned a Bugatti."

Sam arched an eyebrow. "You seem pretty certain."

"I am." The daughter crossed her arms. "Look. My parents won the greatest lotto on earth in finding each other. I mean, they had the real deal. All that stuff modern rom-coms would like to have you believe about finding the one, and living happily ever after. We know it's all rubbish. But every now and again, someone gets lucky. It happens. Just about anything is possible given enough chances and my parents happened to be those people who fell into it. But that's where their fortunes ended."

Sam tried to keep track of her thought process. "You're saying they were rich in love, but poor otherwise?"

"My parents were both driven to help others. Something happened during the war. I don't know what, but they had two driving factors that influenced every single choice in their lives – one was each other, and the other was charity. They spent their lives helping others. It was a good life, but you don't get rich doing good for others. Do you understand?"

Sam nodded. "I do. Thank you."

"I hope you find what you're looking for." The daughter smiled, touched Sam's arm, and said, "Tell my father I love him... and that we miss him."

Sam said, "I will, I promise."

Chapter Seventy-Two

They headed out of the house back to the Citroën 2CV.

Sam was walking just in front of Tom. He felt a little lost and melancholy, as though the story he'd just heard was a tragic and sobering reminder that no matter how wonderful a life may be, it all has an end point.

He wasn't ready to give up hope of finding the Medusa.

The fact was, confused with dementia or not, Nadège knew things about the Medusa. Things that only a person who had actually seen it could have known, and there was no way to know for certain how much of what she had said was true, but right now, her husband was the only person on earth who might be able to shed some life on it, so that's where they were heading.

Sam was mildly lost in his own reverie. He thought about Nadège and decided she was right about one thing…

It was quite the love story.

A moment later, he heard Tom shout, "Look out!"

Before Sam could see what the threat was, he felt Tom's massive frame shove him out of the way. Sam landed hard on the ground, and rolled out of the way. Still standing, Tom had his Glock out.

A middle-aged woman carrying a knife moved toward them, growling and making stabbing motions. Her eyes glowed with the green hue of the Medusa's Curse.

Tom fired three shots in rapid succession.

The woman fell to the ground, dead.

It was a tragedy.

She was probably starving to death. As no one was willing to treat or care for those infected with a deadly and incurable disease. Especially one with a hundred percent mortality rate.

Sam picked himself up. Looked at Tom. "Thanks, Tom. You okay?"

"Yeah, fine. It was just a near miss."

"I'm sorry, I should have been paying more attention. I was lost in the love story of Nadège and Raphaël."

"It's all right. That's why you bring me along."

"All the same, thanks."

"You're welcome."

Sam would have liked to bury the woman, but there was no time. He made a mental note to call someone, but the fact was, they were on their way to try and save the world, and one more body being buried wasn't going to make a difference.

They got in the ugly car and drove back to the airport.

Halfway up the stairs, Tom stopped short, and said, "You better go on without me."

Sam frowned. "What are you talking about? What's wrong?"

Tom made an apologetic gesture with his hands. "I'm afraid it wasn't just a near miss..."

"What are you saying?"

"I don't know how it happened."

"What happened?"

Tom flashed with grief and anger. "Just look at my eyes."

Sam swore... the white sclera was a fluorescent green.

Tom stepped back.

Sam let him go. "We're going to find the Medusa, Tom... and when we do, Firooz is going to make you an antidote."

"I know you will," Tom said, still backing away. "I just wish it would happen in time."

"Twenty-eight days, Tom!" Sam said, "You have twenty-eight days. Plenty of time."

Tom went to close the door to the Gulfstream.

"No wait!" Sam stopped him. "Where will you go?"

"I'll steal a yacht from the harbor. A sailboat. Something French and fancy... a Beneteau or maybe a Jeanneau... nothing big. Something I can comfortably handle on my own. I'll spend my last days enjoying the waters of the Mediterranean." Tom smiled bravely. "I could think of far worse ways to end my last days on earth."

"We'll make it," Sam said.

"I know you will," Tom said.

Freya said, "You can't just leave him to die on his own."

Sam smiled. "It's all right, I have no intention of leaving him long enough to die."

"You can't know for certain that you'll find the Medusa!"

Sam's voice turned cold and hard. "I know, but when the time comes... I'll find him."

Tom said, "All right, if you're going to keep your word, you had better go now."

"Agreed." Sam said, "Are you sure you'll be all right on your own?"

Tom nodded. "Alone? I won't be on my own. I'll take Caliburn with me."

Sam turned to Caliburn. "What do you say, do you want to look after Tom for me instead of standing guard with the jet?"

Caliburn barked and ran past Sam, down the steps. In dog philosophy, it was always better to go somewhere than to be left behind.

Sam drew a breath. "All right. Good luck my friend. When you find a yacht, give Elise a call so that she can keep tabs on where you are. We're going to need to know exactly where to find you as soon as we have a cure."

Tom looked at him. "I'll hold you to that."

With one last longing look, Sam pulled the door to the jet shut.

Chapter Seventy-Three

They flew from Brest to Cassagnes Begonhes Airport.

It was the fastest way to fill the gap between them and Belcastel. Genevieve and Veyron met them at the airport. The plan was for Genevieve and Veyron to fly Firooz back to the *Tahila* so that he could start work on a cure for the virus. Ideally, he needed the Medusa, but there was still plenty to work on if Sam never found the mask.

They had secured a motorbike for Sam. A nightshade, Buell Firebolt XB9R. There was just one bike – transport was scarce. Sam had asked Freya if she wanted to go back to the *Tahila* to ride out the pandemic, but she agreed she'd rather stay by Sam's side. Then, seeing his concern for her safety, she pointed out that with Tom away, she might have to take over the role of making sure he didn't do something too stupid. In the end, Sam had agreed, only too happy to have company and her assistance. With just the one bike, she agreed to ride pillion.

They both carried Heckler and Koch MP5 submachineguns, with Glock 19 pistols as backups. Freya left her grandfather's Holland & Holland Royal Double Rifle on board the Gulfstream, agreeing with Sam's take on things, that the other weapons might be better within the setting of the urban jungle.

Before they all parted ways, Sam spoke to Firooz.

"I got a call from Elise, my tech whizz I told you about. I gave her the details of your father and the alphanumerical code on the medallion. She said it was a special sort of dropbox for undercover CIA operatives, stored at the Pentagon at Langley. In this case, it was your father. He was never a poor Afghani peasant. He was a highly intelligent CIA operative, and he was working on a case of embezzlement in the whole Afghanistan Mujahideen weapons supplies fiasco. Somewhere in the process, he discovered that another CIA operative in charge of the secret program, a man named, 'Michael Gallagher' had become a double agent, and was now working entirely for the Mujahideen."

Firooz looked blank.

Sam said, "Although, the Mujahideen knew him, as Abdul-Azim – Servant of the Knowing God."

Firooz eyes darkened, his expression looked shattered.

He knew the man. Of course, he knew the man. And why wouldn't he? After all, Abdul-Azim was the man who had saved him when he was an isolated, cold, frightened, and starving five-year-old child living on the streets of Kabul. It was Abdul-Azim who introduced him to the world of the Mujahideen. And years later, it was Abdul-Azim's life that a young Firooz Sayyid had saved when he shot down a Soviet Helicopter Gunship. It was because of Abdul-Azim that his entire life had been one long betrayal.

Sam handed him a small dossier on his father. "I know it's a bit late, but I thought you had a right to know who your father really was."

Firooz drew a deep breath, collected his thoughts. "Thank you. I appreciate it."

Sam turned to leave. "Good luck."

Firooz said, "There's something you should know."

"What?"

"I wasn't sure if I should tell you, but you have a right to know."

"What?"

"Tom doesn't have the 28-day strain of the Medusa virus."

"Come again?"

"I'm afraid the fact that his eyes have turned green this quickly means he's got the first weaponized version of the virus."

Sam knew that Firooz had trialed six different strains of the virus. "How long does he have?"

Firooz looked him in the eye. "Seven days."

Teeth tightly gritted, Sam nodded. "Then I'll just have to be quick."

Chapter Seventy-Four

Belcastel, Southern France

It was the early evening by the time the nightshade Buell Firebolt XB9R, glistened silver under the moonlight, as it came around the narrow bend, dropping down the hill and into the Aveyron valley in Southern France. They made an interesting team, with Freya riding pillion and her lithe arms wrapped around his waist. They brought almost no supplies, and were armed to the teeth.

Sam eased off the throttle, down shifted the gears, and the sports bike slowed as they approached the medieval village. They crossed over to the north bank of the Aveyron river along a small, single lane stone bridge. They were leaving behind the blacktop of rural France, in exchange for cobble streets, and a village full of lauze-roofed houses, dominated by the large 1,000-year-old fortress castle commanding prime position behind the village in the steep north bank.

He brought the motorcycle to a stop at the base of the castle. They stood up, stretched their legs, and left their helmets clipped on to the side of the bike.

Freya looked up at the medieval castle. "Nice place. I could imagine coming here for a romantic vacation with a lover one day."

Sam said, "I'm free after we find the Medusa."

She studied his face, her piercing blue-green eyes teasing. "What makes you think I was referring to you?"

"I'm sorry, I didn't realize. Do I have competition?" he countered.

"You don't." She squeezed his hand, leaned in and kissed him on the lips. It was a brief embrace, soft and sweet. She smiled. "Since you asked, yes I'd love to come away with you."

"Okay, it's a deal."

They made their way up the series of stony stairs through a narrow laneway that split the village in two. At the top, they followed a short walkway that rounded the backs of the village houses, before reaching the castle itself. It was easy to imagine a small group of monks avoiding the normal trials of society up here.

There was a small moat, and the drawbridge was drawn.

Sam shouted, "Raphaël Labouchère?"

A tall man slid open a door viewer. "Who's asking?"

"My name's Sam Reilly. This is Freya Capel."

"Are you aware this is a monastery?" The man seemed unhappy for the interruption. "We don't get many visitors."

Sam said, "I need to ask Raphaël some questions."

"What about?"

"The deadly mask he once buried with a Bugatti Type 53."

The door viewer closed.

Sam waited.

After a good minute, he turned to Freya. "Do you think that's their way of telling us he's not interested?"

"It must have been something you said," she replied with a suppressed smile creased upon her lips. "Because I kept my mouth shut."

Sam shrugged. "Must have been."

A moment later, the door opened, and the drawbridge was lowered.

The old man spoke severely, but not with malice. "Let me see your eyes."

They both looked at him.

"Very well," he said, "follow me."

"Thank you," Sam said.

They were guided into the castle through a series of narrow passageways, before opening into a private church.

"Labouchère is in there."

"Thank you."

Sam opened the door to the church.

The Nave was cold and dark. Candles lit the scene fitfully, throwing shadows like restless ghosts. Raphaël Labouchère was an old man, well into his nineties. His face gray and wearied by more than just fatigue. His hands were clasped around a golden cross, holding it to his heart.

The man stood up.

"So, my past finally caught up with me?" He glanced at Sam and Freya. "I've been waiting seventy-five years for someone like you to show up."

Chapter Seventy-Five

Sam listened with rapt attention as Labouchère told the story of the Nazi Steam Train being stolen by bandits, and how the Professor and he stole the Medusa and buried it. When he'd finished telling the long story, and Sam had told his, Labouchère agreed to reveal everything.

Sam said, "The US never knew who betrayed them but always thought it was one of their own people…"

"It wasn't," Labouchère said, "They were German."

"How could you tell?"

"For starters, they were speaking German." He winked and said, "Also, I took one of their service pistols."

Intrigued, Sam asked, "Do you still have it?"

"Yeah sure."

Labouchère retrieved it along with a map for where the Medusa was buried.

Sam looked at the weapon. "That's a Colt M1911A1. That's an American issued side-arm. The Germans were issued with a Luger P08 pistol, or a Mauser C96."

Labouchère looked at him like the guy about to reveal the winning card. "The Colt M1911A1 pistol was a sturdy pistol that was easily and quickly loaded and had the fire power to penetrate body armor, there were about 1.9 million pistols manufactured during WW2."

Sam looked at him, trying to see where he was going.

Labouchère said, "It's true. I've since looked it up on Google since you kids seem so intent on putting everything on the damned internet since it came about."

"Okay, but what does this have to do with German sidearms?"

"Everything."

"Go on."

"There were some contracts made before the war where the Colt M1911A1 was manufactured in Norway. These were still in motion when the Germans took over and occupied Norway. Therefore, there are about 900 Colt M1911A1's that have the Nazi Waffenamt codes stamped on them."

"You're kidding me?"

"The Waffenamt was the German Army Weapons Agency. Inspectors were responsible for the testing and acceptance of all weapons, equipment, and ammunition before delivery to the Wehrmacht. The Waffenamt code is the German inspection proof mark and can be found on firearms and equipment."

"Okay…" Sam said, glancing at the weapon. "Where's the code?"

Labouchère grinned and turned over the Colt M1911A1. On the back of the handle, was the Nazi Waffenamt stamp.

Sam smiled. "Well, we'll probably never know what happened to the stolen treasure, but at least it's nice to finally close the case that American soldiers or our Allies, had betrayed us. Thanks for filling us in on that score."

Labouchère spread his arms. "What do you want to know?"

"Where did you bury the Medusa?"

"It was MacCracken's idea… but I buried it inside a disused mine."

"Where?"

"Machu Pichu."

"Machu Pichu?" Sam was incredulous and also deflated, the distance meant it was unlikely he could possibly recover it before Tom died. "What the hell made you think to bury some ancient treasure in Peru?"

"No, I'm not talking about the Inca Trail." Labouchère clasped his hands together, his eyes looked up at the distant snowcapped mountains to the south. "I'm talking about the Iron Trail."

"Come again?"

"The highest mountain in the Pyrenees is nicknamed Machu Pichu."

Sam's heart raced. They were close. They were getting answers. "You buried it inside an old iron mine?"

"Yeah. High up there in the mountain pass there's an old, disused iron mine. It's mostly banded iron formations. Do you know much about geology?"

"Some. Not a lot."

"These are sedimentary rocks that have alternating layers of iron-rich minerals and a fine-grained silica rock called chert. There's a tunnel that heads due east. After a few hundred feet, it opens into a large chamber. Pass through this one and keep going along the same tunnel. After another fifty or so feet, it opens up to a second chamber. This is the one you want. On the ceiling to the western end of that chamber, a vein of iron ore runs through the ceiling in a south-north direction, and one of chert ran east-west to form a giant cross."

Sam said, "Is it very noticeable?"

He nodded. "Yeah. If you shine a flashlight on it, the iron ore lights up, and the cross reflects like one of those neon-lights out the front of a flashy church."

"Okay, if I find this... then what?"

"There's a pile of iron ore mine tailings – mainly hematite. It's a big pile, but somewhere in there you will find stones that don't belong inside an iron mine."

"What the hell does that mean?"

"Mixed in with the hematite mine tailings, is a pile of white quartz."

Sam scribbled a couple notes. "Then what?"

"The Medusa is buried beneath."

The edge of Sam's lips curled up into a suppressed smile. He arched an eyebrow. "You buried the Medusa beneath an iron cross? Was that for superstition or blind faith?"

"Neither. We weren't pirates, but Colonel MacCracken liked the idea..."

"What idea?"

"You know, X-marks the spot and all."

Sam nodded. He'd been on his share of treasure hunts over the years. "Okay. I get it." Frowning, he met Labouchère's eyes. "Why did the Colonel insist on keeping track of it at all?"

Labouchère's shrugged. "You mean, because he was convinced the thing was evil and would bring ruin to the world?"

"Exactly."

"I don't know. I wanted to destroy the mask, but he wouldn't hear of it. He kept talking about some sort of irrational gut instinct that suggested the Medusa would be important sometime in the future…" Labouchère tone was bemused and tinged with awe. "I guess he was right."

Sam pushed to his feet and Freya followed suit. He shook Labouchère's hand. "Thank you… for everything. You have no idea what this means. For a second time, I believe you might be responsible for saving the world."

"That's good. I don't really care for recognition, but it's nice to know the world is safe. I believe despite its problems, there are many good people who are rather fond of it."

"Yes, they are, sir." Sam turned to leave. "Your daughter sends her love and in a strange way, I believe your wife does too."

Sam almost expected him to argue that his wife didn't remember him, but instead, he graciously said, "Thank you. I'm sure they both do. I miss them with all my heart."

"We'd better be off if we're going to reach the mine and retrieve the mask."

"I hope you've got access to a good industrial water pump."

"No. Why?"

"In mines, all over the world, water seeps into the earth. It requires constant pumping. The iron mine had only recently been disused at the end of the war and was still dry, but when I checked on it a decade later, the entire thing was flooded. It will probably take you a month to pump all that water out."

"We don't have a month."

Labouchère said, "Then I hope you've got gills, because you'll need to breathe all that water."

Sam grinned. "As a matter of fact, breathing underwater is one of the things I can do."

Chapter Seventy-Six

Sam stepped outside.

A rabble had formed down the base of the castle. Someone had rolled the motorbike into the river for fun. Trapped and desperate humans could be relied upon to do very stupid, irrational things that they would otherwise never do in a million years, it would seem.

Freya said, "There goes our ride."

"Yeah… I don't know where we're going to get another one out here."

They stepped back inside the castle.

Labouchère greeted them at the drawbridge. "Forget something?"

"Our ride just got destroyed by a small mob."

"It happens." He turned the palms of his hands outward. "They tend to go through the town wrecking things each night. I'm really not sure what they're trying to achieve. After all, how does destroying things alleviate starvation?"

Freya opened her mouth to discuss the reason profound poverty leads to riots, but quickly closed it again, having realized this was not the time or place for academic discussion about social egalitarianism.

Sam was quicker on his thinking. He turned to Labouchère. "I don't suppose you have a car that we could borrow?"

"Yeah." The man sighed. "It seems fitting. Come with me."

Labouchère brought them around to the remnants of the castle's old dungeon, a place converted to a surprisingly modern garage. They descended more than thirty feet, through a spiral, stone staircase.

It opened up to the garage.

Labouchère pulled back the cover to reveal a green 1932 Bugatti Type 53.

Chapter Seventy-Seven

Freya sat down in the driver's seat.

It seemed only fair that if Sam got to ride the Buell Firebolt XB9R, she got to drive the antique sports car. Besides, if you compared the two vehicles, they were both roughly the same horsepower. She turned the ignition and the powerful Type 50 303.4 cubic inch, straight-eight engine came alive amiably on the first go. Whoever maintained the antique had done so lovingly and admirably. They thanked Labouchère and vowed they would take good care of the car – a promise they really hoped to keep.

She released the handbrake, applied a little pressure to the accelerator, and the engine's smooth supercharger whirred majestically. The four-wheel-drive system engaged, and the sports car pulled out of the driveway slowly. It was dark outside, and although the Bugatti was decades ahead of its time with its four-wheel driveline, using three differentials – front, rear, central – the car wasn't advanced enough to have headlights.

Fortunately, there was a full moon, and the sports car cast a silver shadow as Freya waved goodbye and eased the car gently through the narrow, cobbled streets, crossed the Aveyron river, rounded the bend out of sight of the Belcastel – and gunned the engine.

Freya laughed with pleasure as she pushed the antique sports car to race through the deserted rural roads of southern France. It felt like an overpowered go-kart, or a motorcycle with four wheels. Definitely, nothing akin to a modern car.

While Bugatti bodies are generally lithe and aerodynamic, style appeared to have been an afterthought in the Type 53, with its heavily louvered hood, rudimentary seating area and huge fuel tank behind the driver.

There was good reason for the four-wheel-drive experiment. By 1930, Bugatti's five-liter straight-8 was capable of 300 horsepower in competition form, powering a car weighing around 2,000 pounds. He remembered this was back when shock absorbers used friction instead of fluid, automobile axles were beams, and the width of your palm covered the tread of a race tire. Imagine, then, 300 horsepower . . . on a wet road in a car that light!

They drove through the night, taking turns to sleep and to drive – although not at the same time – and arrived at the southern French city of Perpignan. It skirted the Mediterranean coast on one side and the start of the Pyrenees Mountains on the other.

It was roughly nine a.m. by the time Freya decelerated, taking it slow as she drove into the city. It was easy to see it had once been the capital of the Kingdom of Majorca during the 13th century, and a significant Catalan influence was evident everywhere in its medieval core. South of the old town, the huge Gothic-and-Romanesque Palace of the Kings of Majorca had ramparts with views to the coast. In normal times, it was a mecca for modern adventure tours – with everything ranging from SCUBA diving, boating, whitewater rafting, canyoning, through to paragliding, and most importantly, cave diving.

The place seemed deserted.

Sam exchanged a glance with her. "Not in a million years would I have believed that the world would be plunged into the depths of darkness as it succumbed to a virus, every bit as bad as all the worst dystopian futures thriller writers might imagine."

Freya shook her head. "It's incredible, isn't it?"

She drove another two blocks before Sam's Google maps on his phone indicated that they had reached their destination.

Freya pulled to the curb and parked outside the front of an Adventure Dive Shop.

She glanced at the barred door and the closed sign. "There's no way the dive shop's going to be open."

"Then we'll just have to open it ourselves."

"And what, just take what you want?"

"What we need," Sam said, as though it was all about the wording. "But yeah, taking what we want will work."

She shook her head. Licked her lips and laughed.

Sam met her eye. "What is it?"

"You guys steal a lot of stuff, don't you?"

Sam suppressed a grin. "Hey, we're still trying to save the world."

She lifted her hands. "I'm not complaining, just saying…"

He laughed with her. "I'll leave them an IOU, I promise."

Chapter Seventy-Eight

In the end, they stole two sets of dive gear and another tank of fuel.

Sam wished they had been able to find another, more suitable car to use. Promises to Labouchère be damned, they were trying to save the world, and cars could be replaced. But unfortunately, they were in a ghost town, completely devoid of people and cars.

They had to tie the dive tanks to a small steel rod that extended out from the engine bay. Sam wished they could have brought more tanks, but would have to reach the medusa on their first dive. By Labouchère's description of the mine, it would be an easy dive, and the Medusa shouldn't be too difficult to locate. The dive gear itself was all packed into a large dive bag. That had been strapped onto the car's massive gasoline tank behind the driver's seat.

It took them the better part of the day to climb the winding roads through the Pyrenees Mountains, before finally reaching the gravel track to the entrance of the mine at 3 a.m.

Sam parked the car, began to empty the dive gear, and set it up. He switched on his flashlight and took a walk to the entrance of the underground mine. It was a horizontal opening, known as an adit, and led slowly deeper into the earth. Freya followed. Their twin flashlight beams flickered on the narrow walls. The place seemed dry for a hundred or so feet, before the light finally reflected on the water up ahead.

Sam stopped and studied the natural gradient of the mine. "We'll have to walk another hundred feet before we dive. It shouldn't be too bad."

Freya sighed. "Didn't Labouchère say something about it being a hundred feet in?"

"Yeah, but…"

She crossed her arms. "What?"

"I was going to say, he's an old man. I mean really old, and he buried it seventy-five years ago. Let's give him a little benefit of the doubt that his numbers might just be a little off."

Freya's mouth dropped open. "A little off? We're going to descend into a flooded mineshaft in search of an artifact buried long ago, and you're not concerned about the mental map we've been given being a little off?"

"Hey, I'm working with what I've got." Sam shrugged. "It should be an easy dive."

"Really?"

"Sure. We head east until we find a chamber, pass on straight through it until we reach the second chamber, retrieve the treasure, and then dive west until we're no longer diving." He grinned. "Child's play."

Freya ran her eyes across the narrow walls of the mine shaft, her eyes flashing with a shadow of fear. She swallowed. "I don't know what you did for entertainment as a kid, but my childhood sure as hell didn't take me down flooded hell holes."

Sam shrugged. "If you'd rather wait outside and mind the car, I'll try not to be too long."

Freya thought back to the rebels in Africa, the woman who attacked Sam in Brest, Tom's infection, and the rabble who destroyed their motorcycle in Belcastel. She forced herself to take a deep breath and exhale. "No, I think I'll come with you."

Chapter Seventy-Nine

Machu Pichu, Pyrenees Mountains – France

It was four a.m. by the time they had fully set up their dive gear, donned their wetsuits, and were ready to dive. Despite Freya's protestations that maybe they should wait until daylight to dive – an idea Sam had mercilessly rebuked on the argument that they couldn't wait until midday. Besides, it would always be cold and dark deep inside and underwater in the mine.

They switched on their dive flashlights and slowly entered the mine. Freya drew a breath.

It was insane what she was about to do, but what choice did she have?

The temperature was icy as they traipsed through the shallow water. It ended up being a hundred and fifty feet before the water was so deep that they needed to dive.

Sam glanced at her. "Are you all right?"

"Fine. I've got my open water dive ticket. I've done… twenty dives with tour guides in beautiful, warm, exotic locations…" She bit her lower lip. "Did I mention they were always warm and filled with light? I'm sure I'll be fine."

"Really?"

She drew a breath, feeling a little claustrophobic. "Yeah, I'm afraid of sharks and other creatures in the dark… but I can do freshwater caves."

A couple of bats, spooked by their flashlights, turned and flew over her and Sam's head. They made an awful clicking sound that she felt belonged inside some sort of Stephen King novel.

Sam clasped his hand on her forearm. "It's going to be okay. I'll be with you the whole time. I'll take care of everything."

Freya found Sam's voice calm and soothing. She looked into his blue eyes, and saw they were filled with the certainty of experience. She nodded. "All right, Sam. I trust you."

"Good. I'm right here if you need me."

"How will I get your attention?"

"I'll be right next to you. If you start to panic, I'll know."

The curves of her lips dipped inward with nerves. "What if I'm a silent panicker?"

Sam shrugged. "We'll just have to hope that I'm so well connected to you, that I'll just happen to pick that one up. Okay?"

She nodded, "Okay."

Although she felt anything but.

Freya placed her dive-mask on her face, put the regulator into her mouth, and slowly dipped beneath the water.

With her flashlight in her right hand, it cast a narrow beam through the crystal-clear waters of the mine shaft. The tunnel looked like it might go on forever. Her pulse kicked up, she fought to slow her breathing.

Beside her, Sam motioned for her to start swimming.

It had been a while since she'd gone SCUBA diving, and she'd never cave dived. It took a few seconds for it to all come back to her. Adjusting the air in her buoyancy control device, she slowly made her descent. She equalized the pressure in her ears by swallowing until they popped. It was all a giant balancing act built on frequent, minor adjustments.

She could do this.

All she had to do was forget about the fact that a mountain was above her instead of open water leading to the surface. Forget that if she messed up her buoyancy control, she would disturb the silt, turning the clear tunnel into a silt-out, leading to instantaneously achieving zero visibility.

She glanced at her dive gauge, feeling reassured that the numbers had barely shifted. She remembered Sam pointing out the fact that the dive would be shallow. Under ten feet the entire time. At such shallow depths, they would have plenty of air time. She kept kicking her fins, keeping pace with Sam. It felt nearly impossible to judge how far they had swum.

The mine tunnel seemed to go on forever.

Freya shifted the beam of her flashlight around in a wide arc. The light bounced off the constricted walls, and then stopped. She waved it the opposite direction, and the beam disappeared into a void. Her heart raced.

They reached the first chamber.

The thing seemed massive. It was impossible to orient herself and her mind quickly teased her with terrifying images of being lost in the open expanse. Trapped underwater until her air supply inevitably ran out.

Sam marked a couple arrows onto the floor and ceiling.

She fixed the beam of her light on one of the arrows. It appeared woefully difficult to see. Trying to suppress the fear that kept rising in her gut, she swallowed hard. She had to trust that Sam knew what he was doing.

As if in confirmation, Sam began eagerly swimming again.

They passed through the large chamber and were soon traveling inside the main horizontal tunnel. Freya didn't know if she felt better or worse for being confined to the narrow passageway again. It was nice to have proof that the old man hadn't completely lost his mental mind map of the mine site. But then again, having the walls literally closing in on her didn't do wonders for that whole, trying not to panic claustrophobia type thing.

Sam appeared to notice her.

He squeezed her left hand in his right.

There was affection in the gesture, but also a whole gamut of reassurance. It was almost as though he was acknowledging with her that she was frightened, but it was okay, because he would be by her side no matter what happened.

The moment of panic passed quickly.

Sam kept them moving. After all, shallow water or not, there still was a limit to how much air their tanks would hold before it ran out. The horizontal passageway opened up to an enormous chamber – the second chamber.

Beside her, Sam maneuvered the flashlight beam toward the ceiling. In the clear water, they could clearly see the outline of the iron belt in the ceiling. Sam moved to the northwest section of the chamber, although how he managed to tell where that was, seemed like magic to her. They hadn't gone far, before he stopped.

His flashlight was fixed on the ceiling above.

And there, reflecting back at them, was an iron cross.

Chapter Eighty

They found the pile of iron ore tailings.

The rock pile seemed to go on forever, all filled with the distinctive, dark gray color of hematite. Their two flashlight beams reflected against the pile of tailings. Everything looked nearly identical.

And then it didn't.

There was a small outline of white quartz.

Sam quickly removed the rocks by hand. They were round and fit roughly in his palm. He glanced at his dive computer. They were taking longer than he would have liked. He then glanced at Freya's gauge. She was breathing through her air faster than he expected. And he'd expected her to panic a little.

There was no option "B."

If they didn't retrieve the mask today, they would need to return to the coast and get more air tanks. The turnaround time would be greater than twenty-four hours and that would put Tom perilously close to dying.

Sam removed the rocks fast.

Freya came in close and began to help.

He imagined Labouchère digging a hole deep enough to bury the Medusa, and then placing the white stones on top. The question was, how deep would the man have been prepared to go? The ground was solid, which meant he must have used a pickaxe to chip his way into the ground.

Together, they kept removing the stones.

Finally, Sam reached down for another one, and his hand was greeted by the smooth shield of a canister. Labouchère had told them that the Medusa was sealed in an airtight metal container. 75 years of silt had built up, obstructing any movement of the case. He ran his fingers across the gap at the edge of the case, trying to free it. It only took a minute or two, but he was already mindful of the fact that Freya was running low on air.

At last, he got a grip around the back of the case and pulled.

The case broke free, and he won the Medusa.

In the process, silt stirred, and the entire chamber became blacked out in a shroud of debris. Visibility dropped to zero.

Sam instinctively reached for Freya. His hand was greeted by nothing but a void.

And in that one moment his world turned to hell.

Freya had disappeared.

Chapter Eighty-One

Terror. Cold, clammy skin. Rapid breathing. Nausea. Freya tried to suppress her panic, but she might as well have tried flying without a parachute, for all the good it did for her.

Everything happened so quickly. She replayed the events in her mind in an attempt to retrace her position. She was helping Sam remove the quartz, they had found the container holding the Medusa, it had come free, and in the process, silt had filled the chamber.

In that instant, she had somehow become disoriented.

All she had to do was stay still, but in the fine mist of slit, that was too difficult. She'd read long ago that it takes just thirty seconds for most pilots who aren't instrument rated, to crash once their aircraft is shrouded inside a cloud. Like so much in life, an inability to find anything firm upon which to navigate, will quickly lead you to spiral without control.

What she needed to do was find something to orient herself. Something solid.

She swung her arms around in a wild arc, hoping to connect with something. She didn't. Instead, she found herself spinning in a void. There was no way to tell if she was right side up or upside down. Her gut churned like crazy. Her breath was ragged.

Bubbles poured across her face.

It was the first sign that she was hyperventilating. Her hands and fingers were tingling. Her chest hurt and she felt like she'd just run half a mile. But she needed to stop, because every excess breath she inhaled, was one that she wouldn't get to take once she ran out of air.

She needed to settle and orient herself.

Then she remembered, she was in water.

All she had to do was expel some air, and she would naturally become negatively buoyant, and would sink to the bottom. The chamber was less than ten feet in height. She depressed the air release valve on her buoyancy control device, and she quickly sank to the silty bottom of the chamber.

It wasn't much but it was something, and she felt pitifully grateful for it.

Now she needed to find a wall.

The chamber was large by diving standards, but it wasn't enormous. The fact was, if the chamber had been dry, it wouldn't have taken more than ten seconds to walk from one end to the other. She glanced at her compass, and without caring the direction she was going, she focused on remaining in a straight line.

It didn't take long.

She reached a wall.

She drew a deep breath, and then consciously exhaled slowly.

Once more, she'd added another bit of information to her gradually improving database about her location. She knew where the ground was. Also where a wall was. The question remained, which direction?

That's when it hit her.

Sam had made a comment about it being an easy dive. Head due east into the tunnel, and then return due west.

Even in a complete whiteout, she could still see her dive compass.

All she had to do was follow the wall around until she reached an open tunnel that headed due west. Freya felt inordinately pleased with herself.

She had gotten herself into the worst type of diving accident. Now she was on the verge of getting herself out of it, all by herself.

She slowly followed her way around the chamber, keeping her right hand on the wall at all times until she finally reached a west facing passageway.

Freya drew a breath.

It felt great.

She'd done it.

Now all she needed was to swim out of the mine.

She went to draw another breath.
But she couldn't.
Everything became tight.
Because her tank was out of air.

Chapter Eighty-Two

Freya thought she had panicked before, but that was nothing. THIS was panic.

Off the charts, frenzied, hysterical terror!

It was a worst-case scenario. Everyone's nightmare of horrific ways to die type of dread. Her lungs begged her to hyperventilate, but there was no air to do so. Instead, her diaphragm kept on spasming, as her closed mouth refused to allow her to breathe water.

Freya held it as long as she could.

One of the last thought's she had was no longer one of fear.

Instead, it was that of a strange curiosity. Call it mild interest, if you will? She wondered, of all the stupid things she'd done to reach this precise point in her life, to run out of air SCUBA diving in a fucking disused mine in the Pyrenees Mountains seemed the most ridiculous.

And with that thought, her cognitive mind began to fade.

Terror turned to comfort.

Everything seemed okay.

She was ready… for whatever came next.

Darkness pervaded everything, but it no longer scared her. Instead, it felt like a warm blanket, gently draped over her.

Freya opened her mouth, dropping the regulator, and took a breath, welcoming the inevitable flow of water that beckoned.

Only the water never seemed to come. Instead, she felt the soothing rush of air entering her lungs, flooding her with a sense of immortality.

It tasted cool and surprisingly refreshing.

She drew another breath.

It felt good.

At some sort of primitive level of the brain, Freya thought, *hey… I'm doing this! I can breathe water. We've been conditioned all our lives to believe that we can only breathe air, but I'm breathing water, and I feel fine!*

There was a light approaching at the end of the tunnel.

Freya thought, well... I guess that was it. I'm dead.

Then she recognized Sam Reilly's face.

He was shining a flashlight on hers to get her attention.

Reality struck her like a sledgehammer. Her eyes flashed wide open in fear once more. She was still trapped in the flooded mine.

Sam held her tight, focusing on her eyes.

She stared into his eyes.

Those deep, piercing blue eyes.

He then pointed in the direction they needed to go. On the compass, it showed them on a bearing due west.

They kept going, sharing Sam's air supply.

Time stood still and she just kept swimming.

At some stage, she didn't know when, or how, they broke free of the water's surface. She kept trying to breathe from the spare regulator.

It began to panic her again, until Sam pulled it out of her mouth.

Freya held her breath for a second, and then realized she was out of the flooded section of the mine. She inhaled sharply. The air was cool and delicious.

In an instant, she felt Sam's hands wrap around her lower back in an intimate embrace. He was kissing her face, her eyes, her ears, her cheeks. There were tears in his eyes, and she saw – for the first time – abject fear in his eyes, followed by joy when he realized she was okay.

Freya looked at him and smiled.

And a second later, she wrapped her arms around his neck, and kissed him like mad.

Chapter Eighty-Three

Genevieve came to pick them up that night.

All in total, it had taken them just four days to retrieve the Medusa. On the flight home, Genevieve filled him in that Firooz Sayyid locked himself into the biolab room and had injected himself with the terrible virus. He argued that he too, now had just twenty-eight days to find a cure or suffer the consequence of his actions.

Sam felt ambivalent. It was a little extreme, but probably no more insane than developing a virus capable of turning the world to stone.

On board the *Tahila*, Sam slid the Medusa in through the double vacuumed chamber where Firooz worked on a cure. He thanked Sam and quickly began to take apart the Medusa and retrieve the original virus.

It was a painstakingly slow process.

The *Tahila* sailed through the Strait of Gibraltar, rounding the point, and heading to the coast of Bordeaux.

Firooz called Sam down to the biolab room.

With Firooz infected, no one was allowed to enter the biolab room without wearing a fully enclosed biohazard suit. Sam didn't need to enter to talk.

He pressed the intercom and the doctor answered. "Sam, I have some bad news."

"What is it?"

"I can make the cure, but it is going to take longer than I expected."

"Why?"

"I am working on my own. I didn't take into account the fact that I don't have a full team of experts working with me."

"How long?"

"It might be another seven days. Definitely, no longer than ten."

"But Tom will be dead in three!"

A look of pure sorrow washed over Firooz's pale face. "I'm so sorry."

"No. I won't let it happen."

"You don't have a choice."

Sam said, "Yes I do."

"What?" Firooz asked. "I can't speed up my work anymore than I am. Believe me, I am working as fast as humanly possible."

"No. Not you. Tom can have a kidney transplant."

Freya, having heard the commotion stepped into the room. "What's wrong?"

Firooz was the first to speak. "The cure isn't going to be ready in time. Sam's hoping Tom can have a kidney transplant to buy him time."

"Not just buy him time," Sam said. "His life."

Freya, who knew firsthand where those kidneys came from, said, "Oh Sam... I know he's your best friend, but you can't buy him a kidney. You'd be no better off than the people who tried to steal my kidneys."

"Yes, I can." Sam's voice was defiant. "He can have one of mine."

Her voice caught on her throat. "Sam. It doesn't work like that. You need to be a match. There's no telling that anyone on board this ship is a match."

"That's where you're wrong. I have records of blood types and other matches for every person on this ship. It was planned in case someone had been shot or mortally injured, and needed a transplant, but..." He shoved his hands in his pocket, took a deep, steadying breath. "Well, all the same... I'm a match for Tom."

Freya said, "You can't be serious!"

Firooz was the one to answer, "But he can, and he must, if he wants to save his friend's life."

Chapter Eighty-Four

University Hospital, Bordeaux

Sam woke up from the surgery feeling high as a kite.

The drugs they had given him surged through his veins, giving him a warm sensation that everything was wonderful. It was a mirage. After all, he'd just lost one of his two kidneys. The doctors said it would be six to eight weeks before he could return to most normal activities. That was, until he mentioned what his normal activities looked like. In the end they settled on "Twelve weeks and see how you go."

The virus treatment was coming along well. Firooz assured them that within the next week Tom would be able to receive the injection that neutralized the Medusa virus. The chemical recipe would then be sent to every pharmaceutical company capable of manufacturing such a drug. Then the entire world could come together to mass produce the treatment.

Tom rolled over in his bed. "Thanks, Sam. I owe you one."

Sam gripped Tom's hand in his. "No. After all these years, I figured it was about time I saved your life for a change."

Chapter Eighty-Five

Brest, France

It was a warm night.

Raphaël Labouchère was incredibly happy. Nadège Rousseau, his wife, and the love of his life, who suffered with dementia, was having a good day. One of the best she'd had in years. He'd come by that afternoon in the Bugatti and picked her up. They had driven out to Saint-Brieuc for some ice cream. It was just the sort of crazy thing two 96-year-olds should be doing for fun as far as he was concerned.

Afterward, they drove to a nearby lookout, and parked.

The place overlooked the harbor, with Tour Tanguy in the foreground, and Château de Brest in the background. There were a few small, sailing boats moored along the harbor. And on the far side, an old train line, and an old water tower, the historical remnants from WWII.

They looked fondly on the medieval city in which they had spent most of their lives, and watched the sun go down. The world was filled with beautiful harbors, but this just so happened to be theirs, and they loved it with all their hearts.

Nadège looked at the water tower. Then, turning to meet his eye, asked, "Do you remember that night?"

"Of course! How could I forget? I was so frightened."

She held his hand with the gentle affection of two people who had had the good fortune to share a lifetime together. Her brow furrowed, the deep creases of age, knitting together at the top of her forehead. "Because of the Medusa?"

"That too," he admitted. "But no... I was frightened of what we were about to do."

"Why?"

"I don't know. Because we were kids."

Her tone took on a harder edge. "And you didn't want to?"

"Goodness, no! Of course I wanted to. I was just nervous."

"Of what?" she asked, her eyes wistful, full of distant memories that felt like yesterday.

He smiled at her. His eyes full of love. "Because I was afraid that I wouldn't be enough for you."

She moved in close, and held him. "Oh darling, you were always enough for me. In every single way."

They sat there, in silence for hours.

Not saying a thing. They didn't have to. They just knew.

It was Nadège who finally broke the silence. "Everything we've had in our lives. We've been so incredibly lucky."

"I agree. Most people don't get to enjoy what we've shared together."

"No. We are the lucky few."

Raphaël said, "Do you know, I always knew I wanted to grow old with you."

"Growing old sucks!" She laughed and then shrugged. "But I never could find a way around it. Fact of life."

"Yeah, but we sure did have some good times."

Her eyes locked on his. "And I'm glad I got to share them with you."

Raphaël said, "Did I ever tell you about the time I saved the world?"

"You did," she said in a voice that suggested even with her dementia, she could remember him telling that story more than once. "Something about a terrible monster with green eyes. You did well. You saved the world!"

He smiled with a bemused look. "Twice."

"Really?" Her tone took on the sound of patient interest, like a parent hearing a story from their child for the seventh time that day. "Good for you. I always knew you had it in you."

He laughed. She was poking fun at him, but she loved him. He wished the day could go on forever. But he knew it was getting late. She would tire soon, and then she would have a series of bad days as fatigue tended to make her dementia worse somehow. But he didn't want to. And then he felt guilty about choosing to stay with her, even though it would inevitably result in her having some bad days. Finally, he said, "Should I take you home?"

"No. This is a good night. Let's stay out here all night long. What do you say?"

"With you, darling?"

She smiled at him. "Yeah."

He closed his eyes, opened them again, and stared at her. "I'll happily do anything you ask."

Chapter Eighty-Six

Sam was recuperating well on board the *Tahila*.

It had been nearly four weeks since Firooz Sayyid had produced a cure for the Medusa virus, using the original strain found on the ancient mask. The chemical formula for the medicine had been taken up by pharmaceutical manufacturers globally.

He got a call from his friend, the marine biologist, regarding the whale sharks.

The biologist said, "We think we've got some answers."

"Go on. There was some debate about what could be causing them to dive so deep. I'm really interested to hear the truth."

"We believe the whale sharks are diving deep as a unique means of navigation, possibly involving some sort of synchronization with the magnetic poles."

Sam frowned. "Not mating with the queen whale?"

"What? No. That's a crazy idea. Of course not."

"Right," Sam said, without attempting to conceal his disappointment. "I just thought it would make a better story if the whale sharks were part of a nest, where the queen lived at the bottom of the ocean."

"Nice story. But I'm afraid it's not based on any facts."

"Okay, thanks for letting me know."

"No, thank you and your crew for helping with the tagging."

There was a knock at Sam's quarters.

It was Elise. "Firooz has asked for a word with you."

"Okay. You can tell him I'll be down in a minute."

Sam headed down to the biolab. Firooz was in the process of packing up all his works, including a detailed list of all his processes. Something that any decent biochemist could work with for years in case the Medusa strain ever reared its ugly head to the world again.

Sam greeted him through the glass barrier. Firooz was still working inside the biolab, and so Sam would have had to don special biohazard suits to enter.

Firooz looked up. There was a soft melancholy in his eyes, mixed with the wonder of great achievement, and if Sam had to guess, he saw a certain level of peace in the man's face. A type of comfort and acceptance that hadn't been there, even a few days earlier. Next week, he was going to be picked up and transported to The Hague, where he would be tried for Crimes Against Humanity.

Everyone knew the inevitable outcome.

Sam said, "What can I do for you, Firooz?"

"I just wanted to thank you, Sam." Firooz met him with a candid gaze. "For everything. Not just for saving my life, but for allowing me to put some of this right again. Help me save my soul."

Sam didn't know what to say. What do you say to the worst terrorist the world's ever seen, who just so happened to also have saved more people's lives than any other single person in the history of the human race?

Taken aback, Sam said, "You're welcome."

"And thank you for finding out the truth about my father. Some might say it's a little too late, but better late than never. I can now meet my maker in peace, knowing the truth. I heard they found Michael Gallagher?"

Sam nodded. "Yes, he retired from the CIA three weeks before Medusa was released and the attacks on Russia and Pakistan took place. His house in Washington was raided, but nothing to incriminate him was ever found. He was the perfect double agent. He had compartmentalized his life so well, that his wife and children never suspected the truth."

Firooz looked up. "But they got him?"

"No. A stray bullet in Tajikistan got him."

"Where?"

"In the head. He would have been killed instantly."

Firooz nodded. "That's good. I know he did some bad things, but like me, he believed in what he was doing. He thought what he was doing was right. I should feel hatred toward him for what he did to me. He orchestrated the murder of my father, and set me on a path of radical religious indoctrination. Then he helped me plan a deadly assault on humanity that may have even made Hitler shudder."

Sam had no words to say, so he simply listened.

"But do you know what?" Firooz asked. It was rhetorical, and Sam continued to listen in silence. "For all that, he was still the father I grew up with. The kindest, most supportive person I've ever known. I'm glad he's dead, but I'm also glad it was a single bullet to the head. My pseudo father died instantaneously, without the humiliation of trial, or a slow, painful death."

Ah, Sam thought... *so this is where this was heading.* "The Hague may look favorably upon your efforts in the treatment of the pandemic."

Firooz raised a hand, waving aside such thoughts. "You misunderstand me, Mr. Reilly. It is not my goal to be saved. I just wanted you to know that I appreciate everything you have done."

A moment later, the Albino began to squirm.

Inside the makeshift biolab, the doctor wet himself.

Sam put his hand to his mouth, feeling he might vomit with fear. His eyes narrowed, but he couldn't look away.

Firooz's face twisted and distorted in agony.

Sam said, "You never took the cure yourself?"

He made a gesture of apology. "I'm sorry, Sam. Monsters don't get to have happy endings."

Chapter Eighty-Seven

Kwibisa Plains, Zambia

The Eurocopter landed in the large open space in the front of the clinic.

Sam shut the engine down and helped carry Freya's bags into her home. She was greeted by Amakusana, a young woman with dark skin, and expressive blue eyes, who worked at the same hospital clinic as her. The two women hugged each other excitedly. It seemed to be a happy reunion.

Sam sat down with her.

They drank coffee.

Sam said, "So you're determined to keep working here?"

"I have to establish the clinic. Once it's running, and Amakusana has been trained to take my place, I'd feel better about leaving."

"Where would you go?"

"I'm not sure. Wherever the wind takes me."

He met her with a candid gaze. "Were you aware that there's a vacancy for you on my ship?"

She laughed at that. "Oh yeah, how many babies are born each year on your ship?"

Sam thought about that for a second. "Not many."

"Didn't think so."

Sam held his breath. "That's a no then?"

She returned the frank look, with a little contemplation thrown into the mix for good measure. She smiled. "You're serious, aren't you?"

"Why not?"

"What I would I do?"

Sam shrugged. "I don't know. What do any of my crew do?"

She exhaled. "Oh, it's so very tempting. But I think I'm going to have to pass on this one."

"All right," Sam said. "If you ever change your mind, give me a call."

"I will. And I'm still going to hold you to that romantic weekend away to some French Castle."

"It's a deal." Sam's expression became serious. "Speaking of calls, I forgot to tell you about our ancient French couple. You know the two who had the true love story?"

Freya's brow knitted together. "Nadège Rousseau and Raphaël Labouchère? How could I forget? Do we know how they're doing?"

"They're both dead."

"Really?"

"Afraid so. Apparently, they relived one of their first dates. It was a warm summer's day, and Labouchère took her for ice cream in his Bugatti…"

"Ice cream?" Freya asked, incredulously.

"Yeah, what's wrong with ice cream in your late nineties?"

"Nothing. Go on."

"Afterward, they went to a coastal lookout…"

Her hand instinctively went to cover her open mouth. "And?"

Sam said, "They stayed there, cuddled up together all night – dying in their sleep."

Freya stared at him, almost too stunned to find the right response. "That's tragic… and a little sweet."

"They had something, that's for sure," Sam said, a little wistfully.

Sam stood up to leave.

Freya wrapped her long arms around his neck, kissing him passionately on the lips. Just like always, they kissed like it was the last kiss they would ever have.

Only this time, it probably was.

She squeezed his hand affectionately. "It's been a blast." With one last sisterly peck on his cheek, she said, "Thank you, Sam. For everything."

"You're welcome. And yeah, it's been a lot of fun."

"I'm sorry you never found your lost Spanish treasure."

"That's all right. Sometimes you get lucky and sometimes you don't."

Freya said, "You never did end up showing me that photograph."

"Oh yeah, do you want to have a quick look at it for me?"

"Sure."

Sam pulled out his phone and brought up the image. "Ever seen a place that looks like this?"

She stared at it. Examining it for a few seconds.

The image depicted three granite stones. They were high up on a little island, formed by a large U-shaped bend in a river. There was no wildlife in the image. Two of the stones were almost identical in size. They were massive, and rounded, almost like the outline of a pair of giant elephants facing each other. The third one was about a quarter of the size, more like a baby elephant following its parents. The three stones fell upon each other, to form a small, hollowed section at its base, and presumably an opening to the secret cave of the Gods.

Freya bit her lower lip, place a hand over her mouth. "You're not going to believe me."

Sam stared at her, a wry grin on his face. "What?"

"I've seen that place before."

"What?" Sam shook his head. "No way!"

"No. I have."

"Could you still remember how to get there well enough to show me?"

"Show you?" She met his gaze. "I've been there dozens of times, I can take you there myself."

Chapter Eighty-Eight

Sam stared at the river from the nearby rocky outcrop.

It formed more of an oxbow lake. It would be easy to imagine that it was a U-shaped bend in the river a hundred and ninety odd years ago. Natural erosion and flooding having widened the river. His eyes narrowed in on the two granite boulders.

They were roughly twenty-five feet high.

The image in the cave of the scene didn't do the size of the boulders much justice. The shapes were right. They looked like elephants, but they were much too large for even the biggest of the African beasts.

Sam said, "We seem to be missing one of the boulders."

Freya took off her glasses and stared at the water. "The baby elephant?"

"Yeah, that's the one."

She frowned. "It's funny. I could have sworn it was there too."

"I don't think it washed away."

"No, no... different times of the year the water level changes with seasonal floods and droughts. I'm almost certain I've seen the baby there, too."

"Come on, let's go find out."

They made a unique sight.

Freya was a fit hiker, with strong legs in sturdy leather boots. In her hands, she carried her grandfather's Holland & Holland Royal Double Rifle. Sam, more of a traditional hiker, was carrying a large backpack, with a pair of snorkels, fins, and flashlights. He figured, if they got lucky, the water would be shallow enough that he could free dive to check it out.

After a few minutes they reached the bank of the river. There was a small dugout canoe pulled up along the shore, where a local fisherman worked with his nets. Freya spoke to the man. His English was broken, but he seemed to get the idea of the three stones, and when Sam showed him the photo on his phone, the man nodded and pointed at the twin granite boulders.

Sam grinned. There was something about the fisherman's face that reflected certainty.

Freya chatted to the man and within a few minutes she thanked him and told Sam that the fisherman had agreed to lend them his canoe. They thanked him and climbed into the canoe. Sam placed his backpack in front of him.

Sam looked at the fisherman and asked, "What about crocodiles?"

He shrugged. "Lots downriver. Some upriver. Here. Not so many."

Sam smiled and thanked him. He turned to Freya. "Well, that's reassuring, isn't it?"

Together, they slowly paddled out to the boulder outcrop in the middle of the lake. It was a warm, clear day, and beams of sun shone through the clear water, penetrating to the rocky bed some ten to fifteen feet below.

It was a good sign.

If they were in the right place, it would be easy to confirm or debunk by simply free diving overboard.

They reached the first of the two boulders.

It was uncanny how, once up close, the stones appeared even more like a pair of elephants. There were no signs of human carving in the rock, just the natural fractures of time and erosion that shaped it in such a way.

They paddled around to the opposite side. Light rays from the sun penetrated the water all the way to the rocky bed. And there, in no more than a few feet of water, was the outline of a third boulder – the baby elephant.

Within a couple minutes, Sam had his shirt off, his dive mask and fins on, along with a flashlight secured to his wrist, and a Go Pro mounted to his mask to record the event.

He turned to Freya, "Are you sure you don't want to join me?"

She shook her head. "I'll wait here and keep an eye out for crocodiles."

"All right. Suit yourself."

A second later, he rolled back into the water.

He surfaced, took a couple of deep breaths and disappeared far below.

Chapter Eighty-Nine

The freshwater was so clear its depth was deceptive.

Sam dived all the way to the bottom of the boulders, where the three of them formed a hollowed section at the base. He could just make out the opening from the surface, and as he neared it, he became infinitely certain he was on the right track.

The opening was big enough to comfortably squeeze an adult inside. Several old tree roots from a long since expired tree, were draped over the top of it. Sam used his knife to cut through these, and poking his head in, he peered inside.

The beam of his flashlight shone deep inside the cave's opening to reveal a void of unknown depths. For a split second, he imagined the place being a perfect home for a crocodile, or any number of Africa's deadly river monsters.

Curiously, he wondered where crocodiles slept, and whether or not they even made burrows. Seconds later, he dismissed the entire concept as mad speculation. Then his focus returned to the task at hand.

Reaching under the rocky ledge, he quickly pulled himself through.

The opening leveled out after just a few feet, before heading upward. The flashlight cast beams in a steady arc through the upward tunnel.

Sam's head broke the surface of the water, and he found himself inside a large chamber. The air was relatively fresh, and there were several gaps in the stone above, through which dappled sunlight shone through – onto an enormous hoard of treasure.

It looked like the entire chamber was an ancient air bubble.

Almost like a pyroclastic air pocket, although he knew that granite had nothing to do with volcanoes, and thus, the idea of it forming such a pocket was absurd. Perhaps the entire thing was a rare anomaly and the slaves of the *Midas*, had worked away to make the natural opening bigger?

Whatever the cause, it didn't matter. The fact remained; he'd found the secret chamber of the Gods.

Sam pulled himself free of the water, and onto the solid rock. He surveyed the room, really taking it in for the first time.

There were piles of gold and silver coins in leather bags, minted in Spanish, Portuguese, English, and French. Several bars of gold ingots. Resting on top of the gold ingots, was a single rolled scroll, made of vellum, and sealed by a heavy wax pendant.

Sam stared at the scroll.

There something about it, despite all the treasure of the chamber, he couldn't help but feel that the most valuable treasures of all were yet to be discovered, contained within that very scroll.

Chapter Ninety

Kwibisa Plains, Zambia

Sam opened his laptop, connecting it to the internet via satellite phone.

He sat at the table on the deck of the clinic overlooking the grassy plains. He had left the treasures safely inside the elephant chamber to retrieve later, only taking the vellum scroll. He had opened it and discovered the vellum contained a large map of the world, centered around ancient China.

The entire document had notes written in an ancient Chinese script, named Xiaozhuan. A quick google search identified it as a type of Lesser Seal script, developed c. 700 BCE and still in use today. This script was less pictographic and more logographic, meaning the symbols represented concepts themselves, not objects. For example, if one now wanted to write "Should the king go hunting tomorrow?" one would inscribe the image for the king and the sign which represented 'hunting' and 'tomorrow'.

There were three locations highlighted.

At a glance, one was in the Mongolian Steppes bordering Russia, the other the heart of Africa, and the last one, China.

His eyes narrowed as he tried to make sense of what he was looking at.

Freya stood behind him, her arm over his shoulder, staring at the Xiaozhuan script. "Any idea what it says?"

"Not a clue."

He took an image of it and put it into a search engine.

It came back with an expected blank. Apparently, Google's Translation teams never got around to working on the Xiaozhuan script.

But two words did appear.

Whether it was a Google type of anomaly, as the program refused to accept that it was incapable of supplying an answer, or not, he couldn't tell.

He stared at the two words.

Dragon's Breath.

Freya said the words out loud. Then, "Any idea what that means?"

Sam shook his head. "None."

He typed *"Dragon's Breath"* into a search engine.

Dozens of pages of the term associated with everything from computer games through to mythological movies involving dragons came up.

Sam frowned.

"What if you include the term Xiaozhuan script, too?" Freya suggested.

He added that to the search term.

And was rewarded with a translation of a small ancient seal script. It was dated 247 BC, during the beginning of the Qin Dynasty.

Sam read it out loud. "Dragon's Breath. A weapon so devastating, that it is believed that anyone who wields its power will be capable of ruling the world..."

Freya frowned. "Huh."

"Wait! That's it!" Sam said, his voice excited.

"What's it?" Freya asked, looking at the map.

"This is what the slaves were looking for. They weren't interested in gold. Their success in the Caribbean had made them all rich. No, what they wanted was the power to inflict revenge. And they hoped that could be found in Dragon's Breath."

"But they never found it?"

Sam shook his head, eyeing the strange map. There were three separate locations. One in Mongolia, another in China, and the last one – presumably the one the slaves were searching for – was right there in Africa.

Sam searched the locations on the internet.

It came up with a giant crater. The sort of thing a meteorite might have caused millions of years ago. Only this one occurred much more recently.

Freya said, "It looks like they found it..."

"Yeah, and whatever it was, Dragon's Breath was unstable and killed them. Judging by the shape of the mountain range destroyed, it appears that the weapon was more like a medieval equivalent to an atomic bomb."

"What about the other two?"

Sam frowned. "Other two?"

"Yeah, the one in Mongolia and China."

Sam brought up the rough GPS location of the Mongolian one.

There was a massive hole in the ground. Again, the sort of thing that looked like the remnants of an ancient meteorite or half a dozen A-bombs leveling the mountainside.

He then flicked across to the location in China. More specifically, Lintong District, Xi'an, Shaanxi province of China.

Freya asked, "I don't see any sort of destroyed mountain range like the other two locations. Maybe Dragon's Breath hasn't yet been retrieved there?"

"I don't know. Wait a second I'll see what the region is known for." He typed a few words into the search engine and an image of Terracotta Warriors came up.

She drew a breath and said, "The Mausoleum of the First Qin Emperor – Qin Shi Huang."

"Oh, my goodness!" Sam couldn't contain his elation.

"What is it?"

"I just had a thought."

She pressed a hand against his shoulder. "Well, let's hear it. Don't keep it to yourself."

Sam said, "I'm thinking that those ten thousand strong Terracotta Warriors were never there to guard the Emperor's Mausoleum."

"No?"

"No, they were there to prevent the evil inside – Dragon's Breath – from being released into the world."

Chapter Ninety-One

The Eurocopter was loaded with the *Midas* treasures.

Freya had ducked inside to grab a pen and paper to write down his details. It seemed strange after all this time that neither of them had exchanged phone numbers and email addresses. But the truth was, neither had their phones for most of the time. And there was no point trading physical addresses, because they both moved so frequently.

There was a slight rustle in the long grass. A shadow of a fear stirring the primitive part of Sam's brain into survival instincts. He leaned into the helicopter to retrieve the Mossberg 590A1 pump-action shotgun from where it was kept beside the pilot's seat. He withdrew it, turned, and was greeted by a fist to the head.

The force almost knocked him out.

His world turned to darkness, and if it wasn't for someone moving in quickly to grab him, he doubted he would have remained standing. He licked his lip. There was blood in his mouth.

Sam opened his eyes.

There were five people.

Most likely of Chinese background.

And if he was going to guess that much, then it was fairly safe to say, they were all part of Yuxia.

Five motorbikes were parked in front of him. All black ARC Vectors. Electric motorcycles. Super-fast. Entirely silent. That explained how they closed in on him so quickly without making much of a sound. These men, like the ones he met in Zanzibar were fast, too.

Sam opened his arms outward. "I was wondering how long it would take for you guys to show up."

A tall man, in charge of the group, said, "We hoped you would have given up by now, Mr. Reilly."

Sam shrugged. "I'm sorry to disappoint. If we're going to be friends, you'd better get used to it."

"No one is said anything about being friends."

"I suppose we'd better get this over and done with." Sam gestured toward the helicopter. "The gold is in the back."

"We haven't come here for the gold."

"Now there's a surprise." Sam smiled. "So this really was a social visit?"

The leader shook his head. "We came for the map."

"The map?"

"Don't play games, Mr. Reilly. We've come for Dragon's Breath."

"Oh. Sure." Sam nodded. "If you Google Qin Shi Huang Mausoleum, it will give you the address."

"You know very well what I'm talking about!"

Sam said, "Oh, or you could Google Vredefort crater in Africa and Tabun-Khara-Obo crater Mongolia, if you want to see some of the damage of the remnants of Dragon's Breath."

Sam didn't see the punch.

But he sure as hell felt it.

It was a quick, decisive hit to his solar plexus, sending his diaphragm into a spasm.

"I mean the map to the center of the Qin Shi Huang Mausoleum. A secret so well-guarded that no one has managed to penetrate the 2,300-year-old tomb to this day."

Sam gasped, finally catching his breath. "Oh, that map."

The tall Yuxia stepped toward him.

Sam said, "All right, all right. Now I remember seeing that thing."

He reached in, and grabbed a small, sealed bag containing the velum scroll. The Yuxia took it and stepped back.

All five of the men were armed with QSZ-92 pistols – the same handgun used by the People's Liberation Army.

The Yuxia said, "I'm sorry it had to end this way. You seem like a decent man, although a touch too obstinate for your own good."

Freya stepped into the arena. She was carrying the Holland & Holland Royal Double Rifle. The weapon looked every bit as deadly in her hands as one would expect of something designed to take down Africa's largest game animals. Loaded with .577 Nitro Express, it was the sort of weapon that would leave little left in the way of resembling a human body.

She wore the expression of a hunter, looking forward to a good fight. "Hello gentlemen."

Nobody spoke.

And no one moved.

Freya gave a short laugh. Somehow, it sounded genuine, yet sardonic. Just like a crazy person might sound. And crazy people were the most dangerous of all, because there was no way to know how they might respond.

In a calm, collected voice, she said, "Right now you're all guessing how many rounds this thing carries?"

Still no answer.

"There's just two." She spoke loudly. A wry confidence in her voice. "So now you're probably wondering, do I just carry this thing for show, or am I one of those girls who loves to shoot, and is going to kill two of you before you make a move?"

The tall Yuxia said, "You're going to do this. There's five of us. One of you. And you just said you don't have enough rounds to..."

Freya fired.

Two shots in immediate succession.

Perfect shots.

Two people were dead before they knew the gunfight had begun. The tall guy and the shorter one holding onto Sam were gone. In a split second, Sam stepped forward and grabbed the tall guy, pulling him in close. He used him as a shield, while the other three took their shots.

Freya dropped the double rifle.

And drew the Glock 19, from behind her back.

With a steady and well-practiced aim, she didn't even have to think. Her actions were fast. Smooth. Instinctive. She shot the guy farthest on the left in the head. Then the one on the right, got hit in the throat next.

A round slammed into the side of her abdomen. Barely reacting, she spun, and shot him in the chest. The fifth opponent was already on his bike, and accelerating hard. If she had another round in the Double Rifle, she could have placed it in him for sure. But with the Glock it was a near impossible shot.

She took it anyway.

A small spark flicked off the back of the bike, but the motorcycle kept accelerating into the distance.

Sam looked at the four Yuxia sprawled in various positions in the dirt. He checked to see if any were still alive, or posed further threat. None of them moved.

Sam shook his head in wonder.

Her talent seemed supernatural. Freya, true to her word, was one of those shooters with an innate ability. Every single round had been placed perfectly, every single shot taken had been a kill shot.

She looked at him. "You okay?"

"Yeah." Sam licked his bloodied lips. "I'm fine. You?"

Freya touched the small hole on the side of her abdomen. There was blood on her hand, but not a lot. It had gone in and out, skimming her side, and missing any vital organs. "First time I've been shot, but I think I'll live."

Sam stepped forward to embrace her. "Hurts like hell, doesn't it?"

"You've been shot?"

Sam shrugged. "A few times."

"Really?"

"Call it an occupational hazard, as much as intermittent stupidity."

Freya looked at the leather satchels that contained the pirate gold. "At least they didn't get anything."

Sam said, "But he stole the map to Emperor Qin Shi Huang's Mausoleum!"

"Oh, that's bad," Freya said, her eyes narrowing. "They know about the weapon?"

"It would appear so."

"They have the map to find a weapon more powerful than a modern nuclear bomb?" Freya frowned. "You know what this means, don't you?"

"Yes." Sam nodded, his jaw set with defiance. "It means we're going to have to beat them to it."

Printed in Great Britain
by Amazon